CRIED OUT

TROPHY DOMS NEW YORK #3

KATE HAWTHORNE

Cried Out
Trophy Doms New York #3
by Kate Hawthorne

Copyright © 2024
Kate Hawthorne

Edited by | Jordan Buchanan

Cover Design | Amai Designs

CRIED OUT

KATE HAWTHORNE

DEDICATION

For those who know it's tears that make the best lube.

YOU'RE EYE-FUCKING ME LIKE YOU CAN HANDLE ME," I MURMURED softly to the man kneeling near my feet, leaning back and crossing one leg over the other. I had a whiskey in one hand, propped gingerly on top of my knee while I gave an appreciative once over to the pretty little thing currently on his knees between where Ford and I sat.

Kale had been too caught up with his own shit to notice the way Ford had negotiated his way into the deal, reaching back at one point and patting his billfold before the stranger had followed obediently behind him to our table. Ford had no place soliciting anyone at The Black Door, but being in a secret relationship with your best friend's brother drove people to desperate measures sometimes, I imagined. I'd never know because I wasn't stupid enough to fuck Kale's baby brother, but I did enjoy watching Ford try to dig himself out of the mess he'd made.

"I can," he answered simply, tipping his chin up in what I imagined was an attempt to make him look more powerful than he was.

"You don't know a thing about me."

"I know your name is Astor Brooks," he countered, arching a golden-brown brow.

Fucking Ford.

"You don't know anything you haven't already been told," I corrected.

"Enlighten me then."

I sighed, uncrossing my legs and leaning down closer to his face. In one swift motion, I set my drink on the table and collared my hand around the gorgeous, slender throat of the presumptuous man Ford had paid off. His eyes went wide when I grabbed him, but beyond that he barely moved an inch.

"I'm not a sadist," I whispered, letting my lips dust across his ear.

"Brooks, play nice," Ford warned from his seat beside me.

I gave him the finger, not even bothering to turn my attention upward.

"You can tell him to stop if you want him to stop," Ford went on.

"He knows." I gave his throat a squeeze. "Don't you? Since you know so much?"

"I know," he rasped, swallowing. His Adam's apple bobbed against the palm of my hand and, like a reflex, my cock throbbed. "Tell me the rest now."

"I'm not a sadist," I said again, "but I like it rough."

"I can handle that."

"I get off on making people cry," I warned.

Even thinking about tears streaking down this man's cheeks was enough to get me halfway to hard. I had to count backward from ten in my head to stop myself from tightening my hand around his throat so I could watch him scramble for air.

My confession was as much the truth as it was a lie. When I'd been younger and just learning the ropes of my kinks, lots of people had called me a sadist, but the pain I inflicted wasn't anything more than the cause to the event. I loved making my partners cry. There was something so vulnerable, so revealing about it, and there wasn't a thing in the world that made me more aroused. Breath play, though...breath play was a *very* close second.

I wondered sometimes if I played too close to the edge, because my kink was rarely safe and sane, but always consensual. I tried to pick my partners well, finding men—or women—who understood what my end goals were so they didn't get scared off while we were heading there. I often got mean during sex, rough, and I'd even been called cruel once or twice.

But I always softened in the end.

I would take the time to kiss the bruises I'd left behind, trace the outlines of them with the tip of my tongue and commit them to memory, even if I'd never even bothered to learn my partner's name. I provided water, a warm shower—sometimes a bath—and I always, *always*, paid for their car ride home at the end of the night. And once I was alone again, I'd replay the events of the night and get myself off a second... or third, or fourth time before going to bed.

Alone.

"I'm not scared," he said, blinking slowly at me. "My name is Tate."

I grimaced, shaking my head. "I don't care."

That was half a lie. It was a lot easier to think about him

with his name instead of referring to him as the trouble-making piece of ass that Ford had all but dropped into my lap.

"That's fine."

I flexed my hand around Tate's throat and then let go, moving so my back was tucked into the corner of my chair. At the loss of my touch, Tate had the decency to look bereft, which earned him almost enough points to get him home and into my bed.

"Are you done playing with my food, Brooks?" Ford asked, feigning insult. I knew he was putting on a show because I knew he was in love with Kale's younger brother, Boston. I knew he was pretending because Ford was one of the best negotiators I'd ever met. When we were in school, he aced Business Econometrics without even stepping foot inside the classroom. Some things just came easily to some people, and if he played his cards right, Tate was going to be coming easily for me in less than two hours.

"He's so tempting, though," I said, finishing off the last of my drink. "I think I'm taking him home."

Ford's eyes went wide before he closed them. His shoulder sagged and he managed a nod.

"It's early," Kale complained from his seat beside us. "Can't you take him into one of the rooms in the back?"

"However long you think you can stay sober enough to want to be here, I promise you I'm going to fuck him longer than that." I stood up, patting my hand on top of Tate's soft brown curls. "Better luck next time, Ford. I'll see the lot of you next week."

Tate exhaled a slow breath, like his brain was finally catching up to the next steps of our itinerary. Even on his knees, he swayed a little bit, eyes already glassy like he was naked with my cock up his ass.

"You don't have to take me home," Tate said, licking his lips like the seductive little devil he was. "I don't know if I can wait that long."

I huffed, grasping hold of his hair and giving his head a rough tug. The way the dark neon lights reflected off his eyes made it look like he was already well and close to crying, which meant I might not even have enough time to get him home before needing to take him.

"You're pushy."

"I just know what I want."

"Please, get out of here." Kale groaned and waved us off dismissively. "I thought I wanted to come out with you, but this is just making me miss Christian and now I'm turned on and alone."

"Sad and horny," our otherwise quiet friend Alex said from Kale's other side.

In all honesty, I'd forgotten Alex was even there. For the whole night, he'd sat beside Kale, looking like he wanted to be anywhere but where we were. There had been a time when The Black Door was a sanctuary for us, but times were quickly changing and with Kale and Ford both in monogamous relationships, and with Alex still silently mourning the departure of our other friend, Beamer, it wasn't the same as it had been before.

"You can go FaceTime Christian," Ford suggested to Kale.

I tuned them out, looking down and finding Tate's stare still focused on me. The grip I had on his hair was barely enough to keep him there, and I appreciated that he hadn't moved from the position I'd put him into. Not that I was looking for a submissive, but I did enjoy when my partners had those qualities.

"Get up," I said.

Tate climbed to his feet with the grace of someone whose knees were still on the right side of thirty. Up close, he was taller than me, I realized, but most people were. I shot up to five-foot-eight in high school, long before my friends had even dreamed of a growth spurt that substantial, but that had been it. I stopped growing while all of them continued to inch up past me. It got old, being the short one in a group of six-foot tall giants, but I more than made up for it elsewhere.

"How old are you?" I asked, realizing for the first time that those young knees might have been closer to twenty than comfortable.

"Twenty-four," Tate answered.

"Is there anything I need to worry about with you?" I asked.

He shook his head.

"Do you have any limits I need to be concerned about?" I hated how clinical the introductory line of questioning always felt, but I appreciated the necessity of it.

"I don't want to kiss," Tate whispered. "I don't want to bleed."

That all felt reasonable, if not a little adventurous for a first time with a new partner.

"What's your safe word?"

"Stop."

I shook my head, lower lip pushed into a frown. "I like to play hard, Tate. That's not going to work with me."

"Red," he said instead.

"Unoriginal, but fine. Red it is."

"What about yours?" Tate asked.

I cocked my head to the side, eyes narrowed into a squint. "What do you mean, what about mine?"

"If you need to stop," he said.

"Then I'll stop."

"But how will I know if you're stopping to stop, or stopping to take a breather or something?"

Tate needed a cock in his mouth immediately.

"I'll say red," I conceded. "Is that fair?"

"It's fine." Tate lowered his hands, splaying his fingers out a little bit in front of him to cover what I imagined to be his bulge.

"Please leave," Kale whined. "I'm not above begging."

"That's what Christian told us," Ford teased.

I'd honestly forgotten they were there, but I'd had enough. Turning my attention back toward Tate, I jerked my chin toward the elevators.

"Let's go downstairs and get a room," I said.

He nodded quickly, scampering off. I gave all of my friends a mock salute, then slowly strode after him. I caught up just as the elevator doors opened, and Tate turned to walk backward into the small space, watching me follow him inside.

"I'll make sure Ford pays you whatever you two agreed on," I said once the doors closed.

Tate grunted, folding his arms in front of his chest. "I'm not a prostitute."

"I didn't say you were."

I pressed the button for the main floor and the elevator dropped us down in under ten seconds. I didn't say another word to Tate, stepping onto the main level of The Black Door and trusting he would be close behind. Sure enough, I felt him on my heels as I snaked my way through the crowds near the bar, the anticipation rolling off of him in waves once we reached the back hallway where the private rooms were located.

The Black Door was built for voyeurism and exhibitionism, which was another one of my favorite pastimes, but the owners appreciated that not everyone wanted to get down and dirty in the open. The back hallway was dark, save for the lights on the ceiling in front of the doors, lit up red and green to indicate whether they were occupied or available. The room at the very end had a green light, and I pushed the door open, waiting for Tate to step inside.

It had been awhile since I'd used the club facilities, normally preferring to take my partners home. That was contrary to how my friends tended to operate, but I found aftercare was easiest when I had all the necessary tools at my disposal. The Black Door had generic bottles of water and nice enough washcloths in the utilitarian bathrooms, but it wasn't quite the same.

I gave the room a quick scan, registering all of the usual sex club suspects—a nondescript bed fitted with O-rings on every corner, a small couch against the opposite wall, a St. Andrew's cross in the corner, and a closed door that led to the equally depressing bathroom.

"Are you sure you don't have another half hour in you to make it back to my place?" I asked, turning to already find Tate half undressed, hand braced against the wall while he struggled his way out of his sneakers.

"Here is fine."

I dragged my tongue across the front of my teeth, amused at the fight Tate was having with the rest of his clothes. Before

I could even bother to get condoms and lube out of the cabinet by the bed, he was naked before me, fingers twisting together nervously in front of his dick.

"Let me see your cock," I demanded, my voice already slipping into that lower register that went hand in hand with my own arousal.

Tate swallowed, fidgeting his hands one more time before letting them fall away. He tapped his fingers against the outside of his thighs, cheeks flushing pink to match the darkened length of his gorgeous, swollen cock. He was already hard, his erection short and thick, and I found it almost a shame that I was exclusively a top.

"What are you hoping for, Tate?"

Tate was frozen at the foot of the bed, and I moved across the room, making sure to undo the fly of my own pants before sitting down on the couch. I spread my legs, giving my dick a slow stroke as I pulled it out of my underwear, and Tate shivered. His eyes were focused on my cock, so I pointed it toward him, pressing down on the crown with my thumb.

"I just wanted to fuck," he said, fingers gripping the outsides of his thighs.

"That sounds very selfish of you."

Tate licked his lips, stretching his fingers. It was amazing to watch him fight against his own insecurities. He stood naked in front of me, like livestock being appraised at an auction. I wondered if he felt like a piece of meat, wondered if he would find that humiliating.

If it would be enough to make him cry...

"I want to get fucked," he said, the barest rephrasing enough to make precum leak from the tip of my dick. "I want another man to come inside of me."

I glanced around the room, pretending to be offended at his generalization. I wasn't offended in the slightest—the back and forth was turning me on more than he'd ever know. The way Tate wanted to curl in on himself with every question had me feeling like I'd just scaled a mountain. Vulnerability bloomed in those uncomfortable truths, and insecurities were my favorite place to dig.

"Another man, Tate? I'm right here."

"I want *you* to come inside of me," he said, voice scratchy and cock jerking. "Why do you keep doing that?"

"Doing what?" I asked, knowing full well what he meant.

"Calling me Tate."

"Isn't it your name?" I tilted my head to the side, perplexed by his growing levels of discomfort at the situation.

"It is, but nobody ever uses it."

"I'm not nobody," I assured him. "So, you want to get fucked. You want to make me come?"

"Yes."

"Are you going to cry for me, Tate?" I asked him next, giving the base of my shaft a constricting squeeze.

"If that's what will make you come, yes."

"Do you want me to make you cry with words or with my hands?"

Tate closed his eyes, chest puffing out a little as his shoulders pulled back. It wasn't a proud move, but more of a submissive concession, the first twitch of muscles before a man fell to his knees.

"It's up to you," he whispered.

"No, Tate. It's not."

He nodded. He moved like he was going to cover himself

again, but couldn't decide where to start. Like he wasn't sure what needed to be hidden more—his cock or his face.

"Both," he conceded.

"Is it kindness or humiliation then?" I asked.

Tate shook his head. "I don't know."

"A little of both?" I proposed, giving a slow pull up the length of my erection. "We can see what feels best?"

"Yes," he whispered. "Thank you."

"Don't thank me yet," I warned, knowing it was fully possible he wasn't ever going to thank me at all. "Get on your hands and knees, Tate. Crawl to me and then put my cock into your mouth."

When Tate went to his knees, a flush raced down his spine. It was more of that beautiful pink that matched his cock. He hesitated once his hands hit the ground, and with his face turned downward, he started to crawl toward me.

"Arch your back, Tate. The point of this is to seduce me."

He flicked a quick look at me. "I thought the point of this was to humiliate me."

I chuckled, tracing my tongue across the corner of my lower lip. "Like I said."

He was breathing so loud it was the only sound in the room, and when he settled the arch into his spine and resumed his path toward me, I thought he looked like a work of art. He hated the way it felt to crawl to another man, but his cock was still hard and heavy between his legs, swaying back and forth as he closed the space between us.

I shifted toward the edge of the couch and pointed my cock right at his face. When he reached me, Tate came to a stop and looked up, and I smacked my dick across his cheek. He sucked in a breath, eyes immediately welling with tears, and I traced my tip across his chapped lips, willing myself to not come on the spot.

"Open," I growled.

Tate's chin quivered as he spread his lips, and I shoved right past his teeth with one lift of my hips from the couch. I forced my way right into the back of his throat, and those tears immediately spilled and began to run down his cheeks. It wasn't quite the same effect as making someone burst into actual tears, but my body barely registered the difference.

I grabbed Tate's head, holding my cock in the back of his throat. He gasped and sputtered around me, hot puffs of air filling his cheeks while he tried to breathe around me. Spit shot out of his mouth and he fought against the hold I had on him, struggled against the way I impaled his mouth. He looked frantic, and that kind of fear was like flipping a switch for me.

"What a loose fucking mouth, Tate." With my erection still pressed against his tongue, I stood up from the couch and dragged him back toward the bed. I took us both down to the floor, his head landing against the carpet, but still cradled by my hand. I wanted to hurt him; I didn't want to concuss him. Once I was sure it would be a soft landing, I grabbed the sides of his head and leveraged myself over his face, fucking straight into the back of his throat with my cock.

His tears flowed freely, sliding straight into his ears. I could feel the warm wetness of them over my fingers and the hot press of his tongue swirling around my cock while I fucked his face. He looked like a debauched cherub on the ground like that, all naked and flushed, covered in sweat and spit. He moaned around me, screwing his eyes closed when I dipped deeper into his throat than I'd managed to reach before.

I glanced quickly over my shoulder, pleased to find that his cock wasn't just hard, it was *hard*. Tate's thick shaft was nearly purple, the skin pulled tight like it was ready to explode. I wondered how close he was, and I reached back and grabbed him. His cock was burning hot against my hand, like I'd grabbed a fire poker. His eyes flew open and he whimpered, the sound sending a desperate vibration through my whole body.

I gave a stroke down his length, and his back bowed off the floor. He tried to thrash his head, but my knees kept him in place, my own dick spearing him. I pulled on his cock, twisting my wrist around the thickest part of his shaft, getting harder by the second in response to every sound he made. I'd never been with a man as responsive as Tate, and when he opened his eyes, I found him drunk on lust and fear in a way that spoke to the very heart of who I was.

"I can't come like this," I lied, tearing myself away from his mouth and standing. The condoms and lube were on the couch, and I pointed toward the place I'd previously been sitting. "Crawl over to the couch and put your ass in the air so I can fuck it."

Tate cried, a soft little mewl that made it sound like he was barely restraining himself from bursting into absolute tears. I stroked my cock, rubbing his spit into the skin as I watched him roll onto his hands and knees and crawl to the couch. He had his ass in the air, just like I'd told him to do the first time. He was a quick learner, it seemed, but not quick enough if he was still trying to hold back the only thing I wanted more than his release.

"Are you scared?" I asked, fitting myself between his spread legs and rolling the condom down my length.

"Yes," he whispered.

I poured lube over the first two fingers of my right hand, grabbing the back of his head with the other and yanking so he had to face the back of the couch instead of trying to bury his face in it.

"Is there a color you wanted to share with me?" I asked, smearing lube over his pucker and pushing one finger into him all the way down to the last knuckle.

Tate cried out, a shocked and gasping noise that sent another spurt of precum to the slit of my own dick. His ass was so hot and so tight, muscles gripping and fighting as I started to prep him for my cock.

"Don't stop," he panted, shaking his head furiously. "Please don't stop."

I pushed the second finger into him and his back went rigid. I dug my elbow down into his spine, forcing him back into an arch.

"Does it hurt?" I asked.

"Yes."

I teased a third finger against his rim, popping the tip inside along with the other two. A shiver tore through Tate's entire body and he moaned, the longest and sexiest purr I'd ever heard in my life.

"I'm going to fucking ruin this tight little hole of yours, Tate," I warned, drawing all of my fingers out and letting go of his hair. I poured a ton of lube down my cock and slathered more down the crack of his ass. It was messy and it was going to be slippery, but I had always found the best sex was the dirtiest. It also made aftercare and clean-up a necessity, which was like foreplay for me, but after the fact.

"Please," he whispered, nodding his head before shoving his face against the seat of the couch. "Please fuck me."

"Put your arms behind your back," I said, and he did, aligning his forearms over the small of his back.

I curled my fingers around his wrist, pinning him down to the couch and using my hips to push my cock inside of him. Tate was beyond tight, and that didn't just apply to his ass. Even his mouth had been tense and warm around my cock. I said I couldn't come in his mouth, but that had been part of the game, part of me trying to find a way to get the tears I was so very desperate for.

Turns out that using my body was enough, though, because once I shoved my dick all the way into Tate, his entire body shook with the force of the first sound that burst out of him. I shivered, growling as I pulled away and then fucked back into him with a sharp snap of my hips.

Tate absolutely fucking wailed, his muscles gripping around my cock as I fucked him with a relentless and unsustainable pace. I wasn't worried about going for a long time. He was already in tears and I was going to come sooner rather than later. Releasing his wrists, I slid my arm around the front of his chest and rocked back onto my heels. It dropped him down onto my cock at a new angle that had him whimpering and trembling in my lap like a fucking dream.

"Go on, Tate," I coaxed, bumping him with my hips. "Ride me."

It took a little bit of fumbling, but Tate found a rhythm with short lifts off my lap. My crown dragged across the soft bundle of nerves just inside of him with every jolt of movement, and Tate dropped his head against my shoulder with a groan. I dragged my hand up, covering his mouth with it and angling his face to the side so I could see him better.

Tate's face was tracked with tears, like a goddamn rainstorm had burst out of his eyes. I stuck out my tongue and flattened it, licking alongside his cheekbone and over the crook of his nose to catch as many of the salty tears as I could. With my other hand, I grabbed Tate's cock, not entirely surprised to find it soiled with cum already.

"You came?" I asked, nipping his ear.

Tate nodded, sucking in a gasp of a breath that vacuumed against the palm of my hand. He still rode me as best he could, fresh tears slicking over my knuckles and trying to race into his mouth. His hole convulsed, and I chuckled in his ear. The reaction to a lack of air was one of my favorites, and I teased his nostrils with my thumb and the side of my finger. I didn't go so far as to actually block his air, but the promise of it was enough. Tate's body spasmed, another trickle of cum leaking out of his cock, his asshole doing everything in its power to suck me inside of him.

With his orgasm already out of the way, I was ready for my own.

Even though our liaison had been brief, Tate was one of the best—and most willing—lovers I'd ever had. I hated we were at The Black Door and not my home, because the way I would have fucking cleaned him up afterward would have been the absolute pleasure of my life. I didn't want to think about what I was missing out on, though, not with his tears and his body and his desperate little sounds filling the space like an aphrodisiac designed especially for me.

"I'm going to fuck you now, Tate," I warned.

He made a confused sound, and I shoved him face first

into the couch. It was easy to grab his hips, to dig my fingers in, to draw my hips back and slam into him, bottoming out. The couch muffled Tate's cries, and it didn't take more than a minute for my own release to wash over me like a tsunami wave. I shot my load into the condom, spurt after spurt of cum filling the tip as my body wrung pleasure from every nerve ending I had. My back ached from how hard the orgasm had torn through me. My fingers cramped for how hard I held Tate's body against mine.

"Just like that," I said, panting and out of breath.

I pried my fingers off his hips, stroking them instead down his sweaty and trembling back until my own breathing returned to normal. I was still hard, still inside of him, and with a reluctant grunt, I withdrew. With our bodies no longer connected, Tate's knees finally gave out. He collapsed against the couch at the same time I fell onto my ass with a loud exhale.

Swallowing hard, I swiped the back of my hand across my face, flicking the sweat out of my eyes and onto the floor. Tate reached blindly for me, one hand patting around until he found my thigh, and then he relaxed further into the leather of the couch, his knees splayed out beside my thigh.

"I wish you would have let me take you home," I finally told him, pulling him up off the floor so I could give him a post-sex inspection.

Tate looked to be in as good condition as when I'd gotten him, if not better. The flush did wonders for his skin, and his hair looked even better after it had my fingers in it. His eyes were puffy and swollen, tears still damp against his cheeks.

"Home felt personal," he said, voice hoarse and cracking

from all the screaming and crying he'd done. Tate cleared his throat and shrugged.

"Sex is personal."

With far older knees than his, I climbed up from my seat on the floor and went to get a wash cloth from the bathroom so I could start the process of cleaning him up. I tucked my dick back into my pants and flipped on the light in the bathroom, grateful it wasn't bright white. The water ran hot quickly, and I wet a rag, grabbed a dry towel, then headed back into the room. Tate was still on the floor, but he'd shifted onto his ass, legs splayed out in front of him.

I dropped the towel on the couch, then went back down to the ground beside him.

"You don't have to do this," he said, raising a hand to stop me.

I batted him away. "I want to."

"But you don't—"

"Are you going to safeword?" I interrupted, brow arched in challenge. My dark blond hair had fallen loose from its styling, and I tried to settle it back with a rough jerk of my head.

"No," Tate whispered, shaking his head. "I'm not going to safeword."

"Good." I wrapped the warm cloth around his cock and gently cleaned the drying cum from his shaft and from his balls. He got hard again under my touch, but I did my best to ignore it. I also tried to ignore my own resurfaced erection, because if I was going to fuck Tate again, it sure as fuck wasn't going to be here.

He closed his eyes and sniffled, letting me clean him up as best as the tools would allow. Another tear slid out from the corner of his eye and I knew he'd said no kissing, but I leaned forward and kissed his closed eyelid anyway.

"There," I said, tossing the towel and rag into a pile on the floor. "That's a start."

I stood up and held out my hand for him. Tate blinked up at me, chest still heaving as he slid his hand into mine. I helped him to his feet, then gently brushed his curls away from his face. The puffiness in his eyes had already started to go down, but his lashes were dark and clumped together from all the tears. Heat pooled low in my belly, and I cleared my throat, taking a step away from him.

"Why don't you get dressed and we can have another drink, then I'll make sure you get home all right?"

"Okay," he said softly, nodding.

His clothes were scattered across the room and I collected them into one place for him.

"I'm going to clean up and take a piss, then we'll grab a drink?"

"Yes." He nodded. "Thank you."

I headed into the bathroom where I tore off the condom and flung it into the trash. I rinsed my cock off in the sink, then I took a piss and washed my hands. There wasn't much to be done about my hair, but I wasn't the first person to get fucked in this club and I surely wouldn't be the last. When I'd gotten myself in as much order as I could manage, which wasn't much at all considering the front of my pants were smeared with Tate's sweat and cum, I turned off the bathroom light and stepped back into the room, cursing under my breath when I realized what had happened.

Tate was gone.

"Harder."

Both syllables of the demand fell out of my mouth with ease and I readjusted my hands against the expensive rug beneath me. I was on all fours, the man behind me in desperate need of a dictionary because instead of fucking me harder, he only started to thrust into me faster. Sweat dripped down from his forehead, splattering against the small of my back, and I wanted to crawl into a hole and die.

My knees didn't even burn from the friction.

The whole encounter was a waste of time.

"Are you close?" he asked.

I think his name was Jack. Or maybe it was James. Jim. I didn't care because after he finished and got off of me, I wasn't ever going to see him again.

"Yes," I lied, shifting my weight to reach between my legs and stroke my cock. I was barely hard, the slit moist with precum because I *was* getting fucked, though not well.

Behind me, Jim/Jack's breathing stuttered, and I closed my

eyes and stroked my cock. I didn't have to think about Brooks for long before I was fully hard, and even less time after that before I found myself coming into my hand. The rough way he'd handled me was a high I'd been chasing since our first—and only—night together. Six months later and I was yet to meet a man who had the audacity to fuck me with such a dedicated level of reckless abandon.

I wanted to cry for the misery of it all, not the pleasure.

James went still behind me, fingers barely digging into my hips as he finished into the condom. The aftershocks of his release hadn't even died down before I was crawling away from him and pushing onto my feet.

"I'll be right back," I muttered, giving a tight pull down my shaft to clear the rest of the cum from my slit.

The en suite was against the far wall of his bedroom, all glaring white marble with gold veins, plush white towels, and gold hardware. It felt like a gaudy hotel, and I should have known from first sight that the night was going to be an absolute bust. Kicking the door closed behind me, I rinsed my hand and my dick off in the sink, then used one of the expensive towels to dry myself off.

I tried to not take too long to study myself in the mirror because I knew I wouldn't like what I saw, but it was impossible to ignore my reflection entirely. Catching my own stare, I found my cheeks flushed a light shade of pink and my hair barely mussed up out of place. With damp fingers, I smoothed the light brown strands back into place and frowned.

"Better luck next time," I told myself, tossing the towel onto the floor and heading back into the bedroom.

Jack was on his back, cum filled condom still on his cock

and an arm flung over his face. He was spread out on the carpet like a starfish and his chest heaved with every breath.

"Are you all right?" I asked, bending down to gather my clothes up from the floor so I could get dressed and leave.

He breathed out what sounded like a laugh. "Am I all right? Are *you* all right? I was really going at it pretty hard at the end."

I buttoned up my jeans and tugged my shirt over my head.

"I'm fine," I assured him.

I couldn't find my socks, so I shoved my feet into my sneakers without them. I didn't care enough to stay and look. In the middle of the floor, Joe struggled to pull off the condom, wincing as the tight latex tugged at his sensitive skin.

"I'm going to head out," I said after the condom ripped off with a painful-sounding pop. Jim tied it into a knot with one hand and dropped it on the carpet. My eye twitched, grateful that he hadn't been better in bed because that probably meant my face would have dragged through some old cum stains on the carpet, which...my depravity didn't go that far.

Yet.

I wondered if it ever would.

Sometimes, when I let myself fantasize about my night with Astor Brooks, I imagined I let him take me home like he wanted and then my mind really ran wild. There were no ends to the ways he would try to make me cry to get himself off, and I loved every fucking second of it. I'd been chasing the high of that adrenaline and arousal since then, but I hadn't come close to catching it. Instead, all I had was a laundry list of men who thought they knew how to fuck.

They were wrong.

"You don't have to go," John said to me, still splayed out in the middle of his rug.

My shoes were already on, though, and the shame was quickly creeping in.

"I know." I gave him as much of an honest smile as I could manage. "But it's late."

"Can I see you again?" he asked, rolling onto his side to get a better view of me.

Brooks hadn't asked to see me again. The oversight had been a thorn in my side for over one hundred and eighty days, and I knew I should have been flattered that Jerome wanted another round with me, but I didn't have it in me to pretend his brand of sex was something that I found interesting.

"We agreed," I reminded him, tapping the pocket of my jeans to check for my phone. "This was a hookup, not a date."

"I know." He sighed. "I just—"

"Not a date," I interrupted, confirming my wallet and keys were where they belonged.

Josh was still on the floor, showing no signs of moving anytime soon. It felt rude to step over him, so I maneuvered my way around him to get to his bedroom door.

"Alright," he said, sounding resigned.

"Have a good rest of your night..." I was ninety-nine percent sure his name was Josh. "Josh?"

Behind me, he groaned. "It's Jason."

"Right."

I slipped out of the bedroom and closed the door behind me with a quiet click of the latch. At least I knew with the name snafu that he wasn't going to come after me and beg me to stay. The rest of Jason's apartment was as horrible as his bathroom, and I wondered, if not for the first time, fucking rich men was where I was going wrong. Sure, Brooks obviously was dripping with money, as were his friends, but maybe they were outliers.

Maybe what I needed was to get another guest invite to The Black Door, but the friends who had invited me earlier in the year and I had fallen out, so they wouldn't be able to get me in. I knew all I would have to do was finagle my way back into that club and if I didn't find Brooks, I'd find someone much closer to his sensibilities than the internet was providing me.

Pulling Jason's door closed behind me, I decided to take the stairs instead of the elevator. When I reached the ground level, I checked my email, as if somehow the waiting list at The Black Door had decided to cut itself into pieces so I could find myself at the top of the list. Last time I had checked, there were well over a hundred people on the list in front of me, and the admission rate crept along slower than a snail's pace.

On the sidewalk, I oriented myself and flagged down a cab to go home. It was walkable, and the night air was warm enough, but I didn't want to have too much time alone to myself to think. If I got home, my roommate, Dylan, would be there. He was a good enough distraction to keep my mind off how absolutely horrible my sex life had been since Brooks.

The car zipped through the city to Chelsea, dropping me off in front of my building. We lived on the third floor, and my legs showed the strength that came with four years of going up and down those stairs. I shouldered my way through the door on the street that was always stuck, then took my time to climb the stairs up to our cramped third-floor unit. From the outside of the locked door, I could hear the familiar sounds of Dylan playing his guitar, and I couldn't stop myself from smiling as I unlocked the deadbolt and let myself in.

Our apartment was beautiful, but small, and Dylan wasn't more than twenty feet away on the couch, hunched over with his fingers strumming over the strings. I headed toward him, dropping my keys and phone on the kitchen counter before plopping down across from him on our extremely small sectional. Dylan smiled, soft lyrics I couldn't make sense of falling out of his mouth while he continued to play.

Dylan and I had started as roommates four years earlier, but we'd quickly become friends. He was a trust fund kid from Connecticut who only used his family money for rent and food, which was more than I had, but it ensured I never had to worry about eviction so I didn't begrudge him for it. Dylan was a talented musician, thanks to a lifetime of lessons, but he was making a decent amount of money on his own from the random gig on top of his usual bartending job.

Propping my feet up on our thrifted coffee table, I rested my head against the wall, listening to the gentle lilt of his tenor voice and the way it wrapped around the sounds coming from his guitar. A few minutes later, he finished, softly tapping his palm against the neck before setting the instrument down on the floor.

"Short night?" he asked, reaching for a beer bottle that looked like it had been sitting neglected for well over an hour.

I glanced at the clock on the wall over the stove, a perk of having your kitchen and your living room in the same small box of space, I supposed. The kitchen was also the laundry room, but I'd never complain about all the times we'd drunkenly mistaken the dishwasher for the washing machine, tossing shirts onto the plate rack and glasses into the dryer because I knew how rare it was to have laundry in our unit.

"He wasn't my type," I said with a shrug.

"They never are."

"He's like a unicorn." I waved my hand like I could magic Brooks out of the air. "No one will ever believe I saw him, and the longer time goes by, the more *I* will begin to wonder if he's real."

I needed to get used to having boring sex. I knew there was no way around it, but I couldn't bring myself to do the mental gymnastics required to get there. Every week The Black Door sent me an email with an unchanged update to my position on the waitlist.

"I believe you saw him." Dylan traded his beer for his guitar and he strummed a chord, batting his eyelashes at me as he started to sing. "Tate found himself a unicorn, a man who liked to fuck."

I reached behind me and grabbed a throw pillow to fling at his face. He used his shoulder to deflect, standing with his guitar in hand and heading toward his bedroom near the front door.

"He got himself fucked through the floor, since then he's been out of luck!"

I crawled over the couch and snatched the pillow again, lobbing it down the hallway at him. It bounced off the back of his head and he played some dramatic noise on his guitar before setting it on the stand in his bedroom and coming back to join me in the living room. He kicked the pillow in my direction and got us fresh beers out of the fridge before sitting back down on the couch.

"Besides the bad sex," he said, twisting off the bottle cap, "how was your night."

"My night *was* bad sex," I lamented, taking a swig of the IPA Dylan had brought home from work the night before. "How was your night?"

"Good," he said with a nod and a grin. "I actually picked up a second bartending gig that I started tonight. The tips are way better than at Tryst, so I might have to switch my hours out."

Tryst was a bar in Manhattan that Dylan had been working at for two years. The owner, Marigold, was a sweet little hippie chick with bleached hair and a heavy pour. She had been great to Dylan from the start, always flexible with his schedule if a music gig came up, and that was worth more to him than any paycheck would ever be. He loved it there, and I loved that he loved it there too. Marigold let him bring home beer and liquor almost every night, which didn't seem like a good business model to me, but it was definitely a perk that kept her turnover rate near zero.

"I can't believe I'm hearing you right," I said, pressing at my ear like I was trying to pop it. "Tell me about this new spot."

Dylan pushed a breath out of his nose, his cheeks turning a little dark and he picked mindlessly at the label on his beer. If I didn't know better, I would have said he was embarrassed, but there wasn't anything embarrassing about slinging drinks.

"It's not too far from Tryst." Dylan worked his jaw a little, one of his eyes squinting a bit in the corner.

"Why are you being so weird?" I asked, leaning in toward

him, elbows resting on my knees. "Is it a strip club or something?"

Dylan groaned, scrubbing a hand down his face and falling sideways onto the couch with this head in my lap and his arm outstretched, beer still in hand.

"Not exactly."

I arched a brow.

"It's a sex club," he stage-whispered, scrunching his nose. "It's called The Black Door."

CHAPTER 3

BROOKS

Life wasn't what it used to be.

A year ago, Friday night would have found me and my group of friends out at The Black Door looking for trouble. Now, though...Ford was upstate fucking Boston on a farm, Kale was probably wearing a flannel pajama set and doing a crossword puzzle while Christian sucked his cock like a pacifier, and Alex...

Getting Alex to socialize since Beamer moved to Los Angeles had been worse than pulling teeth, but over the past handful of months, he'd started to show his face more. When I found him leaning against the bar at The Black Door, chatting with a bartender and wearing an actual smile on his face, I momentarily worried he'd been body-snatched. When he saw me, Alex raised his hand to wave, the smile actually widening instead of disappearing.

"You look like you're in a good mood," I said, sliding up beside him at the bar.

"My favorite bartender from my favorite bar just got a job

here," Alex said, gesturing toward whom I assumed to be the newest addition to the staff at The Black Door.

I gave the man a quick onceover, decidedly unimpressed with everything about him save for the way he made my closest friend smile.

"Great," I said, grabbing Alex's drink out of his hand and taking a swallow. It was the strongest martini I'd ever had in my life, and I was fairly certain it had far more liquor in it than it should have. "I'll have one of these, Alex's favorite bartender."

The man's mouth quirked up in the corner, but he made the drink with quiet and practiced ease.

"My name is Dylan," he said, sliding the glass toward me.

"So it is." I clinked the edge of my glass against Alex's, then hauled him away from the bar. "Let's get some air. It's so nice out tonight."

"It's nice inside tonight," he said, letting me drag him toward the elevators.

"The bartender is paid to be here," I reminded him. "He'll be here when we're done."

Alex huffed, but the smile hadn't quite disappeared from his face, which I took as a good sign. We rode up the elevator together, getting smacked in the face with the scent of sex as soon as the doors slid open on the upper floor of the club. It was mostly enclosed, but there was a patio on the west side of the building for when weather allowed, and weather was definitely allowing.

"Tell me about your favorite bar," I said, finding a table for us outside and settling into one of the upholstered patio chairs. It wasn't as comfortable as inside, but the smell of cum and sweat was going to send me into a frenzy if I didn't get a break from it. I hadn't had sex in over a month, and I was practically chomping at the bit to get someone home and into bed. No matter how much my friends wanted to tease me about being easy, I was far more discerning with my partners than they ever gave me credit for. I liked to fuck hard and often, but it was a special kind of partner who could deliver the reactions and the responses I wanted.

I wasn't cut to everyone's tastes. I'd learned that by accident at a very young age.

Growing up with the internet had been a blessing and a curse because early internet porn had done far more harm than good to my sexual development. At least, that's what I had grown up thinking. Now, as an adult, I understood there wasn't anything wrong with me or the way I liked to get off. It simply wasn't the way *most* people chose to get off.

My sexual tastes made relationships hard, but not impossible. I craved the established intimacy of a long-term partner because I'd found my brand of aftercare and attention made strangers far more uncomfortable than the rough sex on the front end. There was a certain kind of vulnerability that came with tenderness, and lots of people were terrified of it. I couldn't blame them. It was terrifying to be known, but I'd long since committed to abandoning things that didn't serve me, that fear included.

In the end, it was that brand of exposure that had sent my last long-term partner, Tyler, running for the hills. We'd split up two years earlier, and I had finally started to settle into what felt like a new normal for me. Things with us ended as amicably as a one-sided split could, and the day he gave me back the key to my penthouse was the last time I'd seen his face.

I owed him thanks, though. It was through the breakup with Tyler that I solidified my own relationship limits. The eighteen months he and I spent together helped me to find more comfort in my kinks and myself, and the solitude that came after our breakup had been welcome and easy. I knew what things I could compromise on and the things I never would. For that, I owed Tyler a debt of gratitude. Unfortunately, he wasn't interested in me owing him anything. I imagined he'd learned some hard truths about himself as well.

"You're not even listening," Alex said, the first words I'd heard out of his mouth since we'd sat down.

I managed a small laugh, raising the martini to my lips and taking a small drink of it. "Guilty as charged, but I'm trying not to get alcohol poisoning here."

My friends had been invaluable as I navigated life post-Tyler, and it hurt my heart that Alex hadn't allowed us to give him the same level of care after Beamer left. It wasn't like the two of them were anything serious, or even anything at all, but the newness between them had been secretive and beautiful, and as fast as it appeared, it was gone. Alex turned reclusive and had only just started to reappear in our weekly outings. He did better one on one, which I imagined was because, as a group, the lot of us could be *very* intense.

"I said it's a bar named Tryst. Not far from here."

Right.

We'd been talking about his mystery spot and his mystery man.

"And the bartender is from there?"

Alex nodded, eyes flashing. "I met him outside of the bar, though."

"And then you followed him inside like a wounded dog?"

"God." Alex rolled his eyes, half-smiling at me. "I almost forgot what an asshole you are."

"I think you've confused me with one Kale Sheffield."

He laughed, folding one leg over the other and resting his ankle on top his other knee. "He is a bit of a prick these days."

"Ford did a number on him with the Boston thing," I said.

"Kale did a number on himself," Alex countered. "He got huffy about me and Beamer, even worse about Ford and Boston. He has more opinions than money and I don't want either of them."

"Jesus, Alex." I scratched my chin and took a small drink of the martini. "Tell me how you really feel."

He sighed, shrugging and setting his drink on the table between us.

"Sorry." He traced his tongue across the front of his teeth. "That wasn't fair."

"It's okay to have feelings about the things he's done," I said.

"He was horrible to Beamer when he found out that we'd started playing together, when he found out that I'd marked him."

"The way you play is no surprise to anyone," I reminded him, knowing what it was like to be on the outskirts of acceptability myself. "He was more caught off-guard because he didn't understand the depths of Beamer's submission."

"If you say so."

"I know so." I curled my fingers around Alex's wrist and lifted his glass toward his mouth. "I don't want to talk about our overbearing counterpart right now. I want to enjoy the night with you and then see what happens."

"The bartender is what's happening," Alex said, grin turning feral.

"Don't break him," I teased.

"He didn't complain the first time," Alex said, "or the second."

"Did you have a hand in getting him a job here?"

I leaned back and stretched my legs out, rolling both of my ankles to give them a little crack. It wasn't like I was old, but when I wasn't being active, my body showed more signs of wear than not. Outside of sex, the only exercise I got was from my morning runs. I'd never wanted to bother with weight training or anything like that. When I was in school, I'd been a swimmer, good enough to make the team but not good enough to win any awards or scholarships. My mind had always been more focused on things that were complicated, like financial review and contract negotiations and I excelled academically. My interest in extracurriculars didn't manifest until college when I realized it was possible to have sex in real life that matched the sex I'd grown up jacking off to.

"I knew there was an opening," Alex said. "I put in a good word and let him know about the posting."

"The next great philanthropist," I muttered.

"I'm a creature of convenience," he said back. "I like it here."

"How did you know there was an opening in the first place?" I asked. "You hardly come out anymore."

Alex tilted his head to the side, a sad smile flitting across his face before he answered, "I don't come here with you."

"I want to be offended."

"The royal you." He gestured to the empty seats across from us.

I made a knowing sound in the back of my throat. "You have been doing better one on one lately, that's the truth."

"Less questions."

"Is that why?" I arched a brow. "Or is it easier to hide when there are fewer eyes on you?"

Alex tipped the rest of his drink down his throat and thrust the empty glass at me. "Go get me another martini if you're trying to be so serious tonight."

I laughed, taking it and standing.

"I'm not being depressing. You're my friend. I worry about you and I miss you."

"I promise it's not as bad as you think it's been," he said. "Maybe at first, but I'm really doing okay."

"I believe you."

"It's nothing like when you and Tyler broke up." Alex laughed, leaning back and switching the position of his crossed legs.

"Maybe Kale is fine," I said, knocking the rest of my drink back. "Maybe you're the prick."

"You wouldn't be the first to make the accusation. Get drinks from Dylan—they're stronger."

"I am not in the market for a two-drink limit," I said, heading toward the door.

Alex was lucky the line for the upper level bar was enough to make me want to tear my hair out, so I rode the elevator down, stuck in the small space with a pink-haired little twink humping the thigh of a bear of a businessman. My cock twitched at the noises falling out of his mouth and the thick smell of precum that quickly filled the space. I dropped my head back and rubbed the bridge of my nose. The doors slid open and I stepped off the elevator. The doors closed behind me with the couple still inside.

For the first time in a long time, the air in the first floor was more breathable than the top, so I didn't rush when I made my way through tables and around the dance floor toward the bar in the back of the space. The music was low, the bass heavy, and everyone seemed to be having an enjoyable night. I was still half-hard from the elevator ride, and I stopped against a pillar beside the bar to adjust myself before filling my hands up with drinks.

Alex's little bartender leaned over the bar top, laughing at a slender man with a mess of brown hair that wasn't short or long, but enough length to get my fist around. I hadn't even seen his face, just the build of him from behind enough to spark my attention.

Discerning or not, I still had a type.

The bartender glanced up, still speaking to the man in front of him, but when he saw me with my hand on my dick, his nostrils flared with recognition. I was quick to unhand myself, coming up to the bar and setting the empty glasses down in front of me. The last thing I wanted was for him to get the idea I was rubbing myself off in public *to him*. Even if I found Dylan attractive—which I didn't—Alex had good as claimed him already.

"Where's your friend?" Dylan asked me, head cocked to the side like the coy little flirt he was.

"Upstairs waiting for you to get off work, I think." I leaned my hip against the bar, half-facing the patron whose conversation I'd been rude enough to interrupt. "Who's *your* friend?"

When the man turned to face me, the recognition flared up my spine like a bolt of lightning. I knew this man. I'd been inside of this man before. It had been months ago, but I'd remember the way he looked as he came for the rest of my life.

"Tate," I said his name, licking my lips as a smile formed on my face.

"You know each other?" Dylan asked. Tate glared at him and Dylan's eyes went wide like he knew a secret. Like he knew *me...*

"That might be an understatement," I said, swallowing down the pleasure that came with seeing Tate's face again.

He looked similar to the night I'd met him, but maybe a little more tired, his hair a little bit longer than before. That would explain my initial thoughts, though. I'd already had my hands in his hair; I knew how soft it was, how silky it felt against my palm. We'd had a great time together, and then he'd snuck out on me without a word, which had broken my heart because that breach of trust meant one thing and one thing only.

I was never going to sleep with Tate again.

BROOKS LOOKED EVEN BETTER THAN I REMEMBERED, WHICH FELT LIKE the second greatest unfairness of my life. The first of which, of course, being losing my virginity to him—the best fuck on the planet.

There was a fleeting second where Brooks looked like he was pleased to see me, but it was gone in a flash. His expression immediately shuttered like the sound of my name had pressed a panic button that sent him into an emotional shutdown.

"Is this..." Dylan started, but trailed off. I knew the question he was getting ready to ask, and both of us knew the answer.

Yes, this was Astor Brooks in the flesh, the man I'd been obsessing over for the past six months. The best sex I was never going to have again.

Brooks collected the two drinks Dylan had made for him, then looked at me with a polite dip of his chin toward his chest.

"Good seeing you again, Tate. Have a good night."

With that, I was dismissed. He turned quickly on his heel and headed toward the elevators without so much as a glance back in my direction.

"Is that really him?" Dylan asked, expression equal parts horrified and curious. "I didn't even know you'd heard of this place before."

"Some friends from work…" I explained, brow furrowed.

The first night I'd found myself at The Black Door, I'd been with some coworkers. They'd gotten me in as a guest, then promptly ditched me for funner pastures. Brooks' friend Ford had propositioned me to play the part of a good little boy on my knees, but that only lasted long enough for Brooks to set his sights on me and then all bets were off.

Brooks had taken me to a back room at the club and proceeded to fuck me to within an inch of my life. I'd never felt better, more alive. He'd told me to stay put, said he'd make sure I got the money I was owed, then he'd gone into the bathroom and left me there, dressed in cold clothes and feeling more like a whore than was comfortable. Even as I'd gotten up and snuck out of the room, I'd known he hadn't meant it that way. Ford owed me money and Brooks was going to make sure I got it, but didn't he understand the money didn't matter? What he'd given me counted for far more than a few hundred dollars ever could.

"So, when I told you I got hired here, you knew about this place?" Dylan asked.

"I've only been here once," I said. "I've been trying to get a membership, but the waitlist is a mile long."

"Knowing an employee has its perks then." He raised a brow.

"Apparently."

The truth was I could have found Brooks if I really wanted to. I knew his first and last name, but I hadn't found the courage to look him up on the internet. And even though I was desperate for more of his brand of sex, I wasn't going to show up at his house or his work for it. That would have been positively unhinged, and I was only in the beginning stages of being sex-crazed for him.

"Are you going to go after him?"

"He clearly doesn't want to talk to me."

Dylan narrowed his stare, giving me a disapproving shake of his head right before getting called to the other end of the bar to mix a drink.

I should have gone after Brooks. For as long as I'd spent chasing after the high of being with him, as many fantasies as I'd built and stacked on top of each other, I was stupid to not run after him. But what would I do if I found him again? If he was willing to speak with me?

Brooks, please. I need you to fuck me again because no one since you has ever come close and I'm starting to think I'm losing my mind and creating fake memories because there's no way you could be that *much better in bed than every man since you.*

It sounded crazy.

It felt crazy.

But my feet carried me toward the elevator anyway, and I was shocked to find Brooks lingering there, two drinks still balanced in one hand. He was looking for me when I got there, expression pulled tight and very close to miserable.

"Can we talk?" I asked.

I didn't remember he was shorter than me, didn't recall the graying blond around his temples. For me, it was the strength of his hands, the pulse in his cock, the things he'd said to me...

"How are you liking the weather, Tate?"

I scoffed. "Are you serious?"

"It's warm for this time of year," he said.

"I don't care about the weather."

Brooks traced his tongue across the front of his teeth. "What *do* you care about? Because it's clearly not respecting other people."

My jaw hit the floor, and I bracketed both hands over my hips, in absolute shock at the accusation. "What the fuck are you talking about?"

"The last thing I said to you, Tate, was that I was going to go piss and then we would get a drink. Do you remember that?"

"Of course."

"And what did we actually end up doing?" he asked.

Embarrassment burned my cheeks, reminding me of the way I'd fled the back room when he wasn't looking. "I left."

He nodded. "You left."

"I was intimidated," I tried to explain, but Brooks just shook his head and rolled his eyes at me.

"I don't want your excuses."

"It's not an excuse," I snapped, a cold sweat breaking out against the back of my neck and sliding down my spine. My shirt stuck to my skin, but I didn't dare move to dislodge it. Even though the conversation was tentative at best, it was better than nothing, and I worried any sudden movements or exclamations would ruin that.

Brooks sighed, shifting the martinis from one hand to the other. I didn't know how he was able to balance both between his fingers in the first place, but it was just one more thing for me to add to the list of things about Astor Brooks that made no sense and blew my mind all at the same time.

"What do you want, Tate?" he finally asked, sounding resigned.

"I don't know," I said, even though it was a lie. I wasn't brave enough to ask him for what I really wanted, which was another round or ten. I wanted to let him take me back to his house and show me how he would have fucked me the first time if I'd let him have his way.

"I know what you want," he said, biting the inside of his cheek and hollowing it out. "You want to fuck again. You want me to take you home and do all the things I would have done that last time."

My breath caught in my throat, but I managed a nod. "I wouldn't hate that."

"It's never going to happen." Brooks moved his weight from foot to foot.

"Why not?" I asked the question so quickly, I didn't even give myself time to think about how out of order it was. Brooks could have a boyfriend, or a girlfriend, or something. There were a thousand reasons for him to tell me no, and he didn't owe me an explanation, but I'd spent so long dreaming and wanting, and it felt cruel to have him here now but also so out of reach.

"I don't fuck people I can't trust, Tate," he said simply.

That was one thing I'd forgotten. The way he used my name, how it rolled off his tongue like a kiss.

"I was a stranger," I rasped, "the first time."

"I had no reason not to trust you then," he said. "I give people the benefit of the doubt, but now I know you aren't a man of your word, and I can't sleep with people...I can't fuck people the way I like to fuck if I don't trust them."

"I was scared!" I practically shouted at him, my voice echoing loudly over the noise of the club at my back. The exclamation startled us both, and I slapped my hand over my mouth to stop myself from another ill-timed outburst. He watched me carefully as I swallowed back down any other protest, a thousand follow-ups racing through my head as I fought my own body to take my hand away.

"All the more reason," he said sadly, sidestepping toward the elevator.

"Not during," I said quickly, holding up my hands like I was surrendering to him.

Again.

"Not during," I repeated, shaking my head. "I wasn't scared then, just..."

Brooks swallowed, stare flickering toward the elevator doors that slid open to my right. He didn't make a move to get on and after a beat, they slid closed. I exhaled, relieved that even though his words said he was finished with me, he wasn't done yet.

"After?" he prompted.

I nodded.

"The end of it is my favorite part, Tate," he said, tilting his head to the side. The weight of his stare was as heavy as the memory of his hands in my hair.

"You don't understand," I stammered, eyes going wide as he pushed the call button again. The elevator was still right there and the doors immediately opened. I jumped in front of the gap as if I could stop him from getting on. Like I wouldn't move out of the way if he told me to.

The doors closed again, and Brooks sighed heavily.

"I have a friend waiting for his drink," he said.

"I know, I'm sorry. I just..." I was fucking it up. I had the chance I'd been waiting months for and I was absolutely ruining it by somehow saying both the right things and the wrong things at the same time.

"You just what, Tate?" He blinked at me slowly. "Call the elevator back."

I pushed the button without thinking because he'd told me to, and I promptly cursed myself for being the one to deliver him his escape vehicle. The doors didn't open, which meant it had headed toward the top floor. There was still more time.

"You have until it's here to say your piece, then I'm going upstairs to finish my drinks with Alex and enjoy the rest of my night," he said.

The only wrong thing to say was nothing, I decided.

"You can't just..."

Brooks arched a brow at the implication he'd been the one at fault here.

"You can't just fuck someone like that and then leave," I said.

"I didn't leave," he said dryly. "You did."

"I know, and I shouldn't have." The doors opened behind me and three men got off, stepping around me to get out. "I'm sorry. I'm sorry."

Brooks cocked his head to the side, chin angled toward the empty elevator waiting behind me. I moved out of the way and he brushed past me into the small space, smelling like gin and lemons and everything I wanted every partner I'd had since him to smell like.

"Have a good night, Tate," he said, turning to face me once he was safely in the elevator.

"You can't just leave," I pleaded, angry at myself the words wouldn't come out.

For all the times I'd imagined wild and new fantasies of sex with Brooks, I'd never once given a single ounce of thought to what *this* conversation would go like. If I had, I would have known what to say, I could have handled it better and said the right thing to make him understand.

"Good night, Tate," he said again.

The doors started to close and I shouted the only thing that came to mind, which was probably also not the right thing, but...

"You can't just take my virginity like that and expect me to be okay fucking boring vanilla men for the rest of my life, Brooks!"

The doors were closing by the time I told him I'd been a virgin, but the rest of it happened in slow motion. His eyes went wide and his grip faltered. One of the martini glasses slid out of his otherwise steely grip and fell, shattering at his feet. Neither of us looked down at the mess. His gaze was instead fixed on me, whiskey-brown eyes filled with a horrifying level of shock and alarm.

And then the door slid closed, and he was gone.

CHAPTER 5

BROOKS

I DIDN'T BREATHE UNTIL THE ELEVATOR DOORS CLOSED AND PROBABLY not even until the upper floor of the club was reached and they slid open again. There was glass all over the floor, a pungent mix of vodka and vermouth along the outside of my leg. Alex was standing in front of the elevator doors when they opened, his expression immediately switching from annoyance to concern.

"What took you so long?" he asked, frowning at the glass beside my feet.

"I was waylaid," I said, switching the one remaining drink to my free hand so I could shake the other one dry.

"By whom?"

Alex shoved his foot against the elevator door to stop it from attempting to close between us. He flagged down someone behind him, who showed up with a little broom and dustpan to clean up the mess I'd made. I stepped over the broken glass, apologizing profusely to the employee and handing the one remaining drink to Alex.

"I ran into someone I slept with before," I said.

"That's not uncommon for you," he teased, "especially not here."

"Months ago," I said, watching as the employee finished cleaning up after me. I apologized again, and he waved me off.

"Also not uncommon." Alex took a sip of the martini and then smiled when he realized it was Dylan-made. He handed it to me and I took a larger drink to calm my nerves.

I watched the elevator doors slide closed for what felt like the tenth time in as many minutes. I held my breath, needing to know if Tate was going to step inside and ride it up. If he was going to come after me again. That would have made twice in one night he chased after me, neither of which would make up for the time he walked away unannounced.

But it was a fair start.

"That man I stole from Ford," I said, still staring at the doors. "The one he paid off before Kale knew about Boston."

"That was forever ago."

"I know."

Alex took the drink back out of my hand, smirking as he watched me watch the doors.

"I was surprised you sent him on his way that night," Alex mused, pressing his shoulder into mine so we could both face the elevator.

"I didn't," I muttered. "I told him to stay and he left."

"Ah. The trust was broken then."

The doors opened and, as expected, Tate was there. Beside me, Alex let out a low chuckle and stepped forward at the same time Tate stepped toward me.

"Exactly," I said.

"Sounds like it's worth a conversation," he suggested.

"I doubt it."

Alex was already walking away from me, he and Tate passing midway between me and the elevator. They locked eyes, and I couldn't see the look Alex gave him, but Tate's expression immediately soured.

"You're a piece of shit," I said, throwing my voice so Tate would know I was talking to Alex and not him, even though the sentiment wasn't far off for either of them.

"So I've been told on more than one occasion." Alex raised his glass just as the elevator doors closed behind him and Tate came to a stop right in front of me.

I studied him quietly and carefully, trying my best to focus on his face in front of me and not the memories of his face while my dick was buried in his ass. My mind was quick to wander, though, which wasn't going to be good, considering it was imperative I remember the bomb Tate had dropped on me just as the elevator doors closed between us.

"Let me explain," Tate said.

I frowned, shaking my head. "You lied to me."

"You didn't ask if I was a virgin."

"I asked if there was anything I needed to worry about," I reminded him, whisper-yelling across the short space left between us. "That's generally something to worry about."

"It was something for me to worry about, not you."

"I beg to differ."

Tate stopped, tilting his head back and rolling his eyes at me like I was a child who had told him I wanted to argue about the color of the sky.

"What if I *had* said something about it?" he asked, cocking out his hip and resting his hands on the slim and protruding bones.

"I wouldn't have fucked you," I said.

"Exactly."

I pursed my lips, having just proved his point.

"That's not..." I bit my tongue, flicking my stare up toward the ceiling like the answers were there instead of tangled in my throat. "The way I fuck isn't for beginners. Your first time shouldn't have been so..."

"Amazing?" he supplied.

"Aggressive."

"It was perfect." Tate clasped his hands together in front of him and took another step toward me. He was painfully close, the tops of his knuckles barely inches away from my chest. I hated that he was taller than me, that he had the upper hand physically when we were vertical and not horizontal.

"It was wrong," I said.

"We'll have to agree to disagree." Tate shrugged.

"We don't have to do anything."

I made a mental note to murder Alex over brunch the next day for leaving me alone. Turning on my heel, I did my best to walk away from the conversation, but Tate reached out quickly, stepping forward with one long leg and closing the space between us. He curled his fingers around my arm and brought me to a stop.

"Let go," I warned, not turning.

The release came quickly with a curse under his breath that sounded pathetic enough I turned back to face him, folding my arms over my chest with a tired sigh.

"I haven't been able to stop thinking about you," he

muttered, letting down whatever bravado he'd been wearing before. "I've fucked my way through half the city, it feels like, and no one makes me feel the way you did."

A surge of jealousy flared in the center of my chest. "You what?"

Tate rolled his eyes at me. Again.

"Well, not really half the city," he said. "I think that's physically impossible."

My jaw twitched, and Tate swallowed nervously.

"You can't act this way," he whispered. "It's not fair."

He wasn't wrong, but it wouldn't have been the first time I did something selfish when other people were involved. I had no right to care what he did on his own. I had no ownership over him. I didn't even know his last name, but there was something about the thought of it. Picturing him chasing down strangers around the city, running after the high of my kind of sex? It made me feel equal parts triumphant and furious all at the same time. My shoulders pressed back and my chest puffed out, and a tight knot of anger burned in the pit of my stomach. "I'm not a fair man, Tate."

His nostrils flared.

"And I never claimed to be," I said softly, taking a step away from him.

I didn't need to look down to know we were both hard. If we'd been any closer together, our cocks would have probably touched. I could already feel the heat radiating off of him, from his breath to his body, to the way his fingers trembled between us.

"I don't want fair," he said. "I want you."

"You lied to me."

"I omitted the truth," he countered.

"You disobeyed," I whispered.

Tate's lips parted, his chin quivering. I closed my eyes and swallowed, fighting back the urge to hook my fingers over the visible tops of his teeth and tug him to his knees so he could suck my cock. The way I wanted him was dangerous, considering he'd already proven himself to be untrustworthy. I knew better than to fuck partners I didn't trust, and he'd already shown me...

"I'll do better."

"Don't say things you don't mean." I flexed my hand into a fist at my side, releasing it and stretching my fingers against the outside of my thigh. Tate held his ground, unwavering in the pursuit of what he wanted, which was apparently now... me.

"I haven't met anyone else like you," he said, stare dragging over my face. "And I've tried."

Another knot in my stomach.

"Don't remind me," I said, before immediately asking, "How many?"

He managed a laugh, mouth twisting around the corners like he knew he'd already won his prize. "Do you really want to know?"

No.

"How many?" I asked again.

"Seventeen."

I rolled my neck, tilting it back to get a stretch after it finally cracked, releasing some of the pressure I'd been carrying since running into Tate at the bar. Seventeen was far from egregious, and if he expected a dramatic reaction out of me at the number, he was going to be disappointed.

"Maybe you should have tried harder," I suggested.

Tate scoffed. "Are you going to fuck me again or not?"

"I haven't decided." I ran a hand through my hair, shoving the strands away from my face. It was a lie. I had decided before he'd even come after me the second time.

"Maybe go piss and we can get a drink," he suggested, throwing back what I'd said to him at the end of our first encounter like the cocky little virgin he was. "See what happens."

"You're not in charge here, Tate."

"I know." His cheeks flushed and he flittered his eyelashes at me, playing coy.

"You go get me a drink," I said instead, "since it was your little confession that ruined mine."

"I think your fingers ruined yours," he interjected.

"I think my fingers ruined *you*."

His eyes went wide, and for the first time all night, he looked appropriately chastised.

"Go get me a drink, Tate," I said again, infusing all of the demand into the request I'd originally intended.

"Should I call you Sir?"

"I'd honestly rather you didn't," I choked out, clearing my throat.

My friends were the ones into those kind of games. I preferred being in charge of a far more level playing field.

"Another martini?" he asked.

"It's Alex's drink of choice," I said.

"What's yours?"

I dragged my tongue across the front of my teeth, finally reaching down to adjust the aching bulge between my legs. Tate's nostrils flared, but he didn't look down.

"Make your best guess."

Tate stepped back and looked at me from my shoes to my hair, gaze dropping back down to linger on the erection between my legs. He smirked and nodded, then disappeared into the elevator, undoubtedly returning to his friend, Dylan. I sucked in a breath and finally walked away from the elevator, needing to find a chair before my legs gave out entirely.

Everything in my body wanted to fuck Tate, but my brain was screaming no at the top of its lungs. He hadn't proven himself to be trustworthy. If anything, I felt far more than deceived over his failure to disclose something as important as being a fucking virgin. If I had known, I never would have...

And that, I realized, was the problem.

Tate was a twenty-four year-old man, and when I met him, he'd been a virgin. If I had known, I wouldn't have touched him, and he was probably tired of getting that response over and over and over, so he'd picked someone and decided not to share that integral piece of information so he didn't get shot down again. He could have just as easily found himself with a man who had much blander tastes than me and everything would have been fine.

Knowing he'd been pursuing men, trying to replicate the feelings I gave him, did more for my ego than I'd ever be willing to admit, but I needed to decide if I had it in me for another go with him. I needed to be honest with myself about what I wanted in a partner, if I even wanted a partner...

It had been so long.

Before I could make up my mind one way or another, Tate was back, an Old Fashioned in hand.

"I thought you left," he said, sounding almost out of breath with worry.

"I make a habit of showing up where I'm meant to be," I said. "You should try it sometime."

Tate set the drink on the table beside me, then sank down into the open chair across from me.

"Okay, Brooks," he said, drumming his fingers on the arms of the chair, looking up at me from beneath the fan of his lashes. "I think I will."

On the cab ride to Brooks' penthouse, I replayed the end of the conversation we'd had on the patio at The Black Door. I apologized for leaving the first night we'd met, then he asked me if kissing was still a hard limit for me. Shocked he even remembered that, I told him no, and he looked like he wanted to lick the word out of my mouth right then and there.

To say Astor Brooks was intense was an understatement, and to think, with all the fantasizing I'd done over the past six months, I'd almost forgotten just how overwhelming he could truly be.

As the cab pulled to a stop alongside the curb out front of a steel and glass skyscraper, Brooks turned to me in the back seat and studied me earnestly.

"How hard is too hard, Tate?" he asked.

I swallowed nervously. "I don't know."

"And the other way?"

The driver came around and opened my door, waiting for me to get out.

"What do you mean?" I asked.

I climbed out onto the sidewalk, smoothing my hands down the front of my jeans while Brooks followed me out. He tipped the driver, but I didn't think he'd even looked away from me for a single second.

"How soft is too soft?"

"I also don't know," I rasped.

No one had ever been soft with me before. That wasn't what I'd tried to chase after, and judging by how well I liked Brooks' hard, I didn't envision myself craving anything soft, least of all from him.

"It's still red," he said, striding past me toward the building. There was a doorman built more like a bouncer than a concierge, but I didn't want to judge. My building didn't even have an elevator, let alone a doorman.

"What's red?" I jogged to catch up to him before the brick wall of a man in front of us shut the door in my face.

"Your safe word."

Somehow, without Brooks even pressing the call button, the elevator doors slid open and he stepped inside. Again, I followed after him, heart trying to escape my body via my mouth. The organ felt like it had lodged itself in my throat, battering its way toward the nearest possible exit.

"Okay," I agreed. The doors soundlessly slid closed behind me. "It's yours too."

He scrunched his nose at that, corner of his mouth tugging up into half of a smile. "You're still the only person who's ever cared about my safe word."

I tangled my fingers together in front of me because I didn't know what to say.

The elevator raced up so fast, my stomach floated around inside of me and, on top of my nerves, I worried I was going to throw up all over both our feet. Thankfully, the numbers on the panel flashed *PH* and the car coasted to the smoothest stop of any elevator I'd ever ridden in before. The doors whooshed open into a private lobby with a single white door on the opposite wall. It reeked of modern new money, and I was thankful Brooks hadn't brought me back here the first night because there was no way I could have gone through with it. Even now, knowing what I was in for, understanding how badly I wanted it, every nerve in my body wanted to turn around and run the other way.

"You look like you're going to be sick." He pulled his wallet out of his pocket and held it up against a small black pad beside the door knob. A light flashed and beeped, and a lock in the door disengaged.

"This is a lot," I muttered.

"Last time I fucked you at The Black Door, you ran out on me," he said, twisting the knob and pushing open the front door of his home. "I figure I'm doing us both a favor by bringing you back here."

"How do you figure?"

"I get to treat you the way I want to and it's harder for you to leave." Brooks gave me a boyish grin and tilted his head toward the door.

"I hope you know that sounds far worse than you meant it to."

"Does it?"

I groaned, reaching out to grab the door before it closed. Brooks was clearly done waiting for me to get my act together, which was more than fair. I'd chased him down twice at The Black Door, and when he'd given in to what I wanted, I started to drag my feet.

"Has anyone ever told you you're intimidating?" I asked, letting the door lock itself automatically at my back.

"Often." Brooks turned to face me, hands clasped behind his back. He worried the corner of his lower lip with his tongue, and I pressed my shoulder blades against the door. "Would you like a drink?"

A laugh fell out of my mouth, and I unceremoniously slapped my hand over my face as if it would be enough to stop the noise. Brooks bit his lip between his teeth and I cursed myself, the word muffled against my palm.

"I don't want a drink," I finally said. "You know what I want."

"Demanding little thing now, aren't you?" he murmured.

"Let's not pretend this is anything other than what it is."

"And what is it?" he asked.

"Sex," I answered, the word scratching against my throat like sandpaper.

"You make it sound so transactional." Brooks took the smallest step toward me, long fingers working to pop the top button of his shirt undone. "So perfunctory."

"Isn't it?" I croaked.

"Not if you're doing it right, which we've already established you haven't been."

"Oh, fuck you."

He plucked open another button on his shirt, then another, sighing heavily.

"Take your shoes off," he said slowly, "and get mine while you're down there."

Maybe it was the nerves or the lack of blood left in my brain, but I kneeled down at Brooks' feet and carefully tugged at the waxed laces of his shiny black shoes. He balanced himself against my head to get free of them, and then I carefully tucked both of the shoes against the wall. Kicking off my black sneakers beside his made me feel poorer than I ever had before, but I didn't think there were many people in the same tax bracket as Astor Brooks...not even his own friends.

When I straightened back up to my full height, which was a handful of inches taller than him, Brooks asked me, "How did that make you feel, Tate?"

"Small," I said.

"Did you hate it?"

I shook my head, cock aching between my legs.

Actually, I opposite of hated it, which was just one more thing about myself I'd have to unpack when the night was over. It wouldn't be the first time the man standing in front of me unlocked something groundbreaking inside of me, and if all went well, it wouldn't be the last either.

Brooks made a thoughtful noise in the back of his throat and undid the final button on his shirt. He yanked the tails out from behind the secure bind of his belt, then huffed a breath in my general direction before setting to work on his cuffs. I hadn't realized he'd been wearing cufflinks, which was...

Honestly, indecently fucking sexy.

After he'd loosed them, he tossed both pieces into the air, catching them in his palm and snapping his fist closed around them. He shoved his hand into his pocket and cocked his head to the side, still studying me.

"No drink?" he checked again.

I shook my head. "No."

"Just..." He scrunched his nose again, and it was the cutest thing I'd ever seen, such an absolute contrast to the way he carried himself. "Here for the sex then?"

"Mostly," I managed to answer.

"We'll put a pin in that." He scratched the bow of his upper lip. "Come on."

As soon as Brooks started into the apartment, I saw it for the first time. Past his entry, the space opened up into a massive floor plan that didn't have any exterior walls, just floor to ceiling windows that spanned as far as I could see. The place was decorated like he'd hired the job out, with curving cream-colored couches and low, light wood tables in comparable shapes. A massive and modern chandelier hung from the twenty-foot ceiling, and an open staircase led to what I assumed must be his second floor. Through the window, I could see the entire city lit up and sparkling, the view a far cry from the brick walls and fire escapes of the apartment Dylan and I shared in Chelsea.

"My bedroom is upstairs," Brooks said, grabbing onto the handrail and waiting to make sure I was close on his heels before heading up. I glanced back over my shoulder as we made our way to the top, overwhelmed by the expansive views and the space itself.

The second floor was just as impressive, a massive landing that opened into what I assumed to be the primary bedroom. The other doors were closed, but I imagined they shared the same view as the main level. Brooks' bedroom had the same expensive taste as the downstairs, but it at least appeared lived in. His bed was low to the floor and unmade, a navy blue blanket tossed haphazardly over the bottom edge. The bedroom itself was on a corner, offering two sides of completely uninhibited city views, and the building was so tall, there weren't any neighbors close enough to even think about peeking inside.

"Tate." Brooks cleared his throat like it wasn't the first time he'd said my name.

"Yeah?"

He shrugged out of his shirt, revealing a golden skin and a soft-looking torso. He didn't have a dad bod, but he wasn't overly fit either. The shape of his body was the only relatable thing about him, and I was almost sad he'd started to strip down. Not because I didn't want to see him naked—I did—but because one of my favorite things about our first time together had been the fact he stayed entirely dressed.

"Is there anything I need to worry about?" he asked me the same question from before and embarrassment burned my cheeks.

"Well, I'm definitely not a virgin."

"No," he said quietly. "I imagine you're not."

"There's not," I said. "I know I've slept around, but I've gotten tested. I'm not careless."

Brooks frowned, holding up his hand to stop me. "I didn't think you were. That wasn't the point of the question."

"What was the point then?"

"It's a chance for you to tell me any limits, Tate, any triggers." The use of my name again sent a shiver up my spine. "If I blindfold you, hold you down by your throat, is it going to scare you? That sort of thing."

My breath caught, and I shook my head quickly. "It won't scare me."

"It was an example."

"I'll say red if I have to," I promised.

"Okay," he conceded, carefully opening his belt. He didn't take it off, and I fought against my eyes trying to roll back in my head. Half-dressed was better than naked, and watching the way he raked his eyes over me with a want that felt tangible was enough to send my earlier nerves running for the hills. "Take off your clothes, Tate."

"I think I love it when you say my name." I tugged my shirt over my head and dropped it onto the floor.

"I think I love it when you do what you're told."

Brooks unzipped his pants and slid his hand down over the top of his black boxer briefs. He cupped his erection in his hand, practically growling as he adjusted himself. I scrambled out of my pants and socks, shucking my underwear down my legs and straightening back up. I cupped my balls with one hand and the base of my shaft with another, groaning at the feel of my own touch.

My vision narrowed down to black pinpricks, sensation overwhelming my body and Brooks hadn't even gotten his hands on me yet. I closed my eyes and tugged my cock away from my body, a rough over-handed tug that felt better than anytime I'd ever touched myself before.

What was it about this man that amplified all of my feelings?

Both physical and emotional, when it came to Brooks...I was constantly at a loss.

I opened my eyes, finding him staring at me like a predator who'd spent months tracking his prey. The intensity of his stare took my breath away, but I managed to beg, just the same.

"Tell me what to do, Brooks. I'm ready."

Something in my brain misfired.

The physical position I found myself in with Tate wasn't new. It was far from the first time I had a man naked and hard in my bedroom, asking me to tell him what to do, but to the best of my knowledge, it was the first time that man was someone I'd been responsible for deflowering. Even the thought of it felt antiquated, and Tate was vocal that he hadn't been waiting around to find me again for another round, but knowing that the first time I met Tate he'd been a virgin...

My brain wasn't speaking to my hands, wasn't speaking to the rest of me, and what should have been muscle memory was more work than it had ever been before. Every molecule in my body wanted him. I could feel it in the way my blood burned and how my weight swayed toward him. I knew I watched him like a better version of myself, a version who didn't care about the past, but still.

"Get on your knees, Tate," I finally said, and he was on the ground before the words were all the way out of my mouth.

Going through the motions, I fished my cock out of my underwear and gave it an overhanded stroke, closing the space between us. Tate's eyes were hooded and glazed like a man who'd finally been given the one thing he wanted more than anything else in the world. I saw the same expression when Ford talked about Boston, when Kale pulled Christian onto his lap at the end of the night. Something unfurled in the middle of my chest, and I swallowed, doing my best to push it down where it belonged.

I traced my cock over his parted lips, precum leaking out of my tip and pearling against his mouth. From left to right I dragged my cock over his face, slapping it roughly against the hollow of his cheek until he opened his mouth. With his tongue stuck out and flat, I tested the heat of his mouth, sliding in just an inch until the flared crown was past the backs of his teeth. Tate let out a low groan, head tipping back, and I was quick to fist his hair and yank him into place. Between his legs, his cock slapped against his stomach, clearly approving of the rough handling.

I'd been so hard on him the first night.

Frustrated with Boston and Ford keeping their secret and forcing me to play along because they weren't ready to tell Kale yet. The whole night had been a mess and I was definitely in a mood. I'd been extremely aggressive with Tate, which I wouldn't have done if I'd known him to be a virgin. But that was exactly the problem, at least, as he'd explained it to me. Tate didn't want to be fucked like he was inexperienced. He wanted to be fucked the way he was built to be fucked, the way he deserved.

I pumped my hips forward, sliding my dick into his

mouth. Once I passed the halfway point, he started to sputter and choke, and we both knew what came next.

"Look at me," I growled, tightening my fist in his hair.

Tate blinked quickly, wide eyes staring up at me as I finished my first hot slide into his throat. With my free hand, I pinched his nostrils closed, shivering with the first gasp of cold air he tried to suck in through his mouth. Having a dick halfway down his throat made it predictably hard to breathe, and his eyes grew large with an initial burst of panic, then he fought against the hold I had on his hair. I doubled down, pushing my cock so deep into his mouth my balls rested on his chin.

"Breathe through it, Tate," I coaxed, giving his head a twist to the side. I pulled out enough so I could watch the tip of my cock drag against the inside of his cheek, then I pushed back in. "Give me what we both want and then you can breathe again."

He sputtered, spit bubbling out of the corners of his mouth, and I had a front row seat watching the way his emotions warred to get the better of him. Beyond the initial flash of panic, there was fear. Deeper still, working its way to the surface the longer I deprived him of air, came the arousal. That one was quickly followed with confusion, and then… then the tears began to flow.

It was the first predictable thing Tate had done.

I released his nose and his hair, and Tate fell backward, gasping and sucking in desperate breath after desperate breath. His body was bowed forward, nearly frenzied for the tension that rolled off his shoulders, and I fisted his hair again before he could recover and threw him onto the bed. He let out a high-pitched whimper when he landed, and I dove between his legs before he had time to formulate a protest. I took his balls into my mouth next, sucking and lapping at the hot sac until he reached for his own dick.

"Don't," I warned, and he dropped his hand to the bed with a groan, gripping the sheets instead of his erection. I'd planned on eating his ass until he cried from the overwhelm of it all, but seeing how needy he was to touch himself gave me another idea entirely.

Climbing off the bed, I finally stripped the rest of the way out of my clothes, then I leaned against the floor to ceiling window across from the bed and folded my arms in front of my chest. My cock ached from how ready I was to fuck, but it would have to wait.

"There's lube in the drawer of the nightstand," I told Tate, my gaze flickering toward the sleek wooden stand at my side of the bed. "There's also toys. Pick the one that most closely matches the cock of the last man you fucked when you should have been here with me."

Tate's entire body flushed a bright and beautiful shade of fuchsia, but he reached for the drawer, just like he'd been told. The drawer opened quietly, and Tate moaned when he looked inside, digging around the contents until he found the toy of his choice. I didn't have a lot of sizes to choose from in there, but he picked one that sat near the smaller end of the range, going so far as to test it in his hand before making his final decision. I reached down and stroked my cock as Tate brought the lube and the dildo back into the center of the bed.

"Trade me places now," I said, pushing off the window.

His brows knit in confusion, and I met him halfway, taking the toy cock out of his hand and slamming it down hard against the window. The suction cup base would hold, and the length of the fake cock bounced as it settled into its new position. Tate still had the lube in his hand and tear tracks drying on his cheeks when I sat down on the foot of the bed and gave him his next instruction.

"Prep yourself with that cock," I said. "Show me what you've been getting this whole time, instead of what you've wanted."

I wasn't an arrogant man.

I was a competent man. I was confident, and I was rich. I knew what I brought to the table, understood what I had to offer, but I would have been a liar if I said it didn't do wonders for my ego to know that Tate had been fucking his way through the eligible bachelors of New York for the past six months trying to find one who fucked as well as I did.

"Are you serious?" The question scratched at his throat as he asked it, and I gave him a serious nod in return.

"Very."

"That's embarrassing."

I smiled, stroking my shaft in his direction. "There's more than one way to make a person cry, Tate. Did you want to stop?"

"No." He frowned, pouring lube into his hand and slathering it up the length of the toy dick. "But I didn't come here to fuck myself with a dildo. I have those at home."

"You're more than welcome to go there if you don't want to fuck the way I want to fuck," I reminded him. "You're the one who chased me down, not the other way around."

"That's mean," he said under his breath, reaching around behind him to slick his ass.

I didn't have a clear view of his reflection in the window, but the sky was dark enough for me to see him shove one finger straight up his ass. The skyline glittered out beyond the apartment, and Tate cursed under his breath while he fucked his ass with his own fingers. His skin was still bright and glaring pink, and my entire body was alive with excitement. I scooted closer toward the edge of the bed, stroking my erection slowly so I didn't come before I had a chance to get inside of him.

"Did you want to cry about it?" I teased.

Tate swallowed nervously, shifting to replace his fingers with the dildo on the window. He screwed his eyes closed and stared down at the floor, giving me a gorgeous view of his tangled hair, but that wasn't going to do at all.

"Look at me, Tate," I demanded.

He glared up at me, both hands behind him to spread his ass apart to accommodate the toy. When the tip breached him, he grunted, and I licked my lips, leaning toward him like a moth to a flame. He looked like he wanted to beat me to death with the dildo, but he had a safe word and I was yet to hear it come out of his mouth.

"How does it feel? I asked, absolutely enraptured by the view in front of me.

Tate was nothing more than coiled rage and arousal, all tucked into the same lithe body. Sweat had already started to bead against his temples, the flush in his chest giving way from embarrassment to pleasure. No matter how bad the sex for him had been, a cock in the ass was still a cock in the ass. It was the burn and the stretch and the fullness that started everything off. The movement was important, but secondary.

"Cold," he grumbled.

"Move faster," I suggested. "Warm it up."

Bent over at the waist, Tate began to fuck himself on the

toy, and the rage bubbled up and out of him with every harsh pump of his hips. He was beyond angry with me, but he wasn't going to stop it. I was going to get a thousand tears out of him before the end of the night, from every range of emotion possible. The promise of it had me yanking my balls down hard enough to stave off the impending waves of my own pleasure.

"Tell me what it was like to fuck other men, Tate."

"Boring," he grunted, pace stuttering.

"Unfulfilling?"

"Yes."

"Did these other men know they were bad in bed?" I asked.

He shook his head.

"Did the last one fuck you as slow as you're fucking yourself?"

"No."

"Show me how he fucked you," I said again, curling my fingers around my thighs so I didn't grab my cock.

Tate started to move faster, body slamming back against the toy in what should have been a rough and punishing pace...if the man had known how to fuck, that is. The longer I watched, the higher Tate's frustration ratcheted up, the pleasure and the shame of the whole thing quickly becoming too much for him to manage.

The signs were all there.

He squeezed his eyes closed, clenched his jaw, and fucked himself faster with the dildo. His cock swung hard and long between his legs, but nowhere near ready to come.

"Tell me how it feels, Tate," I said again, licking the corner of my lip with my tongue. He wasn't looking at me, and that was fine.

I saw him just the same.

"Miserable," he rasped, eyes blinking open in a flash.

The unshed tears were right there, ready to spill, but he was stubborn and proud, and he was so very angry to have a plastic cock inside of him instead of my own.

"Unsatisfying," I offered.

He nodded, still pumping back against the dildo, jaw clenched so tight I worried he was going to break a molar.

"Boring," he said again.

"Predictable."

Tate gave me a jerky nod as a string of precum leaked out of his cock and raced toward the floor. I let my gaze follow the trail of it, humming happily when another kind of wetness splattered beside it, then another, and another.

"It's all right, Tate," I promised, crawling back on the bed until I reached into the drawer in the nightstand where I kept my condoms. I found one without taking my eyes off the sight in front of me, using my teeth to rip open the foil.

At the sound, Tate's head jerked up, fresh tear stains visible on his cheeks.

"All seventeen of those men were just prep for this," I promised him, pointing my cock toward the ceiling with one hand and beckoning him closer with another. "Come over here now, Tate, and I'll remind you how a real man fucks."

CHAPTER 8
TATE

THE ONLY THING THAT HURT WORSE THAN MY ASSHOLE WAS MY PRIDE, but that was exactly what Brooks had been after. I'd been foolish thinking it was only hands and words that would make me cry. Feelings could make me cry too, and I'd never been more embarrassed in my life than I was in front of the window, fucking myself on that mid-size plastic cock while Brooks watched me and jerked himself off. Thinking about all the miserable sex I'd had over the past six months while watching the one thing I wanted most in the world was torturous and mortifying simultaneously. I wanted to lean into feeling good, because even if it wasn't Brooks, there was still a cock inside of me. I was still being stretched and filled, but the shame of it all had brought about the exact reaction he'd wanted.

I cried.

Swiping a violent rush of tears out of my eyes, I stepped away from the window and crawled onto the bottom of the bed. Brooks sat against the headboard like a king, like his cock was a scepter that gave him authority to rule the land...to rule me. I figured he wanted me to straddle him and ride him, but as soon as I reached his feet he launched toward me like a cat, flipping me onto my back and using his body weight to press my legs against my chest.

With a clearly practiced motion, he filled my gaping hole with his thick and talented cock, bottoming out with the first snap of his hips. I cried out, the force of it sending me backward so my head hung off the edge of the bed, giving me an unrestricted—if not upside down—view of the city.

"Tell me about the first time you tried to find a man who could fuck you the way I did," Brooks demanded, the breath rushing out of his lungs with every sharp thrust of his hips. He grabbed me around the waist and hauled me up so my head was flat on the navy blue blanket I'd been admiring earlier, then he set back to work with the same punishing pace he'd started with.

I screwed my eyes shut, shaking my head side to side so fast it made me dizzy.

He collared his hand around my throat, thumb digging into the underside of my chin to stop the movement. Another thrust so extreme I shouted, tears pouring from the corners of my eyes.

"Tell me about the fifth one then," he offered. "The tenth. How many men would you have fucked to find this feeling again?"

Brooks threw his head back, the corded muscles of his neck tight and bulging beneath his skin. Power rippled through him, from his hard and small nipples to the barely visible ridges of his abs and farther to the tight press of his fingers against the delicate swell of my throat.

The man was a force of nature, taking what he wanted, when he wanted.

"The seventh almost made me cry, but only because he was so bad at it," I admitted.

The corner of Brooks' mouth quirked up. "Almost?"

"Almost," I rasped, eyes rolling back in my head.

"So, you didn't cry for him?"

"No."

"Did you cry for any of them?" he asked, hand flexing against my Adam's apple.

"No."

Brooks bent forward and licked my face, from the side of my jaw to my lower lashes, his entire body trembling as he erased the tears from my cheek.

"Good," he growled, pulling out and yanking me onto all fours so fast I barely had time to register the absence before he was back inside of me.

I called out his name, and he grabbed me around the waist, using my body to fuck himself instead of using *his* body to fuck me. My teeth rattled together from the force of it, an ache blooming from how hard he had his hands on me.

It was perfect.

"Harder," I begged, burying my face into the sheets to wipe away the tears and snot.

"Gladly."

And for the first time in six months, I got fucked the way I wanted. Brooks slammed into me with so much force that in under a minute I was off the bed. He was halfway there behind me, one leg flat on the floor, the other still somewhere on the bed, still pounding into me violently. I sucked in a breath that was nowhere near enough to fill my lungs. Every time Brooks thrust into me, he punched the air out of my lungs, and it was impossible to breathe, impossible to speak, to talk…impossible to do anything except be fucked the way I'd been dreaming about for months.

"Tate," Brooks grunted my name, fucking us all the way off the bed. We fell onto the ground, my legs spreading out and dropping me with a thud against the floor. My cock smashed between both of our weights and the sleek wood planked floors of his penthouse, and even still he didn't stop.

He braced one hand against the top of my spine, hiking my right leg up with the other. I was half on my knees, cheek sliding against the floor, slicked by snot and spit and tears. My cock was still tight against my stomach, the friction of Brooks' steady and hard thrusts enough to send flares of pain through my whole body.

"Brooks, it hurts. Oh fuck, I'm going to come, " was the last thing I remembered saying before I shot embarrassingly thick and hot bursts of cum onto the floor. I'd never gotten off from being in pain before, the tears I'd shed for him in the past not quite feeling like the same thing as the physicality of the current moment.

Beneath Brooks' weight, I thrashed and gasped, crying for more and for less, for air and for him to choke me again. Every muscle in my body went taut, and then relaxed. There wasn't any fight left in me—no want, no need, just exhaustion and perfect happiness. Brooks slammed into me one final time, leveraging his weight against my back and my waist as he buried himself to the hilt inside of me.

He came so forcefully I could feel his cock swell inside of me and the heat of his cum pooled in the tip of the condom, resting heavy and wet. Even after his orgasm finished, Brooks trembled behind me, sweat falling from his forehead and spattering against my back. With a reluctance so palpable I could taste it, he withdrew from my body with a pained grunt.

My body wasn't listening to my silent commands to move, so I stayed put with one leg bent and the other stretched out behind me, listening to Brooks tie off the condom and drop it on the floor. He sat down and pulled me half onto his lap, tracing shapes against my back through the sweat he'd left behind. The only sounds in the room were the syncopated beats of us both trying to catch our breaths, and then Brooks let out a quiet chuckle.

"If I leave you alone for two minutes, are you going to run away again?" he asked, trailing his finger down my spine and into the crack of my ass. He swirled his fingertip around my tender entrance, then pushed it inside. I gasped, and there were my muscles, my body instinctively trying to scramble away. He must have expected it, because as soon as I lifted off the floor, he bent forward and banded an arm around my chest, keeping me in place and lodging his finger deep inside of me.

"I won't run," I promised.

I couldn't have run if I tried.

"You won't crawl?" He tested another finger against my hole, pressing the tip in and then stopping.

"I'm not leaving," I assured him.

Brooks answered that with a thoughtful sound, and then with a surprising show of strength, he picked us both up off the floor and he sat me down on the bed.

"I'm going to run a bath and come back for you. Don't get too comfortable."

"I don't need a bath," I whined.

He gave me half of a frown, brushing my sweaty and damp hair back from my forehead. "You don't even know what you *want*, Tate. Let alone what you need."

"I want you," I said quickly. "I wanted that."

"If you want that, then you get this."

Brooks kissed my forehead and padded away from me, naked and covered in a sheen of sweat so shiny I could make out the lights of the city reflecting on his back as he went into the en suite. He didn't turn on any lights, just the taps, which roared to life out of sight.

I fell back onto the bed and flung my arm over my eyes, taking the momentary reprieve as an opportunity to continue working on catching my breath. Brooks wasn't gone long, and I hadn't had nearly enough time to replay through the chain of events that had gotten me to the point where I was sprawled out naked on his bed like a starfish, knowing I could have fucked two hundred more men and none of them would have ever come close to him.

"Can you walk?" he asked.

I snorted a laugh, letting him pull my arm away from my face. When he saw my expression, he rolled his eyes and hoisted me to my feet. It turned out the answer was... no. I couldn't walk. Brooks took all of my weight against his shoulder and ushered me into the bathroom, which was just one more thing to add to the list I needed to start called *Things about Astor Brooks that take my breath away.*

His bathroom was unreal, with windows just like the rest of the house in lieu of walls and a giant, white marble soaking tub tucked into the corner, the sprawling view of the city just beyond. The bathroom was one of those wet room deals, with an uncovered shower head beside the tub and a long and sleek counter made of matching white stone. It was elegant and expensive, much like the soft scent of the candle that was lit beside the sink, smelling like linen and lemon. A strong tap ran into the tub and steam had already begun to waft up into the expansive room.

Brooks helped me into the tub, which was an immediate balm on my weakened muscles. I lowered myself under the water and scooted forward when he gestured that he planned to join me. He settled himself with his back against the edge of the tub and arranged my body between his spread legs, fussing over me until I sighed softly and let my weight lean against him entirely.

"There," he whispered, pressing a kiss against the top of my temple.

When the water neared the top, the tap shut off automatically, which had to be some kind of sorcery I'd never be able to afford, let alone understand. The room went silent, save for our hushed breathing and the soothing lap of water against the edges of the tub.

"What now?" I asked, eyes closing.

"This." He gently looped his hands around my thighs, fingers dancing nimbly across my still shaking muscles.

"What is this?"

"Aftercare," he murmured, digging his fingers in, not to hurt, but to soften the tension that my thighs carried from the position he'd had me in earlier.

"I don't need aftercare." It was a lie, but...

"I do," he said simply, and I snapped my mouth closed, not interested in arguing the point with him.

Instead, I leaned against him the way he wanted and let him knead his way across every muscle he could reach. When he'd run out of body parts, he switched from using his hands to using a soaped-up washcloth, taking extra time between my legs and between my ass cheeks. The way Brooks cleaned me up was far from clinical, but it was hardly sexual. He tended me like his only goal was to care for me, and that was a whole new level of attention I didn't know how to deal with.

Unexpected tears sprang into the corners of my eyes, and I moved so fast to swipe them away I accidentally splashed water over the edge of the tub and onto the floor.

"Sorry," I muttered, letting him push my hands back beneath the surface.

"Don't apologize." His voice was so soft, so contrary to how it had been in the bedroom. And he turned my head to the side and gently kissed the tears off of my cheekbones, the fringe of my eyelashes. The actions were so tender, I sniffled, unable to stop more tears from falling free.

Brooks hummed quietly, content to catch them with his lips and his tongue, not even bothering to reach between my legs with his hand to find out if I was hard or not. His own cock sat hot and heavy against the small of my back, very hard and very ready, but he ignored it, seemingly satisfied to manhandle me with tenderness until the tears ran dry.

"Better?" he asked long after I'd finished, his fingertips tracing wet swirls across the front of my chest and the bottom of my throat.

"I don't know," I admitted, remembering his accusations earlier in the night about not being able to trust me.

I wanted him to trust me. I needed it almost as much as I needed *him*.

"Thank you for being honest." He let out a quiet groan,

then reached out of the tub toward a white cylindrical container I hadn't noticed before. "Up you go."

With an unhappy grunt, I shifted forward, giving him room to stand. Brooks climbed out of the tub, looking every inch like a God carved from marble himself, then reached into the white container and pulled out one of the thickest and softest-looking towels I'd ever seen. Heat rolled off of it, and I stood as quickly as my legs would allow. Brooks helped me out of the tub, then he wrapped me up in the warm and soft terrycloth, making sure I was well on my way to dry before he bothered to throw one around his own waist.

"I'm not through yet, but...will you stay the night?" he asked, staring at a point on my face that wasn't quite my eyes. It was the first glimpse of insecurity I'd seen from him, and I wanted to wrap it up and seal it tight...save it forever, this gorgeous slice of vulnerability that I knew he didn't mean to share.

I blinked, scrunching my nose and letting the towel fall to the floor.

I was nowhere near done with Astor Brooks, and I didn't think I ever would be.

"Will you fuck me again?" I asked.

Brooks licked his lips, tilting his head to the side as he took in the sight of me, freshly rubbed and washed, my skin pink from the water and the pressure of his hands.

"Eventually," he murmured, stare flickering up to my face. "When I'm good and ready."

"Then, yes." I swallowed nervously, all signs of Brooks' earlier hesitance gone. "I'll stay the night."

BROOKS

I sent Tate to bed, naked and flushed, then I dropped both our towels into the hamper and went to the kitchen to get us both some water. Leaning against the counter with both hands, I bent forward and let my head drop down toward the floor. If I closed my eyes and held my breath, I could hear the sheets rustling from upstairs, and knowing Tate was in my bed...that he did what I asked, that he stayed...

I didn't want to push my luck, so I grabbed two bottles of water from the fridge, a pre-made charcuterie tray my private chef had tucked in the back earlier in the week, and then went back up to my bedroom.

Tate looked like an angel tangled in my sheets, fingers clutched tightly around the top while he struggled to decide whether he should pull them up or leave them around his thighs. I walked in when he had them pulled up over his hips, and when he heard me, he startled, letting them fall to reveal the thick bulge between his legs. He was still half-hard, and I wanted to know why.

"You're still hard," I said, crawling into bed beside him. I balanced the food on my lap and twisted the top off one of the bottles of water before passing it to him.

He tapped the edge of his nail against the glass. "This is really bougie."

I gestured vaguely at the view ahead of us and he grinned, tipping his chin to take a sip while I pulled the plastic wrap off the top of the tray of food.

"Eat too," I said.

Tate twisted the top back onto the water and picked apart a flower made of salami.

"I'm still hard," he agreed after chewing and swallowing his first bite. I slid the plate toward him so he would take another.

"Why?"

He snorted, arching a brow at me. "Should I not be?"

"A cock like yours should always be hard," I assured him, "I just meant...what part of the night is encouraging it to stay that way?"

Tate hummed, picking a pearl of mozzarella next and popping it into his mouth. I was close to begging him to eat a carb, but a cracker was next on his list, so I swallowed the request down.

"All of it," he finally answered, turning back to the water.

The longer he picked at the plate, the more comfortable he became, his shoulders sinking back against the wall, his hips starting to wiggle when he tasted something he particularly enjoyed.

"I think it's obvious I like the sex," he said, finishing off the salami flower and moving on to the prosciutto bundle next. "But the bath was...nice."

"Nice."

"No one has ever…" he trailed off.

"I don't want to say the after is my favorite part, but…two sides of the same coin I think," I said.

Tate chewed some more, then turned his face toward me, expression earnest.

"Do you always fuck that way?" he asked, scrunching his nose in curiosity, not disgust. "Like…to make someone cry. Do you always need that?"

I swallowed, twisting open my own bottle of water to take a drink. It wasn't that I was trying to buy myself more time, but it was a question no one had asked me before. Not even when I'd crossed the bridge from hookup to relationship, no one had cared about what I wanted in bed, only what I could give. Some people wanted the roughness and some people tolerated it for the parts that came after. Tate, it seemed, desired them both in equal measure.

Like me.

"I don't need to make you cry to get off."

"But you like it."

"Don't you?" I asked.

"I wasn't trying to cry."

I set my water on the nightstand. Tate had devoured half the charcuterie and he seemed to be slowing down, so I moved the plate to the side as well. He passed me his water, and I added it to the mess.

"It just happens sometimes," I told him, reaching up toward his face. When he didn't flinch away, I brushed some of his wet hair back off his forehead. He smiled softly, stare flickering down at his lap. "Doesn't it feel good? Like its own kind of release?"

That was how it had been described to me years before.

Like the stress and tension had grown so strong there was nowhere else for it to go until it burst forth in a fit of tears. I knew men like Alex used physical impact to bring his partners to the same end. And, in a way, I was physical too, though I'd always recognized the differences in our preferences and styles.

It was more than delivering that release for me, though. The tears...they definitely did something for me. Whether it was the power that came from knowing I was the one to unleash all those feelings or recognizing the vulnerability and raw emotion that came with tears. It was a lot to unpack and it was too late to have the whole conversation with Tate.

"Yes," he agreed with a yawn. "What about the aftercare part?"

"You cried then too."

"It was different," he murmured.

"Was it?" I asked.

Tate shifted his weight and I pulled him down flat onto his side, kissing the back of his neck until he moaned and pushed his ass against my still-hard cock.

"It felt different," he whispered.

"What about it was different?"

I reached behind me to find the lube and another condom, rolling one down my length to be done with it.

"They were softer," he said, following the statement with a quiet moan when I dragged a lube-slick finger between his ass cheeks.

"They tasted the same to me," I assured him, pushing inside of him.

Tate was practically panting from the first tease of penetration, and I bit the inside of my cheek to stop myself from rutting into him like a wild animal. There would be another time for that—I was sure of it. This was the end of the night, but only the beginning of our time together. I saw myself in Tate, and I hoped he saw himself in me, in those puzzle piece kind of ways that people always hoped for but rarely found.

"Oh, God."

I had two fingers inside of him, pumping slow and steady. He was still soft and ready, but I used my hand until he was begging.

"Brooks, please," he whined.

"Please, what?" I smiled against the back of his ear, dick pulsing at the scent of my own soap and shampoo on that most hidden part of his body. I pulled my fingers out of him and moaned at the way his muscles tried to bear down and hold me in.

"I want you again."

"I'm here."

"Your cock." He groaned, breath dragging out of his lungs in a long exhale.

I curled my arm around his chest and held him against me, nosing the tip of my cock against his hole.

"It's here too, Tate," I told him, easing my way back into him. "I've got you."

He pressed against the arm I had banded around his chest, but there wasn't any real fight in it. A long and low sound escaped him, and he sank into my bed and my arms like he was always meant to be there.

I fucked him for the second time that night with lazy and gentle pumps of my hips. I wasn't chasing after tears or an orgasm, or any sort of end at all. It was only for pleasure in its most perfect form. I didn't complain when Tate reached down between his legs and made a loose fist around his cock, content to let the power of my hips fuck his shaft into his hand.

He picked up the gibberish again, and I closed my eyes, kissing the back of his neck and his slowly drying hair. The sheets were wet and our bodies were damp again, but his back burned hot against mine. I fought the urge to move faster, to chase after a release, satisfied instead with the groans and sighs that fell out of Tate's mouth in a near constant stream.

Time blurred into nothing and everything, and Tate let out a soft cry when he came. I slid my arm down so I could feel the hot and sticky mess he'd shot all over his stomach, tracing it up with my fingers. His entire body shivered and spasmed, and I brought my hand to his mouth. I didn't need to tell him what to do. He was quick to open his mouth and suck his cum off his fingers and my palm, asshole clenching down around me the whole time.

"You're a dream," I whispered into his ear, counting down in my head from one hundred to zero, when I went still, locking him down onto me with one final rut of my hips.

Tate whimpered when I finished, back bowing forward as I buried myself thick and deep inside of him. I pumped my load into the condom, wanting more than anything to tear it off next time and spurt across the small of his back, the gorgeous globes of his ass.

"How do you do that?" he muttered, pressing back against me and his face into the pillows at the same time.

"Hmn?"

"Make it all so good."

I wanted to fall asleep like this. With Tate in my arms and my cock in his ass, but the condom was sticky and gross, so with all the reluctance in my body, I pulled out of him and rolled onto my back. Tate didn't go far, doing a complete one-eighty-turn onto his other side and tucking himself against my ribs with a pleased little sigh. I tied off the condom and dropped it onto the floor, reaching my arm around Tate and making a bigger spot for him to cocoon himself into.

"I'm selfish, Tate." I kissed the top of his head. "I just fuck the way that feels good to me."

"Well, it feels really good to me too."

I hoped he couldn't feel the way my breath hitched in my throat at his simple statement, but that was what I'd always wanted, what I'd silently hoped for. That kind of partnership and connection.

That synchronicity.

"Then I'm the luckiest man in New York," I said.

"I wish you'd taken me home the first night," he said next, words almost lost around a long and drawn-out yawn.

"I should have. Would have."

"Don't let me leave again," he whispered.

I pulled my lips between my teeth, staring up at the ceiling instead of looking at him. My brain wanted to argue this was all too good to be true, but I'd watched perfect partners fall into my friends' laps out of nowhere. Why was it so hard to believe the same could be true for me? Why did they deserve it and not me?

"Don't say things you don't really mean, Tate."

Tate pushed up on a shaky arm until he hovered over me, forcing my stare away from the ceiling and onto him. He was so tired and so beautiful, cheeks permanently flushed and pupils still dark as charcoal. I wanted to give him everything he'd ever wanted and everything *I* ever wanted, all at the same time. The need to possess him, to cherish him, to spoil him, was a near visceral feeling, and I fisted the sheets with my free hand to try and quiet the urges that threatened to overwhelm me.

"I do mean it."

Another yawn, and he collapsed back into the crook of my side.

"What does that look like for you?" I asked, relaxed enough to draw spirals down the back of his neck and the top of his spine as he settled into the sheets again.

"I don't think these are things I should ask for."

"I asked you to let me make you cry the first night we met because that was what I wanted from you," I said. "Surely you can ask for what you need now."

"I want more," he answered, pressing a kiss against my ribs. "I want everything."

"You don't even know me."

"I'll learn," he said. "And you don't know me either."

"I'll learn," I whispered back to him.

"Then it's settled?"

I huffed out a breath, closing my eyes and focusing on the way my heart slowed to beat in time with Tate's.

"I think so," I finally agreed, a soft smile spreading on my mouth just before sleep was ready to take me under. "Now get some sleep, darling."

Stretching out like a cat, I luxuriated in Brooks' soft and sleep-warm sheets tangled around my legs. Beside me, he let out a low rumble of a groan, looping his arm around my waist and hauling our bodies flush. He kissed the back of my neck, upper lip dragging over the short hairs at the nape, and I shivered, burrowing closer to him.

"You're still here," he mused quietly, fingers tracking down my chest and my stomach, toying with the short and curly hairs below my navel.

"I asked you not to let me leave again," I reminded him, slowly blinking my eyes open to take in the color of the morning as it washed over his room. "So you slept like an octopus."

He chuckled, pinching my waist before rolling away from me. "I'm a man of my word. Do you want breakfast?"

I turned toward him, reaching out for the small of his back. Brooks was sitting on the edge of the bed, naked, and tanned, and soft.

"You don't have to make me breakfast."

"I know." He glanced at me over his shoulder. "I asked if you *wanted* breakfast."

I want everything.

"Yes, please."

His mouth quirked into a smile, and he pushed himself to his feet and disappeared into what I imagined had to be a walk-in closet...a door near the bathroom that blended in so well with the wall I hadn't even noticed it the night before. When he reappeared, he had on a pair of gray sweatpants that looked as indecent on him as I would have hoped, and he dropped a pair of black sleep pants and a white t-shirt on the bed near his pillow.

"Take a shower," he said, bending down to kiss my forehead in a surprising display of tenderness. "Then come find me."

"I'm going to go through your medicine cabinet," I warned.

Brooks' smile grew. "Have at it, Tate."

And then he was gone, leaving me alone in his bed to overthink the past twelve hours. The kiss on my forehead had been the most shocking part of the whole thing, and I pressed my fingers against the place his lips had just been. It wasn't that the kindness had caught me off-guard—he'd shown me more than my fair share of tenderness the night before—it was the timing. Brooks had only shown that kind of softness *after*, though I supposed the morning after was still very much after.

"Do as you're told," I chided myself, kicking the sheets down, even though they were warm and smelled like sex and I wanted to bury myself in them. Grabbing the borrowed lounge clothes, I made my way into the bathroom and spent far too long trying to figure out how to get the water for Brooks' shower turned on, but once I managed it...

It was the best shower of my life.

The water pressure was perfect, the temperature divine, and I used Brooks' soap and shampoo until I was confident the scent of him had soaked its way into my bones. There was a single towel left in the warmer near the tub, so I made sure to use it, then dressed myself in Brooks' clothes, which were barely too small and short, and stopped to look at myself in the mirror.

I had wondered if there would be proof visible of the night before on my skin, but save for some dark red ovals around my waist shaped like Brooks' fingers, I was unscathed. The state of my skin had me frowning, because how could my body remain so unchanged when my mind and my heart were already irrevocably new? That should have been an outlandish and crazy thing to say, but it was true. I knew it down to the marrow of my bones that my life was about to change entirely.

Hopefully for the better.

Brooks was like a wildfire, fast and all-consuming, sucking up all the air around him and making it impossible to breathe, impossible to see anything besides the majestic power of his flames.

"Did you die in there?" he called, sounding closer than I imagined the kitchen to be.

"No." My voice cracked and I cleared my throat, heading toward him. "I was just admiring your handiwork."

Brooks was in the doorway to his bedroom, and I raised my shirt to show him the scant bruises he'd left around my hips. He immediately frowned, rushing toward me and dropping down to his knees. He pressed and pulled at the skin, manipulating it taut and laying his fingers against the bruises as if he was checking the shape to confirm he was the one who'd left them.

"I'm sorry," he whispered, looking up at me with hair still messy from the fucking and the sleeping, though he looked far from tired. "I didn't mean to."

I laughed, swatting his hands away.

"I was just upset there weren't more," I told him.

Straightening back to standing, he said, "I didn't have permission."

"Didn't you?"

He shook his head. "Not specifically."

"Implicitly," I told him.

"That's not how it works."

I worried the frown was going to take up permanent residence on his face, so I grabbed his hand and brought it up to my mouth, kissing the tops of his knuckles with as much reverence as I could manage.

"It wasn't a limit," I reminded him.

"Just kissing and bleeding," he recounted.

"Maybe just bleeding now," I whispered, giving his hand a squeeze.

Brooks swallowed, eyes flashing with understanding, and then he was on me before I could breathe. He grabbed my face with both hands, slanting his head to the side and angling our mouths together like I was going to change my mind. I parted my lips for him readily, groaning and leaning my weight onto him as he licked his way into my mouth with a happy sigh.

He kissed the way he fucked, all consuming, all *deserving*, and it didn't take more than ten seconds for my cock to jump, pressing against the expensive cotton of my borrowed pants. I slid my hands around Brooks' waist, just to steady myself, and he responded by going onto his toes and spearing his tongue deeper into my mouth. Brooks kissed like the answers to every question he'd ever wanted the answer to were behind my teeth, and when he spun me so my back slammed into the wall, I was thankful for it because my knees weren't going to hold me up for much longer.

From somewhere else in the apartment, a timer echoed, a loud and piercing beep that had Brooks breaking the kiss and groaning against my swollen lips.

"Breakfast is ready," he said with a noticeable hint of regret.

I swallowed, thumping my head against the wall and sucking in a breath, realizing my comparison of the man in front of me to a wildfire was far more accurate than I originally thought.

"Okay," I rasped.

We both looked down, our cocks hard and jutting out from our bodies, crying for attention even though I wasn't sure my hole could take another round of rough fucking without a little more recovery time.

"Tuck it up," he said, reaching down and adjusting himself behind the waistband of his sweats.

My shaft was burning hot against my palm, but I situated myself as best I could, then gave him a nod. He smiled and exhaled through his nose, taking my hand and leading me out of the doorway and back to the stairs.

Somehow, I'd forgotten that Brooks' penthouse was as big as it was, and I didn't even understand the scope until we descended to the first floor. He had to have near five thousand square feet, with sprawling open spaces that stretched what I imagined to be at least half the length of the building.

I cursed under my breath when he brought me to the kitchen, which was basically a long island made of the same marble in the bathroom and a counter that faced another wall of windows. I climbed onto one of the tan leather stools, ignoring the city behind me for the view of Brooks' back muscles flexing as he reached up to turn off the timer on the oven and open the door. He pulled a glass casserole dish out and set it on a black trivet, then used the pot holder to fan some of the steam off the top.

"I hope you're not vegan," he said.

I laughed. "Far from it."

"I made a frittata."

"That sounds great," I said softly.

And it did. It smelled even better, but the one thing I really wanted more than anything in the world at that moment was coffee.

"Cream and sugar?" he asked, like he was a goddamn mind reader.

"Black," I answered.

Brooks poured two coffees from a pot beside the oven, adding two spoonfuls of sugar to his. I watched the careful and practiced way he moved around the kitchen, cutting and serving our breakfast onto plates that matched the counter-tops, then he came around the island to sit on my right side.

My stomach growled as soon as he slid the plate in front of me, and I cut into the frittata with an embarrassing speed, shoveling two quick bites into my mouth, even though the temperature was enough to burn the taste buds off my tongue. Brooks watched me with an amused expression, eyeing me over the rim of his coffee mug while he did the responsible thing and waited for his eggs to cool down. When I finally managed to chew and swallow, he smiled at me, and I melted just like the cheese.

"This is delicious," I told him, finally taking a drink of my own coffee.

Brooks smiled at me, nose scrunching a bit in that unguarded expression I'd glimpsed the night before.

"Did you mean what you said last night?"

My brow furrowed. I'd said a lot of things the night before, and while in general I was sure I meant most of them at the time, I was a little sex-drunk and hoped he wasn't going to hold me to something embarrassing.

"What did I say?"

"That you wanted more," he said, spinning his mug handle from one hand to the other and back again. "With me."

I exhaled, shoulders sagging. I remembered saying that, and I'd meant it with my whole chest. "Yes," I said.

Brooks matched my relieved posture, a smile flickering across his mouth before he hid it by taking another drink of his coffee.

"You called me darling last night too," I said after I'd replayed the rest of the conversation in question through my head.

"Did you hate it?"

I cocked my head to the side, wondering why he always jumped to the worst conclusions when we talked about his behavior.

"I really like when you call me by my name," I admitted, "but darling was...nice. Unexpected."

"It just slipped out."

I believed him. Both of us had been in such a raw and vulnerable state after the bath, after the second round of sex, it was like the sweat and the tears had washed away every defense that existed between us. And I was thankful for it, because even though I'd spent the last six months fantasizing about one part of the man in front of me, I was quickly beginning to realize the entire package was so much better.

"What does more look like for you?" I asked him, taking a bite of my breakfast, relatively confident it wasn't going to sear the rest of my taste buds out of my mouth.

"More of last night," he said quickly, using the edge of his fork to cut a piece of his frittata free. "But also more of this."

"Sex and breakfast."

"And dinners." He studied my face, mouth pulled taut with seriousness. "Lunches. Dates."

"Dates," I repeated softly.

"I'm either on or off, Tate," he said, almost apologetically. "I don't know how to do things in half measures."

I slid my hand down to the blooming bruises on my hip. "This was a half measure," I murmured.

"That was an overstep."

I shook my head.

"I want more of it," I said. "I want to remember you when we aren't together."

"I'd rather just be with you all the time."

"Not practical." It was hard to speak for how much the conversation had me smiling. A foreign emotion burst in the center of my chest, feeling a lot like hope and a little bit like love.

"Fair enough," he agreed, tugging the edge of the shirt up

to inspect the bruising one more time. "We can definitely talk about that part of it, though I would prefer to have you here."

"I have an apartment," I told him. "I have a roommate."

"I imagine you have a job too."

I laughed, leaning away from him and gesturing at the massive penthouse we found ourselves in. "I imagine you have one also."

"I have rich parents." A smile pulled at his mouth, a relief from the worried tension that had been trying to sneak up around the edges. "But, yes, I have a job."

"These will last a few days," I assured him, "so we can start with dinner next weekend?"

Brooks licked his lips like he wanted to protest, like the following weekend was too far away, and holy fuck the way that made me feel stronger and more powerful than I ever had before. I was having breakfast with a man I imagined to be one of the richest in the entire city, and he was unhappy at needing to wait another seven days to take me out, to take me to bed.

"The timeline is up for discussion," he finally said, chewing and swallowing the last bite of his frittata. "For now, just finish your breakfast."

"How did you know Boston was the one?" I asked Ford, four days later over a mid-week lunch in a small restaurant down the street from my office.

In response, he arched a brow and smirked at me.

"I'm not sure I *know* anything," he said, "but I *want*."

"You know what I mean."

"And I know there's a story." Ford lifted his iced tea glass and dragged the straw around until it reached his mouth. "So, start there."

"Do you remember the man you paid to pretend to be interested in you? Before Kale knew you were sticking it to his brother?"

"I'm not sti—" Ford snapped his mouth closed, glaring at me. "What about him?"

"You know I fucked him that night."

"I'm aware."

I pushed the last of my salad around my plate until I could get a decent amount onto my fork.

"I ran into him at The Black Door last week."

"What's his name?" Ford asked.

"Tate." He nodded for me to go on, so I did. "I took him home Saturday night."

Ford's mouth tugged into a smile that he actively tried to fight down until it was impossible for him to keep the turned-up corners of his mouth at bay.

"And you're in love?"

"I wouldn't take it that far," I muttered, stabbing the last bite of salad onto my fork and shoving it into my mouth.

The more accurate thing to for me to say would have been I *shouldn't* take it that far, but I was already well on my way to being head over heels for Tate, and I didn't even know his last name. He knew mine, which was thanks to the man currently sitting across from me, but I made a mental note to remedy the situation as soon as I was able to get my phone out of my pocket.

"But you are," Ford teased, "or you wouldn't ask me how I knew Boston was it for me."

He had me there.

"He's special," I said.

"Aren't they all?"

"No. I mean—"

Ford threw up a hand to cut me off. "I didn't mean all of them as in everyone. I meant all of them as in Boston...Christian...Tate."

"Maybe."

Ford sighed.

"I cooked him breakfast on Sunday," I said. "He's too tall to wear my clothes."

"Are those two things connected?"

I dropped my fork onto the empty salad plate and ran both of my hands through my hair, dropping my head back to stare up at the ugly light fixtures that hung overhead. "I'm trying not to rush," I said.

"Him or you?"

I thought back to the conversations Tate and I had shared between rounds of sex and refills of coffee. He was the first to say he wanted more from me...more than just rough fucking. We were going on a proper date in two days, one with dinner and maybe flowers, and hopefully more sex, but...it was a real date and I couldn't remember the last time I'd cared enough to bother. I had to have dated casually after Tyler and I split up, but none of the men had mattered enough to make any lasting impression. Tate had made an impression, though. From the first night all the way through to the second. I'd remembered him then, and I'd never forget him now.

"It's been how long since Ty left?" Ford asked, cocking his head to the side and squinting at me like he was trying to remember my past harder than I was trying to forget it.

"Couple years."

"So, it's about time then."

"It's not an issue of time," I said. "I wasn't holding out or anything."

"I know."

"I haven't met anyone worth dating until Tate," I told him, and it was true. "I feel a little out of practice with the whole thing."

"It's a lot easier than riding a bike."

"I don't know how to ride a bike."

The waitress came over and collected our empty plates, topped off our drinks, and dropped the check. Ford and I both ignored it. We weren't in a rush, but I did take time to pull my phone out and text Tate before I forgot.

Me: What's your last name?

He answered quickly.

Tate: Why?
Me: Because I want to know.
Tate: Are you going to run a background check on me?
Me: Should I?
Tate: Barlowe
Me: I like it. Thank you.

I turned my phone face down on the table and tried to ignore the bobble-headed and lovesick expression Ford was wearing.

"There's not a timeline for any of these things and you know it," Ford said. "It happens when it happens. Do you think that if I had control over it, I would have fallen for Kale's brother?"

"I can't imagine you with anyone else."

His eyes went soft, revealing the truth of my comment. There wasn't a person in the world better suited for Ford than Boston, and I imagined the fit went just as well in reverse too. The two of them balanced each other in unexpected ways, and it was a real delight to watch Ford fall as hard as he did.

"That's fair, but you know what I mean."

"I do," I agreed, sliding the check toward Ford's side of the table.

He scoffed, pushing it back toward me. "I just bought a farm less than a year ago."

"If it's not profitable then that sounds to be a bad investment."

"It makes Boston happy," he said, giving the check another push in my direction. "And we aren't trying to make money off of anything yet."

"That's why I'm richer than you, because I know you should make money off everything."

"You made all your money off your name and you know it." Ford laughed, and I pulled my wallet out to drop my Amex on top of the check. As soon as the black metal card landed, the waitress was there to snatch it up, undoubtedly hearing her tip echo through the restaurant.

"I just don't want to scare him off," I said.

"If he's the one, he won't get scared."

Everything Ford was saying made sense and, in my gut, I knew it to be true. If Tate didn't accept me fully as I was, then there wasn't going to be a future for us. The thought reminded me of something I'd wanted to hold true to after the breakup with Tyler, but so much time had passed that I'd forgotten. I'd sworn to myself—and probably to Kale as well—that I wasn't going to compromise myself for a partner in the future.

I'd tried for so many months to pretend the aftercare wasn't important, to let up on the way I wanted to touch Tyler and be near him, but it hadn't been enough for him. In the end, we'd both been miserable and bitter over the things I expected from the relationship. Him, because I wanted them at all, and me, because I'd spent so long trying to pretend I didn't. I didn't want to be with anyone I couldn't be honest with, with anyone who didn't accept the full and focused intensity of me in whatever way that manifested.

Ford was right.

I had to put my cards on the table with Tate and let them fall however they might. There was no point in tempering or diluting myself for an extra date or two if the end was going to come around sooner rather than later anyway.

My phone vibrated, and I flipped it over to check the screen as the waitress returned with the check for me to sign. The alert had been another message from Tate.

Tate: My middle name is Benjamin, and I live in Chelsea.

I chewed at my bottom lip, fighting back a smile.

"You're so gone for him," Ford said with a laugh.

He finished his drink and I signed the check, leaving a good enough tip because the waitress left us alone without managing to ever let our drinks run dry. I slid my card back into my wallet and grabbed my phone, pushing my chair back and glowering at one of my closest friends. "I am fond of him."

We walked outside and I reached into the inside pocket of my suit coat to get out my sunglasses. Spring was in full effect, with all of the sunshine and none of the temperatures, though it was only a couple of weeks away before things started to get hot.

"Bring him to the farm one weekend," Ford suggested.

I rolled my eyes. "I haven't even taken him out in the city yet."

"Not *this* weekend."

"I'll see how the first date goes and we can talk."

"Fine," he agreed.

"Fine."

"Does Kale know?" At his own question, Ford's face soured, even though he tried to hide it under the dark lenses of his own sunglasses.

"Alex was with me when Tate chased me down at The Black Door, but no, Kale doesn't know."

"You should tell him soon," he suggested.

"Why? Tate isn't his brother." I gave Ford a small chuckle that fell flatter than I intended. Smoothing a hand down the front of my shirt, I sobered. "Is he still being a prick about Boston?"

"He's not being horrible, but he's not being gracious."

"He'll come around."

"Boston hates it," Ford said.

"You definitely snagged yourself the kinder of the two brothers," I teased.

"Christian would probably disagree."

"There's no fight to be had. He can fuck Kale all he wants, but Boston will always be the nicer of the two." My lip was swollen from where I'd been biting it earlier, so I rubbed my tongue over the spot a few times before I voiced my next thought. "Do you want me to talk to him?"

"You don't have to."

"That wasn't what I said."

Ford inhaled sharply, shaking his head and setting off down the street. It took me four long strides to catch up to the tall bastard, but I managed it.

"If it comes up, I wouldn't hate for you to put in a good word about the man his brother loves," Ford grumbled.

"I'll do what I can," I promised.

We walked the few blocks back to the building where Ford

—and Kale—worked, and then we parted ways with a promise of a farm visit before the weather turned unbearably humid. The walk to my own office was another five minutes, so I turned my attention to my phone so I could re-read the messages Tate had sent me over lunch.

The implication I'd run a background check on him was laughable, but it did have me wondering if there were any skeletons in his closet worth hiding. I wasn't above finding out the old fashioned way, with a conversation over dinner and drinks, which was finally only two nights away. When we'd settled on the date, Tate had answered yes without any hesitation at all, and that had me wondering about his job.

That should have also been a date question, but I had a few minutes left and a curious itch. His roommate was in the service industry and I knew sometimes those kinds of people flocked together. I hoped my desire for weekend plans wasn't cutting into his ability to make hours and money.

Me: Are you a bartender too?
Tate: I'm an administrative assistant.
Tate: Why?
Me: I was worried you were losing a good shift to let me take you out on Friday.
Tate: I get off work at five.
Me: Okay, good.

He didn't say anything after that, and I realized it was because it was quarter after one and he was probably busy trying to do his job while I was worried about keeping him from it in the first place. Ford and I had taken a long lunch, which wasn't unusual, but a sharp reminder of how different our lives were from the people around us.

My money had never been an issue for Tyler. In fact, he was content to spend it as freely as I was. It was the rest of me he found problematic. I would give just as much to Tate, if not more, but he had to take the whole of me to get it. I hoped that wasn't going to be a deal breaker, but in two days, I was going to find out.

CHAPTER 12
TATE

Dylan caught up to me on Wednesday.

I'd managed to avoid him most of the week on account of him sleeping most of the time while I was at work and me doing anything I could except be home when I knew he was going to be there. I was on the couch reading back through the texts with Brooks from earlier in the day with a stupid and undoubtedly googley-eyed expression on my face when the front door opened.

"You're home," Dylan said, closing it quickly behind him.

He was in his spot on the couch before I even had time to think about getting up and fleeing to my bedroom.

"Have you been avoiding me?" he asked.

"Not exactly."

"That's not believable." He raised both his eyebrows at me like a disappointed parent. "Was that man from The Black Door your unicorn?"

Brooks had been my unicorn, but now that he was back in my life, he was proving himself to be very, very real. Even though the fingerprint-shaped bruises were all but gone, I knew the touch of his hand, the press of his mouth. Brooks was no longer just a figment of my imagination.

"Yes," I answered, because it was close enough.

Dylan's face twisted with the most excitement I'd ever seen and he practically bounced up and down on the cushion like an over-eager toddler.

"And you left with him on Saturday?"

"Yes."

"Was it everything you hoped it would be?" Dylan asked.

To say yes would have been another understatement.

"More than," I admitted with a soft smile. I set my phone down beside my thigh and thumped my head against the exposed brick wall behind me.

"I don't know if I should be mad you'd been to that club before and you didn't take me with you. And I don't know if I should be mad that you didn't tell me you met the man of your dreams at a fucking *sex* club."

A week before, the comment would have made my cheeks flush with embarrassment, but for some reason, I didn't see the shame in it anymore. I used to worry there was something wrong with the kind of men I'd tried to pursue in Brooks' wake, but when I was with Brooks, I knew that couldn't be the case. There wasn't a single thing wrong with the way our bodies moved together, and I never wanted to find shame in sex ever again.

"Don't worry about me meeting men at a sex club." I pointed a playful and accusatory finger in his direction. "Let's talk about you going through the whole interview process and never telling me."

"I didn't interview!" Dylan threw up his hands and laughed, tucking his legs beneath him and leaning toward me.

"How did you get the job then?"

"A guy I know from Tryst," he said. "He's that friend of your unicorn."

"And he just...got you a job at a sex club?" I asked.

"It's not like I'm having sex there. I'm just a bartender."

I squinted at him, feeling like there was more to the story, but also feeling confident that I wasn't going to get any answers out of him. Dylan was far too fixated on Brooks to entertain my line of questioning.

"Did you go back to his house when you left?" Dylan asked next, changing the topic back to me as I expected. "Actually, answer that while I'm changing. I have a gig tonight."

"Where at?" I asked, watching him get up and shuffle into his bedroom. The apartment wasn't big and there wasn't going to be any problem continuing the conversation no matter what room either of us was in.

"Some little coffee shop, nothing big. Answer the question."

"I went back to his house," I said, a smile flickering across my face. "His penthouse."

Dylan stuck his head out from his bedroom, eyes wide. "Shut up."

I shrugged helplessly. "He has a huge penthouse apartment with the most amazing views of the city. The bathroom and the bedroom are all windows."

There was the burn in my cheeks, thinking about the dildo Brooks had suction-cupped to the window for me to fuck myself on.

"Did he fuck as good as you remembered?" Dylan stepped back into the hallway dressed in a light wash pair of jeans and a tight black t-shirt.

"Better."

"Love that for you." He grabbed his guitar and case, bringing them both out to the couch to get everything packed up and ready. "Are you seeing him tonight?"

"Not until the weekend."

"Did you want to come with me to this gig?"

I checked my phone. There really wasn't anything for me to do besides sit around and pine over Brooks, and I didn't want to text him or call him and make things weird a clingy. We'd talked about being together like *being together*, but I didn't know what that looked like for him and I didn't want to fuck anything up by being a stage five clinger right off the bat. It wasn't like I could fuck that way every day, but I wouldn't have said no to the rest of the things he liked.

"Is it far?"

"Brooklyn."

I sighed, and Dylan laughed at me.

"Come on. It'll be an adventure."

"Alright." I shoved up from the couch, needing to change out of my work clothes if I was going to some random coffee shop in Brooklyn for the night. "Let me get changed."

In my bedroom, I managed to find a clean pair of jeans and a band t-shirt I'd picked up at a concert a few years before. There wasn't any help for my hair, still sticky with product from when I'd styled it in the morning, so I shoved my feet into a pair of Vans and waited for Dylan to finish getting his shit together for the gig.

An hour later, we found ourselves at a coffee shop called Beans, and I leaned against the wall in the back while Dylan busied himself getting situated on the stage that looked like it had been built out of plywood and dreams. My phone vibrated in my pocket and I juggled my coffee into my other hand so I could pull it out. The screen flashed with a text message from Brooks, and across the room, Dylan strummed his guitar to check the tuning.

Brooks: Is it bad to say I don't know if I can wait until the weekend to see you?

I smiled, thankful that we were apparently on the same page about that.

Me: I was thinking the same thing.
Brooks: Did you want to come over tonight?

"Hey everyone," Dylan said, his voice amplified through the small microphone in front of his face. He tapped it a couple times to check the feedback before speaking again. "I know I'm a last minute addition, but I'm happy to be here to play some songs for you tonight. My name is Dylan Rivers, by the way."

Dylan immediately started with a song I recognized as a cover of a late nineties pop song.

Me: I'm in Brooklyn.
Brooks: That wasn't an answer.
Me: My roommate has a gig and I'm here with him.
Brooks: Still not an answer, Tate.

Me: Of course I want to come over.

Brooks: Then come over when you're finished in Brooklyn.

He sent me his address next, and my phone went silent.

Dylan finished his first song and went straight into another cover. Some people were singing along, which was good for him. One song later, he finally lapsed into some of the pieces he'd written himself. Those were the ones I knew the most and liked the best. Still against the far wall, I hummed along and finished my coffee.

His set was just under an hour, and I helped him pack up so he could make room for whoever was coming after him. Money exchanged hands, and then Dylan and I were on the way back home. He always had a great afterglow around him when he had a good gig, and the happiness practically rolled off of him the whole way back to our apartment.

"I'm going to head out," I said, after helping him up the stairs and making sure everything made it home in one piece. Dylan bent over the fridge, a beer already in his hand and a knowing look on his face.

"Your unicorn calls?"

"He's not...yes."

"I don't blame you," he said, twisting the bottle top off and tossing it into a mason jar on the counter filled with a rainbow of other bottle tops. "Be safe."

"Always," I said, even though it might not have been the truth.

I checked my pockets for all my things, realizing how late it was when the time flashed on my phone. I fired off a quick text to Brooks again.

Me: Should I plan on staying over?
Brooks: If you want.
Me: That's not an answer.

I smiled at the screen, apparently my new favorite hobby.

Brooks: I want you to stay the night.
Brooks: If you can.

I could. It just meant I would have to pack clothes for work, which took about ten minutes to get all my toiletries together. Dylan smirked at me from the couch when I came out with a bag slung over my shoulder, but he didn't say anything.

The trip to Brooks' penthouse went quick enough, and the doorman let me in before I even had a chance to tell him my name. His massive size was just as off-putting as it had been the first time, but he must have had a photographic memory if he remembered me. Or maybe Brooks had called down and let him know I was coming. Either way, a weird tangle of expectations and promises festered in the pit of my stomach.

It wasn't unwelcome—just new.

The elevator raced me up to the right floor, and when the doors slid open, Brooks was in his doorway, leaning casually against the doorframe with his arms folded in front of his chest, one leg crossed over the other at the ankle. His hair was messy, falling down around his face, and when he saw me, he pushed it back and smiled at me like I was the sun after a long winter.

"Hey," I said nervously, suddenly feeling like I should hide my bag even though he was the one who said he wanted me to stay over.

He reached his arm out, and I knew what he was asking.

I gave him the bag and followed him into the penthouse, door closing behind me with a soft latch as the lock automatically slid into place. Brooks carried my bag into his bedroom and I followed behind him up the stairs like a puppy. He dropped the bag in his closet and then turned back toward me, closing the space between us and taking my face into the cradle of his hands. He pulled me down to his level and slanted our mouths together with the most satisfied sigh I'd ever heard in my life.

"I missed you," he whispered against my lips.

I curled my fingers around his wrists, groaning. "I missed you."

"Friday is a lifetime away."

"I'm here now." I said, chasing after another one of his breathtaking kisses.

Brooks kissed with the same level of practice and attention he'd shown through everything else we'd done together, using his tongue to wipe all sense of practicality and propriety out of my mind.

We had started in the doorway of his bedroom, but he used his body to move me to the bed, and the backs of my knees hit the mattress. I fell onto his sheets, just as soft and cool as I remembered, and Brooks climbed on top of me, the burning heat of his body quick to set everything around him on fire. He was only wearing that sinful pair of gray sweats again, and his cock stabbed through the material, poking a wet and instant spot against my hip that had me riled up for him like it was our first encounter again.

By the time he broke for another breath, my own cock was hard and hot, pressing against the fly of my jeans and weeping with want. Brooks reached between us and palmed my dick with his hand, giving my shaft a rough squeeze when it pulsed against his fingers.

"Yes, darling. You most certainly are."

Crawling out of bed when Tate was wrapped in my sheets all soft and warm and smelling like cum was the worst kind of torture. But I started the coffee and went for a run, just like I did every other weekday morning. I was only gone for half an hour, and Tate was still breathing heavily with his face buried in my pillow when I returned. I knew he had work because he'd brought work clothes over with him the night before, but apparently his morning routine wasn't as time intensive as mine.

I showered and dressed while he continued to sleep, and I was downstairs in the kitchen with my coffee when I heard the sharp trill of his alarm echo through my penthouse. Five minutes later, Tate's feet appeared on the stairs, a pair of basketball shorts slung sinfully low on his hips. He shoved his hair away from his face and yawned, giving me an embarrassed little smile when he shuffled into the kitchen.

"Coffee?" I asked.

"Can I shower first?"

"You can do whatever you want," I told him, setting my

mug down on the counter and folding my arms in front of my chest.

"Can I have coffee in the shower?" he arched a brow, playful in his sleepiness.

"You can take your coffee in the shower," I confirmed. "You can take it in the bath and I'll wash every inch of your body before getting you dressed if that's what you want too."

Tate swallowed, suddenly far more awake than he'd been moments before.

"Too much?" I asked, reaching again for my coffee.

"Maybe just enough," he said softly. "But I'll stick with shower then coffee for now."

"As you wish. Can you find your way around up there?"

He nodded.

"I'll be here when you're ready for coffee then."

Tate gave me an odd and lingering look before he turned and headed back up the stairs. I watched him go, sipping my coffee until I heard the shower turn on in my en suite. Letting out a breath that I'd been holding since I realized I couldn't read the look on his face, I wondered if my last comment had gone too far.

It was one thing to dote and tend to a partner after sex, but maybe first thing in the morning might have been a little overwhelming. Tate's reaction was just proof that he and I needed to have a clear conversation about what it meant for men like us to be together. Hopefully, he would have time when he got out of the shower, but if not, the conversation would at least keep until our date on Friday night.

Fifteen minutes later, Tate was downstairs again, dressed in a pair of charcoal gray, off-the-rack slacks and a white button-up. His hair was still damp, dripping down his temples, but he didn't seem to have a care in the world about it. I made a mental note he didn't have his overnight bag in hand, but he did have hot pink socks on his feet, and his toes curled around the rungs on the stool as he sat at the island and gestured for me to pass him his coffee.

"When do you have to leave for work?" I asked.

"From here?" Tate glanced over his shoulder at Manhattan, sprawling out below us. "Probably not for a while. It takes a bit longer from home."

"Thank you for coming over last night, " I said, refilling my own coffee. "I know it wasn't planned."

"It wasn't a hardship." He smiled, tipping his chin toward his chest. "Are we still going out this weekend?"

"Yes."

His cheeks burned a gorgeous and bright pink, and he nodded quickly, lifting his mug to his mouth and taking a drink.

"Will you stay the whole weekend?"

"If you like," Tate whispered.

"If *you* like."

"I think I would like," he said, setting his coffee down and framing the mug with both of his hands. He let out a choked-off laugh, then shook his head and bored holes into the counter with his eyes. "I'm sorry I'm being so awkward."

"Why don't you just tell me the why of it?"

"You make me want," he said quickly, pulling his teeth between his lips and turning that sharp and focused intensity on me.

"I don't think that's inherently a problem."

The feeling was mutual because to say that Tate made *me* want…it was hardly enough of a descriptor. Tate was the first person in a very long time who made me feel like I could *have*, which was just as potent and ten times more dangerous.

"Is it just you and me? Together, I mean."

"Are you asking me if I'm sleeping with other people?"

Tate worked his jaw back and forth like the question hurt him. "Yes."

"It's just you and me," I answered. "I have to warn you that I don't share well."

He cut me off before I could finish the thought. "I don't want you to share."

"This is as good a time as any to tell you that I'm not interested in something fleeting, Tate. This...the way I am...it doesn't wear off. This is me and that isn't going to change a month from now or a year from now. I know that can be int—"

"I like it," he cut me off again.

"Intense," I finished, sucking in a much needed breath. "Are you going to like it once the novelty wears off?"

"I spent the past six months spending far more time than I'd ever admit out loud thinking about you. The way I want you...it hasn't changed," he said, swallowing nervously. He sucked down a swallow of coffee and then dropped the mug down onto the counter with a little more force than would have been inherently necessary, but it was a hard conversation. At least he was sitting down.

I leaned against the counter, legs crossed at the ankle and knees threatening to give up and send me to the floor. "That sounds settled then."

I wanted to trust it, but it was hard to believe that Tate wouldn't eventually follow in Tyler's footsteps. The novelty always wore off, sooner or later, and all I could do was trust and hope that Tate knew himself better than the men who'd come before him. That there was truth in his promises, where everyone else had fallen short.

"Would it be presumptuous to ask you to go get tested?" I asked.

Anger flashed across Tate's face, and he shoved the mug away from him, mouth pulled into a tight frown. "Are you worried I have something?"

I chuckled at his indignation, scratching the side of my chin.

"No, darling," I assured him, "I just want to fuck you raw and come inside of you."

"Oh," he rasped.

Something tight and hot constricted in the center of my chest, and I watched helpless as Tate pushed the stool back from the counter. He stood somewhat awkwardly, all gangly limbs, then he went to the window, staring out at the city waking up all around us.

"How do you afford this place?" he asked, still staring out the window.

"My parents are rich."

"Are you not?"

"They're richer than me," I said, setting my mug on the island next to Tate's. "I wouldn't have anything if it wasn't for them."

"Oh," he said softly.

"Is my money an issue?" I came across the room to stand beside him, shoulder to shoulder, and he glanced at me from the corner of his eye, expression almost wary, but not guarded.

"I live in a two bedroom apartment the same size as your kitchen. Is *that* an issue?"

"I want to say as long as your apartment has a bed I can fuck you in, it doesn't make a single bit of difference to me where you live, but I don't even need a bed, so..."

Tate scoffed, shaking his head, but it was enough to wash all the apprehension from his face.

"I need to get going to work," he mumbled, finally looking at me.

"Before you go." I held my arms open and he walked right into them like he belonged there. "To summarize."

Tate laughed and rocked his forehead against my shoulder. I curled my hand around the back of his neck, massaging at the bent muscles. I loved that he was taller than me, but yielded just the same.

"It's just you and me," I said, talking my way back through the rest of our conversation. "We're hoping to soon forego condoms, and I don't need a bed to fuck you."

"That sounds about right," he whispered, rolling his head to the side and dropping the softest kiss against the thin swatch of skin behind my ear.

I tightened my arms around him, letting my fingers splay our against the small of his back and stray down toward his ass.

"I'll go get tested on my lunch break," I said.

"I'll find a place."

His cock twitched against my hip.

"Eager much?" I teased, pushing against his growing erection before reluctantly working my way out of his arms and putting some necessary space between us. I could have spent every hour of every day naked with Tate, but I didn't want to interfere with his job or his income. Nor would I force my own money on him unless he asked for it.

"Six months, Brooks," he muttered, reaching down and adjusting himself. "You have a lot of lost time to make up for."

I threw my head back and laughed, kicking at his sock-clad toe before heading back into the kitchen for another refill of my coffee. Tate grinned at me, then went back upstairs, undoubtedly for his shoes. Instead of joining me again in the kitchen, he made a turn in the other direction and went for the living room. I followed after him, enjoying the sight of him making himself at home in my home.

"How many bedrooms?" he asked, tying up the laces on his left shoe.

"Four."

"Bathrooms?"

"Five," I answered.

"I've never understood why expensive homes have more bathrooms than bedrooms," he said, setting to work on his other shoe.

"Variety is the spice of life, I imagine."

Tate let out a breath and stood up, smoothing his hands over the front of his slacks, no doubt checking for any visible sign of the erection that I hoped hadn't already gone down.

"What time do you leave for work?" he asked.

I checked my watch, frowning. "Normally, half an hour ago."

"Oh, my God." His eyes went wide and he patted down his pockets, spinning around like a little tornado in the middle of my living room. "You're late."

"I'm also the boss," I reminded him. "I can stay home and work from my office here if that's what I want."

"Then why don't you?"

"The spice of life, or something like that." I shrugged. "Today I'm going in because I have a meeting with a local charity and one of their donors, and also because I have to go slip in to see my doctor around noon."

Tate hummed, a nervous smile flashing across his face.

"I don't even know what you do for work," he said.

"Admittedly, whatever I want. But I have too much money and too much time. I help facilitate relationships between other rich assholes and charities in need."

"That doesn't sound like it pays well."

"It doesn't." I grinned. "That's why it's a good thing my parents are rich. Come on, I'll head out with you. Just give me five minutes."

Tate nodded and flung himself back down onto the couch with a groan. It was a comfortable couch, shaped like an elongated kidney bean, that I'd spent many nights sleeping on, curled up in the opposite direction and tucked against the back of it. That had been years before, though, and now all I wanted to do was bend Tate over the back of it and rail him to within an inch of consciousness.

Instead, I went upstairs and put on my shoes.

Tate had made my bed, which...riled up a whole new host of feelings I would have to process after my meeting with Boston, Ford, and Boston's best friend, Shawn.

Before I could overthink anything, or worse, warn myself off, I took the stairs down two at a time. As soon as Tate came back into my line of sight, I could breathe again. He hadn't moved from the couch, and he stared out the window, expression a little awestruck as he fidgeted with the sleeve of his shirt.

"Are you ready?" I asked.

He stood quickly, like I'd caught him with his hand in the cookie jar. "Yep."

"Everything okay?" I asked, gesturing toward the front door with a jerk of my head.

"Very," he said, and I believed him.

"Overwhelming?"

"Sometimes."

"For me too," I said, holding out my hand. "Time for work, Tate. Let's go."

DYLAN LEANED AGAINST THE DOORFRAME OF THE BATHROOM WHILE I tried—to no avail—to do something presentable with my hair.

"You're overthinking this," he said, an amused smirk playing across his lips.

"I want to impress him."

"You impressed him six months ago." Dylan rolled his eyes and took the pomade container out of my hands, screwing the lid back on and dropping it on top of the toilet. "You impressed him last weekend, and probably again on Wednesday night."

Staring at the reflection of myself, my cheeks burned pink at the insinuation behind his comment. I knew Dylan was right. I didn't have to impress Brooks. He was already impressed, or at least interested. He wouldn't have let me come over in the middle of the week or asked me out again in the first place if the connection wasn't there, and he surely wouldn't have asked me to go get tested so we could fuck without condoms. That wasn't something casual or passing—that was commitment.

That was real.

"Are you coming home before work on Monday?" Dylan asked, laughing when I shoved him out of the way.

Our apartment was small; it always had been. Being on top of each other wasn't something new, but all I needed in that moment was a spare square foot to catch my breath before Brooks arrived. I brushed past Dylan into my bedroom, and I sat down on the edge of my bed, staring at the brick wall only a few feet away from my knees. He stopped himself in the doorway, taking up the same pose he'd held when I was in the bathroom.

"I don't want to assume," I said.

My overnight bag was still at Brooks' house from Wednesday, with a dirty pair of jeans and underwear shoved behind the zipper. My toiletries were sitting damp in the leather bag that used to belong to my grandfather, all of it tucked into the corner of Brooks' otherwise pristine closet. I should have taken the bag with me on Thursday, but I didn't want to raise questions with my friends from work, and also there was a part of me that wanted to make sure I got to come back. I'd seen that little trick on the internet that women sometimes did, leaving small things behind as an excuse to come over a second time. I imagined an overnight bag full of clothes wasn't as discreet, but I worked with what I had.

More than that, though, I knew what I really needed to do was trust Brooks. It was something he'd talked about the first night we met and when we ran into each other again at The Black Door. Being able to trust a partner was of the utmost importance to him, and now that we'd been together a handful of times, I understood why. If he could trust me, I needed to trust him too. I needed to trust the thing between us.

"Just be safe either way," Dylan said, glancing over his shoulder when we both heard the steady and sure knock on our front door. "He hoofed it up three flights to get you?"

"Shit."

I jumped off the bed, having expected Brooks to text about his arrival, not make the three-story hike up to our little apartment. I didn't even have my shoes on yet, and I shoved my feet into them as fast as I could manage. Checking my pockets for my wallet, phone, and keys, I didn't see a message from Brooks letting me know he'd arrived.

"I'll get it," Dylan said, ignoring the desperate noise that fell out of my mouth in place of a *no*. He yanked the door open with so much force, it wafted the rich and spicy smell of Brooks' cologne through the hallway and right into my nose. I stumbled into the couch, deciding there was no point in trying to intercept Brooks in the doorway. The apartment Dylan and I shared wasn't small by New York standards, but it was small by billionaire with family money standards, and with that thought, another wave of the doubt I'd just started to fight off slammed into me.

"You must be Dylan," Brooks said.

The door closed behind him.

"We met at The Black Door," Dylan said.

Shoes against the wood floor getting louder with every step.

"I don't recall," Brooks said, sounding bemused. He

stepped around Dylan, a small smile settling on his face when he caught my stare. "Tate."

There was something about the way he said my name that was always going to do it for me. He managed to infuse an unfair amount of competence and control into it, like there was no argument for whatever words came with it. Whether he used it in or out of the bedroom, I was weak for it. And those few times he called me *darling*? I couldn't even think about it and remain decent.

"I would have come downstairs," I said in lieu of a greeting.

Brooks glanced around the very small living room before looking back to me. "I know you would have, but I wanted to see your apartment."

"It's the size of your kitchen," I muttered.

"My kitchen is unnecessarily large," he agreed. "Show me your room before we go?"

"It's nothing."

"I'd still like to see it, Tate."

There he was again with the demand permeating through the four letters of my name.

I pointed behind me, helpless to argue with him about it. The clack of his shoes against the wood grew louder as he reached me in front of the couch. Brooks took my hand and pulled me the remaining few feet through the living room until we were both in my bedroom, barely large enough for a queen size bed, so I'd tucked a full into the corner and hoped for the best.

"It fits you," he said, taking in my unmade bed and the garment rack shoved into the corner.

"It's what we can afford."

"The only one here who cares about the difference in our living situations is you," Brooks said quietly. He reached into his pocket and pulled out his phone, tapping through a series of apps until he found what he'd been looking for. He read through whatever had come up on the screen, then slipped his phone into my hand.

I tore my stare away from his face to look at whatever was on the screen, finding a lengthy list of test results, ranging from HIV status to LDL cholesterol. Every line item had a green check mark next to it, confirming test results had returned as expected.

"Healthy as a horse," I rasped, passing the phone back to him.

I didn't have an app for my doctor, but there was a folded up sheet of paper on my nightstand that covered the basics, which I handed off to Brooks awkwardly. He unfolded it with long and skilled fingers, making a pleased little hum when he reached the bottom of the page. He folded it up and tucked it into the hidden pocket of his suit coat.

"Are you ready for our date?" he asked, like the silent conversation we'd just shared didn't have anything to do with the fact that we both planned for him to come inside of me before the end of the night.

Another first to Astor Brooks.

I should tell him, I thought, not wanting a repeat of the breach of trust from our first night together.

"I've never," I blurted, scrunching my nose in embarrassment at how loud my voice came out between us in the very small space. "I've never done it before."

Brooks smirked, one of his eyebrows quirking toward his hairline. "You've never gone on a date?"

"No. Yes. I mean, I've dated before," I said. "I meant the no condom thing. I've never done that before."

He worked his jaw back and forth, then curled his fingers around my elbow and pulled our chests together. Our noses brushed, and he tilted his head up just enough to see my face.

"Seventeen men and none of them had you like that?"

I shook my head, lashes fluttering at the way the humiliation over the callout made my blood boil. I wasn't ashamed of the number of partners I'd had, but something about the way Brooks always talked about it so casually turned me on in ways I didn't dare stop long enough to make sense of. He wasn't trying to shame me. I knew that. He was setting himself apart from them, on top of them.

On top of me.

"No."

Brooks smiled, brushing his lips over mine in the barest tease of a kiss. "What other firsts do you have for me, darling?"

The answer rushed out on a heavy exhale. "Quite a few, I'm sure."

"Perfect." His fingers trailed from their spot around my elbow, down to my hand. He threaded our fingers together and took one last look around my room. "Is there anything you need for the weekend?"

In the living room, far closer to my door than he should have been, Dylan snorted.

"I left my bag at your house earlier in the week."

"I know. There wasn't enough for a weekend in it."

"I don't have another bag, and I don't—" I snapped my

mouth closed, feeling silly for leaving the bag in the first place, for doubting Brooks.

"Your clothes are already washed and hung up," he said. "We'll sort the rest out. But maybe you can prepare better next time."

"Next time," I repeated, words rough against the back of my throat.

"Are you ready, Tate?" he asked again.

"I'm ready," I lied.

Brooks led me out of my own bedroom, tipping his chin at Dylan on our way toward the door.

"I will not have him home before midnight," Brooks said.

Dylan laughed and flung himself down onto the couch, reaching for his guitar. "I would most certainly hope not."

"I'll text you," I said to Dylan.

"You better not." He strummed a C-chord on his guitar, effectively ending the conversation.

Brooks pulled me out of the living room and into the hallway, then we were at the door, we were down the stairs, we were in the back seat of a black town car with tinted windows and warm leather seats. His fingers were still curled around the top of my hand, and I couldn't breathe. My body didn't want to hold itself upright anymore, and I sagged against Brooks' shoulder, pressing the fingers of my free hand against my lower lip.

"Are you okay?" Brooks asked, shifting sideways. Our knees brushed together and I was forced to hold my body up on my own.

"I am, yes." I cleared my throat and gave my head a shake to clear it. Our hands were still joined, resting in the small space between our thighs.

Brooks' pants were blue, I realized. A dark and lush navy and the material was so soft against the tops of my knuckles. I hadn't even seen him when he walked in, instead I'd been overwhelmed by the idea of him. Navy slacks, brown dress shoes and a matching belt, crisp white button-up tucked in with the sleeves rolled up to his forearms. The top button was undone, revealing a small V beneath his clavicle. His face was a few hours away from clean shaven, and it was impossible to not imagine the beard burn I was going to end up with before the next morning.

"Are you sure?" he asked, lifting our joined hands to kiss my knuckles. His lips were softer than his pants, and my brain threatened to short-circuit from the feel of it all.

In the back of the car, all I could smell was leather and Brooks, and the way he watched me promised a level of interest and attention that I'd never found myself deserving of before. But he was there just the same, giving it freely. Giving it to me.

"You just take some getting used to," I answered honestly.

"Do you think I'm out of your league?" he asked.

I nodded.

"If it's any consolation, there isn't a single person in this city who is out of *my* league, and regardless of what you think about yourself, I want you, Tate. Just you." He pressed another kiss against the top of my hand, lips warm and wet.

"I hear you," I croaked, gnawing mindlessly at the inside of my cheek. "You're a lot sometimes."

"I can't be less," he said, eyes dark and serious, tone almost biting. "I won't be less."

"I don't want less." I pressed my free hand against the center of his chest, feeling the way his heart slammed violently against his sternum. "I'm just getting used to you. That's all."

Brooks swallowed, heart still pumping madly beneath my hand like it had something to say separate of whatever words he was going to put between us.

"It's me," I promised, curling my fingers against the soft fabric of his shirt. "And I'm not complaining."

"I won't compromise," he said, covering my hand with his. "Not who I am and not what I want."

"I'm glad for that." I licked my lips, leaning in an inch. My arms tingled, skin like a live wire about to be touched. "I don't want you any different than you are."

Brooks closed the rest of the space between us, slanting our mouths together with the neediest-sounding groan I'd ever heard him make. He shook our fingers apart and grabbed my face with both of his hands, using his body and his tongue and his mouth to deepen the kiss like he was searching for the truth of my confession behind my teeth.

It was easy to yield to him, to turn soft and pliant beneath the demanding way he kissed and touched and took from me. When he reached down into my lap and pressed his palm against the quickly thickening erection growing between my legs, sparks exploded against the backs of my eyelids. I threaded my fingers around the short hairs at the base of his neck and kept him close, lifting up into his hand as he found new and dangerous ways to deepen the connection between us.

"We have to stop," he murmured, giving my cock a squeeze and reaching up to pull my hand off the back of his neck. I whimpered, chasing after him, but his expression—save for his dilated pupils and flushed cheeks—was stoic.

"Do we?"

He huffed a laugh, lifting both of my hands to his mouth and peppering grateful kisses against each fingertip.

"I promise I'll take you apart later, Tate," he said, nipping at the pad of my thumb, lips twisting into a devilish grin. "But first... dinner."

CHAPTER 15
BROOKS

BUT FIRST, DINNER, TURNED OUT TO BE A LOT HARDER TO GET through than I'd expected. Normally, I prided myself on my self-control, but absolutely everything about Tate drove me wild.

Earlier, at his apartment, I'd told him he was the only one who cared about the difference in our incomes, but as I watched his calloused fingers roam over the multiple forks and knives on the table, the way he averted his gaze when it came time to order wine, it was impossible to ignore how out of his element he was around me.

"Do you hate this?" I asked after ordering a bottle of Caymus Cabernet for us to share.

"What part of it?"

"Any of it."

Tate gave me a crooked smile and let his finger fall away from the salad fork. He reached across the table to touch me instead, and I had to admit that was where I preferred his attention.

"I'm just unfamiliar with the rules," he said. "But I don't hate it."

"Is it too much? Too overwhelming?" I asked, flipping my hand palm up so he could trace his way down the pads of my fingers toward my heart line.

"Everything about you is overwhelming." His cheeks flushed again. "But this is good. It's perfect."

"I would have taken you to Italy, but you work on Monday," I admitted.

It wasn't so much a lie, but it was a stretch on the truth. I would have one-hundred percent put Tate on a plane and flown him across the globe for better Italian food and better wine, but I had been trying to keep myself in check and not terrify him off the bat. Though, if I hadn't already, I wondered if a flight for dinner really would have scared him off.

"I have PTO," he whispered, pulling back.

The sommelier returned with the wine and poured a sample into my glass. It wasn't corked, so I gave him a nod to fill our glasses. He was finished and gone before Tate had even managed to get his hand under the table.

"Are you saying you'd let me take you to another country for dinner if that was what I wanted?" I raised my glass and he mirrored the action, gently clanking the rim of his against mine.

"I'd let you try." Tate took the smallest sip of the wine, lashes fluttering. "But I don't have a passport so I'm not sure how far you'd get."

"You should get one."

Tate scoffed, laughing at me. "Does my unworldliness hinder your spontaneity?"

"I want to feed you and fuck you on every continent, Tate. So, yes."

He swallowed, unsure of what to make of my comment, but I wasn't going to take it back. I told him I wasn't going to throttle myself or try and be less. This was who I was and *how* I was. It was better for us both if he knew it now instead of coming to terms with it later and breaking both of our hearts in the process.

"I'll have to ask my mom for my birth certificate," he muttered.

The comment felt like a consolation, that I hadn't scared him off yet, so I washed my nerves down with a drink of the wine.

"Tell me about your parents," I said.

"Nothing special to report," he answered with a small shrug. "Working class from southern California. I moved out here for college, made it a semester and dropped out."

"Why?"

"School wasn't for me. It was for them."

"How did they take it?" I asked.

Tate frowned, scratching behind his ear. "Not great at first, but they aren't mad about it anymore. I think they would prefer that if I was just working a boring office job that I did it in California, but I like it here."

"How long have you lived with Dylan?"

"Two years," Tate answered.

"And he's a bartender?"

My question might have had ulterior motives because I didn't know how a bartender could afford his half of that apartment of theirs, and also because Alex was circling a little too close to the man and I wanted to get a read on him before things got out of hand. They were both adults, but Alex was still heartbroken over Beamer and I didn't want anyone getting hurt as part of that rebound process, physically or otherwise.

"And a musician," Tate said.

"How does he know Alex?" I asked next.

"I think they met at another bar Dylan works at, Tryst," he said.

I bit the back of my tongue and managed a nod. Reaching for my wine, I took a decent swallow of it, settling into my seat.

"Why?" Tate asked, head cocked to the side.

"I think Alex likes him," I admitted. "Just trying to feel it out."

"Dylan is a good guy," Tate said. "His parents pay for his rent so he can pursue being a musician."

I wanted that to be a massive red flag, but I lived in a penthouse bought by my parents so I choked off any protest that might have managed to formulate itself in the back of my mouth.

"That's good." I cleared my throat. "Back to you."

"There's not much to say. I don't have a great relationship with my parents, I'm replaceable at work...there's not much of note."

I raised a hand to cut him off. "Stop that. There's plenty of note with you."

Tate snorted, ready to lean in and whisper something only to find himself interrupted by the arrival of his food. He'd ordered pasta with shrimp, and the smell of garlic wafted heavy through the restaurant when the plate was set in front of him. I'd gone with chicken, and my stomach growled after the waiter had walked away.

"This smells amazing," he said, using his hand to circulate some of the scent off his plate and toward his nose.

"There's plenty of note with you," I repeated.

Tate's shoulders locked and he looked up at me, jaw clenched. "If you say so."

"Don't argue with me," I warned, leaning over my steaming plate so I could whisper the next part, "I know what you look like when you come, Tate. That's a miracle in and of itself."

"Oh, shut up."

I grinned, fanning my napkin across my lap and grabbing my knife and fork to dig into my dinner. It was fine if he didn't believe me yet, he'd believe me eventually. I'd make sure of it.

The rest of our dinner passed amicably enough, with casual conversation where we shared mundane things like favorite movies and favorite colors. Tate liked to play video games and I collected whiskey. He couldn't even boil water. I'd learned to cook at the knee of one of the best private chefs in the state. We couldn't have been more different on paper, but maybe that was why we fit together so well in person. By the time we finished dessert—and the bottle of wine—I was ready to remind us both just how *well* we fit.

In the back seat of the town car, Tate dragged his thumb back and forth against my palm, almost like a nervous twitch. I clamped my hand down around his, and the little breath he sucked in was enough to make my cock spasm against my thigh.

"Why are you nervous now?" I whispered into his ear, lips dragging across his skin.

"It's not bad nerves," he murmured, turning toward me and bumping our noses together. "Just...anticipation."

"What are you anticipating?"

"The end of the night," he whispered.

"I know that, but I'm asking you to tell me, Tate. What specifically are you thinking about?"

The hitch in his breath was audible, and I kissed the corner of his mouth with a soft smile.

"How you're going to make me cry tonight."

I moved my hand into his lap, curling my fingers around the hot bulge between his legs. "I'm thinking about that too."

"How far until we're back at your place?"

I squeezed, and he lifted off the seat, his entire body arching into mine like he couldn't decide if he was trying to get more from me or get away. Keeping my hand between his legs where it belonged, I wrapped my other arm around his back, holding him close against me while his brain waged that war.

I glanced over his head out the window, recognizing the modern lines and tall glass panels of my building coming into view.

"We're here now," I told him.

Tate collapsed against me, then slowly unfolded himself from my lap, making sure to adjust himself before the driver had time to get around the car and get the back door open. It was an absolute pleasure to watch his ass stretch the material of his slacks as he climbed out of the car in front of me, and I thanked the driver and the doorman on our way to the elevator.

I managed to keep my hands to myself, but by the time we got to the front door of my place, my mind was racing with ideas. My dick was so hard it hurt, and I practically shoved Tate through the front door. He fell against the wall, using his hands to yank his shoes off instead of trying to catch himself. One of his shoes hit the floor and I was on him, using my body to support us both. He knew what was coming next, understood what I was after, and he opened his mouth so I could slide my tongue past his lips.

Curling my hand around the back of his head to keep it away from the wall and close to my mouth, I kissed him deep, grinding my hips against him slowly. His other shoe hit the floor and then both his arms came around my waist, barely resting there like he knew I was prepared to do all of the heavy lifting.

"Have you decided yet?" he asked, tilting his head up when I moved my mouth down the sharp angle of his jaw to his throat. "How you're going to make me cry?"

"I have a thousand ideas." I nipped at the skin beneath his ear. "And all of them involve you being naked, so let's start there."

Tate groaned, and I helped him out of his clothes, leaving them in a messy pile in the entryway. Once he was fully undressed, I reached for my own belt, but he stopped me with a desperate whimper.

"I like when you're dressed," he whispered, letting his head fall against the wall.

Tate was going to be the death of me, but at least I would die a happy man.

"Living room," I managed to tell him, pointing in the general direction of the room in question.

We moved into the space in sync, and I lowered myself

down onto the couch, brain having already decided how the night was going to start.

"Sit on the table," I told him, spreading my legs to accommodate him between them.

Tate stepped around me and dropped his ass right onto the table without any protest, which was admirable. It was a ten thousand dollar table he was dragging his ass across, but that was my problem, not his.

"Touch yourself," I said next, busying myself with the fly of my slacks. He'd asked me to stay dressed, so I would, but there was no way I was keeping my cock in my pants.

When I gave myself a long and overhanded stroke, Tate licked his lips, his own cock slapping wet and hard against his stomach. He gripped the base of his shaft and stroked from root to tip, his head falling back with a groan.

"That's good, Tate," I whispered, pressing against the back of the couch to keep from throwing myself onto him and rutting into him so hard that I broke the table beneath our shared weights. "Do it again. I want you as close to the edge as you can get... and then I want you to stop."

Four minutes later, I my fingers gripped the edge of Brooks' coffee table, cock jerking madly against my stomach. Precum dribbled down the length of my shaft, and I dropped my head back to curse at his ceiling.

"Are you crying yet?" Brooks asked softly. His voice was low and sinful, in complete agreement with the unaffected posture of his body and the leisurely way he stroked his dick. I, on the other hand, wanted to crawl out of my skin and bury myself in the center of his chest and never leave.

"Not yet," I choked, letting my chin fall down and doing my best to avoid looking at his thick and hard cock, the teasing way it protruded out from between his legs. I loved that he'd stayed dressed for me, but the memory of his slacks and the way they abraded the backs of my thighs our first night together wasn't doing me any favors.

"Well." He dragged his thumb through his wet slit and raised it to his mouth, sucking it clean with a loud pop. "Then go again."

"That's mean," I muttered, licking my palm and wrapping it around my cock.

"That's the point." Brooks leaned back again, his legs spread wide so he took up as much space on the couch as his short frame would allow.

I gave a tentative pull up the length of my cock, sweat beading and dripping down my spine.

"This is going to be over before it's started," I warned, testing a quicker pace with my wrist before slowing back down.

"It's over when I decide," Brooks said, worrying his tongue against the corner of his lower lip, his stare locked on the dark and swollen head of my cock. "Now do as you're told, Tate."

"I am."

"Do it like you mean it."

I managed half a dozen more strokes before I was on the edge again. I squeezed hard around the base of my dick, letting out a strangled groan.

"I can't," I pleaded, slamming my eyes closed.

I knew the easy way to the finish line was to cry from the want of it all, but the tears remained locked away.

"You're not even trying."

Brook slid off the couch and sank to his knees between my spread legs. He wrapped his fist around mine and started to stroke both of our hands up and down my length. I was achingly close to coming all over us, but every time I opened my mouth to warn him, Brooks found a way to back the orgasm off. He either loosened our grip or banded our fists tighter. One time, he twisted roughly around the tip of my cock and I rose off the table with a whimper for how shocking the pain was. He managed to bring me right to the edge and back again another half dozen times before I was able to give him what he wanted.

Trembling and covered in sweat, with Brooks' steady and cruel hand working its way around my cock, a cry tore out of me, echoing through the hollow expanse of his penthouse. A single tear leaked from the corner of my eye and I sucked in a gasping breath as the dam finally broke.

I mumbled incoherently as Brooks unwrapped both of our hands from my erection, but if the words had made sense to either of us, they would have said, "I want you. I need you *now*. Please, oh God, *please*."

And I had no idea where the lube came from, but Brooks hauled me to the edge of the table and pushed two slippery fingers into my hole. It was tense and throbbing, all of my muscles prepared for the relaxation that came after an orgasm, even though it had been so long that Brooks had denied me. He pressed his fingers against my prostate and more wetness leaked out of my slit, sliding down my crown and sticking to my stomach and thighs. I was embarrassingly wet from the precum and the sweat, and when he pulled his fingers out of me—the tears.

"Sssh," he soothed me, crawling onto the table and notching himself in place between my legs. He was still dressed with his cock in hand, and I couldn't even imagine what the sight of us there must have looked like. Me, buck naked and quivering on his coffee table, and him, fully dressed in a suit that cost more than my rent, ready to shove his bare cock into my ass.

"Brooks," I managed to choke out his name as he brushed my damp hair back out of my face.

"Tate," he whispered my name back to me. "Darling."

He purred at me, easing inch after inch of his cock into my hole, and I wrapped my arms and legs around him before he even had a chance to seat himself fully inside of me. Brooks kissed my cheekbone, humming happily at the saltiness he found there. His table was awkwardly shaped though, and it only took a couple of his rough thrusts before I was halfway off of it, head hanging over the edge and upside down entirely. Out the window, I could make out the glittering lights of the city, but Brooks snapped his hips against mine so hard my teeth chattered, and I closed my eyes with a contented little groan.

"Harder," I begged, taking my cock back into my hand. I didn't even need to touch myself. I was going to come without any assistance, but the weight of my dick was somehow comforting in my hand, so I held on tight anyway.

"Harder," he repeated, pulling out with a low growl. He stood, looking taller than I'd ever seen him before, erection jutting out proudly from between his legs, and he walked around to the other end of the table to come near my head. Brooks bent down and grabbed my hair, yanking most of my body off the table entirely. My left leg bent at the knee and my calf rested on the slick wood, but my back was firm on the floor, my other leg splayed wide.

Brooks towered over me, stroking his cock and looking down at me. His eyes were dark and wide, nostrils flaring with every labored breath. He popped open the top button of his shirt and was back between my legs, pushing the swollen tip of his cock into my body again.

"Harder," he grunted again, falling forward and collaring his hand around my throat. "Earn it, Tate."

Brooks tightened his hold, and out of reflex I tried to tear his fingers away from my throat, but he held steady, completely undeterred at my intent to fight him off. With his free hand, he hitched my other leg around his hip and slammed our bodies together, cock threatening to split me open for how deep he reached with every pump of his hips.

His upper lip curled into what almost looked like a scowl and he did, in fact, fuck me harder. He slowed his pace almost to a crawl, fucking me so hard my back slid across the slick wood floor with every thrust. Sweat dripped off his forehead, splattering into my eyes and my mouth, and every second that passed, his hand tightened around my throat.

Everything was perfect. It felt so good, so right, and even when the edges of my vision started to darken and sparkle, I was hard. Gasping for breath, the top of my head crashed into the window, and Brooks finally let go of my throat. The breath that came after was sharp as a bucket of cold water, and I gasped and cried out like I'd been drowning. He hooked my other leg around his waist and fucked into me once, twice more before falling forward and whispering my name into my ear like a prayer.

His cock throbbed and pulsed as he emptied inside of me, and I sobbed like a baby in his arms. Not because I was scared or in pain, but because even though I hadn't yet finished myself, I was so unbelievably happy, I didn't have words for it. All I had were my tears and my slippery fingers against his back and a thousand whispered words that probably didn't make any sense.

Brooks hummed, kissing my cheek and my eyelashes before tracing his fingers over my face and reaching down between our bodies. His fingers, covered in my own tears, were hot against my erection, and he stroked me off with the same level of focus he paid every other part of sex. He waited until I blinked up at him, tipping my chin back and parting my lips to let him know I wanted a kiss.

I needed it.

He crashed our mouths together, and that was all I needed to reach the end he'd been teasing me with all night. My body bucked off the floor when I came, hot jets of cum streaking between our stomachs and over his fingers. The orgasm fucking hurt, unleashing another torrent of tears that I simply didn't have the fortitude to stop.

"You're perfect," Brooks whispered into my ear. "Did I go too far?"

I choked on a tear-stained breath. "No."

The relief was so tangible, it washed over both of us, and I tightened my grip around him so he didn't get any ideas about pulling away from me.

"Swear it."

"Not far enough," I rasped, nuzzling my face against his cheek. "I want all of you."

Brooks swallowed, untangling his messy fingers from my dick and shifting enough to get his hand up to his own mouth. He sucked my cum clean from his fingers, his own cock pulsing inside of me with every taste he caught of my release. After he cleaned off his hand, he turned his attention to my throat, tipping my chin back to inspect me clavicle and my Adam's apple.

"I liked it," I told him, needing him to know the truth. I squeezed my muscles down around him, confirmation of the promise.

"The way you cried for me..." He trailed off, tracing the

shape of his fingers around my throat before rocking back onto his heels.

I tried to slide down with him, but half his cock eased out of me with the shift, and I whimpered over the emptiness of it.

"It felt so good."

"Did it?" He smiled gently, smoothing his hand down his sweaty chest and making an upside down V around the base of his cock with his first two fingers. "*You* felt so good. Hot and bare."

"I can feel your cum inside of me."

It might not have been the whole truth, but when he'd shot into me, I felt it. Every burning hot jet as he painted me like no one else ever had before. I shivered, closing my eyes and letting my hands fall away from his waist.

"I want to see," he said, easing the rest of his still-hard cock out of me. I whined at the absence, at the way it hurt to gape after being fucked so rough.

Brooks moved me around, spreading my legs on either side of his and bending them at the knee so he had a down-stream view of my well-fucked asshole.

"How's it look down there?" I managed to ask, a scratchy laugh coming out after. "Did you ruin me?"

He hummed, stare flickering up to my face before settling back down between my legs.

"For everyone else, hopefully," he said, "but never for me. Oh, there it is. Fuck."

Brooks lifted his hand to my hole, two of his fingers tracing a circle around my tender rim and the cum that had just bubbled out of me. He hesitated before pushing his fingers back into my body and taking the escaping cum with them. I raised off the floor and gasped, groaning as his knuckles stretched my still sensitive rim.

"That's the hottest thing I've ever seen, Tate." Brooks slowly fucked his fingers in and out of me, hauling me into a seated position on his lap. It wasn't long before gravity did its job and more of his load leaked out of my ass and down the backs of my thighs. I was hot and messy, sticky and dirty, and I collapsed into Brooks' waiting arms, knowing that the best part of our night was yet to come.

IT WAS TOO SOON TO SAY OUT LOUD, BUT I WAS QUICKLY FALLING IN love with Tate. My feelings for him went so far beyond the sex, and with every step we took together toward my bedroom, I forced myself to choke down all of my doubts about those feelings. Tate's legs trembled and locked, barely able to hold him up as we climbed the stairs, and he leaned into me with soft little moans and tired sighs. He was still slick with sweat and burning hot from the fucking but, for some reason, the thought of putting him into a bath was the last thing I wanted to do.

"Shower tonight," I said, walking him into my bathroom and helping him to sit down on the short stone bench that jutted out from the wall under the rain shower head. He went down without an argument, eyes still closed like he was seconds away from sleep.

I stepped out of the spray to get my clothes off, which earned me an unhappy grunt from the near-lifeless body tucked against the wall.

"Did you want me to shower in my clothes? Does your

kink go that far?" I asked, working open the buttons on my shirt.

Tate pried one eye open. "If I said yes, would you?"

I licked my lips, swallowing back what felt like a bundle of emotions the size of a softball.

"Yes," I admitted.

Tate opened both of his eyes and regarded me silently from his perch. I had stopped undressing myself at the displeased sound he'd made, hands still in the middle of my shirt, only my chest exposed, and my cock still hanging out of my pants.

"Stay dressed," he murmured, reaching for me.

I found myself under the water before the last word even left his mouth. My shirt plastered itself to my back, and I shoved my hair back out of my face when I reached where he sat. Scooping him up off the bench took considerable work, but I managed it just the same. I turned and dropped my soaking wet, slacks-covered ass onto the bench. Arranging Tate on my lap with one knee on either side of my thighs, I cradled the back of his head and pressed him toward my shoulder. He slipped his hands around the small of my back and snuggled into me, the water raining down on the top of his head and his bare back.

"What about it do you like?" I asked.

"The sex?"

"No." I kissed the side of his head. "Well, yes. But I meant about me staying dressed when you're naked."

Tate hummed, fingers pressing against my skin. "It makes me feel like you're desperate for me."

"I am."

"Like you couldn't even be bothered to take your clothes off. You just need to have me."

"I do," I rasped, closing my eyes.

"Just like you need this? The aftercare?"

"Yes," I agreed.

Tate didn't have anything to say to that, so I reached for my shower gel on the far wall and squirted some into my hand. It wasn't ideal, but I lathered as many bubbles as my fingers would allow and began to drag my hands over every inch of his skin I could reach. I dug my fingers into his muscles, earning me tired and deep groans with every stretch.

"I loved it earlier when you choked me," he said, breaking a drawn-out silence between us after my hands had made their way to his shoulders.

It was the last thing I had expected him to say, and it did a little bit more than catch me off-guard. I chewed the inside of my lip, like it would somehow whittle down the discomfort in my chest.

"You just got tense," he mumbled, face still tucked against my neck. "Do you not believe me?"

"I trust you."

"Not the question, but..." Tate trailed off, and I worked my hands up around his throat, pleased enough to find that I hadn't held him tight enough to bruise. He swallowed, Adam's apple bobbing against my palm, and his cock bobbed in tandem against my stomach.

"You were the only thing I could see," he went on, and I flexed my fingers. "I loved it."

I slipped my hand down from his throat to his chest, feeling the steady and loud beat of his heart against my hand.

"And I loved feeling you come inside of me," he went on. "I love the way you fuck me, Brooks."

It was everything I'd ever wanted to hear, but too much at the same time. I wiggled my shoulder to push his head up, stealing his mouth for a kiss far softer and needier than the ones I'd shared with him earlier in the night. Tate moaned, circling his hips and spearing his tongue into my mouth. He was as clean as he was going to get, position considering, so I was beyond happy to indulge the turn of events. I'd planned to clean him up and give his body a decent amount of time to recover, then I'd wanted to take him to bed and massage him until he fell asleep.

"I..." Tate's breath was quiet against my lips, and whatever he was going to say died in the back of his throat, probably in the same place all my own thoughts had set up a graveyard of their own.

"Let's get you dry," I said, pushing up from the bench enough so that I could turn and sit him back down on it. He grumbled when I stepped away to take my clothes off, but no matter how much I wanted to make him happy, I wasn't going to track water from the bathroom into the bedroom.

That was a lie.

If he had asked...

But he didn't.

I kicked my soaking wet clothes into the corner of the bathroom, then got towels for the both of us, wrapping one casually around my waist before turning off the water and holding the second open for him. He stood on far steadier legs than before and shuffled into my waiting arms. I loved these moments when he wanted to feel small, or when he wanted me to feel tall, I wasn't sure which. But Tate tucked his head down and let me fold my arms—and the warm towel—around him. When he was dry enough, I walked him to the bed, folding the bedding down so it wouldn't be a mess to get up later.

"Face down on the bed," I said softly.

Tate complied quickly, arching his back and putting his ass on a perfect display for me. I palmed my cock, already getting hard again at the prospect, even though sex wasn't what I was after, though...

"Can you handle me again?" I asked him, grabbing the lube as soon as he nodded his head in the affirmative.

Tate turned his face to the side, pressing his cheek against the pillow and making room for me between his legs. It was easy to get myself hard again, slick my shaft, and sink home inside of him. Tate whimpered with every inch, mewling like a happy cat once I was fully seated. Instead of fucking him, I dug my fingertips into the small of his back, starting on the massage I'd always intended to give him.

"Oh, that feels so good," he whispered, eyes rolling back and making his lashes flutter.

Fuck, he was a sight.

"Which part?"

"Yes."

I smiled, tucking my chin toward my armpit so he couldn't see how positively giddy his responses and reactions made me. Working my way up the slender length of his back, I didn't worry about fucking him again. I focused on the massage, letting my cock handle the work from the inside when every dig and press of my hands against his back and shoulders.

I was nearing the end of his massage when Tate flicked

one of his eyes open, doing his best to peer up at me, but losing the fight for it when the head of my cock dragged over his prostate.

"How are you single, Brooks?"

"I'm not. I have you."

He groaned, arching his ass against my hips again. "You know what I mean."

I curled my hands around his waist, hauling him up enough that I could get a deeper angle inside of him. I thrust long and slow inside of him, no longer wanting him to fall asleep during the massage, but this.

"My last boyfriend, he...it got old," I explained.

Tate groaned, shoving his hand between the sheets and his stomach. "You'll need to elaborate."

I bent over his back and slipped my arm around the front of his chest, banding our bodies together. The position made it harder to fuck him, but that was secondary to the rest of it. I rolled us both onto our sides and kicked Tate's top leg over mine, opening him up for me.

"He hated this part." I kissed the back of Tate's neck, enjoying the smell of my soap on his skin and in his hair. "I think he hated me."

"He just wanted the..." Tate gasped, a shiver tearing through his entire body. "The rough fucks?"

"At first." I closed my eyes, focusing on the heat of his ass around me and the quick jerk of his fist around his cock. "Then he didn't want me at all."

"Did he think you would get bored of the things you like? That you would be happy with missionary?"

I scoffed, flipping Tate onto his back and sinking back into him. I wrapped his legs around my waist and drove down into him, long and hard.

"What's wrong with missionary?" I teased. "I can fuck you like this too."

He sputtered out a whimper when I hit him with a particularly sharp snap of my hips, and I loved that I could take his breath away. I didn't know what I would do when the novelty wore off for him.

If the novelty wore off...

"It doesn't matter." I brushed my nose against his, brushing a kiss across his mouth. "He got bored of me, and then I was alone. And now, I'm not."

A sated smile spread across Tate's kiss-swollen mouth.

"No, you're not." He wound his arms around my neck and moaned loudly into my ear. "That was the best massage I've ever had."

"I went to school for it," I said.

"Of course you did."

I hooked his legs up over my shoulders, folding him in half and driving him down into the mattress.

"What do you mean of course?" I asked, punching the breath out of him and making it near impossible for him to answer.

Thankfully, he understood the point and stopped trying, and ten minutes later, he came against his chest with a gasping cry. I licked the taste of it out of his mouth, the heat and the shape of him enough to send me over the edge a second time. I came with a low growl, spilling another load inside of him. Tate's fingers scrabbled against the small of my back, the backs of my thighs, trying to pull me deeper with every jerk of my dick inside of him.

I let out a trembling breath, slowly lowering his legs down, all the while keeping my cock inside of him. Rolling us both onto our sides, I kneaded his tight thigh muscles as best I could reach, which earned me a tired-sounding laugh.

"You're insatiable." He yawned, stretching out and clenching down around my cock.

"I am," I agreed, feeling like, for the first time, that it might not be a bad thing. Wondering if Tate saw it as a bonus, not a detraction.

"Can we sleep like this?" he asked, reaching between our bodies and dragging his fingers over the exposed inch of my cock. "I like how it feels."

"Yes, darling." I flattened my hand against the center of his chest and dropped my forehead against his shoulder. My other hand tickled soft swirls through the coarse hair of his thigh. "We can sleep like this."

I woke up to the promise of a slow fuck, Brooks' weight above me, his hands against the small of my back pressing me into the mattress as he slid his hard cock up and down the crack of my ass. He was cool with slippery lube, and I arched my back, consenting. Behind me, he groaned and eased his length into my still tender body. I reached back and grabbed his thigh, steadying the both of us when he was seated fully.

"Good morning," he whispered, falling forward and drawing lines through my hair with his nose. "How did you sleep?"

"Like I got fucked to within an inch of my life, then massaged and fucked again," I said into the pillow, a yawn chasing after the answer.

Brooks hummed happily and wrapped his arms around me, rolling onto his back so I was straddling him. I took the change in position as an opportunity to stretch, then executed the most awkward turn so I was facing his head and not his feet. He threaded his fingers together behind his head, watching me with half-hooded eyes while I woke up enough to find a rhythm.

I circled my hips, fucking him slow and soft while the both of us woke up to meet the day. There were no tears to be found, just groans and gasps, and Brooks' pleased little laugh when I came hard enough to fill the dip at the base of his throat with my release. He scooped it up and shoved his sticky fingers into his mouth before grabbing my hips and driving into me from the bottom until his cock thickened and pulsed, spilling into me.

It was the perfect way to wake up in the perfect penthouse with the perfect man. Even when he lifted me off of his cock to tuck me against his chest and pull the sheets back up to our waists, I would have been hard-pressed to find a better feeling in my memory.

"What time is it?" I asked, stretching my toes past his feet.

"Too early." Brooks kissed the back of my neck. "Go back to sleep, Tate."

So I did.

It was easy to lose track of time with Brooks because everything about him was so far beyond my normal scope of experience. I never knew what to expect with him because even though he'd been clear about his expectations in the bedroom, the sex we'd just had fell out of the scope of every-thing we'd done before. There weren't any tears and it wasn't part of aftercare. It was tender and lazy and the most intimate thing that I'd ever done.

When I woke up again, what could have been minutes or hours later, I was alone in bed, the sheets behind me warm, but far from being hot. He'd gotten up, but not for long. Stretching out and kicking the sheets down to the foot of the bed, I rolled and buried my face into Brooks' pillow to breathe the scent of him in so deep I hoped it would embed itself in my lungs to hold me over after I left.

Downstairs a door opened and closed, and footsteps jogged up the stairs. Brooks appeared in the doorway wearing running shorts and a sweat damp t-shirt which was halfway over his head when he came around the corner. I sat up in bed, happy to watch him strip naked in front of me, but after the shirt was off, he saw I was awake and stopped dead in his tracks. A shy kind of smile spread across his face, completely counter to the way he shoved his shorts down to his ankles.

He wasn't hard, but he was gorgeous just the same, sweaty and tanned and soft skin.

"You're awake," he said, tossing the dirty clothes into his closet.

"I'm glad I woke up in time to not miss the show."

He rolled his eyes and padded barefoot and naked into the bathroom. Out of my line of sight, I heard the water turn on, and then Brooks called out, "Are you coming?"

I scrambled out of bed to join him in the shower, but the sight of him under the spray had my breath hitching in my throat. Bracing myself against the sink, I bit my lips together, admiring the slope of his throat as he tipped his head back to sluice the water through his hair, the way his balls hung between his legs, and the gentle ripple of muscles alongside his ribs.

Brooks was a god.

Mine.

"Come on, Tate," he said, not turning his stare away from the ceiling.

The callout was enough to crash me back to reality, which

wasn't a horrible place to be, and the water against my shoulders was as warm and welcome as his fingers around my wrists. As soon as I was under the water, Brooks backed me against the wall, reaching down between my legs with his soapy fingers and testing the pressure against my hole. He growled into the corner of my neck, sinking his teeth gently into the muscle that stretched across the top of my shoulder.

"I don't think I'll ever get bored of feeling my cum leak out of your perfect little asshole," he whispered.

A shiver ripped through my whole body, and I thumped my head against the wall with a moan.

"You like that, don't you?" he asked, kissing the place he'd just bit.

"What part?"

"When I talk dirty."

"The way you talk matches the way you fuck," I told him, resting my hands on his hips. He pushed his body against mine, both of our cocks getting hard again.

"How's that?"

"Rough."

Brooks licked a hot stripe all the way up to the underside of my chin before sinking his teeth into my jaw.

"I like it," I answered him finally.

He hummed, lips curving into a smile against my face that was so big and true I didn't even need to see it to know it was there. As soon as it registered, it was gone, as was the rest of him. Brooks took a step back, using both of his hands to shove his hair away from his face.

"As much as it makes me happy to give you all the things you deserve, I'm going to leave you on your own for the rest of this shower."

I groaned, reaching down and stroking my cock in his direction.

Brooks gave me an apologetic—if not promising—look.

"I'm going to make coffee," he said, stepping out of the shower and getting a towel out of the warmer. He ran it over the top half of his body before knotting it around his waist. "And breakfast."

"I'm hungry for you," I complained, stroking my cock twice more.

"I like to make you cry, Tate." Brooks licked his lips, stare lingering on my shaft and how it peeked out from behind my fingers. "I don't want to *actually* hurt you. You need some time."

"I have other holes, Brooks."

He bared his teeth, tracing his tongue along them as he narrowed his eyes and nodded at me. "Duly noted, Tate."

Then he turned and was gone.

He took the air out of the room with him, and I sank down onto the bench, immediately falling forward and bracing my elbows on my knees. I caught my head in my hands and made the most pathetic noise, hoping the drain would swallow it before it reached Brooks' ears.

I knew he was right.

My body needed a break, but when it came to him, I was beyond insatiable. I would have given him anything, but worse than that, I *wanted* to give him everything.

"Start by doing what you're told," I reminded myself, grabbing his soap and washing myself as much as I could manage. I knew I should have paid extra attention to my cock and my asshole, but I wanted to leave those parts of myself dirty with him.

I finished my shower and headed back into the bedroom, finding the bed made with a pair of basketball shorts and a clean t-shirt sitting on the pillow that I already considered to be mine. I noticed when I dressed myself that the clothes seemed to fit better than I would have expected Brooks' to fit me, but there was no way he'd had the time or the inclination to buy clothes for me. Was there?

That was a lot.

Even for him.

Right?

From downstairs, I heard Brooks' voice filter up. At first, I thought he was singing, but as I made my way down, I realized he was on the phone. He moved around the kitchen, which already smelled like coffee, his cell phone sitting on the counter, a call ticker flickering up toward the five minute mark. I didn't recognize the voice of the man on the other line, not that I should have. I didn't know any of Brooks' friends. I'd met them all that very first night, but Ford wasn't interested in me for anything beyond a decoy and the others had barely addressed me at all. Brooks had been the only one.

"I have to go, Kale," Brooks said, pouring some coffee into a clean white mug and sliding it across the island and into my hands. He looked at me quickly, mouthing an apology.

"It's fine," I said back quietly.

"Why?" Kale asked, sounding put out.

"I have a guest."

"A guest?"

"A guest," Brooks repeated.

"What poor fool did you coax into bed this time?"

Brooks glanced at me, his expression tight and concerned. The implication in Kale's line of questioning was clear. Brooks was not a relationship man and his bedroom might as well have had a revolving door. I knew that about him, and he also knew that about me.

"He's been in my bed on and off for a couple weeks now." Brooks picked a pan up from the stove and slid some fluffy looking scrambled eggs onto a plate, which he lined up with the coffee he'd just poured for me.

"A couple *weeks*?"

"He's my boyfriend, Kale."

I bit the inside of my cheek, jealous that I wasn't the only person Brooks made a habit of calling by name.

"Excuse me? First Beamer, and—"

"And then you and Ford, now me. Yes, that does seem to be the way of it." He handed me a fork and napkin, then made a plate for himself and walked around the island to sit beside me.

"Where did you meet him?"

"The Black Door."

"Perfect."

I didn't know Kale, but I could hear the smile in his voice.

"When can I meet him?"

"You've met him. He's the one who was with Ford." Brooks sounded tentative as he said the last part, working his jaw back and forth.

"Oh."

Brooks sucked in a breath. "I've got to go, Kale. Do you want to get lunch tomorrow?"

"Fine."

"You can bring Christian."

"Fine."

"Stop being sullen," Brooks snapped. "You're not a toddler."

"Fine." Kale sounded almost as sullen, but like he was amused at the callout.

"I'm going to invite the guys."

"Fine," Kale said again.

Brooks' phone beeped, the call having been disconnected. He stared at it and sighed, picking up his fork and using the side of it to knife some of his eggs into manageable bite sizes.

"What was that about?" I asked. "Do I want to know?"

"Ford is dating Kale's younger brother. It's a sore spot."

"They were together the night we met, right?" I asked, trying to piece the timeline of the chaos in his friend group together with nothing but breadcrumbs.

"It's a sore spot for Kale. He's getting over it, but it's taking forever."

"Why does he care?"

"Kale is a control freak," Brooks said.

I snorted at the description, and he pretended to glare at me, reaching over to pinch my ribs.

"I'm glad the clothes fit."

I looked down, unsure of how I felt that my guess was right. Plucking at the hem of the shirt, I tugged it down into my lap. "You didn't need to buy me clothes."

"I don't need to do a lot of things, but I enjoy them, so I do them." He squared his shoulders, half-angled away from me. "Is that going to be a problem, Tate."

"Stop getting defensive with me." I accidentally knocked our knees together as I turned to get his face into my hands. I needed him to look at me, to see *me*, and to believe that I wasn't anything like his ex. "Do you remember before when you told me that you needed to trust your partners?"

"Of course."

"Then trust me, Brooks." I pulled our foreheads together. "Not just in bed, but out of it too."

His exhale dusted over my face, smelling like mint and coffee.

"Right," he said, nodding. "Thank you for the reminder, Tate."

"Thank you for the orgasms," I teased. Brooks smiled and laughed, the tension broken, and I slanted our mouths together, eager to taste the perfection of it.

WHEN I SAT DOWN AT LUNCH, OPPOSITE FORD AND ALEX, I COULD still taste Tate's cum on my tongue. It was there beneath the coffee and the toothpaste, embedded forever in my taste buds. The waitress brought me a drink while we waited for Kale to arrive, the tension at the table thick enough to cut with a butter knife.

"It's almost like old times," I said, tipping the rim of my glass in Alex's direction.

It was nice to see him out amongst the living again after his depression spiral over Beamer's marriage. At first, I had thought the whole thing was a little over the top, but it was easy now to think about what I would do it Tate were to ever leave me. Tate, who was so perfect for me, like we'd been cut from the same fucked-up scrap of fabric. Alex had just started to find some of that connection once he and Beamer started sleeping together, and then it was gone in the blink of an eye.

"Almost," Alex agreed.

"But Kale is somehow more of a prick than before," Ford said.

"At least he can't harass you about sleeping with his assistants anymore."

Ford sighed, smile pushing the corner of his mouth, but falling away when Kale sank into the seat beside me with a frustrated noise.

"Sorry I'm late," he said to no one in particular.

"It's far from your worst quality," I said.

Kale flagged down the waitress and ordered himself a drink, leaning back after she left to get comfortable in his seat.

"What is my worst quality?" he asked.

"The way you meddle," I answered before anyone else could.

Ford arched a brow and glanced sideways at Alex, but neither of them said anything.

"Don't act like I've personally victimized the whole lot of you," he grumbled.

Then it was my turn to arch a brow at him. "Are you being deliberately obtuse or do you really not see it?" I asked, turning toward him and taking a calming swallow of my drink.

"Do I not see what?"

"You absolutely lost your mind on Beamer when you found out he was sleeping with Alex."

"I was mad he let someone mark him," Kale argued, doing his best to not look at Alex, who was across from me, his stare narrowed and focused on Kale as he spoke.

"You mark people often," I reminded him, giving my head a bobble to either side. "And the fact that you're upset about Ford and your brother is mind-blowing to me."

Kale curled his fingers around the edge of the table and

started to push himself to his feet, but I reached over and shoved him back down on his ass.

"No," I said simply. "You will stay."

"Is this an intervention?"

"It's a reckoning," I said.

"I just wanted to get lunch," Ford said. "I was told there would be food."

"Speaking of food, your best friend"—I pointed at Ford—"bought your brother a farm to keep him here. You owe him a thank you."

"I owe him something," Kale groused.

"Is there really a better outcome, Kale?" I rolled my eyes, tired of Kale's ongoing pursuit to pretend he was holier than the rest of us. "Is there a better man for your brother than Ford?"

He opened his mouth and I raised my hand to silence him.

"Think long and hard before you answer," I suggested. "And think about what Christian's friends would have said about you if they had any inkling of your past. Of the man you were when that prince fell into your arms."

Kale dragged his tongue across the front of his teeth, reaching out with a desperate hand when the waitress reappeared with his drink. He snatched it from her and Ford waved her off, clearly not ready for an interruption.

"I imagine Parrish would not have approved," Kale finally grumbled.

"I imagine not."

Kale looked across the table, his tongue still working in his mouth. He turned his gaze on Ford, who looked amused but tense.

"He's my brother," Kale tried to explain, sounding defeated.

"And I'm your best friend," Ford said simply.

"We're all best friends," I reminded the lot of them. "We want the best for each other, right?"

Kale nodded and the other two gave me verbal agreements.

"We think the best of each other, yes?" I asked next.

"Yes," Kale agreed.

"Then who better to love your brother than the man you hold in the highest regard?" Ford asked.

"I wouldn't say highest." Kale pointed at me. "I like him more than you."

Ford scoffed, but the concession felt like a step in the right direction. Kale was going to take some work, but I knew he would come around.

"And I like him more than you," I said, gesturing to Alex.

"Ford is my favorite," Alex teased.

"I like Beamer better than all of you," Kale said, a smile flashing across his otherwise sullen mouth.

"Now that *that's* settled." I raised my glass, giving it a shake to settle the ice and coax them all into joining me in a toast. "Here's to getting the fuck over this and getting back to normal."

We clanked our glasses together and drank, the tension around the table sinking away enough for us to get through lunch without murdering each other in broad daylight.

"Speaking of normal," Kale said, clearly eager to change the subject off of himself. "Tell us more about your *boyfriend*."

I sighed, and Alex laughed, leaning back and getting comfortable for the show.

"His name is Tate," I said. "I think I might love him."

"Lord help you," Ford mumbled under his breath.

"Love?

"Don't act like it's such a foreign concept." I flicked my hand at Kale. "You fell first, then that one."

Ford huffed a breath, and the table went silent.

"Anyway," I went on. "He's…"

I trailed off, swallowing back any words that came to mind. All of my friends had been around for my relationship with Tyler and the subsequent breakup. They all understood how hard his departure had impacted me, the betrayal of it all, and I hoped they knew how serious I had to be about Tate to call him my boyfriend, to even bring him up in the first place.

"He's Dylan's roommate," Alex said, filling the break and offering me a reprieve from all of the things I didn't have words to explain.

"Who is Dylan?" Kale asked.

"A bartender at a place called Tryst," Ford said. "Alex knows him."

"How do the two of you know him too?" Kale asked next.

"I've been to Tryst with Alex," Ford answered with a shrug.

"And I met him at The Black Door with Alex," I said.

Kale inhaled sharply, biting his cheek so hard between his teeth his expression went hollow. He swallowed, and I watched the muscles of his jaw work back and forth while he tried to process the fact that even though he'd been holed up with Christian alternating between being an idiot in love and just an idiot, life had gone on for the rest of us.

"Okay," Kale said quietly.

"He works next weekend," Alex said. "If you wanted to go."

Kale swallowed. "I'd like that."

"You can bring Christian," I offered.

"And Tate," he said. "I want to meet him."

Ford sucked his teeth and Kale stared straight ahead, his entire body swaying forward and backward.

"Please tell me my brother isn't..." Kale trailed off.

"Don't ask him to lie," I interrupted, patting Kale on his thigh. "Boston should come too."

"I don't know if he'd want to," Ford said with a shrug. "He enjoys the farm now that the weather is getting warm. There's always something for him to get into up there."

"Maybe we should go to the farm instead then," I suggested with a laugh. I didn't entirely mean it, but I did appreciate how awkward it would be for Kale to be at a sex club with his brother, knowing that Boston liked to get railed in unexpectedly kinky and dirty ways by one of his brother's best friends. "Would that be doable?"

"We'd both love that."

"I don't know if I'm cut out for the farm," Alex wavered.

"It's not another planet," Kale said, turning his focus to Alex, who looked uncomfortable with the shift in attention. His eyebrows lifted into his hairline. "There's running water and electricity. I doubt my brother is going to make you get on your hands and knees in the dirt."

Judging by the way Ford looked across the room with a sickening quickness, Boston might have been more than likely fully capable of making someone get on their knees in the dirt. I loved the idea of Ford being into that sort of thing, and I imagined it would only endear him to Kale more than he already was. We all knew the kind of man Ford was, the kind of men we all were, and if he was willing to go that far for love...

Boston Sheffield was luckier than his brother would ever know.

"I'll ask Tate," I said, even though the prospect of bringing Tate around my friends was enough to spike my blood pressure into another stratosphere.

There wasn't anything inherently wrong with the group of them, but they were *a lot* on a good day, and I liked having Tate in a little bubble where we were the only thing that existed. The only thing either of us had to worry about was finding time to be together. Bringing him around my friends would make the relationship more real, and by extension, more breakable.

I swallowed the rest of my drink, hoping it would chase down the nerves that had started to knot together at the base of my spine, and it was pure luck that the waitress came back to the table, a tight smile on her face. We were only on our first round and we hadn't even bothered to order food yet. She was probably worried about her tip, though I had no idea what about the four of us gave the impression she wasn't going to get her gratuity in the end.

We ordered a second round of drinks and some lunch, and after that, the conversation almost felt like normal old times. Back when Beamer was with us and Kale was his usual amount of domineering, not the overbearing piece of shit he'd become after Beamer's husband showed up. I realized as I watched him beside me, it wasn't necessarily the things happening that were the problem for him, but the change itself.

I stood up quickly, hooking my hand under Kale's armpit and hauling him to his feet. "Come outside with me."

"Fuck you, Astor."

"It'll be quick." I pulled him away from the table.

"Do we need to intervene?" Ford asked, sounding like there was no way in hell he would bother. I imagined he actually hoped I was ready to take Kale out back and beat some sense into him because even though we'd talked through a lot of things, he was still brittle between us.

Outside on the sidewalk, Kale brushed me off, mouth pulled into a tight frown.

"What is your problem?"

"You should be so lucky that a man like Ford loves your brother. That a man like Dalton Fox is married to Beamer. They're both good fucking men and you know it. You're just a stubborn piece of shit who is mad he's losing control of the puppet strings. Scared that things are changing—"

"I'm not scared," he snapped.

"You hooked up with Christian and you ghosted us. You were gone, holed up and happy with that prince of yours, and guess what, Kale? Life fucking goes on. It went on, it's still going." The more I talked, the angrier I felt. The rage simmered in my bones, vibrating through my fingers and I sincerely worried if I touched Kale again, I was going to shock him from the force of it. "Love changes people, Kale. It changed you; it's changing us. Stop fighting it."

"I'm not fighting it." His protest was weak and his shoulders sagged on a tired exhale.

"You're going to lose your brother," I warned. "And not

because he's with Ford, but because of how you're acting toward them both."

I'd known about Boston and Ford far longer than Kale knew, and I loved my friend, but I was going to take that secret to the grave. I'd seen firsthand the way Ford agonized over his relationship with Boston, and I'd seen it with Alex when he started playing with Beamer too.

"I don't want to think about anyone sleeping with my brother," Kale groused, "let alone someone whose dick I've seen."

"At least you know where it's been."

He scoffed. "Everywhere."

"Have you told Christian's best friend how many men you fucked before Christian fell into your lap?" I asked, raising a brow. "I bet he would have some choice words if he were to find out how many extra pages your little black book has."

Kale sucked his teeth, shoving his hands into his pockets. He stared down at his feet, but answered that comment with a knowing nod.

"I'm trying," he said, looking up at me. I saw the truth of it in his face, the sadness and the fear all etched together in the corners of his eyes and the tight downturn of his mouth.

"I believe you." I grabbed his face in both of my hands, even though it was a reach. "But you need to try harder."

He licked his lips and nodded, bending down to bump our foreheads together.

"I'll try," he promised.

"I know." I pushed onto my toes and kissed his forehead before shoving him off. "Now go try harder. Come back inside and I'll tell you about Tate, alright?"

"Alright," he agreed, following behind me toward the

door, but pulling me to a stop before we reached the thresh-old. "Thank you, Brooks."

"For what?" I asked.

"Not letting me ruin this."

"You couldn't even if you tried," I assured him, tilting my head toward the door. "Now, let's go eat."

CHAPTER 20
TATE

Dylan came home Sunday with a hand-shaped bruise around his throat, but he refused to tell me who put it there or if it was consensual. Without thinking, I traced my finger across my own throat, recalling the strong press of Brooks' fingers as he pinned me to the floor and fucked me two nights before.

"Are you all right?" I asked, squinting as he moved around our small space, getting a beer from the fridge before throwing himself down onto his usual spot on the couch.

"I'm fine." He smiled at me like he wasn't wearing a handprint as an accessory. "How was your weekend?"

It was impossible to not smile at the question. "It was really great."

"I'm surprised to see you home so soon."

I rolled my head along the wall, turning my attention to the black iron fire escape just beyond our window.

"He had plans with his friends," I said.

"Alex?" Dylan asked.

"I'm sure." I shrugged. "I didn't ask for details, I just overheard a phone call about it yesterday morning."

"Eavesdropper," he teased, stretching his leg across the couch and digging his toe into my thigh.

I smacked him. "Hardly. He had the call on speakerphone when I got up and he kept it that way once I came into the kitchen."

"Good to know he's not hiding anything from you," Dylan said.

I smiled softly, swallowing and imaging the way my Adam's apple had fought against Brooks' palm for breath.

"He's not," I agreed.

"I've known you two years." Dylan shifted his feet to the coffee table. "I don't think I've ever seen you date anyone, though I have watched you fuck your way through the city. What makes him different?"

I held out my hand and clapped my fingers together until Dylan passed me his beer. I took a drink and turned my attention toward the ceiling, trying to parse out an understandable answer to his question. There were a lot of things that set Brooks apart from men I'd met before him—and after him—but I didn't know how to explain them all in ways Dylan would understand.

Before the night Brooks had taken my virginity, I'd tried to date. I just hadn't gotten far. People were either only interested in me because I was a virgin or terribly turned off over the idea of being my first. It was like the sex and the relationship were mutually exclusive, which I knew wasn't true. I'd quickly proven myself right, finding Brooks on an unplanned night out and making the whole problem go away in under an hour. Sex with Brooks had of course created a new problem in that I had turned into an insatiable fiend who chased after one particular brand of sex that turned out to be even more difficult to find than a virginity thief. My plan had always been to get the first time out of the way and move on, but Brooks had been different from the drop.

Best laid plans, and all that.

"He makes me feel special," I finally said, knowing it was enough but nowhere near it at the same time. He didn't just make me *feel* special. He *was* special.

"How?"

I snorted, rolling my eyes at him. "Really?"

He rolled his eyes back at me, snatching his beer out of my hand. "Yes, really."

"It feels like he really cares about me," I said carefully, doing my best to articulate the tangle of feelings in the center of my chest. "He is thoughtful and attentive. He...he enjoys spoiling me."

Dylan's eyes went wide. "In bed?"

I laughed, returning the kick he'd delivered earlier.

"In it and out of it. He's just...he's a good person, I think. To me and other people. I can tell his friends think highly of him, and even though he has more money than God, he puts it to good use."

"How?"

"For work," I explained. "He basically helps connect other rich people with charities and non-profits that need donations."

"So, he creates tax shelters?" Dylan arched a brow, but there wasn't any seriousness in his expression.

"I don't think that's why he does it."

"Well." He poured the rest of the beer down his throat and pushed up from the couch. "I suppose that's good then. Did you want to go grab a drink with me? Someplace that has better scenery?"

What I really wanted was to be back at Brooks' house, in his bed or over his coffee table, but he was out with his friends —or he had been earlier—and I didn't want to scare him off by being a stage five clinger.

"What did you have in mind?" I asked.

"We can go to Tryst if you wanted."

I frowned, looking at the fire escape. "That's so far."

"It's closer to your boyfriend's house."

"I'm not going to his house," I said. "I haven't heard from him since I left this morning."

"You can text him and let him know you're on his side of town," Dylan suggested. "After you have a couple rounds with me, of course."

I fished my phone out of my pocket to check the time. It was barely dinner time, and if I stayed on the couch, time would creep by like molasses. Getting out of the house with Dylan was a surefire way to pass the time, and he wasn't wrong. Tryst was closer to Brooks' house, and a boy could hope.

"Alright," I agreed.

Dylan grinned and clapped like an over-excited kid.

"Just let me change," I said, rolling off the edge of the couch onto my hands and knees, and then onto my feet. It was two steps around the corner into my bedroom, and I changed into a pair of light-wash jeans and a faded black t-shirt. I found clean socks and my sneakers, which were half shoved under the bed, then I met Dylan back in the living room.

He was waiting when I returned, and I followed him out of the apartment and down three flights of stairs to the street. It was a quick walk to the train and less than half an hour later we were seated at the corner of the bar at Tryst, Dylan's boss Marigold making us martinis strong enough to strip paint.

With the first round down, Dylan was feeling good and I wasn't far behind. When Marigold finally got up the balls to ask about the bruise around his neck, Dylan looked like he was about to be sick, and I didn't think it was on account of the vodka in our glasses.

"It's nothing," he said, covering the mark with his hand. I knew Dylan well enough to know that was a lie.

"Dylan," she said, voice wavering.

"Don't make it a big deal, Mari."

She worked her jaw back and forth, unsure of what to say next, but a patron at the other end of the bar called her attention away and saved all three of us from a conversation no one wanted to have.

"Do you want to talk about it?" I asked him once she was finally out of earshot.

He gave me a quick and sharp smile that didn't reach his eyes. "Just bad sex, Tate. You know what that's like, right?"

I did know what bad sex was like, but now I knew what good sex was like too. I knew that Brooks had almost choked me unconscious before making me come, but I didn't wear the proof of it around my neck. Whoever had done that to Dylan either didn't know or didn't care what they were doing. Or, worst case, both.

"Be careful, Dylan."

The smile was gone, and he finished the last swallow of his martini, flagging another bartender who wasn't Marigold down for another. We started our second round, and the vodka went straight to my head while it appeared to go straight to Dylan's bones. He swayed back and forth on his bar stool and by the third round, my head wobbled like a bobblehead in every possible direction. Against my better judgement, I pulled my phone out of my pocket to text Brooks.

Me: I'm in your neighborhood.
Me: ish.

He was quick to respond.

Brooks: Oh? Where?
Me: A bar with Dylan called Tryst.
Brooks: He works there too, right?
Me: How did you know?
Brooks: Alex told me.
Brooks: How long are you there for?

At some point during my texting, Dylan had gotten up from the bar. I scanned the small space, finding him in the corner beside the jukebox, chatting with a man I'd never seen before. They were leaning in close together talking, and Dylan was so drunk I could see the way he slurred his way through the conversation.

Me: I don't know. Dylan is a little shitfaced.
Brooks: Are you?
Me: Well on the way but not as bad.

I turned my phone face down on the counter because the texts were hard to read. Marigold thankfully dropped two glasses of water in front of me, and I took one with thanks, sucking down half the contents in one go. Dylan was still off in the corner doing whatever he was doing, and my phone vibrated beneath my palm. I desperately wanted to turn it over and read the message, but my stomach was dangerously close to revolting. Apparently, the change of scenery had been a bad idea.

It was near eight in the evening and I had work in the morning. Dylan had disappeared from his post in the corner, and so had the man with him, and my phone vibrated again beneath my palm.

"Sorry," I muttered to the device, shoving it into my pocket and stumbling off the stool. Marigold gave me a knowing look as I zig-zagged my way to the long hallway that held the bathrooms. I'd barely gotten the door open when my stomach roiled, and I slammed open the door of the closest stall and fell to my knees. Retching into the toilet, I cursed Dylan for wanting to come out, then I cursed Marigold for her paint-thinner martinis.

Two violent rounds of vomiting turned into five minutes of dry heaving, and I slid down the wall of the stall and bent my legs. I folded my arms across the tops of my knees and dropped my clammy face against my forearms, sucking in small and measured breaths meant to sober me up, not make me want to die.

I closed my eyes, thumping my head back against the wall...the downward angle wasn't doing anything good for my stomach, and my phone buzzed again in my pocket. From the other stall, I heard the sound of someone getting their dick sucked, the familiar noises of regrettable bar bathroom hookups. Scrubbing a hand down my face, I tried to climb back to my feet, barely getting my knees straight when the magical smell of spicy citrus cologne wafted through the otherwise sticky and dingy space.

I hummed, righting myself and blinking Brooks into focus, and found myself immediately feeling sick again. I spun away quickly, dry heaving into the toilet, which I'd never managed to flush. Bracing myself against the wall as best I could manage, I kicked my foot forward to depress the flusher. It was a risky move sober, a worse one drunk, and my legs gave up beneath me on account of not being able to balance.

Stumbling backward, I landed against Brooks' chest with a whoosh of breath. His arms hooked beneath my armpits and he hauled me to my feet. In the other stall, someone grunted through an orgasm, and we both turned our attention to the door. Brooks' eyes went wide and I snickered, leaning into him like I loved to do when we were cuddling after sex.

"How much did you have to drink?" he asked, breath warm against my ear.

"Too much." My body burned from the throwing up and also the embarrassment. "What are you doing here?"

"You stopped answering my texts."

"This feels stalkerish," I mumbled.

Brooks turned me to face him and took my face into his hands, inspecting me for...something I was too drunk to make sense of.

"I won't apologize," he whispered, tone taking that same hurt defense he had when he worried I was going to criticize the kind of man he was.

"I don't want you to," I assured him, swallowing hard. "I would kiss you, but it's gross in my mouth."

"I don't care," he said, pressing our lips together in a

surprisingly chaste and mostly closed-mouth kiss. "Let me take you home, get you cleaned up."

"Need to check on Dylan," I said, even though I wanted to go more than I'd ever wanted anything in my life.

As if on cue, the door to the other bathroom stall swung open and Dylan appeared, the same bruise around his throat as before, but the flush on his cheeks was a near perfect color match. The man he'd been talking to near the jukebox pushed out from behind him, shouldering past me and Brooks to get to the bathroom door.

I was too drunk to drive, but sober enough to recognize the shame that washed over Dylan's face when he saw me gawking at him. Brooks re-situated his hands on me so I didn't fall over, his expression unaffected.

"I'm fine," Dylan said, but I didn't believe it.

"That's it," Brooks said, a definite sense of finality in his voice. "Let's go. You're both coming home with me."

IT WAS A LOT OF WORK GETTING TWO DRUNK TWENTY-SOMETHINGS back to my penthouse. The cab ride was a nightmare, but it made the elevator ride look tame. By the time I got them both through the door, I sent Dylan into a guest room on the first floor, then ushered Tate upstairs to my room.

He was annoyingly apologetic, even though he didn't have a single thing to be sorry for. I let him ramble while I stripped him out of his clothes, shoving any ideas I'd had of dirty back of the bar sex out of my head. I'd definitely headed to Tryst with the hopes of taking him in public...somewhere we were in danger of being caught, where I had to cover his mouth with my hand to smother his noises.

I shook myself out of the fantasy because Tate was far too inebriated to consent to that kind of thing, and his best friend—even with cum still in the back of his throat —wasn't any better off. Tucking Tate into bed, still in his underwear, I slid my water glass toward the side of the nightstand in case he got thirsty, then grabbed the trash can out of the bathroom and set it right by the edge of the bed. The wood would clean, but better safe than sorry.

After I was confident Tate had mumbled his last apology, I slipped quietly out of the bedroom and headed back downstairs. I'd been halfway through a good book and a better bottle of scotch when he'd texted, but I apparently knew how to sip and savor, whereas Tate was a pound it and hope for the best kind of drinker. It shouldn't have surprised me because it was a clear mirror of how he approached most other things in his life. At least, as far as I could tell.

Even though the night had already taken two sharp and unexpected left turns, I came face to face with another in my kitchen. The new one was Dylan shaped, hunched over my counter with my scotch cradled between his hands.

"Normally people can't look away from the view the first time they come over," I said, taking a fresh glass out of the cabinet and taking the seat beside him. He slid my own bottle of scotch toward me, and I scoffed, filling the new glass with two fingers of amber-colored liquor.

"I think it'll make me throw up," he muttered, swishing the scotch around the glass.

"I think that's whatever you were drinking before now," I suggested. "Did someone drug your drink, Dylan?"

He reeled back surprisingly fast, like I'd struck him.

"Why would you ask me that?"

There were a thousand reasons the question was a fair one, but if he was intent to ignore all of the red flags that hovered over his head, I knew better than to argue with a drunk man who carried the weight of a chip on his shoulder.

"Just checking."

"I knew what I was doing."

I took a sip of my drink, spinning on my seat and propping my elbows up on the counter. I wasn't drunk enough to throw my organs up through my mouth, and I quite enjoyed the view. After five or ten minutes of companionable silence had passed, Dylan made a disgruntled noise, turning his head toward me far faster than he should have. He dry heaved, and I grabbed him by both shoulders, guiding him to the kitchen sink before he emptied the contents of his stomach all over my counter.

Another five minutes later, Dylan had finished with the worst of it, and he barely complained while I wet a cloth for him to wipe his face with, and he didn't argue at all when I dumped out his stolen glass of alcohol and handed him water instead. He drank it without complaint, then hesitated before moving back to the counter where we'd been sitting.

"Couch?" I suggested. "Or do you want to go lie down."

"I don't want to be alone," he admitted, a concerning degree of sadness ringing out with his voice.

"Do you want to talk or do you want me to take you up and put you in bed with Tate?" I asked.

Dylan furrowed his brow. "You'd let me sleep in bed with him? Under your roof?"

"If you were going to fuck him, you'd have done it by now. But even if you had, I know it wouldn't be as good for him as I am."

Dylan swayed, closing his eyes and rubbing the bridge of his nose.

"I knew what I was doing," he repeated his answer from earlier, and I knew it didn't have anything to do with how good he fancied himself to be in bed.

"You don't have to explain yourself to me."

"I'm going to have to explain to him." Dylan swallowed, and it was the first time I noticed the bruising around his throat.

"Tate doesn't seem like the judgmental type to me," I hedged.

"Can I go upstairs with him?" Dylan asked, ignoring me.

"Of course." I slid my arm around his waist and guided him toward the stairs.

Dylan stepped up onto the first one, hand braced on the steel railing. His entire body teetered forward and he made a very treacherous sound in the back of his throat before falling down onto his ass on the floor.

"The bed will be there when you're ready," I assured him, taking a seat beside him on the first stair.

Dylan looked beyond drunk. He was miserable and in a state of self-loathing as concerning as Alex's had been after Beamer left for California. He folded himself forward, propping his arms on his knees and his head on his arms.

"Can I touch you, Dylan?" I asked, hand hovering over his back.

I'd been touching him since I made it my job to get him and Tate out of the bar, but the touch I was asking for was beyond the physical support required to move a drunk person from a car to a house to a chair.

"I won't do that to Tate," Dylan grumbled, talking more to the floor than to me. "He's my best friend."

"Dylan, what do you..."

"You couldn't pay me enough to do that to him," Dylan went on, as angry as his state would allow. "I'm going to tell him about this in the morning, I—"

"Dylan, stop."

He stopped, snapping his mouth closed with so much force I worried he might have cracked a molar or four.

"I wasn't soliciting you for sex, Dylan," I said very carefully, returning my hand to my lap. "I was going to rub your back to help calm you down. To get you ready to go upstairs."

"Oh." He sighed heavily, sinking deeper into himself. "That's fine."

I hesitated, but when my delay in contact drew an embarrassed groan from the back of his throat, I committed myself to it, resting my hand against the small of his back and drawing a wide, swooping circle across his slender torso.

"Did you think I was trying to take advantage of you?" I asked, not pulling away when he leaned into me.

"I thought Alex had told you about me," he said, and it was with that short sentence that everything clicked into place.

I knew Alex had been paying for sex, which I inherently didn't have an issue with, but nothing about Dylan screamed consenting, and I had half a mind to take Alex out the back of a building next time I saw him and find out what the fuck he'd been thinking getting involved with someone as messed up as Dylan.

"I didn't know it was you," I admitted.

"Tate doesn't know."

"About you and Alex?"

"About me and any of it," he said, shifting his pose to focus his stare on the wall instead of the floor. It felt like a step in the right direction, and I kept working my hand up and down his back. Dylan was sweaty, almost trembling, but his skin was clammy. He was going to hate life in the morning.

"I won't tell him," I promised. "But now that I know, is

there anything you want to talk about? Did someone hurt you tonight?"

"Friday," he said, pressing his fingers against the bottom of the bruise on his throat. "But it's fine. Tonight was...just to take the edge off."

"I don't know what that means."

"Tate thinks my parents pay my rent. That they support me pursuing my music." Dylan sounded like he wanted to dig a hole through my floor and bury himself in it, never to be heard from again.

"Do you sing?" I asked.

"And I play guitar. And piano," he said with a self-deprecating chuckle, "and violin."

"That's a lot of talent, Dylan."

He made an uncomfortable sound, shoulders wiggling beneath my touch. I went still, but when he didn't pull away from me, I resumed the soft swirls across the top of his back.

"I write songs too."

I nodded, and he sighed out a heavy breath.

"Did your parents cut you off?" I asked.

"I didn't want Tate to worry about my half of the rent," he said, dejected.

"So you..."

"Yeah," he agreed, not forcing either of us to put a name on it, because even if Dylan had gotten into sex work, that didn't change whatever had happened to him on Friday night that left those bruises around his neck. Hell, I'd had Tate halfway to unconsciousness and there wasn't a single mark around his neck to prove it. Whoever had put his hands on Dylan had done so with less than no regard for his pleasure—or his well-being.

"It wasn't Alex, was it?" I had to ask, my pulse spiking. "On Friday, I mean."

"He wouldn't," Dylan said, sounding more miserable than before.

"Why don't you want Tate to know that you're cut off?" I asked him. "It has to be more than the money."

"He would work himself to death to cover my shortfalls," he answered, and we both knew it was true. Tate was gracious and kind, and he would have absolutely worked himself to the bone to cover whatever Dylan needed from him. "I have rent and student loans. Bills. It's a lot."

"I'm not judging you, Dylan."

"Why do you always do that?" He asked, angling his head toward me. The lights from the window reflected off his eyes, and I could tell he was coming around enough to get up to bed.

"Do what?"

"Say my name."

I laughed and pushed up to my feet, taking Dylan with me. He swayed a bit, but overall felt far steadier than he had when we headed for the stairs in the first place.

"What else would I call you?" I asked, wrapping my arm around his waist and using my shoulder to edge him toward the stairs. "Who else could you be?"

Dylan groaned, resting his head on my shoulder. "I'd rather be anyone but myself sometimes."

I didn't have anything good to say to that, so I nodded my agreement with the sentiment and helped him up the stairs. Tate hadn't moved from where I'd left him, curled into a ball on the edge of the bed, his face half-buried in my pillow. The water and the trash can were untouched, which felt like a good sign. I helped Dylan around to the other side of the bed, leaving him fully dressed. He made a mockery of pulling back my covers, but he found his way beneath the sheets eventually. I tucked the blankets up to his chin, watching from the door was he scooted his way across the bed, searching out Tate with a tired and scared sigh.

I closed the door with a quiet click, then went back down to the kitchen to call Alex. We needed to have a fucking talk.

My alarm went off at the wrong time. It had to be the wrong time because I had just closed my eyes when it started to blare in my ear. I was in the middle of making a mental promise to myself that I was never going to go drinking with Dylan ever again when he groaned behind me.

"Turn it off," he begged, voice hoarse.

I blinked slowly, bringing the room into focus, but seeing didn't make things any easier to understand. I was in Brooks' bed, but Brooks was nowhere to be found. Dylan was the one tucked in behind me, and my face was half-smothered into the pillow on Brooks' side of the bed. Grabbing my phone from the nightstand, I silenced the alarm and rolled onto my back.

"What happened last night?" I asked, rubbing sleep from my eyes and making sure my legs still worked.

"Your boyfriend collected us from the bar, brought us back here."

"Why are you in bed with me instead of him?" I asked.

"I was drunker than you," he said, "and I didn't want to be alone."

The worry in his voice served as a quick reminder and a wakeup call far more jarring than my alarm had been. I remembered the bruises on his neck, remembered catching him on his knees in the bathroom at Tryst.

I turned again, rolling to my other side and propping myself up on my palm, elbow digging into the cloud-soft mattress. "What's going on with you?"

"When do you have to be at work?" he asked.

"I have a little," I told him, thankful Brooks lived closer to my office than I did, but eternally ungrateful that I wasn't rich as him and couldn't *not* work today. "So make it work and we can go into details later."

"The short story then."

"You know I don't care if you're just going through your slut era," I told him, knowing I'd spent the past half-year doing things far worse than sucking a stranger's cock in a bar bathroom. "But I want you safe."

Dylan looked miserable, the bags under his eyes almost as dark as the bruising around his throat. His mouth was angled into a sharp frown, and in the two years I'd known him, I didn't think I'd seen him unhappy more than four times. Downstairs, the door opened and closed, and I knew it was Brooks getting home from his run. He'd have to come upstairs to get dressed eventually, but if I'd learned anything about him, it was he was a caretaker at heart and wouldn't make his appearance without coffee for all of us. Rough sex aside, Brooks had nothing but love—and some lingering doubt— inside of him. He was always ready to care and give and attend. It was insanely sexy, even though I didn't have any recollection of him getting me into bed the night before and that should have been shamefully mortifying.

"It started fine," Dylan said under his breath, reaching over me for a glass of water on the nightstand. The smell of coffee drifted from the kitchen up the stairs and I started to feel awake for the first time since my alarm went off.

"What did?"

Dylan let out a long sigh and set the glass down, then yanked the pillow out from behind my head. He clutched it against his chest like a child holding a teddy bear, and I pushed myself into a seated position, propping my back against the headboard.

"My parents cut me off last year," he said, glancing at me from the corner of his eye. It was a quick look, gone as fast as he'd given it to me.

Dylan stayed quiet after the bomb, and I wasn't sure if it was from shame, the hangover, or because he was giving me time to process what he'd just told me. Dylan had always worked shifts bartending and serving because the music gigs were few and far between, but I didn't think any of it would be enough to float the rent in our Chelsea apartment. I tried to think back, to wrack my brain and remember how long it had been since he had started to pick up more shifts than had been his normal amount.

"What's the next bullet point?"

"I didn't have enough money to live."

"Next one," I prompted again.

"I didn't mean to make a habit of it," he said, the pillow pushing against the underside of his chin. "Someone at the bar offered me money to hookup when I got off work and he was cute, so I didn't really see the harm in taking money to suck him off in the parking lot."

"There isn't any," I assured.

"He came back the next night." Dylan turned his head toward me, eyes glassy. "Offered me a lot more money to go the rest of the way with him, so I said yes. And he was so hot and the sex was really good. It was easy money and it made me feel good. I didn't see the harm."

"You already said that, and I told you there isn't any. Sex work is work, Dylan..."

"I added a little code about it on my bio on some hookup app, and it became a steady thing. That's how I met Alex, Brooks' friend. It was him."

I didn't know a lot about Brooks' friends, but none of them had struck me as the type to hire sex workers. They were all rich and good looking, probably decent personalities, and if they fucked half as good as Brooks, then I couldn't imagine they had issues getting laid.

"And the bruises on your throat?" I prompted, pulling the pillow out of his arms so I could see the marks in question again.

Dylan didn't even try to hide them from me. "A client got out of hand."

"You could have died."

Both of us turned toward the door, finding Brooks leaning against the doorframe in nothing more than a tank top and a pair of running shorts. He had a mug of coffee in each hand.

"I know," Dylan grumbled.

"I didn't mean to eavesdrop, but the coffee was getting cold." Brooks brought the mugs toward us, giving Dylan his first, then dipping down and leaving a kiss against the top of my head as he passed off mine.

"I already told you last night," Dylan said. "I don't care if you hear it again."

"I was trying to give the two of you time to talk, but I need to get ready for work soon and so does Tate."

I pulled my phone off the nightstand to check the time, frowning when I realized Brooks was right. Dylan and I had spent more time talking than I'd realized.

"Last night was just a mistake." Dylan scooted up to sit against the headboard, taking a drink of his coffee. "I've never accepted a hookup drunk before."

Dylan looked so pitiful, nestled in Brooks' sheets with the promise of an epic hangover etched across his features. I hated that it was a Monday, that I couldn't stay longer to hear the rest of his story, to make sure everything was going to be okay with him. Dylan was far more than a roommate. He was my best friend in New York and I hated that I hadn't paid more attention, that I didn't see the signs.

"I wish you would have told me sooner," I said.

"I didn't want you to worry about the money," he said. "And I definitely didn't want your charity."

"We're friends, Dylan. What do you mean my charity?"

"You would have paid my rent so I didn't have to start this."

"I would have gone with you!" I snapped, gesturing broadly. Brooks snatched the coffee out of my hand before it sloshed all over me and the sheets. It was then I realized I was stripped down to nothing more than my underwear and Dylan was still fully dressed. That had Brooks written all over it, and my chest twinged with a feeling that had been floating around the back of my head for a few days ignored.

"What good would that have done?" Brooks asked gently, sitting down beside me on the bed. "There's no point in worrying about what either of you could have or would have done. We aren't in the past. We're here right now, and Tate needs to get in the shower and get going to work."

"I'm fine," Dylan promised me, a sad smile on his face. "I'm safe and you know the truth now."

"But you're still cut off."

"That's a longer story and I don't want to abuse your boyfriend's kindness by making you late for work." Dylan kicked the sheets down and shrugged. "Get ready for work, please, Tate."

"You can shower first," I told Brooks, but he narrowed his eyes at me and shook his head.

"No one is going to fire me for being late," he said. "You, on the other hand."

"I'm fine, Tate," Dylan promised. "I won't go anywhere."

The two of them watched me expectantly, and I knew there was no way for me to put off getting my ass into gear to head into work. Brooks was right that time was short, so with a grumbled protest, I left them both to shower.

I didn't think there was anything about Brooks' shower that had been designed for rushing, though. It was impossible to not want to take your time under the instantly hot rainfall spray, and the bench that caught most of the spray was too inviting to sit on when you had four minutes total to wash the vodka out of your pores.

I did the best I could, which turned out to be a ten minute

shower that left me smelling like Brooks, then I grabbed work clothes from the back of Brooks' closet. As presentable as my hangover would allow, I pulled my phone free from the charger and found the two most important people in my life downstairs in the living room, side by side and staring out the window.

"Showered and ready for work as ordered," I said.

Brooks looked at me over his shoulder, a soft smile on his face. Dylan turned completely, coming toward me in a rush. He threw his arms around my shoulders and buried his face into my neck with a sniffle. I wrapped my arms around him and squeezed.

"I should have told you," he said.

"I wish you would have, but you didn't owe it to me," I promised him. "We can talk more about it tonight? Or whenever you're ready."

"Yeah." He nodded, untangling himself from my embrace. "Yes."

Brooks turned from the window and jerked his head toward the kitchen, and I went after him. Dylan returned to his perch at the window, and even though I hated going to work and leaving him, I knew he'd be safe with Brooks.

"I'm so sorry about last night," I said to Brooks once we were alone. He opened his arms for me and I slipped into his hold with a quiet sigh.

"You don't need to apologize for anything, Tate, but I'm curious what part you think warrants it."

"Getting so drunk that I don't even remember you taking me home from the bar. For having a best friend with this kind of baggage. I don't know where the list should start or stop."

Brooks kissed the top of my head, my temple, my cheek.

"Kale tried to kidnap a prince once," he said with a smile. "Being a drunk twenty-something is far from offensive, I assure you."

"Still."

"I won't hear it." He kissed me on the mouth to shut me up. A soft kiss that dripped with command that was impossible to ignore. I nodded and parted my lips, letting him lick past the backs of my teeth until my cock was half-hard and leaking.

"Are you sure I can't be late for work?" I asked, chasing after his mouth when he finally ended the kiss.

Brooks grabbed a sleek black travel mug from the counter and pressed it against the center of my chest.

"I'm sure. I refreshed your coffee and called you a car so you won't be late."

My cheeks burned. "You didn't need to do that."

"I know." He kissed me again. "I wanted to."

"I…"

Biting the inside of my cheek, I forced myself to shut up.

The corner of Brooks' mouth twitched, but if he made any assumptions about what I'd been about to say, he didn't voice them.

"I'll get Dylan home safe too, so you don't need to worry about that."

I twisted the lid on the mug so I could get a drink of the coffee he'd prepared for me. "I don't know what I did to deserve you."

"It probably has to do with the way you let me rough fuck you out of your mind." Brooks chuckled, and a huge smile broke out across my face.

Shaking my head, I countered, "I think it has more to do with the other parts of it, don't you?"

"Go to work, Tate," he said. His tongue, that had just been inside my mouth, darted out to lick the corner of his lip. I surged closer, bending down low and crashing our mouths together, needing one last taste of him before saying goodbye.

CHAPTER 23

BROOKS

After Tate left for work, Dylan was quick to follow. He assured me the two of them had talked and would talk again, but I was still concerned about his well-being. It wasn't my place to worry about Dylan, but it wasn't really something I could turn off, either. After I'd tucked them both into bed the night before, I'd tried to call Alex to see if he had any insight into the situation, but he hadn't answered his phone. The lack of response was reasonable because it was well after midnight when I'd called, but now it was a new day and I didn't have any meetings before lunch.

Before Dylan left, I'd made him drink a cup of coffee and I asked him if he wanted help. He said he didn't know what help looked like anymore, and the despondency in his tone made me want to lock him in a utility room until I figured out what to do with him. It wasn't my place, but he hadn't said no, so I set my mind to the next steps and I was ready to put them into action. As with most things in my life, I would deal with the repercussions later.

After lunch, I was supposed to meet with Boston Sheffield

and his charity of choice, which happened to be a local soup kitchen owned by a prick of a man and managed by a saint. Ever since Boston and Ford bought the farm, the bunch of them had been in negotiations around a contract that would supply fresh fruits and vegetables for the kitchen, except the owner continued to be resistant to the terms.

My job should have been an easy one.

Before Russell Lang, I'd never met a charity that didn't want money, that didn't need the help. But after months of meetings, it had become apparent he was only in the business for a tax shelter and any more incoming money had the potential to raise red flags that he wasn't interested in waving. Shawn, the manager of the kitchen, had been fighting long and hard against his boss, and I'd been doing hours of due diligence to try and find a loophole that would work for everyone.

I had a meeting on the books at one to meet with Ford and Russell about the whole thing. Boston and Shawn both had bleeding hearts that weren't cut out for the kind of talks that we were going to have, but I was confident an agreement could be reached to replace the current supplier with Boston's new farm. The after lunch time slot gave me plenty of opportunity to track down Alex, which was exactly what I planned to do.

After watching the car I'd hired to take Dylan back to Chelsea disappear around the corner, I pulled my phone out of my jacket and called Kale.

"To what do I owe the pleasure?" he said after answering on the second ring.

"Do you still have us all on Friend Finder?" I asked.

He scoffed. "I didn't think you knew about that."

"You wouldn't have let Alex go silent for weeks after things ended with Beamer if you didn't at least know where he was."

"Guilty as charged," he said. "You're all still in here. Even Beamer over in California with that husband of his."

Knowing he'd kept Beamer on the map, even considering the state of things between them, tugged at the strings of my heart. The two of them had been so close and Kale had taken the betrayal over Beamer's marriage particularly hard. He'd been horrible to Dalton, Beamer's husband, and while he'd tried to make things better, he still wasn't great.

"Where is Alex right now?" I asked.

"Is he being weird again?" Kale asked. The call switched to speaker when he spoke next. "I thought he was more himself last time we got together."

"He was. I just need to have a chat with him."

"Have you tried calling?"

"Where is he, Kale?"

Kale chuckled. "Do I need to call the police? Or let Alex know you're gunning for him?"

"I'm not mad. I'm not going to put my hands on him. I just need to talk to him about someone he's been sleeping with and I want to see his face when I do it."

"Who's he sleeping with?" Kale asked, the interest sharp as a bell in his voice.

I decided to keep the answer simple, but honest. "A bartender at The Black Door."

Kale sucked his teeth, taking the phone off speaker. "Alex is at home, so if he's not answering his phone, he's ignoring you."

"Thank you. I'm seeing Ford later. Do you think two weeks from now is good to go up to the farm?"

I'd known Kale for years and I knew that even though we'd all agreed to go to the farm, he was going to drag his feet over the whole thing unless someone—his boyfriend, namely—physically forced his hand about it.

"I have to check with Christian," Kale answered, predictable as ever.

"Ask him and let me know before lunch so I can tell Ford to plan."

"That's not a lot of time," he protested.

"I'll come find you when I'm done with Alex if you drag your feet on this."

"Before two," Kale countered.

"Before twelve." I hung up the phone and swiped open the app I used to reserve car rides. There was a vehicle available right around the corner, so it didn't take more than five minutes until I was on my way to Alex's house. I could have walked. Almost everything in New York was walkable, but I didn't feel like cutting through Central Park to get to Alex's townhouse on the Upper West Side. He had five floors and four bedrooms, which felt excessive, but it was the house he'd grown up in, inherited after both his parents had passed some years earlier. He'd spent near a million dollars on renovations, turning it into something far more sterile than I would have chosen for myself.

The entire upper floor had been converted into a primary suite with a sloping cathedral ceiling and wood burning fireplace. The kitchen had been upgraded with top-of-the-line appliances, and the room that had been Alex's father's pride and joy, the library, had been converted into a playroom. It was the only room in the house that hadn't been painted a glaring shade of white, instead a more muted cream. Even with the overfilled mahogany shelves still lining the walls, I found it all to be far too formal for my tastes. I knew the criticism was rich coming from a man with a panoramic view of the city and a ten thousand dollar couch, but...I never had issues throwing stones from my glass house. All that aside, Alex had one of the best back gardens in the city, and the five of us had spent many summer nights out back drinking and shooting the shit, but it seemed life had changed all of us, and not necessarily for the better.

The car pulled up alongside the curb in front of Alex's house, and I took the steps to his porch two at a time, banging on the door until he answered. He was bleary eyed, but that was usual for him these days. Other than that, he looked almost his normal self. I slid my phone back into my pocket and unfastened the button on my suit coat.

"To what do I owe the pleasure, Brooks?" he asked, mouth pulled into a tight line.

"That's what Kale said when I called him this morning. I'm starting to feel like none of my friends like my company anymore."

"I enjoy sleeping," he said, stepping aside to let me in. I closed the door behind me and followed him up the stairs and into the sprawling eat-in kitchen where he had a plate of bacon and toast on the counter beside a steaming mug of coffee. The *Times* was open and folded into fours, a pen resting on top and the crossword half-finished.

"Can I have some coffee?" I asked, gesturing to the mug.

"You know where to get it."

Alex slid back into his seat and picked up his pen,

scratching out the letters for an answer to the puzzle I'd apparently interrupted. Thankfully, his coffee pot was full, and I filled a mug for myself before joining him at the table. I stretched my legs out and crossed them at the ankle, waiting for him to get bored of trying to pretend the crossword clues were more interesting than me.

"What do you want, Brooks?" he finally asked, setting the pen down and reaching for a slice of overly-browned toast.

"I want to talk to you about Dylan Rivers," I said.

Alex set the toast down. "What about him?"

"I just want to know your history with him," I said, sipping the coffee that tasted like it had been roasted the night before and flown in from Colombia overnight. "He's not just a bartender."

"I know he's not."

"You hired him?" I prompted. "For sex?"

"It's not a secret, Brooks."

"I know it's not." I set down the mug and held up my hands. "I'm not here to accuse you of anything. I just..."

I didn't know what I was doing or what I wanted Alex to do about it. All I knew was Dylan was Tate's best friend, his roommate, and he'd fallen into some dangerous situations because of the choices he'd been making. The night before, he'd sounded ashamed and embarrassed about the whole thing, but I wasn't sure it was enough for him to stop. Even after coming clean to Tate, I didn't think Dylan was going to walk away entirely, and I didn't trust him to start making better decisions.

That was rich, coming from me, but I'd always been a reasonable judge of character. I could tell Dylan was a good person who'd just been having some bad luck, and then some

worse luck. Based off the way he'd been drinking last night, I...
I just didn't want him to get himself hurt, or worse, killed.
Tate would feel responsible, and I wasn't sure if there'd be any
coming back from that.

I was invested in Tate, and by association, Dylan.

This was one of the side effects of being with me, and I
hoped Tate wouldn't think I had overstepped in any way, but
it was my job now to take care of him and right now...that
meant taking care of Dylan.

"What, Brooks?" Alex reached again for the toast, sinking
his teeth in with a loud crunch.

"He needs...help," I said, frowning. "I picked him and Tate
up from Tryst last night."

"Drinking on a Sunday isn't a red flag."

I narrowed my eyes at him while he washed his food down
with a swallow of coffee.

"Is it a red flag to have to pull him up from his knees on
the bathroom floor and make sure he doesn't choke on the
cum a stranger just shot down his throat?"

Alex set his mug down on the table with a little more force
than necessary, but just the right amount to confirm I'd made
the right decision by coming to him about it.

"He's not anything to me," Alex said carefully, eyes
focused on the crossword.

"I didn't say he was."

"He can suck whoever's cock he wants," he said.

"I asked if I could touch him last night and he thought I
meant sexually."

Alex swallowed, his jaw working as he flicked his stare up
at me. "Is that what you meant?"

"I'm in love with Tate, Alex. I assure you it was the last

thing I meant. I wanted to console him, rub his back so he didn't throw up all over my stairs."

Half the fight went out of Alex's shoulders, and he sagged against the back of his chair. I was grateful he let my confession of love go unnoticed because I honestly hadn't meant to say the words out loud. They were an idea, a dream maybe, that I'd played with just before sunrise sometimes, listening to Tate breathe heavily against my shoulder. I worried about speaking them to anyone who mattered because, at any given time, the doubt and the fear were still very sharp and real things in the back of my mind.

"He needs someone to be easy with him," I said.

"That's the last thing he wanted when we were together."

I hooked my finger in the handle of my coffee mug and slid it back and forth in small half-circles.

"Be that as it may, Alex, I think it's what he needs now."

"I'm not the one for that." He clicked the end of his pen and scribbled down another answer to the crossword. "That's never been me, and it won't ever be me."

"You can do both, you know," I reminded him, "I do."

"That's not...Dylan, he..." Alex stumbled over the words and I sipped my coffee, waiting for him to get himself in order.

He wrote in another answer, and one more.

"Have you ever run the Boston marathon?" Alex asked.

"Twice."

He twirled the pen around his fingers. "What is the town at the eighth mile of the marathon? Six letters, second to last one is a C."

I sighed and finished my coffee, pushing back from the table. We'd all been wrong in thinking Alex was back to his normal self. He was playing the part of the man we knew, but wasn't quite reaching all the marks. Alex was a thoughtful friend and a generous partner. Sure, he had unique tastes in the bedroom, but we all did.

"It's Natick," I told him. "Thanks for the coffee. We're taking a trip to Ford and Boston's farm in two weeks, don't think you're getting out of it."

"Is Kale going?" he asked.

I was halfway to his front door. "All of us."

I heard the pen spell out the answer to the clue, and then Alex sighed, resigned as ever.

"I'll call Dylan."

CHAPTER 24
TATE

My head didn't feel much better after lunch, but Brooks texting me for my office address and getting me snacks and water delivered at three did wonders for the ache of it all. Digging through the kraft paper bag to see what all was inside, I swiped at my phone with my other hand, firing off a quick text to him in thanks.

Me: Thank you, but you didn't have to do this.

His reply was almost immediate.

Brooks: I consider it my job to take care of you now.
Me: Your job is just to fuck me until I forget my name, wash my feet, and then take me to Italy for pasta on a date sometime.

Three dots appeared on the screen, then disappeared, reappeared, then they were gone again. Chuckling, I turned my attention back to the bag of goodies he'd had sent to me, finding a package of vitamins at the bottom which were specially selected for hangovers. I took the bundle of supplements, then texted Brooks again.

Me: I was joking about Italy.
Me: I just remembered you said that last time.

He didn't answer right away, and I cracked open a bag of some salty potato chips. The sodium was magic, and by the time I'd eaten my way through them, I almost felt normal again. My phone buzzed with a message, so I tucked everything except a small chocolate bar back into the bag and stashed it under my desk. The message was from Brooks, because of course it was.

Brooks: You're the one without a passport, Tate.
Brooks: I wish you would remedy that.
Me: I don't necessarily have a spare hundred and whatever dollars lying around, Brooks.

My phone rattled with a different vibration pattern, alerting me about a pending hundred and fifty dollar cash transfer. I sighed, giving a quick scan of the office to see if my boss was anywhere in sight. He was holed up in the conference room on the front end of a two-hour meeting with our product development team, so I reasoned I had a little bit of spare time to make a personal call to Brooks.

"Don't be mad," he answered instead of saying hello.

"You didn't have to do that," I said, frowning at the dollar signs on my screen, even as I initiated the transfer to my bank account.

"What if I wanted authentic Italian food?" he asked.

"I'm sure there's restaurants in the tri-state area that could fit the bill," I murmured.

"There's not, but it's cute that you think so."

"You don't need to pay for my passport," I said again.

"Is that not part of taking care of you?" he asked, and I could picture the seriousness on his face with the question. "I'm not trying to pay your rent or move you out of that shoebox apartment you and Dylan share. Consider this a selfish move if it makes you feel better."

"Selfish?" I laughed. "How so?"

"Take pity on a man with no creativity when it comes to dating so he relies on flashy jets and foreign countries to impress the man he..." Brooks trailed off, and my breath caught in my throat. "If it really bothers you, you can cancel the transfer."

We both knew it was too late for that.

"I just don't feel deserving of it," I told him.

"And I don't feel deserving of you, so we'll have to fight through those wrong ideas together, darling."

Again, with the darling.

"Okay," I agreed softly, nodding even though he couldn't see me. "Thank you."

"You're welcome."

"And thank you for the care package. The chips have done wonders for my mental stability today."

On the other end of the phone he chuckled. "Can I see you after work tonight?"

I opened the top drawer of my desk and felt around for the

rolling bottle of ibuprofen, chasing four tablets down with a swig from the electrolyte water that Brooks had sent with the afternoon delivery.

"I would like that, but Dylan..." I groaned, scrubbing a hand down my face.

Dylan and I had talked about the basics of his situation while I was getting ready for work that morning, but it felt like there were still a dozen things left unsaid between us.

"I've asked a friend to check in on him," Brooks said.

"Alex?"

He hummed his agreement.

"That's great, but he's still my best friend."

"Then text him," Brooks suggested. "If you're not happy with the response, go see him after work and come over if you feel better about him."

"And if I don't feel better?"

"Then I'll try again tomorrow."

The answer was so simple, so precise. So *not* demanding.

"Alright," I agreed. "I'll let you know."

"Dylan is going to be okay," he assured me.

The door to the conference room opened and the head of our product development team came out, looking red in the face and far from amused.

"I need to go," I said quickly. "Sorry."

"Bye, Tate."

I barely caught the goodbye before I dropped the phone back onto the base. It clattered a little louder than I would have liked, but my boss was in a heated conversation across the room. They'd clearly just taken their disagreement out for some fresh air. A couple minutes later, they both returned to the conference room and closed the door. I watched it for a beat to make sure it stayed closed, then texted Dylan.

Me: How are you?

Five minutes later, I had my reply

Dylan: My head hurts, but I'm lying in the dark and that seems to help.
Me: Do you need me? To talk or help you at all?

I didn't know what I could do for him, but I wanted to offer. I didn't want him to feel alone after what he'd shared with me.

Dylan: I'm okay for now, but we can talk soon.
Dylan: I'll answer any questions you have.
Me: I don't want to ask more than you're willing to share. I just want to be there for you. You're my best friend.
Dylan: Same.
Dylan: I'm okay, Tate. I promise.

I didn't have much to do besides take Dylan at his word, and if he was alone in the dark, there was no real point in me going home after work for that. Before I convinced myself that was exactly what I needed to do, I texted Brooks again.

Me: I'm free after work.
Brooks: I told you he was okay.
Brooks: Do you need to get fresh clothes?
Me: I should

Brooks: Come over when you're ready then. I'll order in.
Me: Sorry we can't have dinner in Italy lol
Brooks: I'll send you more money to expedite the processing, Tate.
Brooks: See you tonight.

I unwrapped the chocolate bar and popped a bite into my mouth. It tasted like heaven, and I knew without looking up the name of the wrapper on the internet that it was the most expensive chocolate I'd ever had. I'd barely swallowed it when my boss was out of the conference room again with a mile long list of things he needed me to do. The distraction of my job made the day go by faster, and before I knew it, I was home.

Dylan's bedroom door was closed and his lights were off, but I could hear the careful and quiet strumming of his guitar through the door. I reached into the care package from Brooks and found the second chocolate bar, then shoved it under Dylan's door. The chords quieted and he set his guitar down. I didn't hear his footsteps, but I recognized the sound of the paper being crumpled as he tore into the bar.

"Thank you," he said, mouth full. "I'm fine, I promise."

"I'm going to Brooks' place," I told him through the door. "If you need anything, will you call me?"

"I'll call."

I didn't have a choice except to believe him, so I left him with the chocolate and headed across the apartment to my bedroom. There was an empty soda can in the sink, which was infinitely better than an empty liquor bottle, so I called it a win and stripped out of my work clothes. After tossing them in the hamper, I grabbed a clean pair of slacks and a polo shirt for work the next day, then redressed myself in jeans and a coffee shop t-shirt I'd picked up at a gig with Dylan the summer before. I put on my shoes and checked on Dylan once more, then headed downstairs.

The last thing I expected, though I don't know why, was to come out of my building and find a black town car idling alongside the curb, the driver resting against the trunk and scrolling through his phone. When the door closed behind me, he looked up and quickly shoved his phone into his pocket.

"Mr. Barlowe?" he asked.

It was impossible to not smile. Like Brooks and I had made a commitment to each other and it meant all restraint was off. He had warned me before that he didn't do things in half measures, that he worried about being too much, but...as much as I wanted to protest about the level of attention he gave me, I didn't have it in me to do it. It had been so long since I'd had anyone to take care of me, the attention was welcome, even if it would take some getting used to.

"That's me," I said, adjusting my duffel bag on my shoulder.

The driver reached for the bag and I passed it to him, climbing into the back seat of the car after he opened the door. I buckled up and then texted Brooks that the car hadn't been necessary. He told me he knew, but he wanted to anyway. The usual current of defiance was absent from the message, and I pressed my phone against my chest and closed my eyes with a smile.

The doorman let me up as soon as I walked into Brooks' building and when I stepped off the elevator, I found him in the doorway, leaning against the jamb with his arms folded in front of his chest, his legs crossed at the ankle. When he saw me, he smiled, and it took all my self-control to not run head-first into his arms. Instead, I walked a little faster than normal, dipping my face into the crook of his neck and letting him bring his arms around me.

"Glad to see you vertical," he murmured, kissing my ear.

"Your care package certainly helped." I shifted enough that our mouths were in line, and I hesitated long enough so he could be the one to initiate the kiss. With his lips less than a breath away from mine, Brooks smiled, then slanted our mouths together with an intention so clear, I worried I was going to come in the hallway.

With our mouths still connected, he reached around and took my bag out of my hand and tossed it into the entryway behind him, and with his other arm still wrapped around me, he walked us both backward into his penthouse. As soon as the door was closed behind me, my back was against it, Brooks' hands on either side of my face, caging me in while he deepened the kiss. I curled my fingers around his waist and bucked my hips toward him, which earned me a hand down my pants and a rough fist around my quickly thickening shaft.

"I wanted you so badly last night," he whispered against the corner of my mouth, his thumb pressing a hard line against my leaking slit. "You were so drunk, so loose. I couldn't stop thinking about how easy it would be to throw you around and fuck you until you cried for me."

I moaned against him, wanton and unrestrained. My blood burned, setting my skin on fire with every drag of his hand against mine, the wet press of his mouth.

"Why didn't you?" I whispered.

His tongue licked back into my mouth, smile still curving across his lips.

"You weren't anywhere near the level of consent I require," he said, sinking his teeth into my lower lip. I winced, pushing my entire body off the door and right into his arms.

"But now?"

Brooks' hard cock pressed against my thigh, hot and long. "Now, Tate, I think you're just my type."

It was torture to tear myself away from Tate's perfect body, but I hadn't had a chance to order us dinner and if I got his clothes off, we wouldn't be eating for hours. Tate whimpered, chasing after me when I pulled my mouth away, and it took me scrubbing a hand down my face to recover enough dignity to even propose the idea.

"I need to feed you first," I said, reaching into my pants and adjusting my erection behind my waistband.

Tate licked his lips like a desperate man. "I could eat."

Groaning, I wagged a finger at him.

"That's dessert, Tate," I warned. "I didn't have time to order in so I was thinking we could go around the block and get some sandwiches at least."

"Is this a new tactic to make me cry? Because I'm really close."

I chuckled. "Dessert."

"I can't convince you otherwise?"

"It'll be quick," I promised, "but I won't be, so this is better."

"You're cruel," Tate complained, shoving his hand into his pants to fix the placement of his cock.

"I never said I wasn't."

I already had my wallet and keys in my pockets, so I pushed Tate back out the front door. He cursed me under his breath and stabbed at the elevator button, glaring at me over his shoulder. He was adorable when he was angry and it only made me want to fuck him more. The elevator arrived, doors sliding open, and I shouldered him into the small, enclosed space, boxing him into the corner with both of my hands on either side of his face and my body pressed hot against his.

I dropped my face against his neck, licking the sweat and soap from his skin. Working my way up to his jaw, I nipped at the angular bone before licking my way to his ear and sinking my teeth into the lobe. Tate slid his arms around my waist and pulled our bodies flush, moaning as I worked his skin with my mouth.

"I didn't think you were a sadist," he murmured, arching his neck to give me more room.

"This hurts me too."

As if to check, he reached down and pressed his palm against my erection, smashed up hard and pointing toward my stomach.

The elevator reached the ground floor and the doors slid open with a silent glide.

"Maybe we'll both cry tonight," he whispered, sneaking out from behind me and stepping into the lobby like he hadn't been seconds away from going onto his knees and choking on my cock.

In a twist of roles, I followed obediently after him, content to watch the way his ass jiggled in his jeans as he went through the revolving door and onto the sidewalk. It was a bold statement, but I hadn't cried since Tyler left me, and it wasn't an action I planned to repeat. Though if there was anyone capable of bringing those feelings out in me, it would definitely be the man standing in front of me.

"Turn left," I said, taking his hand and heading toward the little deli around the corner.

Tate squeezed my hand and adjusted his cock with the other one.

"You have to stop touching yourself in public," I warned. "You'll get us both arrested for indecency."

"You shouldn't have sent me out with a hard-on," he countered.

"I'm just trying to keep you alive."

He hummed out an amused sound. "Are you planning to fuck me right into dehydration?"

"Someday," I whispered, reaching the deli on the corner and pushing the door open.

The thought of fucking Tate until he didn't have any tears left to cry was like an electric shock that rippled from my spine and out, radiating through every bone and nerve and cell in my body. I'd never *needed* anything, but suddenly I very much needed that. Needed him covered in sweat and tears and cum, absolutely spent and boneless, nothing coming out of him except for air. Tate brushed in front of me, rubbing his ass against my cock, and he knew exactly what he was doing when he tipped his head back and pressed his temple against mine.

"What's good here?" he asked.

"Everything."

There was a decent-sized line, which I assumed had to do

with the fact it was still considered the end of the workday. Plenty of single bachelors grabbing sandwiches to take back to their apartments to eat alone. We got our order in, Tate getting a roast beef and cheddar to my pastrami on rye. The man working told us it would be about twenty minutes, and the misery started to roll off Tate in waves at the prospect of a delay so long. I didn't want to admit it, but I found the timeline far out of reach myself, and so I decided it was time to take matters into my own hands.

"Come on," I whispered into his ear, hauling him to the back of the little deli and into the bathroom. It wasn't anything of note, barely more than a janitor's closet with a toilet and a rickety slide lock, but it would have to do.

"Oh, thank God," he said as soon as I shoved the lock into the latch. He undid his jeans and shoved them to his ankles at the same time I used my forearm to turn him and push him against the door. His chest hit the doorjamb hard and he arched his back, giving me the ass that I was so ready to be inside.

I fussed with my fly, getting my zipper down enough so I could pull my own erection free. I was hard and hot, precum beading against the tip of my dick, and I smeared it around with my fingers, knowing it wasn't going to be enough lube to make it go in easy.

"I want you so bad, Brooks," Tate whined, reaching between his legs and starting to stroke his cock. "Please fuck me."

I licked my palm, then I spit into my hand a couple of times, using my fingers to get into him. It was tight and rough, but the sounds Tate made were far from resistant. There was no way around it. This was going to hurt us both, but I didn't think it was something either of us was willing to walk away from. I'd have to sit down later and examine my growing obsession with him because I'd rarely shied away from sex in any venue, but this moment was far from chasing pleasure. This was an aching and desperate kind of need, like if I didn't get inside of Tate immediately, I'd combust.

Pulling my fingers out of his ass, I spit as much saliva into my palm as I had, then I slicked my shaft and notched my slippery head against his hole. Getting into his ass was tighter than tight, and Tate cried out from the pain of it before I'd even gotten my head inside.

"Do you want me to stop?" I asked, bracing myself with one hand against his hip.

"Don't you dare."

I fucked another inch into him, only to be met with another keening wail from his throat. It was heavenly, but it wasn't going to do. With one quick motion, I brought my hand to his mouth and forced the rest of my length inside of him. Tate's lips spread against my palm, and I did my best to smother the sounds that fell from his mouth.

"You have to be quiet," I warned, tightening my fingers across his face and my hand on his hip. I fucked him with hard and short snaps of my hips, thrusting the air out of his lungs with every pump. His breath burned against the side of my finger and his asshole seared the length of my shaft. Every part of his skin was perfect and burning. His tongue swirled in mindless circles against my palm between the way he whined and cried, the quick jerk of his hand around his cock fighting against the punishing pace I had set from behind him.

Even with my hand over his mouth, Tate was loud and writhing, and it didn't take long for spurts of cum to spill from his cock and paint the bathroom door. He gasped against my palm, lips and teeth working like mad until he moved my fingers around so they were inside of his mouth, pressed flat against his tongue.

"You're perfect," I whispered, sliding my fingers down toward the back of his throat.

Tate gagged quietly, turning his face so I could see the tears slicking down his cheeks. His face was flushed, lashes clumped together, and spit tracked down his chin from the way I'd been holding his mouth.

He looked like a cock slut.

A whore.

He looked like the man of my dreams.

"Tate, I..." I bit back the confession for what had to be the hundredth time, but not for lack of trying.

The force of my own orgasm was insurmountable, stealing my words, my breath, even my vision. I buried myself inside of him, and Tate sputtered around my fingers, my vision going black around the edges. Cum geysered out of my cock and I shoved him against the door, dropping my forehead against his shoulder with a grunt. My entire body pulsed in time with my orgasm, more cum than I'd ever felt before leaking out of me and filling Tate up. He whimpered, reaching around and grabbing my thigh, keeping me inside of him until our breathing returned to something that felt close to normal. My fingers were still in his mouth, and it was with great reluctance that I slid them free. His chest heaved and he thumped his forehead against the door, licking his dry lips and closing his eyes.

I tucked my spent but still hard dick back into my pants, then kissed his shoulder, the back of his neck, the spot behind his ear. He still had his dick in his hand, and he stroked himself slowly with spread and loose fingers like the touch was too much.

"Please take me home," he finally said softly, turning around and pointing his erection at me.

There was a need inside of him that I'd only ever found in myself, and there was no way I'd deny him anything ever again. Whatever Tate asked me for, he could have. Money, houses, sex—I'd give him whatever he wanted.

"Get dressed," I said, voice hoarse.

While he tucked his dick back into his pants, I yanked a few paper towels out of the dispenser and cleaned up the mess he'd left against the wall and tossed the soiled paper into the trash can. Tate unlocked the door and waited for me to turn off the lights, then we went and got our sandwiches, which had been ready for lord knew how long. If the man behind the counter had a judgmental look for us, I didn't see it. I snatched the brown bag off the top of the counter and told him goodnight, practically falling over Tate to get out onto the sidewalk.

The walk back to my building took an eternity, and as soon as we were back in the elevator, Tate started in on the fly of his pants. He shoved his hand behind the waistband of his boxer briefs and fisted his cock, slamming his head against the back wall of the elevator.

"How am I still hard, Brooks?" he whispered, both of us looking down at the swollen organ jutting out from between his legs. He reached over with his free hand, palming my cock, which was also hard and imprisoned. "How are you still hard? When will it be enough?"

"I don't have an answer for that."

The elevator reached my floor and we both scrambled off, more like desperate and lovesick teenagers than grown men. When we got inside, I dropped our dinner on the side table, then ripped off my shirt at the same time I toed off my shoes. Tate followed my lead, making quick work of his clothes before I'd even managed to get my socks off.

"Where?" he asked, stroking his cock and taking a step away from me. "And preferably somewhere with lube this time."

I made a mental note to take extra care of his asshole when we were done for the night, but it was early still and if the erection between my legs was any sign of things to come, the end was still very far off.

"Go upstairs, Tate." I licked the corner of my mouth, staring at the sticky mess of cum already coating his shaft. "Go upstairs and get on your hands and knees. I want to take you from behind."

CHAPTER 26
TATE

I WAS BARELY IN BROOKS' BEDROOM WHEN I WENT ONTO MY HANDS and knees. I was sure he'd meant on the bed, but I'd never needed anything more than I needed him in that moment. So it was on the floor in front of the bed, face toward the window with the city sprawling out before me. The sun had just sank past the horizon and the skyline was a mix of purple and pink, the lights of the skyscrapers beyond our view just starting to blink to life.

"Insatiable," Brooks said from behind me.

He went to the bed for the lube and was between my spread legs before I had time to formulate a response. The bottle snicked open and then the cold and hard tip of his cock pushed against my hole. His entry hurt, more than it ever had before, but he seated himself fully and quickly, the fronts of his thighs slapping loud against the backs of my legs. His balls were heavy and hot against mine, and I arched my back, pressing my cheek against the pale wood planks of his floor.

Brooks fisted my hair and yanked my face off the floor. I cried out, the gesture putting a deeper arch into my spine and somehow allowing him deeper inside of me. It couldn't have been more than an inch, but it felt like a foot, the tip of his cock kissing against my second hole and sending a violent shiver through my whole body.

"Oh fuck," he gasped from behind me, and I knew he'd felt just how deep he'd gotten into me.

My eyes rolled back and Brooks folded his body over mine, batting my hand out of the way and taking over the motions against my own cock. His grip was rougher and tighter than mine, far more demanding, and it was with that touch that he forced a second orgasm out of me. I shouted myself hoarse, cum streaking across his floor as my entire body seized and spasmed.

Normally after I came, he was close behind, but Brooks moved quick, flipping me onto my back and sinking back inside of me. The glint in his eyes was that of a man possessed, and he bent my legs toward my ears, folding me in half and fucking me so hard it pushed my body through the sticky puddles my cum had just left. Above me, Brooks was more disheveled than I'd ever seen him, nearly frantic with his hair falling loose across his face and sweat beading on his temple. His jaw was slack and his pupils dark pools that consumed the golden light of his irises.

We'd had sex plenty of times that wasn't rough, that didn't end in tears and whimpers, but after the way he'd so masterfully played my body, the way he knew what to give me when I hadn't even asked, I found myself desperate to give it to him. All the other times, Brooks had coaxed the tears out of me whether I'd intended for them to fall or not. He knew what to do and how to get me there. It was a thing I didn't think about, hadn't had control over. But half-drunk with lust and maybe something far more potent, I realized the truth of it all.

I *wanted* to cry for him.

"Brooks," I rasped his name, the violent snaps of his hips pushing the breath out of me with every thrust. He must have seen the plea in my eyes, the thing I needed to ask for, even though I didn't have the words for it, because he closed the small space between us, collaring his hand around my throat and giving me a hard press into the floor. My entire body burned, muscles sore from tensing and trembling, my hole, tender and well-fucked. My back ached from the friction and the slide against the floor and my throat from all the crying out and screaming Brooks had made me do.

The sturdy slap of his body against mine, leaving bruises against my ass and my legs quaking from the overwhelm. It was only his hand around my throat that stopped me from telling him I loved him. His eyes scanned my face, lips parted like there was a confession just as damning on the tip of his tongue. I tapped the white knuckles that were cutting off my air, not because I wanted him to let up, but because I wanted more. I wanted him to take me right to the edge and then fall over with me.

His thrusts turned harder, and my vision gave way, sparkling like snow on an old television. The shape of his face went blurry and I blinked slowly, the hand I had around my own cock slowing down before stopping entirely. It took all of my strength to focus on breathing, and I bucked off the floor, folding myself into a neater half-shaped version of myself as I managed one last gasping breath. With spit flying out of my mouth and tears pooling in the corners of my eyes, Brooks let go of my throat with a roar.

He bowed backward and I sucked in a breath so necessary it hurt. Every muscle in my body constricted and seized, and then Brooks cursed under his breath and slammed himself into me once more before going still entirely. His cock thickened and swelled against my rim as he came, and I cried out, a desperate and agonized wail.

"Sssh, now," Brooks coaxed, brushing my sweat-soaked hair back from my face as his dick still pumped me full of cum. Even in the throes of an orgasm that must have left him feeling like a god, his attention was on me and my pain.

My pleasure.

I gasped, my throat on fire, a cold sweat dripping down my spine and mixing with the cum that had started to dry there from my earlier orgasm. Brooks pulled out of me, slowly untangling my legs and pulling me into his lap. It wasn't until I was against his chest and listening to the rapid-fire beat of his heart that I realized I was crying. Not just the kind of leaking tears from my eyes that he normally brought out, but full on, uncontrollable sobbing that vibrated my entire body.

Brooks wrapped his arms around me, stroking through my hair and down my back. I hiccupped against his chest, fingers scrabbling against his ribs like I wanted to crack him open and crawl inside.

"Tate. My darling man," he cooed, kissing the top of my head. "I'm here. You're okay. Did I hurt you too much? Was it too far?"

Even through the haze of the asphyxiation and the orgasms, I could hear the ever-present worry in his voice. I shook my head against him, licking my lips and trying to draw the words up from my heart.

"No," I rasped, clearing my throat, which only sent me into another coughing and crying spiral.

Brooks soothed me until I settled, and I waited until my arms and legs worked again so I could draw back enough to see his face. His stare was etched with concern, from the tight draw around his mouth to the quick way he blinked as he studied me. I huffed a breath out, testing the pressure against my throat, then I traced my fingers over the stubble on his cheeks.

"Brooks." I tested my voice with his name, and it came out scratchy, but clear.

"I'm sorry." He dragged his trembling fingertips over my throat, frowning. "I went too far."

I curled my fingers around his wrist and jerked his hand away. "Brooks, stop."

"Tate." It was another apology, this one in the shape of my name, and I wanted none of it.

"It was perfect," I said before he could utter another word. He blinked again, brows knitting together. "It was perfect and so were you."

"Tate."

Less of an apology there, which felt like a step in the right direction.

"You're perfect for me," I said again, clarifying my last thought. "Perfect, Brooks, and I love you."

There was a pause.

A breath.

A beat.

And I wasn't sure if he was going to push me away or pull me closer. I was ready to open my mouth and take the whole thing back when his eyes went glassy and before I had time to see if it would turn into tears, he crashed our mouths together and knocked me back down onto the floor.

"I love you," I said again, the words garbled around his tongue.

He reached between our bodies and pushed the tip of his cock against my sensitive hole. I shivered and whimpered, scared, but ready. I spread my legs wider and he pushed his half-hard dick back inside of me. There was still enough of a gape that it didn't hurt as bad as I'd expected it to. All of my feelings tangled together in my stomach, threatening to be everything and nothing all at once. I felt like I was a black hole beneath him, ready to expand beyond comprehension and consume us both.

Once he was inside me again, he didn't move, though. He rocked back onto his ass and pulled me onto his lap, my body sinking deeper around him. Groaning, I dropped my forehead into the crook of his neck, shivering as he drew circles and stars up the sweaty length of my back.

"Tell me again," he said softly, kissing the shell of my ear. "Tell me that when I'm home inside of you."

I bared my teeth against his neck, desperate to sink my teeth into him, to take a part of him for myself like he'd taken all of me.

"I love you," I whispered.

He splayed his fingers against the small of my back and lifted off the floor like he was trying to thrust into me again, but his cock wasn't hard enough and it slipped out with a sticky plop. He took my face into his hands, thumbs chasing the tears that hadn't quit falling, and he leaned close, kissing the salt off my skin that his first pass had missed.

"Are you certain?" he asked, breath hot against the tip of my nose.

"Never been more sure." I managed a weak smile. "I think maybe I have since the first night, but I didn't—"

He cut me off with another kiss, this one slower and deeper...as if such a thing was even possible. Brooks kissed me like either of us had enough stamina to get hard again, and when I had to break away to suck in a much needed lungful of air, he collapsed onto his back with a grunt. He pressed one of his hands against the center of his chest, the other to his forehead, and his lashes fluttered as his eyes fell closed.

I sat beside him and studied him quietly, watching his chest rise and fall in time with my own, even though he couldn't have known that. Finally, he sat back up, moving onto his knees before rising to his feet and holding out a hand for me. I knew what came next was his favorite part, but the thought of getting to my feet and walking myself into the bathroom was a bridge too far.

"I can't," I said, swallowing thickly. "I think you fucked the bones out of me."

He grinned, a quick and exhausted thing, then he stretched and bent down, hooking one arm beneath my knees and the other under my arms. Even in our post-sex state, Brooks lifted me like I didn't weigh more than a book, and I flung my arms around his neck with a startled yelp.

"Bath or shower?" he asked into my hair.

The bench in the shower was nice, but there was no question.

"Bath."

Brooks carried me into the bathroom and lowered me gingerly into the tub before plugging the drain and turning the water on. He sprinkled in some bath salts that smelled like lavender and sage, and then turned to go.

"Bath with you," I clarified, stretching my arm toward him with all the strength I could muster.

"Let me get you some water, Tate." He bent down and grabbed my hand, kissing my knuckles before disappearing and leaving me alone in the tub.

It wasn't until I registered his absence that I realized...

Brooks hadn't said it back.

I couldn't breathe.

Even in the open space of my kitchen that smelled decidedly like coffee and not sex, I couldn't catch a breath. Buck naked, I pressed my hand against the middle of my chest, counting the staccato beats of my heart until they slowed to something I didn't think most doctors would be concerned about.

I'd had a lot of sex in my life, with a lot of different people, but I'd never...*never* had sex like that. It was beyond unbridled, and the sheer vulnerability of the act had stolen not just my ability to breathe, but my ability to speak.

Tate told me he loved me, and I...

Fuck.

Grabbing two bottles of water out of the fridge and the discarded bag of sandwiches we'd dropped in the entryway, I raced back up the stairs. Tate was sprawled in the tub, legs bent at the knee and his arms resting on the edge. He had his head tilted back, eyes open and unfocused on the ceiling. I deposited everything on the floor and climbed into the tub, notching myself between his legs instead of behind him as I'd initially planned. The water poured from the faucet against the backs of my calves, and with what seemed like reflex, Tate wrapped his fingers around my biceps to hold me steady above him.

"I don't deserve it." I shook my head and dipped close to him, knocking our noses together.

"Hmn?"

"Your love," I whispered, swallowing. "I don't trust myself with you sometimes."

"I trust you with me."

Our lips brushed together, his swollen from our earlier kisses...soft and puffy and still slick with spit.

"I didn't mean to not say it back."

Tate smiled against my mouth. "It's my feelings, not yours."

"Stop it." I slid my hand between our lips, breaking the kiss, and I covered his mouth with the tips of my fingers. "That's not what I was going to say."

He hummed against my skin, eyes half closed.

"I love you too," I said, the truth of it settling in my stomach like a stick of cotton candy, making me simultaneously happy and sick. "I've loved you awhile, I think, but I didn't want to say it."

"You're not too much," he murmured against my hand. I let it fall into the water, which was finally at chest level. "Or maybe you are for other people, but not for me."

I wanted desperately to believe it.

Turning away from Tate only long enough to turn off the water, I shifted our bodies into the position I'd originally intended. With my back against the side of the tub, I nestled him between my spread legs, hooking my feet around his ankles to keep his legs spread wide. I doubted either of us had another orgasm to spare, but if we were being vulnerable, then...

I cupped some water into my hand and dripped it down Tate's chest, and he groaned, resting his head against my shoulder and closing his eyes again.

"I've dreamed of a man like you," I said softly into his ear, letting my fingers dance across the slender expanse of his chest, the sharp peaks of his nipples, and down beneath the water to the defined ridges of his abs. "I didn't think you were real."

"Think of all the time we wasted."

"Because you walked away," I reminded him.

"Stupid of me."

I worked my fingers through the short hair around the base of his half-hard cock, doing my best to detangle any cum that had dried in the curls there. Satisfied I'd managed to get it all, I wrapped my fingers around his length, stroking down toward the tip, not with the intent to arouse, but to stretch and clean. I dragged my thumb beneath the flared tip of his crown, and Tate whimpered, turning into me as much as the position would allow, pressing a kiss against my clavicle.

"I'll listen now," he moaned, hips giving a quick push back against my tender and well-used dick.

"I know you will."

"God." Tate groaned, and my fingers worked into the muscles of his thighs. "I've dreamed about you for months."

"Do I live up to the fantasy?" I asked.

I'd gotten as far down his legs as my arms could reach, and I settled back, listening to the quiet lap of water around the tub compete against my heartbeat for loudest sound in the room. Tate's breathing quieted, and I bracketed an arm around his chest, keeping our bodies close while I reached over the side of the tub to get him one of the bottles of water I'd brought from the kitchen.

"You're more than I could have ever imagined for myself," he said softly.

"In two weeks, I'm heading upstate to my friend's farm for the weekend. I'd like for you to come with me."

Tate dropped the bottle of water out of the tub, the plastic bouncing on the floor with a loud thump, then he floated his palms against the surface of the water before flipping his hands over and raising one in the air for me to see. "I'm pruned."

I grabbed his hand and kissed each of the wrinkled pads of his fingers.

"Is that your way of asking to get out of the bath?" I asked. "Or your way of telling me you don't want to come to the farm."

Before he could answer, I was up and out of the tub, wrapping a towel around my waist. I didn't bother to dry off, and I dripped water all over the bag of food, which I'd make sure he ate eventually. I tossed it onto the counter, then grabbed him a towel from the warmer and held it open for him. Tate eyed me thoughtfully, using his toe to flip the drain on the bath. Climbing out carefully, he walked into my arms and I folded the warm terrycloth around him, giving it a few rubs up and down his shoulders to facilitate the drying.

"Just because I love you doesn't mean it doesn't scare me," he said softly, letting the towel fall to the floor.

My mouth went dry, tongue stuck to the roof as I forced a

nervous swallow. Tate picked up the bag of food from the counter and carried it into the bedroom. I collected both discarded bottles of water and went after him. He was still closer to soaking than dry, and he plopped himself down on the foot of the bed, unbothered. The bedding darkened from the wetness that rolled off him, but if he noticed, I never would have known. He patted a spot beside him, and I discarded my towel to join him naked on the bed. In an unexpected twist of roles, Tate was the one to dish out the sandwiches from our long-forgotten dinner, his attention mostly focused on the sprawling skyline beyond the window in front of us.

"It scares me too," I told him.

"It scares you because you don't trust it."

"Why does it scare you?" I asked.

The sandwich wrapper crinkled in my hands, a clump of shredded lettuce falling onto the floor between our feet.

"Because I do." Tate took a bite of his sandwich, chewing and swallowing. "I'd do anything you asked, Brooks. Give you anything. Go anywhere."

"I know you would," I rasped.

He'd already given me so much.

"I'll prove you wrong," he said after another bite. "Or right, depending on how you think about it."

I understood what he was saying, that when all was said and done, he'd prove to me that I'd made the right decision by taking a chance on loving him. That when everything was said and done, we'd come through the other side together, in love, and happy.

Happy.

What a strange idea.

For years, ever since Tyler left, I thought I was happy. I'd convinced myself that being with my friends and having the freedom to pick and choose my partners was the most I wanted out of life. What I deserved. But Tate had blown in like a storm and shown me just how very wrong that fallacy had been. Before him, I'd been a shell of the man I'd used to be, a cardboard cutout of the man I *wanted* to be. And he was here now, giving me the opportunity to step into the life I'd always wanted for myself.

The only person standing in my way was me.

"I know you will," I said.

Re-wrapping the sandwich, I shoved it into the bag and leaned back, stretching my legs out in front of me and following Tate's stare toward the city. After he finished his sandwich, he balled up the wrapper and held it in the air between us until I offered him my outstretched palm. He dropped it and I added it to the bag with a sly smile.

"Water," he said, and I handed him the bottle. He drank half of it in one go, then gave his head a little shake, side to side. "I know this is unhinged, but I want you again."

I scoffed, a shocked sound that caught in the back of my throat and shot out my nose. "There's no way."

"I know," he agreed. "And yet."

I didn't think I had another round in me, but I also didn't have the strength to tell him no. I wanted to give him anything and everything. Wanted to prove I was worthy of everything he was giving.

"Get on all fours," I croaked, pushing to my feet. "Spread yourself apart for me."

Tate cursed under his breath, a red flush creeping up his throat before he turned and assumed the position I'd demanded. Digging his fingers into the globes of his ass, he spread himself open, resting his cheek and chest against the sheets. I trailed my fingers up the backs of his thighs, pressing when I found little bursts of bruises from how hard we'd fucked. The pressure caused him to make happy sounds that had my cock thinking we might stand a chance, but when I got close enough to inspect his hole, I talked myself out of that one quickly.

"You're so gorgeous," I whispered, kneeling on the bed behind him so my breath puffed out against the skin in question. "Swollen and pink...and used."

"Please."

I kissed his hole, licking hot stripes from his balls to the top of his crack until he lost the grip on his cheeks and had to fist the sheets instead. He was hard again, cock jutting toward his face and precum pearling at the tip. Tate wasn't that much younger than me, but I admired the magic of youth that had him ready to go after everything we'd done.

"Touch yourself, Tate."

I had to hold him open to get my tongue inside of his asshole, and the sound that tore out of his throat when I punched past his pucker was enough to send my cock back to full mast again. If I fucked him again, though, it would hurt him, so no matter how much either of us wanted it, I had to be strong enough to refuse. Rimming, that I could do. Tate's hand around his cock moved with quick and jerky thrusts while I ate him out, and ten minutes later, he shot a single spurt of cum onto my sheets. His entire body bowed and bucked like he was dropping gallons of sperm out of his balls, and when he looked down before collapsing into the mess, he let out a hoarse laugh.

"Maybe you were right," he muttered.

I chuckled, hauling him up toward the pillows and kicking down the sheets so we could get properly into bed. My cock burned against the small of his back, and I spit into my hand and slicked my shaft before tucking it between the tight press of his closed thighs. His balls were hot against the top of my cock, and I fucked my way through the soft crevice of his thighs until I shot my load against the underside of his soft and sticky cock.

It was hard to breathe, hard to think, hard to do anything except close my eyes and bury my face into the still wet hair at the back of Tate's head. He reached back blindly, pulling my arm over his waist and threading our fingers together. Between his legs, my cock still throbbed in time with my heart.

"Tate," I whispered his name, only to be met with a half-awake sounding groan.

But even in his state, he managed my name.

"Brooks," he said quietly. Reverently.

"I love you, darling."

Tate hummed and nodded, giving his thigh muscles a squeeze.

"I love you too."

After the drunken nightmare that was Sunday night at Tryst, and the love confessions the night after, Brooks and I were pretty much inseparable. I kept waiting for the newness of him to wear off, but every time he smiled at me, it was a breath of fresh air. By the time Thursday rolled around, I was ready for the weekend *and* also ready for a change of clothes. Brooks had been diligent about ensuring the few items I had at his place were always clean and available for me, but I'd been wearing the same clothes for four days and I needed something new.

Much to his disappointment, I made the decision to stay at my own apartment on Thursday night. The intent was twofold because I also wanted to check in on Dylan. I believed Brooks when he said his friend Alex had been checking on him, but Dylan was my best friend and I needed him to know that even though I had a boyfriend, I was still his best friend and I was still available for him. The only reason I'd been comfortable staying at Brooks' for the week was because

Dylan had kept in touch, responding to my text messages, if not my calls.

When I got home from work on Thursday night, Dylan had his guitar case open on the couch. He was dressed in all black, and the bruising around his neck had turned a barely noticeable shade of yellow. I only saw it because I was looking for it. Most people would have probably thought it wasn't anything more than a shadow. He looked up and caught me starting, and I rubbed the back of my neck, averting my gaze.

"Hey," he said, snapping the case closed.

"Are you leaving?" I asked, realizing he had on shoes, that his messenger bag was slung over his shoulder.

"I got a last-minute gig." His cheeks burned and he lifted his guitar from the couch. "I know I haven't seen you in a few days, but I need the money."

"Right." I held up my hands, like I needed to apologize for my presence. "That's fine. Of course."

"Did you want to come?"

I'd spent the whole day looking forward to crashing on the couch with Dylan and sharing a couple of beers like old times, but in light of the weekend revelations, I wasn't going to say no to something that would make him money and help him out.

"Of course." I tugged the tails of my shirt loose from my slacks. "Just let me change and we can head out."

I changed into jeans and a t-shirt and brushed the product out of my hair so I didn't look so uptight. Dylan was halfway out the door when I got my sneakers on, and I jogged after him down the stairs, texting Brooks to let him know where I was going. It wasn't like I needed to account for my where-abouts, but it felt like the right thing to do.

Me: Going to a gig w Dylan tonight. I'll text you later.
Brooks: I'm with Alex.

The message didn't make sense, but when Dylan and I reached the venue, the meaning clicked into place.

The spot wasn't much larger than a coffee shop, with a small black stage tucked into the far corner with fairy lights strung from the ceiling and hanging down the back wall. There was a worn-down Persian patterned rug on the stage, a short black stool, and a singular microphone in the center. The place was decently busy, most of the attendees looking like some sort of copy of Dylan or myself, which was why Brooks and Alex stood out like two sore thumbs.

Even dressed down in jeans and a t-shirt, Brooks looked like if you cut him open, money would pour out of him. There was something about the way he carried and presented himself that made his class and status indisputable. The two men leaned against the side wall, drinks in hand, heads angled together while they whispered back and forth, completely unaware of our arrival.

"I want you to tell me about Alex," I said to Dylan, following him into the very small backstage area that was more like a closet than a dressing room. It wasn't like he had any prep to do, but I appreciated the private space.

"What about him?" Dylan pulled his guitar from the case and leaned against the wall, giving one last run through some chords to check that it was tuned properly.

"Brooks said Alex had called you. That he was..." I trailed off because I didn't know what to say. I didn't know what Brooks had meant with any of the things he'd told me about his friend, just that it meant Dylan was in good hands and I didn't have to worry about him the times that we weren't together.

"I don't want to talk about Alex with you," Dylan said, looking up at me with tired eyes and half of a frown. "But I promise I'm fine. We can talk about the rest of it if you want to after the gig."

"We don't have to," I said. "I don't want to press."

Dylan squared his shoulders. "I'm not ashamed of it."

"I know." I closed the snaps on his guitar case and propped it up in the corner against a dirty mirror. "I don't want you to be defensive with me. You're my friend and I love you. That's all."

Some of the fight went out of him, the frown lines around his mouth softening until he was less than a second away from a very small smile.

"I made some bad decisions, but I'm not going to do that anymore." Dylan angled his head toward the door. "We have time for a drink before I have to play."

My stomach flipped at the mere idea of drinking liquor, and I made a show of clutching my gut like I was going to be sick at the thought alone. That earned me a smile and a laugh, and Dylan let me wrap my arms around him in a quick hug.

"I'll get water," I told him, opening the door. "Did you know Alex was going to be here tonight?"

As soon as we were out of the dressing room, the noise grew exponentially louder. Dylan set his guitar down on the stage and then linked his arm through mine, weaving through the quickly growing crowd to get to the bar. Brooks and Alex were still in the same spot as when we'd walked in, but Brooks had looked up to scan the crowd, mouth pulling into an honest and pleased smile when he saw me.

"Alex got me the gig," Dylan said before leaning over the bar and shouting an order to the woman on the other side. She gave him a thumbs up, and he dropped back down onto the ground.

"Oh?"

I realized there was already far more to their relationship than I had suspected, but with Brooks and Alex both on their way toward the bar, it wasn't the time to ask. Besides, Dylan had already made it very clear he didn't want to talk about his association with Alex, and I wasn't going to push him.

"I didn't expect to see you here," I said to Brooks, stepping into his embrace when they reached us. He wrapped his arms around me and dropped a quick kiss against the side of my head, then loosened his hold enough for me to turn back toward Dylan.

"I told you I was with Alex."

"You did," I agreed.

Alex maneuvered himself halfway behind Dylan, leaning down and whispering something into his ear when the bartender returned with my bottle of water and his whiskey sour. Dylan clenched his jaw and turned his attention toward his feet, nodding with a quick jerk of his head. I grabbed the water off the bar and twisted off the top, taking a long and cold swallow.

"No drink tonight?" Brooks teased.

"I never want to drink again."

Alex reached around Dylan, took the tumbler and drank it in one gulp. The tips of Dylan's ears were red as a cherry, and Alex set the empty glass back down onto the bar and ordered a second bottle of water. The bartender was quick to leave it, and Dylan snatched it with a scowl before storming off. Alex watched him go, and I took a step to follow after him, but Brooks hooked his thumb through one of my belt loops and dragged me to a stop.

"He's fine," Brooks said.

"He's not." I narrowed my eyes at Alex, who definitely looked like he didn't care about me or my opinions.

"He's not supposed to be drinking tonight," Alex said simply.

I scoffed, letting my attention drift from Dylan's quickly shrinking back to Alex's arrogant face. It wasn't the first time I'd seen him, but it was the first time I had enough concern to actually look at him. He was taller than me, close to six feet if not over, with tanned skin and hair as dark as the frames on his glasses. He looked younger than Brooks, and I wouldn't have put him past thirty.

"Do you trust me?" Brooks whispered in my ear, sliding his arm around my waist and hauling me against his side.

"Of course."

"And you trusted me with Dylan on Sunday?"

"Obviously."

"Then trust him." Brooks jerked his chin toward Alex, who was ordering another bottle of water from the bar.

The lights over the crowd dimmed and the stage spotlight flashed to life, highlighting my best friend sitting on that black stool, guitar in hand. The three of us tried to get closer to the stage, but Alex came to a stop a few people back. We had a clear line of sight to Dylan, but he probably would have had to scan the crowd a few times to find us. He gave a test strum of his guitar, and I rested my head against Brooks, trying to decide if Alex was deserving of the same trust I so freely gave to Brooks.

There weren't a lot of facts to be seen, except that Alex had sexual tastes as curious as Brooks because their entire friend group had memberships to The Black Door. I didn't know if they liked the same things, but whatever it was, it wasn't vanilla. I also knew that, for whatever reason, Alex was the one who'd gotten Dylan this set, and that was a decent thing. Right? I didn't know what his intentions were...didn't understand what he was getting out of the relationship with Dylan. It was hard to not worry about Dylan being taken advantage of, considering the state of things up until four days ago. Who was to say that Alex wasn't also taking advantage of Dylan, just in a different way.

"You're thinking so loud they're going to have to pay you instead of Dylan," Brooks said into my ear, smiling. "I trust Alex with my life, and I would trust him with yours."

That sort of blind faith wasn't given freely, and I tried to relax, knowing that just because I didn't understand what was happening, didn't mean it was wrong. There had to be plenty of people who would question the things Brooks and I did together, but it made sense for us. I didn't want to turn around and be one of those people to Alex...or to Dylan.

"He's safe?"

"They both are." Brooks pulled me in front of him, lifting onto his toes so he could rest his chin against my shoulder. "Now be quiet. I'm trying to watch the show."

I huffed, feigning offense, but it was impossible to not listen and watch when Dylan was on the stage. He was one of the most musically talented people I'd ever met, and I couldn't imagine how hard it had been for him after his parents cut him off. He'd explained why he hadn't told me about it, but I hated it just the same. Dylan always put his heart and soul into his music. I remembered the night he wrote the song he was currently singing. He'd scratched out some lyrics on the back of a takeout bag while I'd laid on the couch beside him tapping my fingers against the edge of our coffee table to give him a beat.

The song ended and before anyone could offer him applause, Dylan launched into another one. With my best friend doing what he loved the most, I relaxed into the solid press of Brooks' body against mine and tried to enjoy the show. In the middle of the third song, I let my stare wander to Alex, and I watched him sing along under his breath and wondered how he already knew the words.

CHAPTER 29

BROOKS

By the time Dylan's gig was over, he was somewhat less defiant than when he'd tried to get a drink earlier in the night, but he was still sharp around the edges, angry and lost. Tate could see it, and it killed him to stay hands off. I didn't know what the dynamic of their friendship had been before, but it didn't take a rocket scientist to tell things had changed. Ten minutes after he'd walked off the stage, Dylan joined our little group, guitar case clutched in his white-knuckled hand. Alex passed him a fresh bottle of water, which Dylan drank without complaint.

For as long as I'd known Alex, his kinks had always been something he kept relatively close to his chest. He played on occasion, but never with the frequency or the interest that I expected from men like Kale and Ford. It wasn't until Alex and Beamer started to hook up that I understood for the first time the things that the two of them preferred. Alex played rough. Rougher than me and with a far more serious undercurrent of submission than any of us cared to pursue. That wasn't something that could necessarily come through safely in a club environment, especially with strangers, so watching Alex go through the heartbreak of losing Beamer put the whole thing into clear perspective for me.

Dylan and Tate were chatting about the gig, and I took the opportunity to grab Alex by the arm and pull him aside. He came freely, eyes watching Dylan for any sign of fight. When he was satisfied that the other two weren't going anywhere, he turned his attention fully to me.

"You're taking that one seriously, aren't you?" I asked, resting my shoulder against the wall.

"You asked me to."

"Only if you wanted," I reminded him.

He threw a glance at the back of Dylan's head. "I wanted."

"Does he?"

Alex answered that with a half-shrug. "He doesn't *not* want it. But I don't think he understands the why of it."

"Not many people do."

"Beamer did," he said.

"Speaking of Beamer." I cleared my throat, searching Alex's face for any tells or clues that would betray whatever words were going to be next out of his mouth. "How would you feel if I invited him and Dalton to the farm next weekend?"

Alex could have been a statue, save for the tic in his jaw.

"I don't think it's your place to invite people to Ford's farm," he finally said.

"It's Boston's farm."

"Same idea."

"I have permission," I assured him.

He sucked in a breath. "I don't think Beamer would want

to come across the country to sit on a stranger's porch and pick corn for a weekend."

"I think he'd fly around the world to see his friends again."

"I'm not your keeper, Brooks." Alex dragged his tongue across the front of his teeth. "You can do whatever you want."

"I still don't know the entirety of what happened between the two of you and I don't want things to be weird. I just thought it would be nice for all of us to be together again."

"It seems cruel to lock Kale in a house with the men he's been the most horrible to," Alex murmured, no doubt thinking about the dramatically offensive way Kale had taken the news about Beamer and Dalton being married, shortly followed by the revelation one of his best friends had been sticking it to his little brother.

"Most of those men are also his closest friends," I pointed out. "He can't live in a sex bubble forever with that little prince of his."

Alex snorted, stare flickering to movement from the place we'd left Tate and Dylan. I looked over to see them both weaving through the thick crowd to the place where the two of us stood near the back wall.

"I'm ready to go," Dylan announced.

"Hold on," Alex told him, turning back to me. "If you think it's a good idea, then I support it."

"I'm asking you if it's a good idea."

"I'll be fine, Astor."

I flipped him off. "Don't first name me to prove a point."

The corner of Alex's mouth hitched into a smile, and he took the guitar case out of Dylan's hand. "I'm a big boy, *Brooks*. I can handle a weekend with my friends."

Tate's stare shifted to the guitar in Alex's hand. "Are you coming back to the apartment?" he asked Dylan.

Dylan cracked his knuckles, plastering on as brave of a smile as he could muster in the situation. "I'm going to Alex's for a bit, but I might be home later."

I watched Tate's face as the cogs and the gears clicked into place and understanding washed over him. It was like he'd known there was something happening between his best friend and my best friend, but he didn't know the what of it.

"I want to spend time with you soon," he said, brow furrowed. "Just the two of us again."

"Monday?"

Tate didn't even bother to look at me for confirmation, which I loved.

"I'll be home after work."

Dylan lunged forward, wrapping his arms around Tate in one of the tightest hugs I'd ever seen. Tate seemed startled, stumbling back from the force of it, but he leaned in and returned the embrace with all the force Dylan had delivered. Dylan's mouth moved, whispering something into Tate's ear that I couldn't hear, and Tate nodded furiously before shoving him back, straight into Alex's tall and strong body. He took my hand, and we watched the two of them go, Dylan's guitar in one of Alex's hands, Dylan's hand in the other, fingers tightly wrapped together.

"I guess I should get going," Tate finally said, giving his neck a crack from side to side. "It's a work night and it's late."

"Did you take the train?"

"We walked most of it," he said. "Did you take a cab?"

"Town car," I said.

A smile pulled at the corners of Tate's mouth. "Of course you did."

"Do you want to take a car home with me?"

"I was supposed to stay home tonight," he reminded me, pressing a finger against the middle of my chest. "Get some clean clothes, see my best friend."

"You saw your best friend," I said.

"Barely." The earlier furrow in his brows was back, deeper than before. Watching Tate's shift between emotions was giving me whiplash. "Alex stole him."

"Alex is..." I didn't have a good answer.

"Helping," Tate whispered. "Right?"

"Dylan needs support right now, more than what you can give him, I think. That's no fault of yours."

"And Alex gives him that?"

"Alex needs support too," I said. "He's been sad for a very long time and I think that whatever is going on with him and Dylan is helping to fix that."

"Are they in a relationship?" he asked.

"I don't think I'd call it that," I answered. "At least, not in the way you and I are in a relationship."

The smile was back, and I was dedicated to making sure it won out over the frown for the rest of the night. I curled my fingers around his wrist and raised it to my mouth, dragging a kiss—with teeth—across the thin skin.

"Take me back to your apartment, Tate." I kissed the heel of his palm, nipping into the calloused skin just below his thumb.

Tate's lashes fluttered, and even in the dark of the club, I knew he was blushing.

"I can get my clothes and we can go," he murmured, leaning into me as I kissed my way to the tip of his thumb.

"I want to sleep in your bed," I told him.

"It's small."

I swirled my tongue around the tip of his pointer finger. "I'm short."

"I'm glad you didn't say you were small." Tate licked his lips, other hand sliding down between us. "Because that would have been a lie."

"You insatiable little thing," I teased. "Is sex the only thing you think about?"

"Sex and what comes after."

Even though Tate had shown me over and over that he was in it with me for real, the mention of aftercare sent a bolt of panic straight down my spine. It wasn't as sturdy or as pronounced as it used to be, but the connection was still there...not entirely frayed.

"I love the way you take care of me after you make love to me," he said, pressing our bodies together and sealing his lips against my ear.

That was the first time anyone had ever called the way I liked to fuck *making love*, and my first thought was to protest the absurdity of it...but it was true. Wasn't it? Even before I loved Tate, I loved fucking, and...it made sense in a way that I'd never thought of before. No wonder it was always too much for everyone else.

No wonder...

"I love it when you push inside of me again to fill me up a third or fourth time. When I cry because it's all just so..." His breath against my ear was a wildfire, out of control and all-consuming.

"So what?" I pressed, needing to get him out of a public establishment before we both caught a charge for public indecency.

"I've never felt more loved than when I'm with you, Brooks."

It wasn't the answer I expected, but it was the answer I needed.

"We're getting out of here now." I still had his hand and I turned him toward the door. "And I'm going to fuck you on every surface in your apartment."

"You've seen my apartment. It's a shoebox," he said with a laugh. "There's like two surfaces in the whole place."

"Then I suppose I'll have to make them count."

I wanted to call a car, but by the time I got my phone out of my pocket, Tate was already halfway down the block. Tugging him to a stop at a red light, I flagged down a cab and shoved him into the back. Tate gave his address to the driver and I attacked his neck, sucking a bruise onto his collarbone as the car sped through the intersection. A short five minutes later, we came to a stop. I threw far more cash than necessary at the driver and hauled Tate out of the car.

The stairs to his apartment took an eternity, and I was glad Dylan wasn't home because as soon as Tate got the deadbolts unlocked, I had him against the wall with his pants around his knees. Pressing my forearm against his shoulders, I ripped my belt off and let my pants fall down to my ankles. I didn't know my way around his apartment, and I was far too wound up to wait, so I spit on my hand, spread saliva down the length of my cock, and shoved it between the tight squeeze of Tate's thighs.

"No," he whined, fighting against me. "I want you inside of me."

I thrust my hips up, fucking my cock against the underside of his balls with as much force as if I'd been penetrating his hole.

"You'll get it when I'm ready," I promised, bracketing my spit-slick hand against his bare hip for better leverage.

More than anything, I wanted to bury myself inside of him, but the need to mark him was an urgent and nearly tangible thing. It was rough and raw in a way that felt out of the norm for me, but Tate moaned into it, reaching down and wrapping his hand around his shaft.

"Hands on the wall, Tate," I warned, digging my fingers into the curve of his hip until he spread both of his hands flat against the wall. I shoved his chest into the brick, getting harder when the breath pushed out of his lungs from the landing.

"It hurts," he whimpered, fingers curling around the bricks as I resumed fucking between his thighs.

My own end was within reach, sparkling and close to the periphery, and I knew it hurt Tate to not touch himself. I wanted him to hurt, needed him to endure it for me. I hoped there wasn't something wrong with me, something cruel and unusual about the way I made love—as he called it—but when Tate's eyes rolled back as I fucked against him one last time, I knew if anything was wrong with me, he was just as afflicted.

I painted the insides of his legs and the exposed brick wall in his hallway with hot spurts of cum. My dick still leaked when I fisted the back of his hair and dragged him deeper into his apartment, folding him in half over the coffee table and going to my knees between his spread legs.

"You make me believe I can hold onto things that I don't deserve," I whispered, rucking up the back of his shirt and spreading his ass apart with greedy fingers. I licked my cum from his thighs and his balls, then speared my tongue into his asshole.

Tate's entire body lurched forward, knocking an empty beer bottle and a discarded spiral notebook onto the floor. I sucked and ate his asshole until I could get two fingers inside of him and the precum leaking from his cock dripped down to the floor. With his face smashed into the coffee table, he babbled mindlessly, eyes screwed shut and hips bucking.

My entire body was on fire with need for him—with love—but my fingers shook, making it hard to get deeper inside of him. I was grateful he wasn't looking because the last thing I wanted was for him to see how frantic he made me, how uncontrolled. Tate made me lose my mind, he made me lose myself, and he'd been right earlier.

This thing between us, it was the purest kind of love.

I whispered that into his ear as I notched the head of my cock around his kiss-swollen asshole, and when I pushed my whole length into him, he burst into tears, thanking me over and over as he came all over the floor.

I WAS ONE HUNDRED PERCENT CERTIFIABLY IN LOVE. I'D ALREADY told Brooks, but somehow I woke up every day feeling the truth of it in the ache of my bones and in the satisfaction that wrapped around me like a weighted blanket.

The morning after Dylan's gig, just when I thought things couldn't get any better, Brooks woke me up with my cock in his mouth. He sucked me until I screamed, clamping a hand over my mouth as I thrashed around the bed and spilled into the back of his mouth. Then he crawled up my body, spit my cum into my mouth, and kissed me until all I could taste was him. Sending me to work with an erection the size of the Empire State Building was cruel, but by the time I got to his place at the end of the day, I was ready to explode.

My week again rushed by in a flurry of sex and sleep, and then the weekend was upon us and it was time for our trip up to the farm. To say I was nervous about being with Brooks' friends would have been an understatement. Even though I'd met them all on more than one occasion, the setting of his friend's upstate farm felt more casual than anything we'd done before. Brooks assured me all his friends were teddy bears, but that was only half the worry.

Alex was coming for the weekend and Dylan was not.

"I promise you, I'll be fine," Dylan swore to me in the middle of our kitchen, my duffle bag packed with clothes I wouldn't mind getting dirty.

"I know."

Even though I'd spent most of the week still with Brooks, I'd heard that Alex had been chasing Dylan around, doing whatever it was they'd been doing. Even though Dylan hadn't divulged any secrets about the nature of their relationship, I was under the impression it had to do with Alex making decisions and Dylan taking orders, which I didn't think was going to be sustainable. Maybe for Alex, but definitely not for Dylan.

"I'll check in if it makes you feel better," he said, a half-empty water bottle crinkling as he squeezed it, the tension in his grip not betrayed in the slightest by the cool expression on his face.

"With me or with Alex?"

At the mention of Alex's name, Dylan's face flushed red and his eyes darkened.

"I'll check in," he repeated, not clarifying one way or the other.

I dropped my bag and hauled Dylan over to the couch to sit. It felt like a lifetime ago we'd tucked our bodies into the cushions and shared stories of our weekend adventures. Mine had mostly been chasing down men who could never be like Brooks, and his had been gig after gig and bartending stories that had us laughing until we were blue in the face. Knowing now that he'd been cut off, that he'd been putting himself at risk.

"Are you still doing sex work?" I asked, taking the water bottle out of his hand and setting it on the table. "I don't care if you are. There's nothing wrong with it. I just want you to be safe about it."

"I made a couple of bad decisions, Tate." He touched his throat, the bruising gone. "I'm not making a habit of it."

"Can we talk about this before I go?"

For two weeks, we'd been skirting around all of the problems in Dylan's life, and I didn't want him to think for one second that just because I had a boyfriend I didn't have time for him anymore. He hadn't bothered to share with me in the first place, and that was a trend I wanted to stop as much as the bad decision-making when it came to the jobs he took.

"Fine." He sighed, kicking his legs up onto the coffee table.

It was as if he wanted to look casual, but his fingers drummed nervously against the top of his thigh and his eyes darted around, looking anywhere in our shoebox apartment besides my face.

"Why did your parents cut you off?" I asked.

It was a start.

"They told me my interest in music had gone on long enough," he said.

I scoffed. The idea was absurd. Dylan's parents had funded his pursuit of music for his entire life. It was thanks to their dedication to him and the money they forked out for lessons that he was half the artist I knew him to be. The rest was him, of course. Pure and unbridled talent.

"They said if I hadn't made a go of it by then, by now, that there was no point in pursuing it further."

"What did they want you to do?"

"My dad was pushing an internship with his top VP," he

said, frowning. "Quit the music, drop out of school, quit the bartending, and get a nine-to-five."

"That's not you."

"Something honest." His tone came off mocking, and I knew it had to be a verbatim commentary from his parents.

"And you told them no?"

"I asked for more time," he explained. "I had been enjoying the gigs here and there, but I hadn't been *trying* to make a big go of it."

"Because you didn't have to."

Dylan sighed, shrugging. "I was trying to do both, but they changed the rules. They said I'd had enough time."

"I still wish you would have told me," I said.

"You barely make enough to cover your half, Tate. What would you have done?"

Licking my lips, I hesitated before deciding to reach forward and grab his hand in mine. "We could have figured it out together. You're my best friend here, Dylan."

"I didn't want it to be your burden."

"You're not a burden."

He snorted, rolling his eyes, giving me the impression he'd been told quite the opposite on more than one occasion, and I hated that for him. Hated that he hadn't felt safe to share with me or that I'd been too consumed with my own shit to notice the change in his behavior.

"I saw the way you were hooking up. Not that what you were doing was wrong, but how you were looking for something so specific with it and always falling short. I figured there had to be a market for it."

My blood ran cold, palms going clammy. "Please don't tell

me you were out taking jobs with men who fuck the way Brooks does."

"The way his friends do," Dylan whispered knowingly.

"Have any of them hurt you?"

He was quick to shake his head. "Alex is the only one I've been with, and no. He...well...no. Alex isn't like that."

"I don't know a single thing about him."

Dylan loosed a scornful little laugh. "He's a good man. A little lost is all."

"Like you."

He rolled his eyes at me again. "Anyway, they cut me off and I changed career course. It worked really well for a while, and then I just had a string of bad luck with it."

"You could have died," I said, dropping his hand. "Why didn't you just call your parents and take the job back? It wouldn't have to be a forever thing, just a for now thing."

"You can't really be asking me to settle when you never could."

I reeled back, caught off-guard by the honesty in the comment, and the truth of it too.

"You're right," I agreed. My phone vibrated in my pocket, and I knew without looking that it was Brooks letting me know he was downstairs and waiting for me. Dylan's stare flickered toward the sound, and he pasted a smile on his face that would have read as sincere had it reached his eyes.

"You'll be back on Monday," he said. "So will Alex, if that makes you feel better."

"I don't know how I feel about Alex."

"Neither do I." His eyes sparkled, a flash of sincerity. "But he has helped more than he's hurt."

"I'm sure you could still come with him this weekend if you asked."

"That's not what we are to each other." Dylan stood up, clearing his throat and tossing my duffel bag onto my lap. The weight of it knocked the wind out of me, and I grabbed it to stand.

"Will you call me if you need anything?" I asked.

"I won't need anything."

"But if you do?"

Dylan sighed. "I'll let you know. Maybe Monday night we can hang out and you can tell me all about it?"

It was the first hint of my old best friend that I'd seen in two weeks, and some of the dread evaporated, making way for a pinprick of light at the end of the tunnel.

"I'd like that," I told him, wrapping him into a quick hug before he could get away from me.

Dylan wasn't a hugger and he fought it before settling into my arms and dropping his nose into the crook of my neck on a heavy exhale. His shoulders sagged, and I was happy to hold the weight of him until he was ready to pull away.

"When I get back, I want to talk about the money and the rent," I told him. "You're my best friend and I've been caught up in my own shit. I want to be a better friend to you."

"You're in love," he said, like that excused or explained it.

"And you're my best friend," I repeated. "I can do both."

Dylan wormed out of the hug and I gave him one last look before grabbing my bag and slinging it over my arm. There was a knock at the door, and much like the unread message, I knew it was Brooks.

"There's your man," Dylan said, turning his back on me

and heading for the door. He unlocked it and pulled it open, drawing in a sharp gust of Brooks' sandalwood soap as he did.

"Sorry," I called from the living room, checking my pockets and my bag to make sure I had everything I needed for the trip.

"You're fine, darling," he said. "The farm isn't going anywhere and I'm told the corn doesn't pick itself."

"Are you really picking corn?" Dylan asked, pressing his back against the wall to reveal Brooks on the doormat in a pair of worn jeans and a fitted gray t-shirt. He had on a pair of running shoes, fancy watch still around his wrist and not an ounce of pomade in his hair. The dichotomy of him, half put together and half taken apart, fried my brain. For the life of me, I couldn't decide which version of him was hotter, though I did favor the version of him buried balls deep inside of me, cock spurting cum while he pressed my face into the floor.

Or the pillows.

Or the wall.

"I think the day laboring is to be determined." Brooks held out his hand and I handed him my bag.

"Sorry to keep you waiting," I told him.

"Nonsense." He threw my bag over his shoulder and turned to Dylan. "Are you sure you don't want to come?"

"Did Alex put you up to this?"

"Alex says you're your own man."

Dylan swallowed, nodding. "I don't want to go, but thank you for checking. I already promised Tate that I'll be fine here."

"I'm sure you will be," Brooks murmured, reaching for my hand. "Are you ready?"

"Yeah."

I said goodbye to Dylan one last time, then followed Brooks downstairs to where a black town car idled in the street.

"I know this is a stupid question, but doesn't it get expensive to be driven around everywhere?" I asked.

Brooks opened the back door before the driver could get out and around to us, and I bent over to climb inside, which earned me a low growl from his throat.

"My accountant will tell me if I have to stop, which…I don't expect to ever happen."

He crawled in after me and closed the door.

"I wish Dylan's parents could be like yours," I said.

Brooks hummed thoughtfully, pressing a button on the door that rolled up a tinted security screen between us and the driver. "Everything I have came with more stipulations than you can imagine. But I was brought up knowing how to play the game. I gave them their way long enough to make sure I could get what I wanted out of it."

"They bought your penthouse."

"A substantial investment, but they hated what I do for work. They didn't see the worth in it."

"In helping other people?" I found that hard to believe.

"They were fans of helping themselves. Much like Dylan's parents, I imagine. Though to a lesser degree." Brooks sighed dramatically, dropping his hand onto my thigh. "I don't want to talk about anyone's parents this weekend, though."

"What do you want to talk about?" I asked. "We have a long drive."

"I'd like to spend most of the drive not talking at all," he murmured, turning his head toward me at the same time as he slid his hand around to the inside of my thigh. "But first I want to know if you submitted your passport documents."

His fingertips grazed over my sac and I arched off the seat, hips bucking toward his hand whether I wanted them to or not. "The day after you paid for it."

"Good," he said softly, working his way toward my zipper. He pulled it down with an achingly slow precision, and he moved his hand inside, over the top of my boxer briefs, even slower. "Now, onto the not talking portion of our drive."

Tate tipped his head back, lashes fluttering like butterfly wings when I flexed my hand around his cock. He was half hard, hot and already leaking precum by the time my thumb dragged through his slit, and the moan that fell out of his mouth was music to my ears.

"It's not soundproof back here, darling," I warned, shifting my weight so I could cover his mouth with my free hand. He blinked his eyes open, revealing wide and dark pupils, deep with enough lust that my own cock jerked at the sight of it.

Tate grunted against my palm, teeth bared as I tightened my hold around his shaft. I wanted to fuck him there, more than I'd ever wanted him, I thought, but the logistics of managing that in the back seat of a larger than normal, but smaller than a limousine, town car was something I hadn't put much forethought into.

"Give me your hands," I said, and he lifted his ass off the seat and stuck his wrists at my face. It was careless, but I made quick work of getting him unbuckled, then I wound the seatbelt around his wrists and latched it back into place. It twisted his body to the side, hands restrained against the seat, cock accessible through the fly of his pants. He grunted, and whether it was in protest or approval, I wasn't sure. His face and body told me he wanted it and Tate knew what words to use to make it stop.

I tugged his pants down until his bare ass was pressed against the seat, but the denim was in my way, so I pulled his jeans and his underwear all the way down to his ankles before situating myself back between his half-spread legs. Reaching up, I shoved two of my fingers into his mouth, depressing his tongue and reaching for the back of his throat. He sputtered and gagged, muscles seizing around me as I reached deeper.

"Get them wet, Tate," I said, voice quiet. "And settle down before he pulls over to check on your welfare back here."

He sealed his lips around my knuckles and sucked like if he was good enough at it, cum would spurt out of my fingertips. I appreciated his eagerness and decided that when all was said and done, I'd be sure to let him use the lube after all. But said and done was definitely not going to be in the back of this car. It might not even be this weekend at all.

Spit leaked down his chin, and I imagined they were as wet as he could get them. I pulled my fingers out of his throat, my dick surging at the sounds Tate made when he caught a breath. Teasing behind his balls and lower still, I hauled him to the edge of the seat to allow myself more access. The back seat was bigger than most cars, but still cramped, and the heels of my own shoes dug into my ass, knees resting against the floor. I traced spit-slick swirls around the soft skin between Tate's balls and his asshole, then I teased both fingers into him at the same time.

He moaned, spreading his legs wider and using the

muscles of his ass to grab around my knuckles. Sweat had already started to bead on his forehead and he looked positively debauched...and I'd barely gotten him going.

"Be quiet," I warned again. I was too far below him to reach his mouth and he wasn't going to be able to gag himself with his hands ratcheted to the seat. "Did you need help?"

"I need you," he whispered.

I needed him too. More than he'd ever know.

I tore both his shoes off his feet and then fought his pants the rest of the way down until I could get his underwear off. His boxer briefs were still wet with precum, and I balled them up, shoving them as deep into his mouth as the material would reach. Tate made a choked-off gagging sound, eyes rolling back in his head as I pushed both of my fingers into his asshole again.

"That's better, yes?" I asked, tone teasing.

He nodded fervently, jerking his hands against the seatbelt. He was tied up and tied down, sucking in breaths of his own arousal while I fucked his asshole with my fingers and his cock with my fist. Tate's erection was long and hard, thick with the skin pulled taut and hot to the touch. He'd gotten enough spit onto my fingers that his hole made indecent squelching noises as I pushed into him, spitting down onto my hand so I could add a third.

Tate tried to shout, the sound barely smothered by the cotton in his mouth. I'd told him earlier the driver would stop if he made too much noise, but the truth was Tate could scream the roof off the car and he would have kept rolling on. I paid a lot of money for the luxuries in my life, discretion being at the top of that list.

With three fingers buried to the knuckle, I levered myself

up off the floor of the car so I could get deeper into Tate's body. He thrashed beneath me, fighting so hard he locked the seatbelt in place, which only caused him to fight harder. Against my palm, his cock thickened, and I smiled, kissed his forehead, and pulled away from him entirely. Tate screamed against the gag, tears springing out of his eyes before he even had a chance to think about holding them back. His cock cried too, precum leaking out of his tip and sliding down toward his balls, which were hardly visible for how high they'd lifted toward his body.

"I want you beyond belief," I whispered, fighting my own fly down and taking my cock into my hand.

I laid myself on top of him, as much as the position would allow, stroking my cock against his while leaving his erection untouched. Tate's eyes flew open, wide and frantic, and I pressed a kiss against the top of his mouth, getting more of his underwear against my lips than his skin.

"I want you so much I can't stand it," I told him, stroking myself so the head of my cock bumped against his swollen and slippery head. I repositioned, jerking myself against his tender balls, his stretched and ready asshole.

The seatbelt continued to hold him tight against the back of the seat, so when I stroked myself to completion, he was helpless to do anything besides whine and choke. I shot all over the dark and hot skin of his shaft, using the side of my finger to drag it up to his slit and push it inside.

After gathering my cum with the tips of my fingers, I pulled Tate's underwear out of his mouth. He sucked in a sputtering breath, which I quickly cut off by shoving my fingers into his mouth. He immediately closed his lips and sucked me clean, swirling his tongue around my fingers and chasing after every drop of my release he could catch. His hips bucked again off the seat, chasing after friction he wasn't going to find.

"Look what you do to me," I whispered, kissing my way toward his ear. The salty tear stains on his cheeks were enough to draw another dribble out of my dick, which I promptly rubbed against his asshole. My leg was asleep from the awkward twist of my body, but the way Tate whined and whimpered against my hand made the discomfort worth it. "When we get to the farm, I'm going to take such good care of you, darling."

It wasn't a lie.

Tate would be restless and needy by the time we arrived, even worse off after enduring dinner and drinks with my friends and their significant others. I imagined he would beg for it by the time we made it to bed, and as a reward for his graciousness and his patience, I'd give him everything he asked for.

"I love you," Tate gasped, trying again to get loose of the seatbelt and falling short. "I need you so much."

"I'm yours." I licked my way back down to his mouth. "I'm right here, Tate."

He dropped his head against the back of the seat with a groan, and I smiled against his lips, kissing down his chin to his throat. He tasted like tears and sweat and cum and soap. He tasted like he was mine.

"You're not going to let me come, are you?"

"Not in this car," I said.

Another tear slid from the corner of his eye, outlining the dimple of his nostril before spreading out over his upper lip. I kissed him there too, catching my breath. Once I could hear more than the thunderous beat of my own heart, I reclined off of Tate just far enough to get him re-dressed, sans underwear, of course. I took my time with his shoes and his socks, tightening and knotting the laces before collapsing with a huff into my seat beside him.

Tate rolled his head to face me, expression tight but sated.

"Would you stay like this the whole ride?" I asked, pulling at the seatbelt around his wrists.

He hummed, nodding and closing his eyes.

My perfect, tired, darling man.

"I love you too," I whispered, undoing the latch and unwinding the nylon from his wrists and pulling him over the hump of the center seat so I could reach him better. Tate sagged against me with a groan, and I massaged my thumbs into his wrists, wearing the striped pattern of the belt out of his skin. Minutes passed, and Tate finally cleared his throat.

"I almost forgot how well you massage."

"Then I'm failing you." I brought his wrists to my mouth and kissed each one before moving my fingers up toward his forearms to knead those muscles next.

He pried open one of his eyes, giving me a wary expression before he sighed and settled back against the seat.

"What was that for?" I asked.

"You say things like that sometimes, but you mean them."

"Did I not mean it now?"

"You meant it, but not as a shortcoming I don't think." Tate groaned when I pressed into a knot. "Not in the way you used to."

I traced my tongue across the underside of my top teeth, thinking about how I understood what he'd meant, even if the delivery had been far from clear. Even though our relationship was new, in the earlier days of it, I was filled with doubt, worried that I was going to do the wrong thing or too much of the right thing, and lose him entirely. That fear wasn't gone, but it was a far softer thing than it had been before, and the thought hadn't even crossed my mind when I'd made the comment.

"I really meant I just need to up my game," I clarified, kissing the top of his head.

"A month ago, you would have died before saying something like that."

"You're not wrong," I agreed.

My fingers were starting to cramp from the awkward angle of the massage I'd set up to give Tate, so I forced myself through it until I reached his elbows, then I lowered both of his hands into my lap. He turned his palms up and threaded our fingers together. I tipped my chin toward my chest to admire the way our hands fit together, the way our fingers twined like a braid.

"You know so much about me," I said, turning our hands over to study the connection points from the other side. "But I don't know much about you."

"You know more than most," he said softly.

"I know how you look when you come."

"And you know how to *make* me come."

I chuckled, remembering Tate's fruitless pursuit of a man like me after our first night together.

"So, more than most after all."

He laughed, tucking himself against my chest. I should have buckled him up, but I wrapped my arm around his shoulder instead, trusting myself—maybe for the first time—to keep him safe.

THE REST OF THE DRIVE, I TOLD BROOKS EVERYTHING ABOUT MY LIFE that I could remember. From growing up as an only child and playing baseball until junior high, to making the decision to come to New York for an out-of-school internship that I was sure would be my ticket to a six figure desk job. I told him how I met Dylan and how our roommate relationship had blossomed into the closest friendship I'd ever had, and Brooks stroked his fingers through my hair, telling me the same facts in return. Most of his friends had met in college, the rest of them coming along soon after. He told me about the fifth friend in their group who had moved to California and how much that had affected Kale. Hearing the chain of events that had led up to *our* meeting put a lot of things into perspective for me, and I wasn't sure if I liked Kale Sheffield, but... Brooks did.

Hours after leaving the city, we arrived at his friend's farm. The town car turned down a long gravel road in the middle of nowhere, driving up to a sprawling farmhouse with what had to have been acres of trees and farm spreading out toward the horizon. Based off what he'd told me on the drive, I'd expected a mass of cars in the drive, but there was only one.

Brooks grabbed our bags from the trunk and dropped them on the porch. Light filtered through a glass cut-out in the door, and he didn't even have time to knock before the door swung open. I recognized Ford immediately, even dressed down in a pair of soft looking jeans and a faded NYU hoodie. His feet were bare and he had a knife in one hand, which should have been more alarming than it was, but the smile on his face was sincere when he saw his friend.

"You're early," Ford said by way of greeting, smiling at Brooks, then at me. "Good to see you again, Tate."

"I'm surprised you remember my name," I admitted. "I don't think you even asked for it."

"Guilty as charged, but Brooks hasn't shut up about you. Come in, come in." He gestured toward the interior of the house with the knife, and we followed him inside.

I didn't think I'd ever been in a farmhouse, so I didn't know what to expect, but Ford and Boston's farm looked like just any other house. There were two matching pairs of dirty boots inside the door, but beyond that, it looked like a normal, open floor plan home. Ford gave us a quick—and unnecessary—tour, considering everything was exposed on the main floor. His boyfriend, Boston, was in the kitchen, surrounded by vegetables, a smear of dirt on his cheek.

"Your first guests have arrived," Brooks announced.

Boston glanced up at him with a crooked smile, using the top of his wrist to push a pair of black glasses up his nose.

"Not quite," a voice from behind us said, and Brooks turned so quick, he almost fell over.

"Holy shit," he said, brushing past me to the tall blond man who had appeared in the hallway. "You actually came."

The two men embraced in a hug, Brooks clapping his hand against the other man's back and hugging him so hard they both stumbled into the wall.

"That's Beamer," Ford said to me, folding his arms in front of his chest, eyes trained on his friends.

"Who names their kid Beamer?" I asked.

"His name is Carter Emerson Royce IV," Ford corrected himself. "Kale has always called him Beamer. His husband calls him Ivey."

"What am I meant to call him?"

"Whatever feels right, I suppose. But his husband doesn't enjoy when other people call him Ivey."

"So, Beamer," I said with a laugh.

"Safe bet."

An equally tall, dark-haired man with dark five-o-clock shadow pushed out from behind the tangled friends, hovering to the side until Brooks and Beamer had finished saying their hello's.

"Good to see you again, Dalton," Brooks said, extending his hand for a shake.

Dalton looked like he wasn't sure he believed it, but he returned the gesture with a curt nod.

"This is Tate," Brooks said, hauling Beamer toward where Ford and I stood half in the kitchen. "Tate, this is Beamer and his husband, Dalton."

I shook both of their hands, trying to swallow back the varying levels of nervousness and discomfort that had begun to bloom around the base of my spine. They'd all known each other for years, and I felt like an interloper in their space. My history with Brooks was a short one, and these men had decades between them. Beamer said something to Ford, who pointed at him with the knife before heading around the counter to resume whatever he'd been chopping when we arrived.

"They're more manageable on their own," Dalton said, giving me a cockeyed smile. "Together they're a lot. My friends are the same."

"Am I that obvious?" A weak laugh bubbled out of my throat.

"How long have you and Brooks been together?" he asked.

"Not long. A couple months almost."

Dalton swiped his tongue across his lower lip, mouth twitching into a smile. "When you know, you know, right?"

"You could say that," I rasped.

"Don't let any of them bully you about it," Dalton warned. "Or him."

I nodded.

"Tate," Boston called out to me from the kitchen. "Can I get you something to drink? Or eat? Or did you want to take a quick rest after the drive?"

"I'm good," I said, flexing my fingers to stretch my hands out of fists.

"You look like you want to throw up."

I glanced at Brooks, who was enthralled with whatever story Beamer was telling him. Ford stood beside them, amusement coloring his features as he listened to the story. We'd talked so much in the car about his life and my life and *our* life, and this was far from the first time I'd seen him with his friends, but for maybe the second time it seemed like I was seeing Brooks in his element. The first, of course, being the night I met him at The Black Door, sitting on that overstuffed chair like a goddamn king. Here, though, in his best friend's kitchen, he looked like an uncovered version of himself. And when I'd thought it impossible to love him anymore, he caught my eye from across the room and winked.

"He's fine," Dalton said, knocking into my arm with his shoulder. "Aren't you?"

I smiled back at Brooks, heat burning my cheeks. "I'm good."

"Enjoy it while it lasts," Boston said, pushing a cutting board away from him. "My brother gets here in the morning."

Beside me, Dalton grumbled.

"He's better than before," Boston said, but Dalton's expression indicated he didn't believe it. Boston must have read the confusion on my face because he sighed, then explained, "My brother is a prick who thinks he's in charge of everyone he knows and it's been a steep learning curve for him to learn he's not."

"That's polite," Dalton murmured.

Boston rolled his eyes. "He's more than welcome to stay in the city."

"He wouldn't miss a chance to see Ivey," Dalton said, gazing fondly at his husband.

Whatever conversation Ford, Brooks, and Beamer were having wrapped up, and all three of them turned their eyes in our direction. The intensity and the weight of their stares was nearly uncomfortable, but the corner of Brooks' mouth quirked into a smile and his gaze flickered down to my fly. I moved quickly, covering my zipper with my hand. It was done up, but the weight and the press of my hand might as well have been a vibrator for how fast the pleasure shot through me.

In the noise of our arrival, I'd almost forgotten the torture Brooks had inflicted on me in the car on the drive from the city, but the heat of his stare sent me straight to the back seat, seatbelt knotted around my wrists while Brooks rutted against me to get himself off.

"Drinks on the back porch?" Ford asked, which earned an eye roll from Boston.

"They're something else when they're all together," he said, even as he pulled a bottle of gin out of a cabinet.

"Trophy Doms," Dalton said with a laugh. He moved around Boston to get glasses, already familiar with the kitchen. "At least, that's what my friend's boyfriend calls us back home."

"Ford's head might explode if he hears that one," Boston said.

I scratched the back of my neck, trying to not be in awe of how perfectly the name fit. Brooks had filled me in about enough of the history that I knew from *their* friend group, Beamer had been the exception to the nickname, but Dalton... the man was beyond intimidating, yet anything but scary. He only had eyes for his husband, and Brooks...

He broke away from his friends, watching me like I was a prize. I swallowed, stuck in place as he reached me, taking my hand and dusting a kiss across the tips of my fingers.

"You look like a deer in headlights," he said softly just to me, while the rest of his friends poured and mixed drinks in the kitchen.

"It's a lot," I admitted.

"I'm sure having so much blood between your legs isn't helping."

"I was fine until I touched myself," I whispered.

"Then I didn't do a good enough job in the car." He smiled, then raised a hand toward his friends. "Ford, we want to wash up before we settle in. Where's the guest room?"

I knew Brooks wanted to do anything *except* freshen up, but I also knew better than to protest. Ford took a quick swallow of his drink then headed back for us, grabbing our bags from where Brooks had dropped them on our arrival. He led us down the hallway Beamer and Dalton had appeared from, and I realized the farmhouse was far larger than it looked from the main room.

The guest room was the same size as my bedroom at home, but it was more than enough for the weekend. The oak bed was made with navy sheets, and two matching night-stands on either side held modern-looking black iron lamps. It was a unique juxtaposition of city life outside the city limits.

"We'll be on the back porch," Ford explained. "Bathroom is across the hall."

"Thank you," I said, stepping away when he and Brooks exchanged a quick look that I couldn't make sense of.

Ford closed the door behind him, and as soon as the lock latched in place, Brooks was on me, backing me against the wall and sliding his hands up underneath my shirt. He kissed the curve of my neck, and I bit back a groan, immediately falling back into the same headspace from the car.

"I liked seeing you aren't intimidated by my friends," he said, nipping his way up to my ear.

"I'm very intimidated," I told him, bracketing my hands over his hips so I didn't fall over. "By them and by you."

"I'm a church mouse," he teased, moving quick and slanting our lips together to kiss any potential protest right out of my mouth.

"Please, Brooks."

He tweaked my nipples, a little bit harder than was nice.

"Please what, darling?" He smiled against my mouth. He sucked my tongue, and my knees gave out entirely. He used his body weight to push me up against the wall so I didn't fall, his knee lodged between my legs.

"Please can I come?"

"Of course you can come, Tate." He pressed his knee against my balls. "Later."

"I hate you."

"You love me."

I huffed out a breath that sounded a whole lot like a sigh, and Brooks stepped away, using those cruel and skilled fingers to tuck my erection away so his friends wouldn't be able to see it, though I doubted that much mattered. They were the way they were and we were the way we were. None of them hid the things they liked when they were out at the club, so I didn't imagine they would bother hiding it in the privacy of their homes.

"I love you," I said.

"I promise that I'll give you the best orgasm of your life before bed tonight, darling." Brooks brushed my hair away from my face. "You're so patient and perfect. I'll make it all worth it, I swear."

Screwing my eyes closed, I nodded.

I believed every word.

After running a shower for Tate, I left him to compose himself and joined my friends on the porch. Boston had finished chopping vegetables in the kitchen and he was relaxing on a bed swing with his hands threaded together behind his head and his eyes closed. There were chairs farther down the length of the porch, and I found Ford, Beamer, and Dalton there, a bottle of gin and three glasses between them. Ford kicked his bare foot at one of the open chairs, and I threw myself down into it with a tired sigh.

"Did you fuck Tate into a state of unconsciousness?" Ford asked, passing me his half-full glass.

"He's in the shower." I took a drink, smacking my lips at the sharp taste of the gin before passing the glass back to him. "This is quite a place you've got here, Ford."

He answered with a small smile and a quick glance toward Boston on the swing. "It's a good life."

"You won't say that in the morning when the roosters crow you awake at sunrise," Dalton grumbled.

"Brooks is a runner," Beamer told his husband. "He's up early every day anyway."

"I've been slacking lately," I admitted.

"A good man in your bed makes it hard to get out of it and start the day." Dalton curled his hand around the back of Beamer's neck and squeezed.

"Did Brooks tell you how he met his boyfriend?" Ford chuckled, taking a sip from our shared glass.

"No, but I'm sure there's a good story," Dalton said.

I scoffed, rolling my eyes and glancing sidelong down the porch at Boston, who looked like he'd fallen asleep.

"Ford was sleeping with Boston and didn't want Kale to know, so he hired Tate on the spot to pretend they were going to fuck at the end of the night."

Beamer barked out a laugh, shaking his head.

"Don't act like you don't miss the absurdity that Kale inspires," Ford said, grinning.

"I took him off Ford's hands, fucked him senseless, and then he ran out on me," I explained.

So much had changed in the past few months, that first meeting felt like it was a lifetime ago, like it had been a different version of myself who met Tate that night at The Black Door.

"Did you chase?" Dalton asked, brow raised.

"He's not the type," Beamer said.

I shook my head in agreement. "Ran into him months later at the club again. His roommate had started bartending there."

"*Then* the rest was history?" Dalton guessed.

"Basically," I said, stretching out my legs and turning my attention to my West Coast friend and his husband. "When did the two of you get here, and more importantly, does Kale know you'll be here?"

"Yesterday," Dalton answered for the both of them. My stare flickered to Beamer, who had a soft smile on his face. He was truly happy, which was more than I could have said about his short romp with Alex. Not that the two of them had been bad together, I think they'd been an important stepping stone for each other, but there was an easy sort of relaxation that wrapped around Beamer. He was beyond content to let Dalton take the lead when he wanted it, and I was beyond happy for my friend.

"I would have come up early." I reached over and clasped Beamer's hand in mine. "I miss having you around."

"I miss you too," he said. "I miss a lot of things, but I'm happy in Los Angeles."

"I didn't doubt it for a second," Ford said.

The back door opened and Tate stepped onto the porch, his hair wet and shaggy around his face. He'd put on a pair of sweats, which left me feeling entirely overdressed, but he didn't seem to mind, coming straight for me and crawling onto my lap.

"Is this okay here?" he asked, burrowing against my chest with a yawn.

"More than."

I wrapped my arms around him and rested my chin on the top of his head.

"I'll be better company tomorrow," he said to my friends with another yawn. "It's been a long few days."

"You can go to bed, darling." I kissed the wet mess of his hair.

Tate groaned against me, using his body to remind me of what I'd promised him before sending him off for his shower.

"I think we're going to turn in," Dalton said before I could. "It's going to be exhausting tomorrow with Kale's arrival, and I want to be fresh for it."

Beamer chuckled and stood alongside his husband. They both told us goodnight, then slipped back into the house, leaving Tate and me on the porch with Boston and Ford.

"The walls are not soundproofed," Ford warned, pushing to his feet. "Goodnight, boys."

He weaved his way around the cluster of chairs toward the bed swing. Boston had not—in fact—been asleep. He took Ford's extended hand and followed him into the house. They left the lights on in their wake, and I tightened my arms around Tate, even as I shifted him to a better position on my lap.

"The best orgasm of my life," Tate whispered, wiggling his hips.

"Let's see what I can deliver on," I murmured, standing and holding him under his thighs so he didn't fall. The shift woke him up enough to wrap his arms around my shoulders, and I carried him to the swinging bed Boston had been lying on. I set Tate down carefully, testing the tension of the supports and the sway of the bed before settling myself fully on top of Tate.

I hadn't been to the farm before, but I'd known Ford for years, and the man was nothing if not prepared. Shoving my hand beneath the decorative pillows, I found exactly what I'd been looking for. Tate was still relaxing his way onto his back and I made quick work of cuffing his wrists to the corners of the bed. Of course Ford had cuffs on the bed, and I wagered he had lube stashed somewhere too. Tate tugged on the restraints, hips arching upward just as my fingers grazed over a tube of lube behind one of the pillows.

"Was your friend a boy scout?" Tate asked, eyes open but hooded.

"He knows how to tie knots and start a fire if that's what you're asking."

I made quick work of Tate's sweats, yanking them down to his knees, then fighting one of his legs free so I could wrap them around my waist. He understood what I wanted from him, body hot and willing as I busied myself getting my own cock out of my pants. I had no idea how I was going to make this the best orgasm of Tate's life, considering how out of my element I was and how tired we both were, but all I could do was try.

Inside the house, some of the lights flickered off, and I slathered my cock with lube before notching the tip against Tate's hole. He groaned and spread his legs wider, and I rocked back onto my heels, mind whirring.

"Come back," he whimpered, fighting against the cuffs as he attempted to reach for me.

"Come back," I repeated, turning away from him.

It didn't take a lot of work to find what I was looking for—two additional cuffs at the other end of the swing. I unclipped them and fastened them around Tate's ankles, then folded him back in half and latched his ankles to his wrists. The clips and short chains clinked softly as he settled into position, then he groaned loudly.

"I've never seen you this open," I whispered, sliding down between his legs and licking his balls. "This exposed."

"Your friends could see," he whispered.

"Do you want me to stop?"

He shook his head. It was more of a thrash from side to side, but it was the same answer either way.

I licked his balls again, sucked them, then made my way to his asshole. With his ankles above his ears, he was wide open and ready to be fucked and he acted like it. Tate whimpered and whined, trying to press against me to get more friction or penetration, but the chains held him strongly in position. Between my legs, my cock was already slick with lube and aching to get buried inside of Tate's body.

"Be quiet, Tate," I warned, pushing two fingers into him and bringing my body up and over his so I could see his face.

Sweat beaded on his temple and his thighs quivered.

With one hand inside of him, I brushed the hair back from his face with the other, kissing his closed eyelids, the tip of his nose, his trembling mouth.

"I love you," I whispered, smiling against his lips and sliding my tongue inside his mouth.

I replaced my slick fingers with the head of my cock, pushing into him a few minutes before he was ready for me. I expected the response, opening my mouth wider to swallow down the groan that tumbled out of his throat. With his legs over his head, he was tighter than ever, muscles gripping hard at every inch of my cock I fought to get inside of him. My tip dragged over his prostate and he shivered, a full-body tremble that rattled the bed so violently I worried it would fall out of the beams and drop us both to the floor.

"I love you," I told him again, pulling out a couple of inches and easing back inside.

Tate swallowed, tipping his head back.

I kissed my way down his jaw to his throat, sucking at his

Adam's apple when my hips finally found a pace that felt good. It wasn't slow, but it wasn't fast, a long and smooth thrust that took my cock almost all the way out of his body before burying it back to the hilt. It was hard and slow, every pump of my hips sending another seizure through Tate's compacted body.

Tate and I had fucked in a hundred different ways, and I thought the sex we'd had before leaving the city had been the best sex of my life, but there was something about this moment that topped it entirely. It could have been the humid night air that wrapped around us like a blanket, or the fluid motion of the swing, I wasn't sure. It could have also been me, I imagined, my heart cracked open and bare for the man who was open and bare for me in return.

"I'm going to come," Tate rasped, lips searching out mine.

I pushed his hair back again, holding his head down against the pillows while I kept the pace of my hips steady. Slapping into him with low grunts, the way he shook beneath me was the greatest aphrodisiac I'd ever tasted.

"Can I come?" he asked, eyes rolling back in his head.

"Yes."

I bit his bottom lip, growling as his orgasm crested and took us both under. His body burned against mine, chains probably making enough noise to be heard inside the house, but if Ford didn't want us to fuck on his outside sex bed, he should have said so. There wasn't a single thing in the world that would have stopped me from sinking every inch of my cock into Tate's body in that moment.

He came with a gasp, a far cry from his normal sounds. Hot streaks of his cum splashed against our stomachs, sticking as I continued to fuck him through the entirety of his orgasm. The tremor in his legs turned uncontrollable, and his fingers grasped wildly at the air, and I knew he was fucking flying.

I swallowed, dropping my forehead against his and going still. Cum pumped through my cock, spilling so much inside of him I worried about if I would have to buy Ford a new set of cushions for his swing. With some work, I hooked my arms underneath Tate's armpits, curling my fingers around his shoulders so I could thrust deep into him once more, twice more, before my own legs gave out beneath me.

Tate sucked in gasping breath after gasping breath, then a whimper that had me turning to the side enough so that I could see his face. His eyes were screwed closed, lashes shiny and matted together. His bottom lip quivered, and I moved quickly to take it into my mouth. When I slanted over him, he let out a soft cry, and I thrust into him again.

My dick was well on the way to falling out of him, but I held my length inside of him as long as I could manage, kissing and licking every quiet cry out of his mouth. After my length slipped out, I kissed the side of his neck and raised myself away from him so I could get him unhooked.

"Move slowly," I said, unlatching the first clasp around his ankle. I helped him straighten his leg, then I undid his other ankle, repeating the same help until his legs were stretched straight. I took the cuffs off entirely, kneading my fingers into one ankle at a time, working my way up his legs to work the tension out of every muscle.

By the time I reached his thighs, his cock was hard again, the mess from his first orgasm dry and flaking against his stomach. I picked at some of the dried cum with my fingernail, flicking it onto the porch. Tate moaned and sighed, seemingly content to let me aftercare him to my heart's content, so after I finished on his legs, I gave the same attention to his wrists and his arms, the crook of his elbows and the ticklish dip of his armpits.

I lost track of time, finding myself in the stretch of Tate's limbs and the soft heat of his skin beneath my fingers. I believed every time he told me he loved me, found truth in his promises, echoed through his bones when he let me tend him after we fucked. The sex we'd just had had been far from the roughest fuck, and he'd cried just the same, though I suspected it was for different reasons entirely.

"You still with me?" I asked, the question barely more than a brush of air across his parted lips.

"There's nowhere else I ever want to be."

His wet lashes fluttered open, and he hooked his arms around my neck, slanting our mouths together. He kissed me deeply, using his mouth, his entire body, until I felt the truth of his answer vibrate through my bones.

"I love you," I told him for what had to be the hundredth time that night.

"I love you," he said back, resting his cheek against my shoulder. "But I'm sorry, I don't think my legs are going to get me to bed. You'll have to carry me."

I chuckled, obliging him in the same way I always knew I would.

I woke up Saturday morning to absolute silence. After Dalton's warning the night before about how loud the roosters could be, I worried it was still too far before sunrise for the fowl to be awake, but the sun streaming through the gauzy curtains on the far wall proved otherwise. Brooks' side of the bed was cool to the touch, his clothes from the night before discarded in a pile on the floor.

I rolled to get up, my thighs sore from the night before, along with some other well-used parts of my body. But I stretched through it, the memory of Brooks' careful fingers working their way over my muscles almost as wonderful of a memory as the way he'd fucked me on the porch. The night before, he'd promised me the best orgasm of my life and he'd more than delivered. There was something about the vulnerability of being bent in half like that...outside on his best friend's porch that had heightened every other feeling and sensation inside of me, both physical and mental.

Lured by the smell of coffee, I crawled out of bed and adjusted the waistband of my sweats before I got to the door.

Brooks had gotten me mostly dressed before bed the night before, so I wasn't as indecent as I could be, though as I padded down the hallway, I realized there was still cum dried on my stomach. I tugged the hem of my shirt down and rounded the corner, finding Brooks and the rest of his friends staring each other down from opposite ends of the long kitchen island.

Brooks stood with his back to me, Ford on one side and Beamer on the other, Boston and Dalton flanking them respectively. Alex was alone beside the sink, with Kale and another man—I assumed must be his boyfriend, Christian— on the other side. To say the mood was tense would have been an understatement.

"Good morning, Tate," Alex said, which seemed to snap the group out of whatever rage-induced haze they'd been under. At the sound of my name, Brooks spun, the tension in his face evaporating as soon as he saw me. He held out his hand and I went toward him, scooting in between him and Beamer.

"Everybody sleep well?" I asked, voice cracking.

"A bit windy last night," Ford said, absolutely deadpan. "The swing was creaking for hours after we went to bed."

Brooks slid his arm around my waist and pinched my side.

"Yeah," he said with a grin. "We heard it too."

"Glad to see the party started without us," Kale said with a frown.

Dalton huffed, pressing his hip against the counter and resting his chin on Beamer's shoulder. "Maybe if you weren't so miserable to be around, you would have been invited early too."

"Stop now," Beamer whispered, turning his attention back to Kale.

"I thought we'd gotten past this."

"So did I," Ford chimed in.

Christian's expression was sympathetic, and his hand rubbing soft circles over the middle of Kale's back did little to alleviate the pinched lines around Kale's downturned mouth and eyes.

"I can go back to bed," I offered, gesturing over my shoulder toward the hallway. Brooks tightened his grip on my waist, and I sighed, defeated.

"You can stay."

"Can I have coffee first?" I asked.

Alex was closest to the pot and he poured a mug full for me, and Boston passed it down the line until Brooks slid it into my waiting hands.

"Good to see you again, Kale," I said, giving him a tired smile before turning toward Christian. "I don't believe we've met."

"This is Christian," Kale said, angling his head toward his boyfriend. "That's Tate."

"Nice to meet you," Christian murmured, hand still drawing circles around Kale's back.

"Feels like I walked into a bit of a war zone," I said to Christian, who gave me a sympathetic smile.

"They're all children," he said.

"Fighting about their toys?"

"Essentially." He moved his hand up to Kale's shoulder and squeezed. "The king of the castle over here is upset that people make moves without his approval now."

"Watch it," Kale warned, even though when directed at his boyfriend there was hardly any heat in it.

"It's the truth," Christian whispered. "I'm sorry you don't want to hear it."

I rested my head on Brooks' shoulder.

"Your friends are just trying to live their lives and you're upset because you're not the center of their world anymore," Christian said.

Kale worked his jaw, stare flickering between Christian and the countertop. "We can talk about this later."

"We can talk about it now," Ford said with a weary sigh. "We've all beat around the bush about your attitude for months and all it's gotten us is nowhere."

"If you're here to gang up on me, I'll happily take a flight back to the city," Kale snapped.

"You flew here?" Boston asked, swaying with amusement. He breathed out a quiet laugh and his brother turned his attention toward him faster than lightning.

"Of course I flew here," Kale said.

"The airport is half an hour away," Ford said. "It would take the exact same amount of time as if you'd driven."

"I can go, Ford," Kale reiterated.

"Take a breath," Christian whispered, and surprisingly, Kale did.

"You have to stop being mad that you can't live in everyone's bedrooms, Kale," Boston said softly.

"Or their porch," Ford murmured.

"What about the porch?" Christian asked.

"I fucked Tate on the porch swing last night," Brooks answered with a broad smile. "Apparently the whole house heard."

"The next farm over heard," Boston teased.

The good-natured ribbing seemed to make Kale angrier, and not even Christian's soft touches were enough to walk him back.

"I don't care who you fuck!" he shouted, throwing his hands into the air. "I care that you lied to me about it. That you didn't trust me enough to tell me the truth!"

The confession was explosive, landing like a bomb in the space between the friend group, and I was under the impression it was the first time Kale had voiced the truth of his problems to them. I grabbed my coffee and glanced at Christian, gesturing toward the back door with a quick jerk of my head. He whispered something in Kale's ear, and Kale morphed into a deer in headlights as Christian stepped away from him. The imbalance was clearly visible then, seven men against one, and I found myself feeling strangely sympathetic for the former front runner of the group.

"Maybe you guys should sit down and have a chat," I suggested. The living room space seating was more circular, ensuring that it wouldn't be a showdown that ended with accusations being flung one way or another. "Christian and I are going to go out back and enjoy the weather."

"You're a good man," Brooks said against the corner of my mouth before giving me a kiss.

"You're a better one."

I waited until the group of them sat down, then followed Christian out to the back porch. He eyed the swing warily before deciding on one of the chairs on the other end of the porch. The gin and the half-used glasses were still on the table, evidence of the hasty departure we'd all made the night before. Christian settled into a seat and stretched his legs out with a sigh.

"This reminds me of home," he said, and it was the first time I picked up the subtle and soft accent to his voice.

"The scenery?"

He jerked his thumb over his shoulder toward the house. "The conflict."

I chuckled, closing my eyes and taking a drink of coffee.

"Kale isn't a bad man," Christian said after a while.

"I didn't think he was."

"He's just stubborn. He's scared of losing control."

"They all are," I agreed, knowing Brooks wasn't any different and I doubted Ford or Alex was either. "But they have to grow up sooner or later."

"He's trying," Christian said.

"I believe you, and I'm sure they do too."

He let out a long breath and cleared his throat, soothing the itch with a drink of coffee. We sat together in silence until a few minutes later when Boston stepped outside, hair frazzled like he'd been tugging at it. Dalton followed close behind, a tight frown pulled across his mouth.

"Have you been relegated to the back porch boyfriend's club?" Christian asked mildly.

"I came willingly." Boston took the seat beside me and groaned, running his fingers through his hair.

"Was there bloodshed?" Christian asked.

Dalton took the last remaining chair, looking miserable.

"No, they're friendlier about the whole thing than they've ever been, but your boyfriend can't let it go," Boston said.

"He's your brother."

"I know." Boston took a swallow of his coffee. "Believe me, I know."

"He means well," Dalton said under his breath.

"They all do."

Minutes passed and there were no raised voices from inside, no furniture crashing, or any sounds that would have otherwise indicated there was a fight. Wes sat in a companionable silence, recognizing that even though we were all different, we were all in love with the same kind of man. Even Dalton, who was clearly just as dominant as the men he'd left in the living room, was in love with what had to be a stubborn and defiant streak that ran through Beamer, just like the rest of them.

Making the observation, I'd reached the bottom of my coffee, but didn't dare go back inside lest I disturb the tentative peace the four friends were establishing around the coffee table. A few more minutes passed and then Alex stepped onto the porch, pulling the back door closed behind him.

"They're alive," he said before any of us could ask.

There weren't any seats left so he sank down onto the wood planked porch, his spine pressed against a support post. He bent his legs and rested his forearms on his knees, gaze focused on the ground.

The sound of furniture dragging across the floor had all of us on our feet and running toward the door. I wasn't worried about Brooks, but what I'd heard about Kale and Ford's relationship especially had me worried over the possibility of them coming to blows with each other. Boston pushed his way to the front, making it into the house first and coming to a dead stop so fast the rest of us crashed into him before we could put on the brakes.

Dalton shoved him out of the way, only making it two more steps before he dragged himself to a stop, and we all crowded around in time to see the four men tangled with each other in the middle of the floor.

Except it wasn't a fight.

It was a hug.

Beside me, Boston visibly relaxed, and Christian clapped him on the back, the relief pouring out of both of them like a waterfall. Over the mess of limbs and shoulders, the only thing I could see of Brooks was the top of his head, but I knew that in the tangle of his friends he was more than feeling the love.

Alex snaked his way around us and joined his friends, enveloping Ford and Kale's shoulders as he shoved his way into their hug. He was accepted easily, and I bit my lips between my teeth to swallow down the swell of emotion their display brought to life in the middle of my chest. What a lucky group of men we all were, to have these relationships, to know this kind of love and support.

I thought of all the struggles Brooks had shared with me. How hard he'd fought against the way he was and the things he deserved in order to make himself lesser for more people, when he should have been okay with being too much for everyone except me all along. And I thought of how kind he'd been to Dylan, how much he and Alex had tried to help *my* best friend...a stranger to them. I wished Dylan could have been beside me, wished he could have borne witness to what your life can look like when you let people in.

I pulled my phone out of the front pocket of my sweats and texted him.

Me: I miss you a lot and wish you were here. I want to spend more time with you when I get back home. I want to be a better friend.

I clutched my phone in my palm, the message unanswered. The group of them finally broke away from their hug, all of them wiping their eyes in that secret way when you didn't want anyone to know you'd been crying. Brooks saw the group of us standing there, and he smiled, immediately breaking away from his friends to come to me. I wrapped him in a hug that felt as sturdy as the ones he offered me, tangling my fingers into the back of his hair when he rested his forehead against my shoulder.

"Good?" I asked.

He nodded.

My phone buzzed in my hand and I maneuvered it between our chests. Dylan's name flashed on the screen as an incoming call, not a text.

"Hello?" I answered, covering my ear with a finger to push out the noise of the recently reunited friends behind me.

"Hello?"

It wasn't Dylan's voice on the other end of the line.

"Who is this?" I asked, shouldering open the back door and stepping down onto the porch.

"Yes, hello. This is Dr. Ventura from Chelsea Medical Center. We're trying to reach the next of kin for Dylan Rivers and you're listed as his emergency contact. Can you talk?"

As it turned out, it didn't take as much time to fly between the farm and the city as it took to drive. And for what might have been the first time ever, Kale's incessant need to flash his money around had turned out for the better, getting us back to the city well before lunch time. Tate hadn't said much, and outside of Dylan's hospital room, Alex shot me a nervous look.

"Do you want to tell me what happened between the two of you now or wait until Tate is done in there?" I asked.

Alex leaned against the wall and scrubbed a hand down his face, turning his glare to the soda machine across the hall. "I don't even know where to start."

"The beginning, probably."

"Oh." He arched a brow. "Do you mean the beginning when you called me up begging me to set your boyfriend's best friend straight?"

"It wasn't going to be the first time you'd taken him in hand, or I wouldn't have made the suggestion."

"That was…" Alex snapped his jaw closed, narrowing his eyes.

"What was it?"

"For him?" He raised a brow. "Work."

I leaned in closer, lowering my voice. "Are you trying to tell me he didn't get off with you? That he didn't enjoy it?"

"It was transactional," he said, exhaling loudly and banging his head against the wall. "And you called me up, asking the impossible. I did my best, but…"

I saw the defeat in his eyes and realized what I'd asked of him had been too much. Not just for him, but for anyone. I'd misconstrued the situation between him and Dylan, and in doing so, I'd hoped that he'd have been able to keep Tate's best friend on track. I'd been wrong on multiple accounts. Tapping my thumb and finger together, I turned and leaned against the wall beside my friend.

"I'm sorry I misjudged things with the two of you."

"Thank you, but that's not it." Alex scratched the side of his nose and sighed. "If I didn't think I could manage it, I would have said so. I really just overestimated myself, I think."

"Dylan doesn't strike me as being easy either."

"He's lost and I know the feeling. It should have worked."

"Was the problem the discipline?" I asked.

"How much do you know about how I like to play?"

I stared down at my chest, rolling Alex's question around in my head. I was still in pajamas, I realized, a loose pair of gray sweats and a white undershirt. Tate had been so upset after getting the call he hadn't given any of us chance to get dressed. Thankfully, Kale for once had a level head and was able to get us to the airport in record time and then back to the city before I'd even had time to realize I hadn't put on underwear. Kale and Christian had stayed with Boston, Ford,

Dalton, and Beamer, which was either the exact—or the last —thing the group of them needed.

"I know you play as hard as I do," I said carefully. "But different."

Alex huffed a laugh under his breath. "I think I lean more into punishments and rewards than you do."

"That feels like a polite way to put it."

"It's more than just the..." he trailed off and scanned the hallway to make sure we were still alone. The door to my left remained closed, Dylan and Tate on the other side. "More than just the physical parts of it for me. I like the psychological aspects, the mental strength required for more serious submission. I didn't realize it until I started to play with Beamer."

"So, what happened?" I pressed.

"Dylan wants it, but...he's not ready." He scrubbed a hand down his face. "I don't want to say there's too much fight in him, but...we argued about restrictions, his drinking for one. He told me he'd just been playing along with my stupid ideas to make Tate happy."

I cursed under my breath and pressed my fingers against my eyelids, blacking out my vision.

"I don't know what Tate has told you, but Dylan's parents said some horrible things to him when they cut him off. It's been a lot for him. I don't want to give up, but I can't do anything without his consent," Alex said.

"And he revoked it."

"Vocally," he agreed. "Repeatedly. Emphatically."

The door to Dylan's hospital room swung open and a weary—yet somehow fuming—Tate stopped in the middle of the hallway, an accusatory finger waffling from Alex to me and back again.

"You promised he would be okay," Tate accused, the direction of his stare finally settling on Alex.

"I tried."

"You tried," he mocked.

"It's complicated, darling," I tried to explain, but Tate swiveled on me, full of unspoken vitriol, and I closed my mouth on a long inhale.

"Don't darling me."

"Tate," I said simply. Sharply. "You know as well as I do that nothing can happen without consent and Dylan—"

"Did not," Alex finished.

Tate bracketed his hands on his hips and dropped his head back, turning his glare toward the ceiling. "What did you do wrong?" Tate asked. "Why did Dylan change his mind about being with you?"

"That's not for me to answer," he said, "and frankly, even if I had the answer, it's not your business."

"He's my best friend!"

"You sound like Kale," I said softly, and the fight left Tate's shoulders like my words had siphoned it right out of him.

"I don't know him well, but I know that was an insult."

"You cannot control the lives of the people around you," I clarified. "If you try, you will only push them away."

Tate sighed heavily, spinning on his heel and slamming his palm against the wall. The slap drew the ire of a nurse down at the welcome station, and I sent her an apologetic look and small wave. She looked back at the chart in her hand, and I tentatively reached for Tate, who thankfully didn't shy away. I pulled him across the hallway and into my arms where he willingly buried his face into the crook of my neck. Wrapping my arms around his back, I held him, counting our breaths until he moved next, gouging his chin into my shoulder to stare at the wall.

"I care about your friend," Alex said from beside us. "I wish I could have helped him more."

"You helped," Tate grumbled, and I glanced over in time to see Alex's face twist from the misery of the whole thing.

"Not enough," Alex said, "obviously."

"He's okay," Tate said, to us and also to the wall. "He was drugged and left unconscious on the curb outside the emergency room."

The chin on my shoulder quivered, and I tightened my arms around Tate's back.

"He said I could tell you this, by the way. I'm not—"

"I know you're not breaking his trust," I whispered.

"He's even more worried now about paying his half of the rent." Tate sniffled, a tear falling from his eye and splattering against my shoulder.

"Darling." I pulled away from him enough so I could wipe the tears from his face, but as quick as I cleared them, more fell.

"I didn't want to assume, but I figured you would loan me the money to cover it until he's back on his feet."

"I won't loan it to you, Tate. I'll give it to you."

"I hate that," he said.

"*I'll* give it to you," Alex said, clearing his throat.

"Fine."

Tate exhaled, staring down at the floor, and I was barely able to bite back an amused laugh at how readily he would take my friend's money over mine. Though I supposed coming from Alex, Tate would see the payment as some sort of penance, not a handout.

"Dylan said they want to keep him until tomorrow for observation." Tate scrubbed a hand down his face. "He doesn't want me to stay all day. He said he'll call me when he's ready to go home."

"Do you believe him?" I asked, brushing Tate's messy hair back from his face.

"This time."

"Let's get you home then," I said. "Get you cleaned up and get some food in you and we'll wait for the call."

Tate nodded, frowning at Alex, even as the tight turndown of his mouth softened.

"Thank you for trying," Tate said softly. "I know it's not your fault."

"I'll try again if he wants me to," Alex said.

Tate shrugged.

"We'll talk soon?" I asked Alex, who eyed Dylan's hospital door like it was a venomous snake.

"Soon."

I looped my arm around Tate's shoulders again and led him toward the elevator bank, pulling my almost-dead cell phone out of my pocket to get a ride home. I didn't need to look back to see the debate raging across Alex's face, whether to go in or go home, and when the elevator doors slid open for the two of us, not the three of us, I knew he'd made the right decision.

By the time we made it back to my penthouse, Tate was dead on his feet.

I stripped him down and walked him into the shower, only because it would take less time than a bath. I washed the dried cum off his skin, the physical proof that the past twelve hours hadn't only been a fever dream. After getting him clean enough to drop him into bed, I turned off the taps, dried him as best I could, and walked him straight into bed.

"I'm so exhausted," he said hoarsely, reaching for me.

"I know."

I lay down beside him, pulling the sheets up to our waists. Tate rolled onto his side and tucked himself against me, and I'd have been a liar if I said I didn't get hard over the way he tried to make himself small around me sometimes. I wasn't dominant in the way my friends were dominant. I didn't crave control or submission. For me, it had always been the trust, but with Tate...sometimes we walked the line of it and I didn't hate the idea of sometimes falling over the other side of things.

"So exhausted I can't sleep." He tried to cover his face with his arm, but the light in the room wasn't the problem.

"I'm sorry, Tate."

"Make me come," he begged. "It feels so wrong to get off after everything that's happened, but you make me mindless, Brooks. Please."

"Hush, darling." I shifted him onto his back and braced myself over top of him. "You never have to ask me more than once to come."

"I've had to ask you plenty of times to come."

I hummed, reaching down and cupping his cock and balls in the palm of my hand. "Well, right now you only need to ask once," I said.

Sliding down his body, I kissed my way across his chest, over each small nipple. He barely had the energy to moan, sighing softly and spreading his legs for me when I reached his navel. I swirled my tongue there, wishing I'd done so when it had been filled with his cum. I loved the taste of him, even though I'd never gone down on him before with the intent to make him come. It was a weekend of firsts apparently, and as soon as I swallowed the whole of him into my mouth, I knew it would be over sooner rather than later.

"Oh, God," he rasped, fisting my hair before quickly letting go of me.

Blindly, I groped around for his wrist and returned his fingers to my head, holding him steady until I was sure he wasn't going to let go. Satisfied, I hollowed my cheeks and bobbed up and down his length, sucking him with the intent to make him come as soon as possible.

He was on the cusp of release from the very first moment, and when I slid one spit-soaked finger against his crease, Tate cried out weakly, barely lifting off the bed as he shot jets of cum against the roof of my mouth. I swallowed him down and kissed the tender fold where his leg bent up toward his waist, and by the time I reached his mouth, his eyes were closed, jaw slack.

Asleep, and hopefully dreaming.

I woke up disoriented, sweaty and tangled in the softest sheets I'd ever slept in. Sucking in a breath, I caught the taste of Brooks' skin in the air, immediately settling down when I realized where I was. I was in his penthouse, his bedroom, his bed. Muffled voices drifted upstairs, and it was easy to pick out Brooks' voice, which I'd know anywhere, and Alex's.

The sky outside the windows was gray and pink, but I had no idea of telling whether it was sunset or sunrise. I strongly hoped it was the former because sunrise meant I would have slept through Dylan's phone call to pick him up from the hospital. Kicking down the sheets, I forced myself to get out of bed and find clothes. My cell phone wasn't plugged in, but I found it on the counter in the bathroom, most likely where Brooks had left it before he showered me off the night before.

It was dead.

Of course.

I plugged it in and left it on the nightstand to charge, then headed downstairs, stumbling over my feet on the last step when a third voice mixed in with the two I'd already recognized. Dylan was here. Picking up my pace, I hurried through the living room and found the three of them in the kitchen. Dylan had on basketball shorts and a wrinkled black t-shirt, his left arm secured tight against his chest in the same black nylon sling he'd had on at the hospital.

When he saw me, he smiled weakly, climbing off the barstool and closing the space between us. I wrapped my arms around him and squeezed, letting up when he winced.

"Are you okay?" I asked, pulling back to look at him. "I'm sorry. I was asleep and my phone died."

"I'm fine," he said, voice scratchy. He cleared his throat, brows furrowed. "I'm fine. Alex was there."

I shifted my stare over Dylan's shoulder to Alex in the kitchen, with his arms folded over his chest and eyeing Dylan like he was a landmine. Like we both were.

"How long have I been asleep?" I asked Brooks, who bobbled his head side to side. He was dressed in his usual running clothes, tight shorts and a tank top, but his feet were bare.

"It's just dinner time," he said. "Not long."

"Do you want some water?" Alex asked. "Coffee?"

"Water, I think," I answered, making my way into the kitchen before either he or Brooks could get a glass filled for me.

I wasn't the one who needed tending and care, at least not in this moment. Dylan was the one who'd just been released from the hospital, his shoulder in enough pain they'd had him on a morphine drip earlier in the morning. He should have been the one asleep in bed being doted on by a man with more means than sense.

"Thank you for picking him up," I said to Alex, who gave me a curt nod in reply, his eyes still focused on Dylan.

In the living room, the sky had more colors, and my best friend wandered to the window, staring out at the skyscrapers across the city with a tight frown. Sipping my water, I joined him, leaning gently against his good side until he knocked his head into mine.

"Drink," I said, passing him the glass.

He took the smallest swallow possible, then handed it back. "The pain meds are making me nauseous."

"Right." Of course they were. "I'm sorry I missed your call."

"I'm not." He inhaled. "It's not your responsibility to take care of me. It's my bad choices that got me here."

"It's not my responsibility, but you're my best friend. I want to help you."

"It's more complicated than that," he said. "Alex was the right person to call."

I bristled. "How do you figure?"

"More money." Alex chuckled. "More time."

"He doesn't know you."

"Maybe not." Dylan glanced over his shoulder and I followed his gaze. Alex still watched him, even as Brooks leaned close and said something that looked relatively serious.

We both turned back toward the window.

"Dylan," Alex called from the other side of the kitchen, "it's time for your meds."

From the corner of my eye, I watched Dylan's jaw tic, then without a word, he went into the kitchen. Holding out his hand, Dylan waited while Alex twisted open an orange bottle with a white lid. He dropped a pill into Dylan's hand and slid a bottle of water toward him. Dylan took the pill, then made a show of opening his mouth and sticking out his tongue.

"I'm not going to kill myself, asshole," Dylan grumbled, leaving Brooks and Alex in the kitchen to rejoin me at the window.

Even with the space between them, I could almost feel the cord tying the two of them together, and somehow they both wanted to set it on fire.

"You know," I said carefully, lowering my voice and tilting my head closer to Dylan's ear. "If you don't want his help, you can just tell him no and—"

"It's fine."

"Dylan, it's..." I didn't know how far into the conversation I wanted to tread. How far would be too far. "If you don't want it."

"I know about safe words, Tate. You can stop."

I licked my lips, swallowing back any other protest that had assembled itself in my throat. I'd been wrong for months, thinking I understood Dylan or who he was, and I needed to stop making the same mistakes. When it came to my relationship with Brooks, the things we did in the bedroom, I always imagined if I was mad or if I didn't like something, I would say red and things would end. That was the point of a safe word, wasn't it? Even though Brooks had never even gotten close enough to warrant me needing to use it, the option was there.

Dylan seemed to acquiesce to Alex—again—but he was beyond mad about it, and I didn't understand why he didn't just use his safe word and put an end to it. If he was so angry about being told to take his medicine, being watched, monitored...

"You're an adult," I reminded him.

"It's complicated," he finally said, "but I know how to make it end."

"Okay," I said, because there wasn't anything else to say.

If Dylan hadn't called my sanity into question after all the dubious choices I'd made before reconnecting with Brooks, it wasn't my place to poke and prod about whatever was going on with him and Alex. I also needed to trust that Alex was Brooks' friend, and Brooks would step in if there was anything that wasn't aboveboard.

"I wanted to be here when you woke up from your nap," Dylan said. "I didn't want you to worry. But I'm tired and I want to lie down."

"Right." I cleared my head, upset that I'd spent our first minutes back together worrying too much about myself and not Dylan, who was injured beyond the marks on his body. "I wasn't thinking. Let me grab my phone and we can head home."

I hadn't finished speaking before Dylan shook his head, pivoting on his heels to face me more head on.

"You stay here," he said.

"At least let me get you back to the apartment."

He shook his head again. "I'm going to stay with Alex for a while."

"What?" I blinked slowly, even more confused at whatever was going on between the two of them.

"Just for a little," he said. "I know Alex is paying my rent, so you don't have to worry about losing the lease, but I imagine you'll want to move in here sooner rather than later."

With his good arm, Dylan gestured at the vastness of Brooks' penthouse. I followed his stare around the first floor, so much of it not even visible. There was so much space, so many rooms, all of the windows.

"We haven't talked about that yet."

Dylan rolled his eyes at me, a glimpse of the friend I'd nearly lost, the man I'd shared beers with while he wrote songs on his guitar about the man of my dreams. How had both of our lives changed so quickly?

"I'm sorry that I scared you," Dylan said, pressing his good hand against his bad shoulder. He blinked slowly and sucked in a breath. "You're my closest friend, Tate. I was just so embarrassed about all of it."

"Remember that guy I hooked up with before Brooks?" I asked. "The one who fucked me so hard that *he* passed out?"

Dylan chuckled and I smiled, wrapping my arms around him while making sure to not put pressure on his injured shoulder.

"That was embarrassing," I said, "not this."

Dylan nodded and sniffed. "No more secrets from here on out," he promised.

"So you'll tell me what the fuck is going on with you and Alex?"

He threw a quick look across the kitchen. Alex still watched him, even as he spoke to Brooks.

"That's not a secret," he murmured. "It's just too messy to make sense of."

"Promise me you'll tell him no if you have to."

"It's not like that," Dylan assured me. "We aren't sleeping together."

"Will you explain it to me another day?"

"I promise," he said. "I'm going to go back to Alex's and lie down awhile."

"Are you ready?" Alex asked, interrupting whatever Brooks had been saying to him, which gave me the impression he'd been listening to our conversation the whole time.

"Yes," he answered, snapping his mouth closed before calling Alex an overbearing prick under his breath.

He couldn't have meant it though, or he wouldn't have gone along with it, I reminded myself as Alex herded Dylan's things together and out the door. Even with my best friend on his way across town, I wasn't able to shake the discomfort over whatever he was doing with Alex. It was bad decision-making that had gotten him into the hospital in the first place.

"Alex is just giving him a place to stay," Brooks assured me. "He's playing nurse."

"Why?"

"Guilt, I think."

"Why doesn't he just *hire* a nurse then?" I asked. "If he feels so beholden to Dylan about the whole thing?"

"Alex has never been a good delegator."

"This feels wrong," I muttered.

"I think most people would say the same about the things you and I do in the bedroom," he said gently.

"Dylan said they're not sleeping together."

"Does it matter?" Brooks arched a brow like he was ready to challenge me, but in a flash his expression turned soft and he pulled me against his chest. "Do not be like Kale about this."

I screwed my eyes closed, feeling a glaring flash of sympathy for Brooks' formerly ostracized friend.

"I'm trying," I said, rubbing at my eyes.

"I know." Brooks kissed the top of my head. "Do you want

dinner? Do you want to go back to bed? Do you want to go back to the farm?"

I snorted, shoving him away and walking back into the kitchen to get some more water.

"We can't go back to the farm."

"Why not?" he asked, mouth pulled taut in confusion.

"You're so serious right now, aren't you?"

Brooks blinked.

"Never mind," I said, falling in love with him a little more. "I'm not that hungry, but I think I should eat."

"Do you want to go out or do you want me to order in?"

I climbed onto one of the barstools, spinning it sideways so I could admire both of the views. "I'm tired and I want you to decide."

The corner of Brooks' mouth quirked into a smile, and he dropped his cell phone onto the counter.

"That's essentially where Dylan is at, for what it's worth."

Before I could formulate any sort of reply, Brooks was already on the phone with a Thai restaurant down the street, ordering enough food to feed an army.

And I let him.

IT TOOK A WEEK FOR TATE TO UNWIND ABOUT DYLAN AND ALEX, BUT his de-Kale-ification was a welcome change. Even though Tate had spent most of his time at my place, he was glued to his phone for the first half of the week, ready to swoop in and rescue Dylan at the first hint of unhappiness over the situation he'd willingly put himself into. By Friday, the phone was on charge in the bedroom and Tate was stretched out on my couch with his ankles propped up on the coffee table, and I took it as a win. He'd arrived later than normal, stopping by his apartment to get the mail and make sure everything was still in order since both of them had been elsewhere for so long.

"Good news," he said, which was a welcome relief whatever the news would be.

I gave the ice in my drink a swirl and joined him on the couch. I sat beside him and matching his pose. After that, Tate was quick to slide down onto his back and drop his head into my lap. Humming, I brushed his hair back from his face, my cock twitching at the delicate and content way his lashes fluttered at my touch.

"Tell me everything," I said.

He shoved a six-by-nine envelope into my face, and I didn't need to take out the contents to know it was his passport.

"It's here."

"That was quicker than I expected."

Tate slid the dark blue book out of the envelope and flipped through the pages, stretching his arm out for me to take it.

"Where are you taking me first?" he asked with a grin.

I stretched my arm down his chest and rucked up the hem of his shirt so I could drag my fingernails up his stomach. "To bed?" I proposed.

"I don't need a passport to go there." He arched under my touch, groaning as he settled back into the cushions.

"I'm amused you'll let me take you out of the country, but you won't let me pay your rent," I told him, tossing the passport onto the coffee table.

Tate's relationship with my money was a complicated one, but we all had our hang-ups. I'd spent the first half of our relationship living with the constant fear he was going to get overwhelmed and leave me. The worry was still buried into the back walls of my brain, but it was much easier to ignore than it had been before. Tate had never worried about me leaving him, or about leaving me. He'd never seen my fetishes as a detriment to our relationship. My money had always been the sticking point, but there wasn't much I could do about that. It was as much a part of me as anything else was.

"I'm learning," he grumbled. "You don't care that I don't have money, so I don't think I should care that you do."

"Finally seeing reason." I bent myself in half and dropped a kiss against his forehead.

"I don't know what the future looks like." Tate rolled onto his side, his breath hot against my stomach. I bent my legs at the knee, thighs pressing against the back of his head to sort of fold him into my body as much as the position would allow.

"No one does."

"Alex can't pay Dylan's rent forever."

"I don't think he plans on it," I said softly.

"Dylan isn't going to magically be able to afford his rent again when his shoulder is better." Tate swallowed and hooked his arm over my lap, curling it around my back.

"That's a conversation for the future," I assured him, drawing a long, curving swirl from his forehead down to his chin. "Don't worry about things you can't control."

"I can't control anything."

He wasn't wrong.

"Sounds like a good life, darling." Dropping my head against the back of the couch, I closed my eyes and sighed. "Not a worry in the world to be seen."

Tate snorted, and we both knew it was a lie.

"I'm very worried about where you're taking me with this new passport."

I was very worried about how I was going to convince him to abandon the apartment entirely and move in with me permanently, but I wasn't an infant. I knew as long as there was a chance in hell Dylan would be returning to their apartment in Chelsea, Tate was never going to give it up. I admired his dedication to his friend, and I was glad the two of them had each other. Even though I didn't know what their friendship was like before things had started to go south, I was hopeful in the future it would be better than it had been before. I had that with my own friends, even Kale, who had finally yanked his head out of his asshole on Saturday morning and started to come around to his piece in the breakup of our friend group.

"Tell me where you want to go and we'll go," I told him.

"You keep talking about pasta." Tate rolled his eyes, a mocking gesture that wasn't anywhere close to hiding the smirk on his lips.

"Italy, Tate?" I used my hip to knock him up enough off my lap that I could reach into my pocket for my phone. "We can go to Italy. We can go to Greece. We can go anywhere you want."

"Antarctica," he said.

"We could, but why would you want to?"

"Aren't there polar bears and penguins there?" He smiled. "At the bottom of the world."

"There's polar bears and penguins at the zoo and it's far less cold," I reminded him.

Tate stretched out and lifted himself off my lap, situating himself against my side so he could see my phone.

"New York is cold in the winter," he said.

"Not quite the same."

I had an app on my phone for private flights, and I silently hoped the price tag that was about to flash on the screen wasn't big enough to give Tate a heart attack. He rested his head against my shoulder while I keyed in our destination and our dates, a short trip unfortunately because of work, and Tate swatted my hand away before I could press *Book and Pay*.

"That's like...nothing to you, isn't it?" he asked, brow furrowed while he counted the zeroes to the left of the pay button.

I debated trying to downplay it, but Tate wasn't a fool.

I shook my head.

"Maybe I should have let you pay Dylan's rent," he said, letting go of my wrist.

I booked the flight, and then tossed the phone to the side and hauled him onto my lap. He laughed, throwing his head back as he straddled my thighs, curling his fingers around my neck and pressing our foreheads together.

"I'd pay yours," I reminded him.

His eyes sparkled and he pressed our mouths together. "I know you would."

"I'd pay it and let you live here."

Tate nodded, kissing me again. "I know."

On the other end of the couch, my phone vibrated with the confirmation alert for our trip.

"When do we leave?" he asked.

"Tonight."

"Of course." He chuckled. "We should pack."

"We could buy clothes there," I suggested.

"Do you think I would look good in an Italian suit?" Tate leaned back and smoothed his hands down the front of his chest.

"You'd look good in anything," I said, shoving his shirt up to expose his chest. "You look best in nothing."

"Then what am I doing in all these clothes?"

He took his shirt out of my hands and pulled it over his head, tossing it onto the floor. I wrapped my hands around his waist, grinding his ass down on my lap with a barely restrained groan.

"We do have a flight to catch, darling."

"I've never fucked on a plane."

I hummed. "Can you wait that long?"

"If you tell me to," he whispered, cheeks burning red.

I slid my hands up his sides until I reached his face. Grabbing his cheeks, I slanted our mouths together and speared my tongue into his mouth, kissing him until he made that needy little whimper that he always let loose when his erection was so hard it started to hurt him.

"Is that what you need tonight?" I asked, licking the corner of his mouth. "You need me to drag it out until you can't stand it anymore?"

I kissed my way to his ear, and Tate tipped his chin toward the ceiling, giving me more room to suck and worship. I collared my hand around his throat loosely, noticing the way he bucked on my lap when my fingers wrapped around his neck.

"It feels like it's been forever," he whimpered.

"I fucked you this morning."

"I mean since I cried for a good reason."

There was a very real concern I was going to come in my pants right there in the middle of my living room, Tate still half-dressed on my lap.

"Go pack a bag, Tate." I lifted him off my lap and deposited him onto the couch.

He grabbed me before I could go, nuzzling his face into my crotch and rubbing his cheek up and down the length of my erection. I fisted his hair, yanking his head back to make him stop, but when he looked up at me, his pupils were shot and his eyes were glassy.

"You're in a mood," I said gently, giving him one more shove away from me before letting him go entirely.

"Horny?"

Tate and I had been intimate—repeatedly—over the past week, but it had been muted versions of our normal encounters. That wasn't to say I took it easy on him, because I definitely never had, but I wasn't as aggressive as I could have been. He hadn't complained so I wasn't sure he noticed, but now there was no doubt in my mind he'd caught on.

"Don't let me do it again," I warned, bending down so we were face to face. He was perched on the edge of the couch, hand rubbing slowly between his legs. It was so reminiscent of the Tate I'd met the first night at The Black Door what felt like a lifetime ago.

"Hmn?"

"Don't let me neglect you." I grabbed him again by the throat and hauled him to his feet. He gasped, circling his fingers around my forearm...for support, not to fight. "If I'm not giving you what you need, darling, tell me."

He nodded, swallowing. His throat bobbed against my palm, and I tightened my hold. His cheeks darkened, not just from the flush of arousal but also from the restraint of his air flow.

"I'll tell you," he rasped.

With nothing besides reluctance, I set his feet back down on the floor and let go of his throat. Tate whined, swaying into me.

"Go pack a bag," I told him again. "The sooner you do as you're told, the sooner we can get in the air."

He sucked in a breath and nodded, then turned and scampered up to the bedroom. I liked that he had enough of his things at my house to pack a bag for an overseas trip, though I hadn't been kidding. I would have bought him anything he needed—or wanted—once we were in Italy. I still would.

I'd give him everything.

Something crashed upstairs, and I headed up behind him. My steps were slower, not in a rush at all. Drawing out the end was part of the fun, after all. In the bedroom, I found Tate in the closet, digging out a clean pair of jeans and underwear for his duffel bag. I sat on the edge of the bed and booked a villa at Castelle di Casole, chuckling when Tate threw my own empty overnight bag at me.

"I'm ready," he said.

"You're primed, that's for sure." I slid my phone into my pocket and grabbed the empty bag, brushing past him into the closet. "Don't think that just because you're on the plane you get to come. Are you sure you want to move so fast?"

He groaned, adjusting his cock, which somehow looked like it had gotten harder. "There's no other speed with you."

A smile flashed across my face, and I dug out a pair of handcuffs from the back of my sock drawer, making a show of dropping them into the bottom of my bag.

"I have plenty of speeds, Tate. Maybe we can use tonight to change gears."

I'D NEVER BEEN ON A PRIVATE PLANE BEFORE.

Never been able to bypass security entirely.

Never had a flight attendant know my name before I stepped foot onto the plane.

I'd also never had a man get on his knees in the middle of the plane aisle to swallow my cock down to the back of his throat after reaching cruising altitude.

But Brooks had changed a lot of things in my life.

It wasn't unheard of for him to suck me off, but it was rare, and I don't know if that's why it felt like a treat or maybe it was because the altitude was doing funny things to my brain, but it took less than thirty seconds before I was ready to come down his throat. I told him as much and he pulled off with a pop, an amused smirk on his face and a tent between his legs.

"Maybe time for a drink then," he suggested, climbing to his feet and buckling himself into the seat directly across from me.

The plane wasn't small by any means, but far too big for just the two of us. With a cluster of seats on one side, a table in front of a couch on the other, and a bedroom tucked in the rear, the seating arrangements for the next eight hours were endless. Brooks pressed a button, and less than a minute later the same flight attendant who knew me by name appeared to get our drink orders.

Brooks ordered a whiskey for himself and I was floating too far out of the atmosphere to make a decision on my own, so I asked for the same. She served us expensive whiskey in heavy crystal glasses with round spheres of ice like they had in the drinks at The Black Door. The whole experience was so far beyond surreal, it made me want to cry from the disbelief of it all.

Sipping at the whiskey, I dropped my forehead against the side of the plane so I could stare out the window. It was dark outside, the lights of the city already far behind us as we careened through the air toward Italy.

All because Brooks wanted to buy me good pasta for dinner.

"What are you thinking about?" he asked, kicking his foot against mine.

I glanced at him in time to watch him wipe some of my precum from the corner of his mouth before he sipped his drink.

"How less than three months ago I was sitting on the couch with Dylan and he was singing made up songs about the nameless man who'd ruined me for everyone who'd come after him." I took another swallow of the whiskey. "And now I'm on a plane with him going to Italy *just because.*"

"You're going to Italy because I want to take you to Italy," he corrected.

Somehow, the clarification mattered, but I couldn't explain how.

"Sometimes I wonder if it's a fever dream," I murmured, giving him half a smile.

"That's the delirium from having an erection as often as you do."

I chuckled, finishing off my drink and setting my glass down on the arm of the seat. Brooks still had a few sips left in his, and he cocked his head to the side, regarding me silently. He looked at home on the private jet. Even in jeans and a t-shirt he oozed wealth and class. With his legs spread enough to take up the whole seat down to the careless way he held his drink between his thumb and first finger, wrist bent and swinging. Brooks was a man who knew how to get what he wanted and keep it, except until me...that hadn't entirely been true.

"What are you thinking now?" he asked, unbuckling his seatbelt because he already knew the answer.

"That I want to suck you."

He hummed and popped the button on his jeans, drink still held loosely in his other hand. It didn't take much work for him to get his cock out of his pants and I was on my knees as soon as his tip poked out from behind the waistband of his underwear. Brooks combed his fingers through my hair as I sank down between his legs, taking him as far into my throat as I could without gagging. And then I went the rest of the way anyway. His hips lifted off the seat and he groaned, fingers flexing against the back of my head as I swallowed around him.

"Maybe I'm the one dreaming," he rasped, spreading his hand against the back of my head and holding me down.

My nose was pressed tight against the trimmed curls around his base, the length of his cock filling my mouth and throat. I pressed my hands against his thighs and tried to pull back, to get a breath, but he pushed at me from above and below, making sure there was nowhere for me to go.

"You can do this, darling," he murmured.

The glass in his drink clinked against the side and the swallow when he drank was audible. Brooks smacked his lips and moaned, cock jerking against the roof of my mouth and blocking my air even further. Screwing my eyes closed, I dug my fingers into his thighs. All the while, spit sputtered out of my mouth, soaking his underwear and sliding down toward his balls and his ass.

He took another drink and turned the spread fingers on the back of my head into a fist, yanking me up hard and fast. My next breath came on a gasp, spitty and sputtering. I hadn't realized how much he'd been cutting off my air until it returned, the stars sparkling around the edges of my vision as I blinked him into focus, my entire body covered in pins and needles like my muscles were asleep and just starting to wake up.

"Take a drink, Tate," he said, bringing his glass to my mouth and tilting it back until a swallow of whiskey raced down my throat.

"Thank you."

"Take a breath," he said next, and I did, catching the last of it as he pushed my head back down between his legs.

With his hand in my hair, Brooks used my mouth as it pleased him, which pleased *me*. My cock was hard from his house, hard from the blow job he'd just given me, hard from the rough way he was using me and I was desperate to touch myself. Sliding both of my hands off his legs, I fumbled with my fly. My fingers were numb and clumsy, and by the time I got my dick out of my pants, Brooks had caught on.

He pulled me off of him again with a warning tsking sound against the roof of his mouth.

"I have plenty of speeds," he said, voice a dangerous and low reminder of his warning before we'd left the house. "The whole crew knows what you're doing by the way. I instructed them to stay in the back unless called. They're seasoned, darling. They know what that means."

With my mouth stuffed full of his cock, there wasn't much for me to say, but heat flooded my cheeks just the same. It should have been embarrassing, but I found I didn't care. My brain, my body...it was so singularly focused on Brooks and the pleasure he brought us both, I couldn't be bothered to care.

The statement and my understanding of it was a new shift in the foundation of our relationship. With the exception of our first night together, everything we'd done had been in private. There was no one to see and judge the way we loved each other. Being on the plane, with the crew in back behind a thin door, probably able to hear the way I gagged around his cock, knowing—hoping, at least—they'd hear us both come before the night was through...

"Does exhibitionism appeal to you?" Brooks asked softly, lifting my mouth enough off of his cock that I could get a decent breath.

I hadn't thought much about it until that moment, but I definitely didn't hate it. I didn't know if it was my own incessant arousal speaking, the need to not have my pleasure delayed another second, but I didn't just not care if other people knew what we were doing. I managed a nod around his cock, and he eased me back down, raising his hips to make sure he was all the way inside.

"Does it make you hard to think about choking on my cock in public?" he asked, pulling my head and starting a slow and wet pace that had my lips sealing around the flared tip of his cock before he pushed me back down to the base. Up and down. Up. And. Down.

Up.

"It makes me hard to think about choking on your cock anywhere," I told him.

Down.

Down.

Down.

"I want another drink, Tate," he said, bending over to get his mouth closer to my ear. "Do you understand what I'm saying?"

I nodded, but pushed against his hand until he let me up entirely. He looked just as well fucked as I felt, his cheeks pink and his hair falling toward his face. I could see his pulse in the side of his neck, and I wanted to kiss him there, so I did. Throwing myself onto his lap, I sucked against the artery that caught my eye, and Brooks wrapped his free arm around my back, groaning as I neared the point of sucking a bruise into his skin.

"I don't care if they know," I said, kissing up to his ear. "But I don't want them to see."

"I'm proud of you for speaking up." He knocked his head against mine until I slanted our lips together, opening for him to kiss the taste of himself out of my mouth. "Get in your seat then and put your cock away."

Touching my erection hurt, and as I zipped up, I wondered if I'd made the wrong decision. Brooks hid his own cock back in his pants, pressing the call button with a steady finger. She was there quickly, and I couldn't stop myself from smirking when he told her to just bring the bottle. While I waited for her to return, I closed my eyes, trying to imagine what it would feel like for her to have come at his call while I was still on my knees between his legs, mouth stuffed full of cock. I didn't think she would have called attention to it in any way. She would have taken his order, ignoring me entirely.

I shivered at the thought, at the dismissal.

Since I wasn't on my knees choking on cock, when she returned with the bottle, she didn't ignore me.

"Anything for you, Mr. Barlowe?"

"I'm good, thank you." My voice cracked, and across from me, Brooks smirked.

"That'll be all," he said, dismissing her back to the rear of the plane again.

Brooks watched her go, waiting until she was out of sight to twist the top off the bottle and refill his glass. He gestured to mine, but I shook my head, immediately going back to my knees between his legs. He didn't protest when I tore at his zipper; he only sighed softly when I pulled his hard dick out of his pants and sucked it back into my mouth.

Brooks arranged himself above me, spreading his legs wider and resting his head against the back of the seat. He didn't return his hand to the back of my head, instead curling his fingers around the armrest of the seat and letting me control the pace. I truly loved sucking his cock, whether it was of my own accord or at his preference. The way he swelled in my mouth, pressing against the backs of my teeth, my tongue. It was consuming in the best ways.

"Hands, Tate," he grunted.

I raised them and he bound them together at the back of my neck. It was hardly a restraint, but it was enough control to send a surge of heat between my own legs. I humped the air while I sucked him, chasing invisible friction and the edge of my own release.

Content to suck him for the entire eight hour flight if that was what he wanted, I took my time, kissing and sucking and licking my way up and down his shaft. I tongued his slit and his balls, staring up at him through hazy eyes and a mouth full of his nuts. Brooks gazed down at me softly, drink still held loosely in his hand and his eyes full of admiration. He licked his lips, pulling the bottom one into his mouth on the front end of a chin quiver that turned his entire body rigid.

He was barely inside my mouth when he came, spurts of cum landing against my lips and my cheek, my nose. Brooks blinked quickly, groaning as he continued to spill and spill across the side of my face. My lashes fluttered closed and I sank back onto my heels, chest heaving with every breath.

I heard the ice clink when he set his drink down, and with my hands still restrained behind my neck, he used his shaft to clean the cum off my face before feeding his length back into my mouth. Even as he softened against my tongue, I sucked him greedily.

Sucked him happily.

"Tate," he whispered when his cock finally slipped free of my swollen mouth.

I blinked my eyes open and licked my lips.

He looked at me like I was a ghost, shaking his head and

hauling me onto his lap so fast my leg flew out and knocked his whiskey into the aisle. The ice sphere was the only sound in the cabin, rolling toward the back of the plane as Brooks studied my face with wide and frenzied eyes.

"I love you," I told him, not because I wanted to say it, but because I felt that he needed to hear it.

He released my wrists and took my face into his hands, crashing our mouths together to tell me the same thing in return. I moaned happily against him, my pleasure mounting when he reached into my lap and took my throbbing cock into his fist. He jerked me off with a tight grip and no lube, making me come so hard I saw more than just the stars outside the windows.

I took Tate to bed three hours before we were set to land in Tuscany. He was half asleep by the time I'd wrung a third orgasm out of him, but the whiskey was working double time for us both and a nap was long overdue. When we were woken up for landing, he was beyond groggy, but the sunrise was cresting over the clouds and I didn't want him to miss the gorgeous, rolling hills as we descended into Italy.

With his head against my shoulder and his fingers threaded tightly around mine, Tate squeezed my hand and stared out the window with tired but excited eyes.

"Am I dreaming?" he asked under his breath, but I didn't think he really wanted an answer. I kissed him on the top of his head and rested my eyes until it was time for us to de-plane.

There was a car waiting for us, sent by the hotel, and I would never find enough thanks in the world that Tate never begrudged me—at least out loud—the luxuries my bank account allowed us. He stayed pressed against my side as we were driven to the villa, his posture only turning nervous once we reached the hotel.

"What's wrong?" I asked him.

The driver took our bags straight to the concierge, and Tate vibrated beside me while I got the keys to our villa.

"This is something," he said.

"Is this more impressive than my penthouse?" I asked with a smirk, curious as to how Tate ranked displays of wealth in mind.

"This is *Italy*," he said. "I'm in Italy."

"And you got here on a private jet," I reminded him, leaning close and kissing his ear. "With a belly full of cum."

"Jesus." He banged his forehead into my shoulder.

"You're tired," I told him. "Let's go settle in."

The concierge took our bags and led us through the sprawling hillside estate until we reached the private detached villa I'd booked us for the weekend. If Tate thought my penthouse was too much, lord knew what he was going to think about this, but even though we'd dabbled in some exhibitionism on the plane, I wanted to ensure both of our privacies for the duration of our stay.

"This is..." He trailed off, not finishing his thought while I tipped the concierge and closed the door behind us.

"Let's find the bedroom," I said.

"Which one?"

"Take your pick, darling."

With a burst of energy, Tate disappeared down a travertine tiled hallway. I followed behind him slowly, impressed but far less rushed. From somewhere on the other side of the villa, I heard him curse, and I found him in what I assumed to be the primary suite—if the view and the layout was any way to judge.

One wall was nothing except windows, mostly comprised of a large French door that opened onto a private patio with an uninterrupted view of the rolling hillside. On the opposite wall sat a king sized, four poster bed. An open door in the corner led to what I imagined to be an equally impressive bathroom. The villa was massive, but as soon as I sat down on the edge of the bed, my own exhaustion over the past couple weeks started to get the better of me.

"Tate." I beckoned him away from the doors. "Come lie down with me."

"There's breakfast on the patio," he said, face turned toward the hills even as he walked toward me.

"I imagine when we wake up, it'll be replaced with lunch."

Stripping out of my clothes and leaving them spread across the floor, I climbed under the covers and took Tate with me. He fitted himself against my body like we'd been carved from the same piece of marble, and much to my amusement, he fell asleep before I'd even had time to close my eyes.

Listening to the soft and level sound of Tate's breathing should have been enough to lull me to sleep, but I found myself wide awake, staring at the ceiling, staring at Tate, staring at the lush hills beyond the open doors. The breeze was soft and warm, and I waited until I was sure Tate was borderline unconscious before extracting myself from his arms. He shifted and buried his face into the pillow, hips giving a little thrust toward the mattress before he settled with a snore.

I was simply *too* tired.

The stress of everything that had transpired over the past

year was finally starting to take a toll on me. From Beamer's relocation to Kale's temper tantrums to Dylan's hospitalization...all of that stacked on top of simply trying to *fall in love*. I wanted to extend the reservation in the villa and never go back to the city. I suddenly found myself understanding why Ford had been so quick to buy Boston the farm upstate. It was enough of a break from the stressors of everyday life without being so far removed as to separate oneself entirely.

I took a quick shower, thinking of all the ways I was going to make Tate cry under the rainfall showerhead that took up half the ceiling, then I wrapped myself in a plush robe and padded barefoot out to the patio. Tate snored quietly from the bed, but I closed the doors halfway anyway. He'd been right about breakfast, there a small spread on the table with a net covering the top of it to keep away any bugs.

Pulling out one of the wrought iron chairs, I sat down and stretched my legs out, finding some comfort in the stillness of the landscape, but not enough to fight off the heaviness in my eyes. Too tired to sleep, too tired to wake, I instead found some sort of calmness there with my eyes closed, the wind wrapping around me. My mind raced faster than the breeze, debating if I'd done the right thing when it came to Alex and Dylan, worrying about how near I was to closing a deal for Boston, Ford, and the food bank that meant so much to them, wondering if I was always going to worry about Tate leaving me.

The sun crested over the top of the sky and began to slide down toward the horizon, and I still hadn't slept. Lunch was delivered, and Tate slumbered through it all. I sat at the foot of the bed for a while, watching him. God, he was beautiful, gorgeous, perfect.

He was mine.

Eventually, my stomach growled so loudly I worried it would wake him up. The noise didn't even register, so I ventured back to the patio to pick at the bowl of panzanella. The food was light and delicious, and I ate it well knowing the man I loved was resting well in the bed behind me.

"How long have you been up?" he asked me sometime later, his voice thick with sleep and the weight of jetlag.

"Awhile," I said, stretching my hand for him. "But lunch is here, like I said."

Tate shuffled toward me, wearing nothing more than his cum-stained underwear from the night before. He sat down in the chair beside me and leaned over the table, sucking in a deep breath of all the foods we had to choose from.

"I don't know what any of this is," he said at the same time he picked up a piece of crostini and dug into the panzanella.

He approached the spread with the same eagerness that he seemed to use with all things in his life, me included. Tate was more than brave, he was fearless. Watching the awe in his face as he looked from the scenery before drifting to the food and then to me and the hills again felt as much of a gift as it did when he let me lick tears off his face. The preciousness of it had emotion welling in my throat, and I swallowed back my own tears as best as I could manage, stretching my hands out against the arms of the chair,

"Are you all right?" he asked, noticing the tension in my muscles.

"I'm tired," I admitted, "but I've never been happier."

Tate grinned and set down the uneaten crust of his bread. He took my hand, threaded our fingers together, and turned my hand over in his, kissing my knuckles before pressing my fingers against his cheek.

"It's so beautiful here," he said quietly, scooting his chair closer to mine. "I wish we didn't have to leave."

"We just got here."

"You know what I mean."

"I do," I agreed, twisting our joined hands and mimicking the kisses he'd just given me. "But also we don't have to leave."

"Of course we do," he said, following it up with a laugh that quickly died in the back of his throat.

"We don't." I inhaled a deep breath. "I work because I want to."

"I work because I have to."

"You don't have to work at all," I said, glancing at him from the corner of my eye.

"I don't want you to pay my rent."

"I don't particularly *want* to pay your rent." The corner of my mouth twitched into a tired smile. "I'd rather you just lived with me."

"Are you seriously asking me to move in with you right now?" he asked.

"It was more of a statement, but..."

"Why don't you ask?" Tate smiled, letting go of my hand and reaching for the chilled bottle of wine that I'd managed to ignore for the majority of the afternoon. He poured us each a small glass, and even though I'd drank half a bottle of whiskey on the airplane, the wine was as refreshing as a glass of ice water would have been.

I loved Italy.

I loved Tate.

"Why don't you ask?" I returned the question back to him, the annoying doubt in the back of my head barely louder than a whisper by that point.

Tate pulled his lower lip into his mouth, eyes awake and sparkling, more gorgeous than the landscape behind him. Instead of asking me the question I hoped we already knew the answer to, he took a leisurely sip of his wine, stretching out his legs and sinking back into the chair.

"I could get used to this," he said softly.

"Are you not already?"

"I'm used to you," he whispered. "I'm…invested in you."

Another unfamiliar burn at the back of my throat, a dam of tears in the corners of my eyes.

"Is that so?" I croaked, the words sounding wet as I choked them out.

"I want to spend every night with you," he went on, looking at the sky instead of me. The smallest of blessings. "Every morning."

"Oh?"

"Oh," he repeated it back to me, tone lilting. "Sounds like I should move in."

My lashes fluttered and closed, a single tear sliding out the corner of my eye and pooling alongside the curve of my nose. I didn't even hear Tate move, but he kissed the top of my lip, his tongue dragging up and chasing after the tear. I grabbed him as soon as he moaned at the taste of it, spearing my tongue into his mouth and kissing him until neither of us could breathe. Gasping for air, I dug my fingers into the back of his head, pushing our foreheads together hard enough to hurt.

"That was obscenely sexy," I told him.

Tate grinned and hummed a small laugh. "I don't want to miss a single day with you."

"All my days are yours," I promised him. "Every breath."

"I need to keep the apartment," he said, "for Dylan."

"I'll buy the building." I was only half joking, and he knew it.

"I don't want to quit my job."

"I never asked you to." I kissed him again, and our tongues swirled together, my cock springing back to life like I was a well-rested man in my twenties and not a jetlagged asshole in his mid-thirties.

"So, that's settled then," he whispered against my mouth when I let him up for air.

He was practically naked, and I ran my hand up his bare chest, over his shoulder and around his long throat. Tate sucked in a breath that sounded a lot like a moan, tipping his head back to give me more access to one of my favorite parts of him. I tilted his head back, pressing my thumb against the underside of his chin, then kissing the divot left by my nail.

"It's settled," he murmured, pulling my hand up to his mouth and swirling his tongue between my fingers. "The only thing up for discussion now is what you're going to do with those handcuffs you packed."

I took two days off work so we could stay in Italy longer, and thank God for that because Brooks didn't take the handcuffs out of his bag until Monday after lunch. We'd just gotten back from a private wine and pasta tasting, and I felt like I was walking on air. Brooks needed to check on the status of the contract he'd been finalizing before we left the city and I needed to spend some alone time in the bathroom to make sure everything was in order.

By the time I finished up, I found Brooks' cell phone on the nightstand and his clothes on the floor. He'd practically lived in one of the thick and plush hotel robes since our arrival, and I made a mental note to save up money to see if I could buy him one for Christmas or something. There was always going to be a disparity in our incomes, which would only broaden if I ever walked away from my job. Brooks would have never balked at me spending his own money on him, but I appreciated being able to contribute out of my own account.

After getting out of the shower, I slid my robe up my shoulders, but didn't bother with the tie, instead letting the sides fall open. My damp feet slapped quietly against the tile floor as I made a loop of the villa trying to find Brooks. The past few days had been surreal, I thought, knowing that when we got back to the city my life was going to change again.

But the thought of going back to New York and having to go back to Dylan's and my little shithole apartment in Chelsea was too much for me to bear. I already spent so much of my time at Brooks' penthouse, it made sense for me to be there all the time.

Officially.

It helped knowing that the apartment would still be there. Not for me—I was confident in my future with the man I was looking for, but for Dylan. I didn't think he'd be happy about living on his own after being with me for so many years, but I had to have faith we'd find a new middle ground for what things would look like moving forward.

"There you are," I said, stepping out onto the patio from the living room of the villa.

There was a patio space that basically wrapped the entire back side of the villa, with the view from our bedroom being the highest and the living room the lowest. All the spaces were connected with uneven stairs down the hillside and one of the most beautiful views I'd ever seen in my life. Brooks stood on the far end of the patio, hands braced against the short stone railing. Even with his back to me, I recognized the cool metal glint of the handcuffs hanging off the tip of his finger.

He didn't turn toward me, he simply lifted his hand and pushed the cuffs until one of them clicked through and fell open. It was as much of an order as any words would have been, and I padded toward him, shrugging out of my robe on the way. I easily settled my wrist into the waiting cradle of the cuff, which he quickly latched. With one of my wrists restrained, Brooks spun me, taking out the back of my knee in the same motion. He caught me before I fell, easing me down to the ground while looping the chain of the handcuffs around one of the railing supports and closing the other piece around my other wrist.

Flat on my ass on the warmed Italian stone patio, my first instinct was to test my restraints, which offered me less mobility than the positioning he'd put me in on the bed swing at the farm. He stepped back, rubbing absently at his chin while I struggled, smiling when I gave up and went still. My legs were bent at the knee, feet planted against the ground, my cock jutting straight toward the roofline.

"I was doing some rough math earlier," he said, letting his hand drop into the pocket of his robe. He pulled out a bottle of lube and clutched it in his fist, gaze flickering down to my face. "There's at least one hundred surfaces in my house I haven't fucked you against yet, and at least four on the plane."

"Plenty here," I rasped, swallowing my nerves.

"Time is short, unfortunately." He cocked his head to the side and pulled at his earlobe, lost in thought. "And I think it's been awhile since you've cried out of desperation."

"I cried last night," I reminded him.

I'd cried *and* cried out, the rough fuck he'd given me in the shower enough to have me screaming down the walls. The way Brooks owned my body so wholly was a feat I'd never understand. It wasn't even that he fucked me to the point of pain; it was that the pleasure had been too much to bear. The sharp sting of need vibrating out of every nerve in my body, his thick cock slamming into my prostate with every snap of his hips, the bite of his fingers pinching my nipples when I was on the edge. Everything with Brooks was a combination of sensations and feelings that rolled up into something far more than they'd ever be on their own.

And that was what had been missing from all the men I'd foolishly thought could fill his shoes. They were good at one thing or another, but none of them knew how to tie it all in. They didn't understand how to assemble the thing they'd built. How to use it.

Use me.

"True," Brooks murmured, loosening the knot on his robe and pouring some lube onto his hand.

His cock was already hard, poking at the material of the robe and dragging it to the side. With his free hand, he yanked a chair across the patio, the sound grating. He moved the chair into place, less than two feet away from me, and then he sat down. It didn't take a rocket scientist to know what was going to happen next.

"Please, don't," I begged, testing the handcuffs again, but short of shattering the stone column that dug into my back, I wasn't going anywhere.

Brooks sat down and spread his legs, then slowly stroked his cock from root to tip. Throwing his head back with a low groan, he made me watch while he brought himself to the brink. He forced me to watch him fuck into the loose grip of his fist when the tight heat of my body was so close and more than ready for him.

"God, Tate." He groaned, pointing his cock toward me so I could see the precum leaking from his slit. The handcuffs dug into my wrists and I was seconds away from growling at him out of frustration. "Look how hard I am."

"I see it."

"You're drooling for it so much I bet I'd drown if I put it in your mouth." Brooks managed a smile, but it quickly fell away as he twisted his wrist around the thickest middle part of his shaft. "Bet I'd burn up if I put it in your ass."

"Come over here and find out," I pleaded.

Fighting at the handcuffs, I licked my lips and tried to lean toward him, smacking my mouth like if I made enough noise he'd take pity on me and let me suck him. We both knew that wasn't the case, though. There was no amount of begging that was going to get me what I wanted.

"I'm so close," he whispered, slowing his pace until he went still entirely. Tension rippled up the muscles in his stomach and he grabbed the chair with a grunt, hips bucking into the air chasing after a grip that he'd already abandoned.

"Please," I whispered, lashes fluttering. I dropped my head against the stone railing and sighed, all of the blood and the heat and the need in my body currently centralized between my legs.

"Please what?"

"Please come closer."

"I'm right here, darling." Brooks stood, but instead of coming closer to me, he walked away.

I countered that with a very disgruntled sound that died down when I realized he was only going to the table beside the door. There was another bottle of wine there, two empty glasses waiting. He poured himself a drink and turned toward me, taking a swallow and waiting for me to settle down. There was no calming me, no settling down, and I let out a shaking breath when he started back toward me.

"Closer," I begged again when he came to stop between my body and the chair. His cock was nearly eye level, a handful of inches too high for me to get my mouth around considering how limited my movement was.

"Can't get much closer than this," he teased.

Another swallow of the wine and his cock was back in his hand, this time close enough that I could smell the musky salt of his precum when he stroked himself back to full hardness.

"Brooks."

"Tate," he whispered my name back to me, raising the wine glass to his lips as a streak of cum geysered out of his cock and splattered my forehead.

I cried out, frustrated at the waste of his cum and the nonchalance of the orgasm. He stroked himself until his balls were empty, sticky strings of cum trailing down my eyelashes and my cheeks, then he collapsed back into the chair with a satisfied groan.

"I love you so much," he said after another swallow of wine.

"Let me have a drink," I pleaded, my left eye screwed shut so I didn't get cum on my eyeball.

"Anything for you, darling." Brooks went to his knees between my spread legs and tipped the glass to my lips, just like he'd done on the airplane. The wine was harder to drink, racing down my chin and splattering on my bare thighs. I imagined Brooks didn't care if any of the wine made it into my mouth because he was too busy sliding his thighs beneath mine and shifting my ass off the ground. Wine dribbled down my lips as Brooks produced the bottle of lube from his pocket again, squirting it unceremoniously on his shaft.

"Is that enough?" he asked, meaning the wine.

"More," I demanded, wanting not just a drink, but everything from him entirely.

He hummed a pleased sound, tipping the glass at a steeper angle. I parted my lips and let the wine run into my mouth, swallowing with desperate gasps. Between my legs, I recognized the familiar press of his cock and the sharp burn of penetration. The wine in my mouth cut off my moan, and I swallowed furiously, drink after drink of wine until the glass was empty. Brooks' cock was all the way inside me by then, and my entire body wracked with a shiver when I took the last swallow of wine.

"More?" he repeated, setting the glass to the side and grabbing my waist with enough force to immediately bruise.

"More." I nodded.

Brooks yanked me onto his lap, and the cuffs bit into my wrists, pulling my arms behind me as he fought my body forward. He let out a low and feral-sounding growl, stare focused on the place our bodies were joined. Taking my dick into his lube-slicked fist, he started to stroke me in time with the thrusts of his hips, bringing me to the edge of my orgasm over and over, backing off each time until I screamed out for him at the top of my lungs.

The outburst was unavoidable, and he clamped his hand down over my mouth and nose, his own lips twisted into a rueful smirk. He couldn't keep me quiet, jerk me off, and fuck me at the same time, so with his cock buried in my ass, Brooks focused his attention on my breath and my erection.

"You have to quiet down, darling," he said, pinching my nose and tightening his fist. "We don't want the staff to come find you like this, with a cock up your ass and cum in your eye."

My mouth gaped against his palm, fighting for a breath, even though I knew I wasn't going to find one. That was the way things went between us, and I wanted it more than I wanted air. His fist was a slick vise on my cock and his dick up my ass pulsed in time with my own heart. My movement was limited and my ability to form rational thoughts even more so, but I fucked myself on his cock as much as I could manage. After a whole day of torturous build up and the prep time from my earlier shower, I was more than primed for Brooks and whatever he was willing to dole out to me.

The orgasm was expected and it was fierce.

His fist was like pins and needles around my cock, and my struggle for breath turned from a fight to a death rattle. It was less important to breathe when the only thing I wanted to do was come. In fact, I needed it. I knew I was safe in his hands, even though the pressure mounting in my balls felt positively explosive and insurmountable.

"Come on, Tate," he coaxed, stroking me faster. "You're right there. Just give it to me."

I didn't have the strength to open my eyes.

All I could feel was the weight of my balls, the pressure on my prostate, and then I could breathe. I didn't even think about it, it was reflex, the way my eyes flew open and I gasped for breath. The handcuffs bit into my wrists as I sucked in breath after breath, so much air it made me choke, and when my orgasm finally found its way around, I did as we both knew I would.

I burst into tears.

Brooks bracketed my hips with his hands, letting my cock splatter cum across my stomach, and he fucked into me so rough it made my teeth rattle. Sobbing, tears cascaded down my face, taking his drying cum and cool wine with them. He came soon after, shooting streams of cum into my asshole, bending down and licking the mess he'd made of my face with a contented groan.

His tongue dragged over my eyebrow and eyelid, down to my nose, my cheek, my jaw. And then he was kissing me, shoving all of the mess back into my mouth. My body spasmed, working through the aftershocks of my orgasm, but it was impossible for me to fall against him. I was still bound to the railing, bent on display for his pleasure and his use. If I closed my eyes, I could still feel his hand over my mouth, and that sent another wave of tremors up my spine, another dribble of cum out of my cock.

At some point I realized Brooks was talking to me, whispering praise as he eased his still-hard cock out of my ass.

"It's unbelievable that you're mine," he said sweetly, brushing my sweaty hair back from my face and depositing me back down on the ground. He sat down in front of me, back against the chair and chest heaving.

"My wrists hurt," I finally managed to tell him, and it was half true. I could have endured the bite of metal into my wrist, but there was more... "I want to hold you."

"Oh, darling."

He pulled the key out of his robe and made quick work of detangling me from the stone pillar. I crawled into his lap and wrapped my arms around his neck, peppering kisses up his throat and chin until I reached his mouth.

"You're always so good about giving me what I need," I whispered, the orgasm still vibrating through my bones. "Can you draw us a bath now so I can return the favor?"

Brooks slipped his arms around my back, kissing the top of my head, my temple.

"With pleasure, Tate. With pleasure."

CHAPTER 41
BROOKS

THE FOLLOWING WEEKEND WE WERE BACK IN NEW YORK, SITTING ON the floor of Tate and Dylan's apartment, packing half a dozen boxes of Tate's belongings up. I'd offered to pay for movers, but he'd insisted he was capable of boxing things up on his own. Dylan had come by around lunch and I'd ordered the two of them pizza, then headed out for a walk around the block with Alex.

"How have things been?" I asked when we reached the street, thankful that I'd never have to deal with visiting anyone who lived in a walk-up ever again.

"I'm not sure what I'm doing," Alex admitted. "But Dylan is safe."

"Does that matter to you?"

Alex snorted. "Are you asking me if I have feelings for him?"

"Do you?" I pressed.

"I don't not," he said.

"That's enough," I said. "Have you heard from Beamer?"

"We've talked once since he got back to California. I don't want to get in the way of anything."

"You're his friend."

"It's not that simple and you know it." Alex shrugged. "What would you do if Dylan and Tate had fucked, and Dylan kept trying to come around and be friendly while you and Tate were together?"

"I don't care who fucked Tate before," I reminded him, "I'm the one who's fucking him now."

Alex heaved a sigh. "It's complicated, but I'm fine."

I didn't entirely believe him, but I didn't want to push him away again. "Have you sold the motorcycle yet?"

"No."

"Are you going to?" I asked.

"I don't know, Brooks."

It was a fair answer, all things considered.

"Ford has invited us back to the farm again," I said, changing the subject.

He'd actually done more than invite us.

In Italy, I'd managed to finalize the food distribution contract he and Boston had been fighting so hard for. Ford had offered to rename the property after me and kiss me on the mouth, both of which felt a little excessive.

"Duly noted."

We turned another corner.

"If not the farm, how do you feel about a trip to the club this weekend?" I asked. "Kale texted about it."

Alex huffed out half of a laugh and shook his head. "He's a trip."

"He means well," I said, remembering the fierce parts of

him that had shone through Tate when it came to defending his best friend. "I think any of us would have done the same."

"Within reason," he added.

"Is that a yes?"

"It's a maybe," Alex said, which was as much of a yes as it ever was with him.

Tate and I were looking forward to the outing. Tate, because he was perpetually horny, and me, because I was eager to test the limits of his newfound interest in exhibitionism. I appreciated on the airplane he hadn't wanted the flight attendant to catch him with a throat full of cock, but I wondered if he would feel differently about it in the right setting, which The Black Door definitely was. If he was still uncertain, there were always plenty of dark corners, bathrooms, and private rooms to choose from.

"I'll take it."

We turned the last corner, coming up again on the entrance to Dylan and Tate's building. I glanced at my watch and cocked my head toward the street. Alex nodded, and we took a second lap around the block to give the two of them more time to chat without our presence interfering any of the thousand questions I knew Tate had for his best friend.

Alex and I walked in silence, though, which was companionable and nice. Even before recently, he'd always been the quietest of the group of us. He often bordered on broody, but I personally found it to be part of his charm. A man of few words with the biggest heart of anyone I'd ever met.

We made it back to their apartment, the moving van I'd rented idling in the street. Seeing the slim number of belongings Tate had to his name, it was overkill, but I doubted everything would have fit in the trunk of a town car. I told the driver to give us two minutes, then Alex and I headed up to the third floor.

"If I never walk another flight of stairs in my life," Alex grumbled under his breath when we reached Tate and Dylan's front door. It was still unlocked, and we found the two of them sitting on a couch, Tate's boxes neatly taped and stacked beside them. The pizza was half eaten, which was more than enough.

"The van is downstairs. Are you all set?" I asked, not wanting to rush, but more than ready to get Tate fully unpacked and settled at my place.

Our place, rather.

"Yeah," Tate confirmed, pushing up from his seat.

Dylan's arm was still in a sling, but he hugged Tate without wincing, which felt like progress. They whispered some words to each other that I knew weren't meant for me or Alex to hear. Behind me, one of the movers rapped his knuckles on the door, and Tate faced him with a sigh.

"Just these," he said, pointing to the boxes.

The mover let out an amused laugh, then he and the man beside him collected the boxes in one swoop and carried them downstairs. There was no rush for goodbyes because the boxes would get to the penthouse whether we were there or not, and I still had to call a car for us. I didn't know how Alex and Dylan had gotten across town, and it was none of my business so I didn't bother asking.

Tate closed the space between us and slipped his arms around my waist, pressing a quick kiss against the corner of my mouth.

"I'm ready," he whispered.

We said our final goodbyes to Alex and Dylan, then began the trip back to our new home.

The first thing I wanted to do upon arrival was fuck Tate against in the entryway, half on top of his boxes, but he had other plans, leading me instead upstairs to the bathroom.

"What's this?" I asked, spreading my arms and letting him strip me out of my clothes. After he'd gotten me naked, he turned his attention to himself, discarding his own clothes with far less care than he'd offered mine.

"Aftercare," he answered, pulling me into the shower and turning on the taps.

"For who?"

Tate pushed me under the spray and tilted my head back, letting the water sluice through my hair and down my neck. I didn't even bother trying to hold back a groan. The press of his fingers and the heat of his body were like a salve to cure every single one of my ailments.

"For you," he said, kissing the dip of my throat. "For me."

"Are you needing attention, darling?"

He hummed, turning me and urging me down onto the bench so he could go to his knees between my legs.

"You give me everything I need." He scrubbed a hand over his face, shoving the water out of his eyes before dipping down toward my quickly hardening dick. "I want to make sure to do the same."

He swallowed me into the back of his throat on the first try, his talent for choking on my cock approaching perfection. He'd had enough practice at it, that was for sure. Threading my fingers into his hair, I made sure not to force his speed, letting him set the pace which turned out to be leisurely and slow.

Tate sucked on my cock like he was worshiping it, which in a way, he was. When he reached down to take himself in hand, I didn't protest. I closed my eyes and dropped my head against the back wall of the shower, moaning low and long the closer he got me to my own end.

"I love you," I whispered, voice barely louder than the spray of the water on the back of his head. My grip on his hair was tentative at best, and I had to let go of him and brace myself against the wall. Even as the adrenaline ramped up in my body, Tate maintained his casual pace, sucking and slobbering on my shaft like it was his favorite dessert.

Instead of saying anything back to me, he tilted his head to the side when his lips were closed around my crown and opened his eyes. He cradled my balls in his free hand, body swaying forward as he grunted and came onto the floor. He put my entire shaft back into his mouth, deliberately choking himself with my length until he'd finished coming.

"Want you to come," he muttered, the words garbled.

"Thought this was about me," I teased him.

"Exactly."

I chuckled, taking his head into my hands and lifting off the bench to impale his throat with my cock. Watching him deprive himself of oxygen on his own, all in the name of a better orgasm, already had me careening dangerously close to the cliff. Fucking his mouth and listening to the strangled gagging noises fall out of his throat was enough to send me over the edge entirely.

I came with a shout, shooting against the roof of his mouth. My cum spilled out of his mouth, smearing over his lips and his chin, and he grabbed my thighs and dug in his fingernails as I rode out my orgasm in his throat. When he blinked up at me, his lashes were clumped together and he had a lust-drunk smile on his face.

"I love you too," he said, body going limp. "Thank you for this life."

I swallowed thickly, still not sure that I'd given him anything less than what he deserved, but I knew better than to argue about it. Instead of pulling him into my lap like I normally would, I went onto the floor beside him. Tate chuckled, arranging himself next to me and stretching out his legs. His thighs were slimmer than mine, but his feet reached a few inches past mine. It was easy to see the differences between us even though we were the same in all the ways that mattered the most.

The shower rained down against his face, washing him clean, but I couldn't wait for later when I had the chance to get him well and truly dirty again. All of his moments would be mine, would be ours. His days, his nights, just like in Italy. His body, his heart, his mouth, his hands, as much mine as mine were to him.

"Tate." I turned my head toward him, head going fuzzy at the sight of the man I loved, so happy from the pleasure we shared. "Kiss me, darling."

He flung a leg over my lap and took my face into his hands, kissing me until I forgot how to breathe without his mouth against mine.

And I leaned into it readily.

What a perfect way to live.

ALSO BY KATE HAWTHORNE

———

Trophy Doms Social Club

Humbled

Edged

Praised

Bound

Shared

Trophy Doms New York

All In

Tied Down

Cried Out

Roughed Up

Giving Consent

Worth the Risk

Worth the Wait

Worth the Fight

Worth the Chance

All in Good Time

Necessary Space

Necessary Time

Duality

Dual Destruction

Dual Surrender

Dual Defiance

Two Truths and a Lie

A Real Good Lie

A Cold Hard Truth

A Matter of Fact

Room for Love

Reckless

Heartless

Faultless

Fearless

Limitless

A Very Messy Motel Brothers Wedding

Relentless

Secrets in Edgewood

A Taste of Sin

The Cost of Desire

A Love Made Whole

Secrets in Edgewood: The Complete Series

The Lonely Hearts Stories

His Kind of Love

The Colors Between Us

Love Comes After

Until You Say Otherwise

STANDALONES

Rebound

One for the Road

Daybreak - Vino & Veritas

Unfettered

Dreams

A Thousand Lifetimes

COLLABORATIONS

With E.M. Denning

Irreplaceable

Future Fake Husband

Future Gay Boyfriend

Future Ex Enemy

With J.R. Gray

May the Best Man Win

ABOUT KATE HAWTHORNE

Kate Hawthorne is an author of character-driven LGBT romance, known for crafting emotionally intense stories with high heat and a kinky twist. Creating worlds where passion and angst collide, Kate's books bring you complex protagonists in fearless pursuit of self-exploration and happy—if not sometimes unconventional—endings for everyone.

Visit her website
http://www.katehawthornebooks.com

Sign up for Kate's newsletter
http://www.katehawthornebooks.com/extra

facebook.com/authorkatehawthorne

x.com/katewriteswords

instagram.com/kate.hawthorne

patreon.com/katehawthorne